Praise for Gra

"A compulsively readable thriller that probes the … relationship between sport and crime."
Matt Lawton, Chief Sports Reporter, Daily Mail

"**Fatal Fix** held me to the very end…quick-paced and exciting and very reminiscent of Le Carré. A terrific read."
Gay Courter, author of Code Ezra *and* Flowers in the Blood

"Graham Morse's **Fatal Fix** takes you inside the murky world of football match fixing. This may be a work of fiction, but it lands uncomfortably close to brutal, unblinking reality. So pull up a chair, hunker down, and let this novel take you on its revealing and perilous ride."
Douglas Schofield, author of Time of Departure *and* Killing Pace

"In Matt Riley —an investigative sports journalist —Graham Morse has convincingly created a character who will risk his life to find the killer of his friend and file the story of a lifetime."
Brian Scovell, author of the biographies of Sir Trevor Brooking *and* Sir Bobby Robson

"In **Fatal Fix**, Graham Morse has delivered the goods: a first-rate crime thriller that is enriched by its understanding of the human heart and enlivened by an authoritative look at the influence of gambling on big-time sport."
Les Standiford, author of Done Deal *and* Last Train to Paradise

"Graham Morse's stylish and compelling thriller will introduce many Americans to the seamy side of British football (read soccer). British readers and the rest of the football-obsessed world will experience again with vivid intensity what they hate about the sport they love. Full of keen observation and humanity, familiar yet fresh characters, scenes that snap, and cleverly turned twists, this fast-paced first novel will delight all lovers of crime fiction."
Sterling Watson, author of Suitcase City *and* The Committee

FATAL FIX

A sports crime thriller

Graham Morse

SHIPSTONE
PUBLISHING

All characters in this publication are fictitious and any resemblance to real persons, whether living or dead, is purely coincidental.

ISBN: 978-1-8381317-0-8
eISBN ePub: 978-1-8381317-1-5
eISBN mobi: 978-1-8381317-2-2

Published in 2020 by Shipstone Publishing

A CIP record of this book is available from the British Library.

Cover design by Patrick Knowles Design

Dedication

For Janet. For always being there.

Acknowledgements

I could not have written this novel without the help of experts who gave their time and advice so freely. I would specially like to thank the *Daily Mail* Sports Desk, in particular Matt Lawton and Matt Barlow, who showed me the life of the sportswriter, as well as Sami Mokbel and Laura Williamson, and at *The Times* Alyson Rudd.

I am grateful to Dr. Sue May for her expert advice on pathology and Dr. Sarah Gregson and Dr. Blanca Bolea for guidance on medical matters and psychiatry. Ex-Met detective Dennis Walkington gave me revealing and invaluable insights into police procedures. I must thank Declan Hill for sharing his unrivalled knowledge of match fixing and his indispensable book, *The Insider's Guide to Match Fixing in Football.*

I am indebted to Les Standiford and Sterling Watson for including my story in their *Writers in Paradise* workshops at Eckerd College, Florida, and for the help and support of the many writers I worked with there.

Thanks to Ken Friar at Arsenal F.C., Chris Connor, Alex Wood, Sue Lynch, and my friend and fellow thriller writer Douglas Schofield, who helped keep the wheels on the track, and to my readers, Carol Drake, Bev Batten Simpson, Alyson Medeiros, Peter Kandiah, Tomy Wilkinson, Luke Windle and Fiona Foster.

A posthumous award of my gratitude to Shari Wilson, my mentor, an inspiring source of help and encouragement, who died far too young. Finally a huge thank you to my editor Sarah Williams for believing in the novel, for showing me how to improve it, and for putting it to bed.

Last but not least, a heartfelt hug to my dear wife Janet for her unfailing support, patience and advice on every aspect of this book.

CHAPTER ONE

Matt Riley was still angry. At six thirty on Sunday morning the roads in south west London were clear of traffic and he was pumped up, pushing himself harder than usual on his racing bike. The thin tyres hissed on the black, wet tarmac. It was dark, cold, and it had started to drizzle. Matt liked it that way. It kept his mind focused as he raced round the route that took him through residential areas, over the bridge, and down by the river.

He knew when Bill Wickes had called him into the office that the news wasn't going to be good. But it was worse than expected. The latest round of cutbacks had sent a chill through the newsroom. On the sports desk alone twenty journalists had been trimmed to fifteen. Then Bill told him he was cutting out the time he could have to pursue investigative stories.

An investigative journalist was an expensive luxury, even for a mass circulation paper like the *Daily Chronicle*. Matt knew that. Investigations took time and sometimes fizzled out without any copy being filed. But he had already nailed some big stories that no one else in Fleet Street had got a sniff of. Matt had slammed the door and walked out. A future of only writing match reports and interviews with managers and players was not the career he had planned. He was better than that.

He felt the phone pulsing in the body-belt strapped around his waist and ignored it. Then came an agonising thought. What if he was missing something important? At six-thirty on Sunday morning? No, a wrong number, surely? But what if it wasn't? Cursing under his breath, he braked hard and pulled his bike onto the pavement under the shelter of a shop awning. He looked at the screen. It was Bill. He had never had a call from his sports editor at this time of the morning.

'Christ, Bill, what's up?'

'Tony Barker's dead.'

The bike slipped from his grasp, clattered to the ground, and he slumped against the shop window.

'What!'

'He was found hanged at his home about fifteen minutes ago.'

Matt pressed his back against the plate-glass window. The blood drained from his face. There was a long silence.

'Matt. You still there?'

'Hanged?' he croaked. 'Did you say hanged? Are you sure?'

'Yeah, we just had a call from a freelance who had a tip-off from the police. It hasn't hit any of the news channels yet, but it will any time now.'

He jolted back, hitting his head against the plate-glass window. 'Suicide? Oh no,' he moaned. 'Not Tony.'

'It's always suicide when they're found hanged at home,' said Bill.

He stared at the flashing red neon shop sign on the other side of the road as the memories hammered through his carefully-built defences. He slumped down, his head in his hands.

I wake up. Light is starting to show though the gap where the curtains don't meet. I look at my bedside clock. Five o'clock. The house is still but something has woken me. There it is again. Sam is whimpering and whining. He doesn't do that. Something feels wrong. I get out of bed and creep down the stairs. I must be careful not to wake Mum and Dad. I open the door to the kitchen and Sam runs up to me, pushing his nose hard up against my leg. "What's up?" I whisper. He nudges me again, harder this time and runs to the door, whining, looking back for me to follow. I open the door and Sam darts over to the garage. He is jumping up and scratching the side door, his whining even louder now. My knees are shaking and I feel something is terribly wrong. I reach for the knob and the door creaks on its hinges as I open it. It is dark and cold inside and I am only wearing my pyjamas and I haven't got my slippers on. I start to shiver. As my eyes adjust I can just make out the shape of Dad's car, a blue Ford Anglia. I inch forward between the car and the wall to where I know the light switch is. I reach up, press it down and the room is instantly flooded with a harsh white glare. Something knocks my shoulder. One of my Dad's feet. I look up. It's my Dad. He's hanging in the air, feet dangling. He's got a rope around his neck. I collapse onto the cement floor. It's hard and it's cold and I am sobbing.

An early morning walker crossed the road and bent over him. 'You alright, mate? You look white as a sheet. Do you want me to call an ambulance?'

Matt looked up and shook his head. 'What? No, no. I'm fine.'

'What was that, Matt?'

'Sorry, Bill, I was talking to somebody else.'

Bill's tone softened. 'I'm sorry, Matt. You knew Barker well, didn't you?'

'Yes, we were friends.'

'Mmm-hmm. That's why I called you. When did you last see him?'

'Oh... I don't know...' Matt struggled to focus. 'Umm, actually it was only last week. Wednesday, I think... we had lunch.' They had been together in the canteen at the club training ground in Surrey, sitting at a corner table overlooking the pitches. Players' banter and laughter had filled the room. He pictured Tony's craggy face, his warm smile and his furrowed brow as he made a serious point. He could almost hear his infectious laugh as they shared a joke.

'How did he seem then?'

'Normal, I suppose... just normal. We talked about the Everton game. Who was playing well, injuries, players' loss of form, you know, the usual stuff.' He paused. 'Oh, and he told me he had just booked a surprise trip to take Tania to Venice for their wedding anniversary.'

'Really? That's good. We can use that. I want you down there this morning – you know, cover the personal angle. The news desk is sending James Piggot-Browne. Do you know him?'

'I don't think so.'

'It's sure to get splashed on the front page. We'll probably give it three pages in sport. Talk to his wife, get the inside story – an exclusive. We need to find out what happened Matt. Why he did it.'

The sweat of a few minutes ago had turned cold and Matt felt a chill running down his spine. His Lycra jersey clung to his back. Tony? Of all people – Tony! What could possibly have driven Tony to take his own life? Matt wanted this story but something else was gnawing at his gut. What if he turned over stones in his friend's life and uncovered embarrassing personal revelations? How would he deal with it? Like he handled any other investigation, he thought: truthfully. It wouldn't be easy, but he didn't want anyone else on the sports desk going near it, that's for sure. Whatever came out he could handle it better than they would. He would do it, but he would do it his way.

'You're right, Bill. It's my story. Thanks for the call.'

'Talk to Piggot-Browne; he'll have information from the police. I'll get some of the others to do the career background and statistics. You need to concentrate on the suicide angle, you know, family problems, financial worries, personal issues, depression. And job pressures, of course – it can't have been easy working for Buzinsky.'

Sergei Buzinsky, the owner of London City F.C. was one of the richest men in the world. The Russian oligarch had shocked everyone in football with his naked ambition when he bought a famous but ailing Premier League club in the Midlands, relocated it to Canary Wharf, and renamed it London City F.C. The Wimbledon switch to M K Dons had set the precedent back in 2003/2004, but this was on an altogether different scale. The new stadium, hotel and conference centre complex was stunning. The training centre was state of the art. Buzinsky wanted to outdo the other Russian oligarchs, the oil rich Saudis and Far Eastern tycoons who were competing to have the best team in the Premier League. Buzinsky wanted to win, and he called the tune. Tony was part of his plan – as long as he was winning. Tony had accepted that when he took the job three years ago. Tony had a Midas touch with the team, and Buzinsky didn't often interfere in team matters.

'Yeah, I'll hook up with Piggot-Browne as soon as I get there. What about my schedule?'

'Don't worry about that. I'll reassign your match. You can forget about your diary for the next few days.'

Bill Wickes wasn't a bad sports editor. Matt had known worse. Bill had come up through the ranks as a sports writer himself, and had a nose for a story, unlike some editors who worked their way up in the office. Bill knew what sold papers and had given Matt some license to pursue stories that uncovered corruption... until last week when he had put the lid on it! Still... Tony taking his own life? That could change things.

Matt wheeled his black carbon bike into the hall of his Fulham apartment and wiped it down. He switched on the television – it was tuned to Sky Sports News as usual – and inserted a sachet of espresso into the coffee maker. The kitchen work surfaces were clean and tidy, but his mind was in turmoil.

He gazed down at the street below. It was still dark, but in the orange glow of the streetlights he could see that it had started to drizzle. Puddles had begun to form on the road. An old man walked his dog, raincoat collar pulled up around his neck, hat pulled down over his ears. Matt continued to stare at the empty pavement long after the man disappeared, still unable to accept what Bill had told him.

The ping from his mobile startled him. It was a text from Bill with Piggot-Browne's number. As he poured the coffee and inhaled its aroma, his eyes were drawn to the television and the red bar at the bottom of the screen – Breaking News – Tony Barker found dead at his London home. The female news anchor introduced the story, a sombre expression on her face.

'We have just had breaking news that Tony Barker was found hanged at his luxury home in Wimbledon early this morning. Barker was one of the outstanding figures in English football. As a player he had a stellar career over twelve years, twice leading Chelsea to the Premier League title followed by FA Cup glory two years later. When his playing career ended he quickly built a reputation as one of the best young coaches in England, and in only three years had established London City F.C. as the leading club in the Premier League.'

She turned to the male anchor sitting alongside her, who picked up the story. 'Barker was seen last night by millions of viewers here on Sky Sports 1 after City's home game against Everton, which they won one-nil.' The picture on the screen changed to footage of Tony Barker stalking his technical area. 'The forty-seven-year-old manager was married with two children. We'll bring you more news on this breaking story as it comes in.'

Matt stared at the screen. He couldn't pretend that Bill's phone call had been a dream. Tony was dead. He had to pull himself together. He called Tania on their home number but there was no reply, just voice mail. He wasn't surprised; she had probably left it off the hook. He left a message.

The hot water from the shower eased the tension in his shoulders. The steam cleared his head and he began to think more rationally. He hurried through to the bedroom and pulled on a pair of blue jeans, a black roll-neck sweater and a black leather jacket. He ran his fingers through his wet, short-cropped, thick black hair and rubbed his five-day beard stubble. At forty-two years old, 5'10" and 175 pounds he was in good shape – not much different from when he and Tony had played together at Chelsea twenty years ago. There was no flab round his middle and his muscles were well toned.

He made a last mental check that he had everything he needed, unplugged the laptop that sat on his desk, slipped it into a bag and picked up his phone. The apartment block was Sunday morning-silent as Matt emerged into the artificial glow of the deserted underground car park. He tossed his bag into the back of his car and an image of Tony flashed before him – dangling from a rope, head slumped forward. Matt felt the bile rising in his chest. Quickly stepping away from the car, he bent over and retched uncontrollably. After several deep breaths he stood up, pulled a tissue out of his jacket pocket, wiped his mouth, and slipped behind the wheel. The tyres squealed on the rubberised surface of the car park as he gunned the car up the ramp, heading out into a dark, wet, January morning.

There was still little traffic that early and he made fast progress, crossing the river at Putney Bridge as a pale dawn revealed angry black clouds. On Putney High Street he stopped for a red light. The drizzle had turned into steady rain and the windscreen wipers whirred hypnotically. The rhythmic swish resounded in his head: Tony's dead... Tony's dead... Tony's dead. Staring through the windscreen he saw Tony – wavy blond hair, craggy face – smiling at him. Smiling the way he did the last time they had played football together twenty years ago.

It had been raining like this at Villa Park when Matt had been forced out of the game. An ugly tackle, studs that ripped into his leg, and a sickening crack had silenced the crowd and shattered his dream. The blast of a horn from the car behind startled him. He looked up at the lights. The red light had changed to green, but as he began to ease the car forward it flicked back to red again. He waved his hand to the driver behind in apology.

He pulled away when the light again turned green, but his mind drifted back to the day at Villa Park that had changed his life. Tony had been there for him then, supporting and encouraging him during a year-long rehabilitation program until he finally had to accept that his playing career was over.

Traffic was building up, and glancing down Matt noticed the red warning light: low on petrol. He didn't want to waste time stopping, but the red and yellow canopy of a service station that appeared ahead made his mind up for him. A few men stood in shirt sleeves, shivering, gazing at the pump gauge, eager to be back in the warmth of their cars. He jammed the nozzle into the tank. How often had he done this with Tony on their way to training? When he came to Chelsea as a promising eighteen-year old, Tony had protected him from the worst of the initiation rites: the bullying that went on in training and the taunting because he read the *Daily Telegraph*. Matt had learned quickly and the crowd had taken to him. They had given him the nick-name 'Stinger.' They liked it when an opposition player tried it on with him. They knew what was coming. He would suck it up and then, when his attacker least expected it, he would find himself with an elbow in his face as they went up to head a ball, sometimes even a broken nose. He was a regular in the first team by the time he was nineteen, won a Cup Final medal at twenty, and was already talked about as a future England player. But it was Tony who had been the father figure who had looked out for him – encouraged his talent, taught him how to be more tactically aware and helped him to control his natural aggression.

Some of the customers inside the shop at the filling station were buying the Sunday newspapers. He winced at the headlines: BARKER'S TRIUMPH OVER EVERTON. Tomorrow's papers would tell a different story. Perhaps it was only now that Tony was dead that he was beginning to realise what a big part of his life Tony had been.

Matt had been as competitive in the classroom as he was on the football pitch. He had been offered a place at university, but he had chosen professional football. When that career had been snatched away at the age of twenty-two he had made another choice: to be the best sports writer in the country.

When his application for a journalism degree course was politely rejected he had telephoned the course director. 'I appreciate your determination, Mr. Riley,' the director had told him, 'but other candidates have more relevant experience. I've had two hundred applications for twenty-five places. Playing football is not an alternative qualification.'

Matt had persuaded the man to at least grant him an interview. 'A successful journalist needs determination and persistence,' Matt had said. 'I've already proved I've got those qualities.' The director had sat up and examined the arrogant young man more carefully. 'And what's more,' Matt had continued, 'there is not one of them who wants to be a successful journalist more than I do.' And he had been right. None of his peers on the course had made it to a national newspaper.

While Tony was developing a reputation as one of the most successful young managers in the country, Matt had made his less spectacular way as a sports writer. His first job on a local newspaper in Manchester had soon led to him joining the *Daily Express* as a football writer covering the Yorkshire region. When he had heard that one of the paper's most experienced football writers was retiring Matt had taken the train to London and walked into the sports editor's office. 'I want that job,' he said. 'Just let me tell you why I'm the best man for it.' Five years later he had been poached by the *Daily Chronicle*. Matt had seen less of Tony as they made their way in their new careers. Of course he was there for Tony's wedding to Tania, and he had invited Tony to be his best man when he married Susie, but their careers had left little time for social meetings, and Tony's success as a manager had brought a millionaire lifestyle that Tania basked in.

But inevitably their paths had crossed in the course of Matt's job, although they didn't agree on everything. Like most managers, Tony was critical of journalists. He had reproached Matt when he broke a story about a famous manager who had cut his son in on a transfer deal.

'That's his private life, Matt, and I bet he won't speak to you again.'

Matt had bristled with indignation. 'Tony, that was corruption. His son was a small-time agent who had nothing to do with the deal. He only agreed to the transfer if the player's official agent agreed to share the commission. I had the story verified from two sources.' He shrugged. 'But you're right. It's ruined my relationship with him.'

'Don't you sometimes feel bad about it?' Tony had said.

'No, I don't. I didn't stitch him up. Yes, I investigate people's private lives when I'm exposing lies and corruption, but I'm always straight.'

'There are plenty of journalists that aren't.'

'Yeah, alright,' Matt had conceded, 'but I'm not like some on the red tops. I've never made up a story. Look, Tony, I know I can be aggressive. I won't take no for an answer. I rub people up the wrong way. But it's no different to your job. If you want something enough you've got to kick doors down to get it.'

CHAPTER TWO

It was still only half past seven on a wet and misty morning when Matt pulled into the tree-lined road in Wimbledon where Tony and Tania Barker lived. Dozens of vehicles were parked haphazardly. He found a space to squeeze his car into, stepped out and pulled up the collar of his green Barbour.

The house had been built ten years ago in the classic Georgian style. Constructed on rising land in red brick, with a grey tiled roof and large sash windows it was, to say the least, imposing. An ornate, black, wrought iron gate opened onto a neat gravel drive leading to a detached double garage with accommodation for staff or guests above. The house and grounds had been cordoned off with police blue and white 'Do Not Enter' tape. A uniformed officer stood by the gate to make sure that nobody did.

Inside the taped off area, tents with emergency lighting had been set up. Police vehicles and an ambulance were parked outside the house. The air crackled with static and disembodied voices from VHF radios that had been left on. Television outside broadcast vehicles with satellite dishes and emergency lighting had been parked close to the scene – the noise from their generators shattering the peace of the suburban Sunday morning. A TV reporter, wrapped in a raincoat, one hand struggling to keep her hair in place, was speaking to camera with the house in the background.

A van serving hot tea and bacon sandwiches was doing brisk business. Matt recognised some of the football writers amongst the growing gaggle of journalists. Some neighbours had come along, drawn by a fascination for the drama unfolding on their doorsteps. Television interviewers and press reporters latched onto them, eager to pick up any background snippets that would help fill a story still short on facts.

Matt texted Piggott-Browne, then spotted him chatting with a group of journalists under umbrellas. He was quite tall and somewhat overweight. His thick head of hair was completely white and his upright posture suggested he might have been an army officer. Probably in his mid-fifties, Matt thought as he approached him.

'Hi, you must be James. I'm Matt. Can I get you a coffee?'

James' cheery face broke into a broad grin. 'Thanks, old chap. I'll have tea please, milk and sugar'.

They joined the queue at the catering van.

'The crime desk told me you would be coming. I understand you knew Barker?' said James

'Yes, very well. We played together at Chelsea. He was the best man at my wedding.'

'So, you must know his wife then?'

'Sure, I know Tania.'

'Great! That gives us an inside track.'

Yeah, Matt thought, but it's my inside track, not yours.

They shuffled forward in the queue until Matt ordered the hot drinks. 'One black coffee and one tea with milk and sugar please.'

'Can you make that two spoons, please?' said James, as the woman handed them the cups. He sniffed the frying bacon. 'Smells rather good,' he said to Matt. 'Fancy a bacon sandwich?'

Matt wrinkled up his nose, his stomach still raw from the earlier incident in the carpark. 'No, a bit early for me.'

'There you are, my love,' the woman said, as she served up the sandwich oozing bacon fat.

'Sure you won't change your mind?' James asked as he piled on the HP sauce.

Matt noticed that James spoke with a confident public school tone that reinforced his first impression that he had been an army officer. His accent wasn't one often heard in the press boxes at Premier League games. He'd be more at home at Twickenham, he thought.

Matt shook his head. 'No thanks.'

They walked away from the van and surveyed the hive of activity around them. Matt took a sip of the hot black coffee and clasped his cold hands round the warm cup. 'What do we know so far?'

'Not a lot. What I'm hearing unofficially is that Barker's wife found him hanging in the house early this morning and called the ambulance and police. He was dead when they arrived.'

Matt shuddered. He couldn't imagine what it must have felt like for Tania to have found him. A thought flashed through his mind.

'Where were the children?'

'I don't know. But his wife was alone in the house.'

Matt breathed a sigh of relief. 'Thank God for that.' He looked across at the police officers scurrying in and out of the house. 'When are we going to get something official from the police?'

'They're completing their evaluation of the scene. If they're sure it's suicide they won't be here long. I heard them say they're short handed and I don't think they were too happy about being called out this early on Sunday morning.'

'Has the pathologist arrived yet?'

James laughed. 'You've been watching too many TV dramas. The pathologist would only attend if it's murder. Anyway, a SOCO will be taking photographs of the body and showing them to the pathologist. But I expect the police will make a statement ruling out foul play very quickly. It's got all the hallmarks of a routine suicide.'

'How can you be so sure?'

'Well, I don't know for sure, of course. That's what we're waiting for.'

'How long?'

'Hard to say. But they can't keep this lot waiting for too long,' he said, waving an arm in the direction of the massed TV cameras, reporters and photographers. 'There's bound to be a press conference this morning.'

A plain clothes policeman strode out of the house to speak to a uniformed officer.

'Who's that?' Matt asked.

'Detective Sergeant Maclean. He's in charge. It looks as if they may be getting things moving. When Maclean has finished, the body will be moved to the local mortuary. It's an unnatural death, so there'll be a post-mortem and an inquest.'

Matt shook his head, thinking of the last time he saw Tony.

James frowned. 'Why are you shaking your head?'

Matt shrugged. 'I just can't believe it.'

James studied Matt, who had slumped against the side of a parked car. 'I know. He was your friend, Matt. It's understandable. But I don't think there can be any doubt. Believe me, I've seen it all before. We'll know soon enough though.'

Low black clouds hung in the sky, threatening more rain and there was no shelter from a rising easterly wind that sought gaps in their jackets. They stamped their feet and rubbed their hands. Matt looked at his watch for what seemed like the tenth time in ten minutes.

'We've been waiting an hour already.'

James shrugged his shoulders. 'We get to do a lot of waiting around at crime scenes. It's not like a football match. Fancy another coffee?'

They strolled back towards the catering van. The queue had dwindled and they walked straight up to the cheerful lady at the counter. 'I'll get them,' said James and handed over the money.

'Thanks, love. Bleeding parky, ain't it?' she said, rubbing her hands. 'Cold enough for snow.'

'Have you had any contact with Barker's wife?' James asked.

'What do you mean?' Matt snapped.

'I just wondered if you had phoned her this morning.'

'Oh! Of course. The line was busy. I left a message.' His voice tailed off as he tried to think what he would say when he met her. 'Anyway, I'm hoping to get a chance to see her this afternoon – you know, when the police have gone.'

James grinned at him, 'You're going to make the rest of the press pack jealous – getting an interview with Mrs. Barker today.'

Matt winced. 'Yeah, but it'll be difficult, won't it? She'll be in shock.'

'I know, but you'll be on the inside: never know what you're going to hear.'

A small group of football writers wandered over. 'Hello, Matt. Terrible business,' said Harry, shaking his hand. 'Did you have any inkling?'

'I'm totally gobsmacked, Harry. I was with him last week. I just can't believe it.' Harry Robinson was huddled in a padded jacket, stamping his feet to keep warm. Although they worked on rival papers, Matt and Harry often met at press conferences and matches and had become friends.

'I'm going to miss him,' said Harry. 'It's unbelievable. After all the Barker stories we've done, who would have guessed that his biggest story would be his last?'

Another reporter standing near Harry butted in. John 'Sniffer'

Jackson was a pale, thin, short man with pinched features. His 'red top' paper sold millions because readers liked their sensational stories, and Jackson would turn over any stone to find them. If he didn't find anything, he had been known to make a story up.

'Do you think things were alright between Barker and his wife?'

'Yeah, I think so. Why do you ask?'

'Apparently she was out on her own,' said Jackson. 'Got back in the early hours this morning. And Barker tops himself while she was out.'

'Are you sure?' Matt said, controlling his surprise. 'I hadn't heard that. Where was she?'

'At a party, apparently. You knew Barker. Was the marriage in trouble?'

Matt wondered where Sniffer was going with this. If it was true that she had been out at a party on her own last night, that raised more questions, but he didn't want to give Jackson any encouragement to begin a sensational story.

'Rock solid, mate. I'd have known if there was any trouble.'

But he had heard rumours. Tony had never said anything, but who can tell what really goes on inside a marriage? When his own went through a rocky patch he had never discussed it with anyone. His friends were shocked when he and Susie agreed their trial separation.

'So, what do you think?' Matt asked Sniffer.

Sniffer shrugged. 'Could have been financial difficulties.'

'Really,' Matt replied. 'What gave you that idea?'

'Well, Gary Pearson told me that his financial advisor, Veejay Patel his name was, conned him out of a couple of million – and he hinted he'd done Tony as well. Of course we didn't publish that. Gary wouldn't go on the record but, well, we all know he sails a bit close to the wind. He said Patel came up with investment ideas with fantastic returns, tax free schemes, offshore accounts – I don't think Gary understood a word of it. Just let Patel get on with it. Mind you, Patel was very plausible, smartly dressed, talked a good game. Seemed to know everybody in football.'

Others in the group had stopped talking and were listening to Sniffer.

'So, you think Patel conned Barker?' said Matt.

Sniffer shrugged. 'I don't know. I'm just saying he could have. It's the sort of thing that could drive a man to suicide.'

'Come off it, Sniffer,' Matt said. 'You know what Gary's like. Always good for a quote, but I should take it with a barrel of salt.'

James interrupted, looking up from his phone. 'The press conference is at twelve at Wimbledon Police Station.' They glanced at their watches and began to walk towards their cars. Sniffer turned to Matt again.

'What do you think about Barker's relationship with Buzinsky?'

Sergei Buzinsky had come to prominence in the Brezhnev era in the 1980s, acquiring assets in energy companies cheaply and in suspicious circumstances. Like other Russian oligarchs, he had come under scrutiny in the Putin era, was jailed under corruption charges, and then released some five years later after an appeal. It was rumoured that he was in a legal battle with shareholders in his Russian companies and in conflict with the government.

None of that was of any concern to London City supporters. Buzinsky had brought football to the City of London. Supporters had come from the affluent developments east of the city, and from the catchment area vacated by West Ham's relocation to the London Stadium. City were in the big time: Premier League Champions and competing to be the most successful club in Europe.

'Look, we all know what Buzinsky is like,' said Matt. 'He owns the football club and he can do what the hell he likes. Tony knew that when he took the job. All right, they didn't see eye to eye on everything, but Buzinsky thought Tony was the best manager in Europe and he wants to win the Champions League. Tony was his best chance of doing it.'

'They had a row over Sirocco though, didn't they?'

'Oh for Christ's sake, Sniffer! Yes, Tony was pissed off when Buzinsky made a decision to buy a player without consulting him, but that's hardly a reason to take your own fucking life, is it?'

The group split up to find their cars. James, who had come by train, cadged a lift with Matt.

'Nice motor,' James said, as he slipped into the BMW. 'Hmm,' he grunted, sniffing the leather, 'smells new too. Pay well on the sports desk, do they?'

Matt threw back his head and laughed. 'I wish. No, I made good money when I was playing. Nothing by today's standards, but I made some investments that turned out well. What were you doing before this?'

'Army. SIB.'

Matt looked at him. 'SIB?'

'Special Investigation Branch – operational arm of the Royal Military Police.'

'You were a detective?'

'Yeah. I transferred across from the regular army and it was a good fit for me: enquiring mind, self-motivated, working on my own a lot of the time. And the work was challenging: serious criminal cases, complex fraud, special investigations.'

'Where were you operating?'

'Oh, all over the world. Germany, Libya, Hong Kong; Northern Ireland mostly.'

'Ouch,' said Matt.

'Yes, it's stuff we don't talk about. Not just the Official Secrets Act. I saw things I wouldn't want to tell anyone about.'

'I can imagine. Are you married?'

'I was, but we divorced fifteen years ago. What with endless travel and the unsocial hours, Mary just couldn't take it anymore.'

'Sounds familiar. How did you get into journalism?'

'I'd reached army retirement age, took a pension, and looked for a job. I saw the advertisement and I was lucky. The *Chronicle* thought my SIB background would be useful on the crime desk, dealing with the police. You know, sort of gamekeeper turned poacher. '

Matt looked at James in a new light. This was not the public school/army officer stereotype he had imagined when he first saw James. Despite their age difference, he thought, they had things in common. He found that he liked him and respected him in a way he had not expected when they met earlier.

Wimbledon police station was a modern red brick building in the centre of the town. On a weekday, the shops and restaurants would be busy and parking would be a nightmare, but on a wet Sunday it seemed eerily quiet and the nearby multi-story car park was deserted.

A large utilitarian room had been allocated for the press conference. The space had already filled up with journalists from every British national newspaper, television and radio station, as well as UK-based journalists from European newspapers. Writers chatted to each other as they removed their wet jackets and raincoats and hung them over the back of the black metal chairs. The seats were all taken as even more accredited media crowded in and were left to stand at the back. With the central heating turned up to maximum, the assembly's wet clothes gave off a damp steamy heat and the atmosphere became oppressive.

The buzz in the room died away as Detective Sergeant Maclean entered and took his seat at a raised table flanked by two uniformed officers. Behind him was a large portrait of the queen. He faced a bank of TV cameras and a forest of microphones.

Maclean was in his early fifties, short and stocky. His steel grey hair had been cut very short and his penetrating blue eyes gave the appearance of a man who missed nothing. Deep lines were drawn across his forehead and sallow cheeks. He looked like a man who had seen it all before. Maclean was unfazed by the media barrage and began by reading a short statement.

'On behalf of the Metropolitan Police I would like to extend our sympathy to Mrs. Barker, her family, and all those connected with London City Football Club for the tragic death of Mr. Barker.' He cleared his throat and looked around the room at the expectant sea of faces. 'A 999 call was made by Mrs. Barker at five past six this morning. The police and ambulance arrived at the scene at twenty past six. Mr. Barker was found hanging in his home and was pronounced dead by the ambulance crew. We have completed our investigation of the body, the house and the grounds and have found no suspicious circumstances. We are treating this as a tragic case of suicide. The coroner has been informed, the body has been moved to the mortuary and a post-mortem will be carried out tomorrow. We believe that the time of death was between ten o'clock and midnight on Saturday evening. The pathologist will confirm the time.' He put his down his notes. 'Thank you. I will take questions now.'

As the detective sergeant sat down a hubbub erupted. Journalists raised their hands, competing to get their questions in. Cameras clicked incessantly and dazzling flash photography lit the room.

'Had he threatened to commit suicide before?'

'We are not aware that he had.'

'Had he been suffering from depression?'

'We don't know. That will be a matter for the coroner.'

'Was there a suicide note?'

'No note has been found, but that's not unusual in these cases.'

'Where was he found?'

'Mr. Barker was found hanging in his study.'

'Was there any sign of a forced entry?'

'No, we found no evidence of foul play. We are treating this as a case of suicide.' Matt chipped in. 'Were there any visitors during the evening?'

'No. We checked the CCTV. There were no visitors.'

Everyone had a hand up, trying to get their question in. Maclean pointed to Sniffer Jackson.

'Where was his wife at the time Mr. Barker died?'

'Mrs. Barker was at a friend's party and did not return until after two on Sunday morning.'

'Why didn't Mrs. Barker find the body until six that morning?'

'As I've just said, Mrs. Barker came home alone late last night and went straight to bed in another bedroom.'

'Was that unusual?'

'We understand that, as she came in late, she didn't want to disturb her husband.'

'The Barkers have two sons. Where were they?'

'The two children were away at boarding school.'

'Have you established any reason why he would want to kill himself?'

'No. We don't know, and that will now be a matter for the coroner's inquest.' D.S. Maclean stood up. 'Thank you, ladies and gentlemen. That's all for now.'

Outside the police station, on the paved concourse, Matt called Bill and gave him a run down on the press conference. His response was short and to the point. 'You have to find out why he did it. That's the story.'

'I know. The trouble is, I knew Tony. He's the last person I would expect to take his own life.'

Bill's sceptical snort spoke volumes. 'Sorry, Matt, but I've heard it all before. What about his wife? Why was she out at a party on her own? Got back at two in the morning? Had they had a fight? Was she having an affair? You're the best person to find out.'

'I know, Bill. I'm going to try to see Tania this afternoon.'

'That's good. I want an exclusive.'

'I know but...'

'It's suicide, Matt. Get on with it. What readers want to know is why he did it.'

CHAPTER THREE

Matt disconnected the call to Bill and looked around. The concourse outside the police station teemed with journalists huddled over their smart phones, texting, emailing, phoning or just chatting in small groups. TV presenters were broadcasting live reports. In their studios, editors would be rushing to source new photographs, select footage and find celebrity players and managers to interview. Matt wasn't one of them. His fame as a football personality had faded years ago and no one had yet made the connection between him and Barker.

He ran James to Wimbledon station for the train back to Waterloo. He paused before getting out of the car. 'I don't think there is much here for me after this week. I expect the sports desk will be all over it for weeks, but if I can be any help, old chap, just give me a call. Anytime. I mean it.'

Matt watched him melt into the crowd funneling into the station, pulled out his phone and dialed Tania's number again. It was still busy. He redialed a few minutes later and this time a voice he didn't recognise answered.

'Can I speak to Tania, please?'

'Who is this?'

'My name is Matt Riley. I'm a close friend.'

'Hello, Matt. This is police constable Pauline Edwards. I'm the family liaison officer looking after Mrs. Barker.'

'Oh, right. How is she?'

'She's in shock at the moment, but that's to be expected.'

'I wondered if I could come to see her?'

'You're a close friend, you say?'

'Yes.'

'Could you hold on for a moment please?'

There was a long silence. He assumed she had gone to speak to Tania. After what seemed like minutes she got back to him. 'Mr. Riley, are you still there?'

'Yes,' he said, his pulse quickening as he waited for the answer.

'Yes, Mrs. Barker would like to see you. It's always a help when they have someone to talk to about their loved one. When can you come?' He heaved a silent sigh of relief.

'I could be there in ten minutes. Is that okay?'

'Ten minutes? Where are you?'

'I'm at the press conference at Wimbledon police station.'

'You're a journalist?'

'Yes, I am.'

There was another long silence. She was probably speaking to Tania again he thought. At last she got back to him, her tone suggesting that she did not approve of a visit from a journalist.

'Mrs. Barker said you can come now.'

Most of the police vehicles had left when Matt returned, but the paparazzi were still tracking every movement in and out of the house, hoping for a sighting of Tania. He lowered the car window, and the police constable on duty checked his identity and cleared him to enter. Some of the paps recognised him and crowded round the car.

'Hi, Matt.'

'Are you going to see Tania?'

'How is she?'

'I don't know yet. I'm here to offer my condolences.' The gates swung silently open and the BMW scrunched up the gravel drive.

The front door was opened by P.C. Edwards. Standing behind her, he recognised Tania's sister, Jane. He had only met her a few times. The last time was probably at his godson's christening. Matt guessed she was about six years older than Tania, but she had the same blonde hair and blue eyes as her sister. Although she must have risen very early, her hair had been carefully done and she wore make up. He stepped inside and P.C. Edwards slammed the door shut on the peeping eyes of a hundred telephoto lenses.

'Hello, Matt. Thanks so much for coming.' Jane stepped forward and gave him a kiss on the cheek. 'It's been terrible, but it will be a comfort for Tania to talk to someone who was close to Tony.'

'How is she?'

'Not good. Still in shock as you can imagine. We're just trying to get through today. Come and say hello.' They walked through into the empty lounge. 'Tania's in the kitchen with Emma Griffin. Oh, I forgot, you must know Tony's PA of course.'

'Yes, we've met a few times and we speak on the phone a lot.'

Matt wasn't entirely surprised to find Emma there. Tony had often said that his PA was indispensable.

'Emma's offered to come over and help. She's been a treasure: the phone hasn't stopped ringing,' said Jane. 'The boys are at their boarding school, thank goodness. I spoke to the Head early this morning. Wait here and I'll go and fetch Tania.'

He hadn't been to their new house before. He usually met Tony at the training ground or a restaurant. He looked around. The room was tastefully furnished – a Persian carpet on the oak floor and white leather sofas. The walls were hung with original oil paintings of English country scenes. Hardly Tania's taste, he thought, more likely an expensive interior designer. A grand piano stood in one corner. He hadn't seen it before and he knew Tania didn't play. He smiled to himself. She didn't even like classical music – it was her way of making a statement. There were no football trophies or photographs. He thought Tony probably kept those in his study.

Silver framed photographs stood on the gleaming black piano. He picked up a wedding portrait: Tony, confident, smiling, a football star with the world at his feet; Tania, a slim, beautiful, footballer's wife. It had been a hot July afternoon—Matt's shirt had clung to his back in the black morning jacket and waistcoat—but Tania looked cool. He remembered the time when Susie first met Tania. 'Typical footballer's wife,' she had said, tossing her head in the air.

The door clicked as it closed and he looked up at Tania. She was wearing jeans and a sloppy sweater. Her face was pale and drawn, her blonde hair unbrushed. Her sunken eyes had a haunted look.

He walked across the room and put his arms around her, his cheek softly touching hers. 'I'm so sorry, Tania,' he whispered. It seemed such an inadequate thing to say, but it wasn't something you rehearsed. Her body was shaking and she clung to Matt for a long time.

'How are you?' he said finally. She didn't answer.

Jane came in with a tray of coffee, breaking the awkward silence. They pulled apart as Jane set out the cups.

'It's been very difficult,' Jane said. 'The police have been asking lots of questions but she just can't take it in.'

Tania was shaking her head. 'Why? Why did he do it?' She stood there, helplessly twisting a handkerchief through her fingers. 'Why?'

'I don't know, Tania.' He shook his head. 'I can't believe it either. I had lunch with him only five days ago.'

'Did you? What did he say?'

'He said...' Matt, hesitated, breathed in deeply, then exhaled slowly. 'He told me he had booked a surprise trip to Venice for your anniversary.'

She stared at him for a moment, a tear appearing in the corner of one eye and sliding slowly down her cheek. She picked up a cup, her hands trembling, took a sip and set the cup back in the saucer with a nervous clatter that spilled coffee onto the table. Jane rushed to mop it up with a napkin. Tania stared at the cup, seemingly unaware of the spill.

'We haven't got any biscuits. I must have forgotten them. I'm sorry, Matt. I'm sorry.'

'Don't worry.'

'Tony loved Hobnobs, they were his favourites.'

'I know.'

'Do you like Hobnobs? I'll get some tomorrow.'

Matt smiled at her. 'Don't worry. How are the boys?'

Tania seemed not to have heard. She looked around the room. 'Jane, where's Buster?' She looked back at Matt. 'Tony loved Buster. He always fed him himself: biscuits in the morning and a tin of meat at night.' She seemed lost in her thoughts. 'He loved taking Buster for his walk.' She paused. 'That's if he was here, of course.'

'How are the boys?' Matt asked again.

Tania stared down at her hands. Jane jumped in.

'Thank God they weren't here! Mum and Dad are driving up from Kent now. They'll collect the boys from school and take them back with them. We thought it was best,' she said, waving her hand dismissively in the direction of the media entourage. 'Tania spoke to them when we phoned the headmaster this morning.'

Tania looked from Jane to Matt, biting her lower lip. 'I just told them... Daddy was...' she choked up. Matt waited for her to continue. ‘That Daddy had died... I couldn’t tell them... you know,’ she said, looking down at the floor.

Jane broke the long awkward silence that had filled the room. ‘I think they’ll be better off with Mum and Dad. It’s in the country and the boys like exploring in the woods. We’ll bring them back when things settle down here,’ she said, glancing out of the window at the paparazzi and looking accusingly at Matt. He wriggled uncomfortably in his seat, struggling to find the right balance between being a friend and a journalist.

‘Do you want to tell me about it?’ he asked Tania.

The ticking of the grandfather clock measured the silence. He waited. Finally, Tania said softly, ‘I looked in the bedroom.’ Her voice trembled, like a child playing tentative first notes on a recorder. ‘He wasn’t there... or in the bathroom. I called out... ran down the stairs... I thought he might be in the study.’ She had been staring glassy-eyed into space, but now she turned to face Matt. ‘He gets up early, you know. He likes to work then...’ There was a long pause while she took a deep breath and summoned up the strength to go on. ‘And there he was... hanging... like a rag doll.’ Her shoulders slumped forward, her chin sagging onto her chest, perhaps subconsciously mimicking how she found him. Nobody spoke and Matt’s skin tingled as he imagined how she must have felt. After a while she recovered her composure, and continued, unnaturally calm. ‘He was dead, of course. I knew that. I just dialed 999.’

Matt hesitated before bringing up the question he knew he had to ask. ‘Why didn’t you find him until six this morning?’

Tania jerked upright. Her mood changed. ‘I told the police,’ she snapped. ‘I’d been out at a party and didn’t get back until two. I went straight to bed in another room.’

‘Wasn’t that a bit odd?’

‘What? Sleeping in separate bedrooms?’

‘No, going to a party on your own.’

She slumped back in her chair, avoiding looking at him. ‘Look, Matt,’ she said in a monotone voice. ‘It was a crowd of friends we know in Wimbledon. He didn’t mind. It was just a party!’

‘What time did you go out?’

‘Oh, I don’t know. Around eight I suppose.’

'Why didn't Tony want to go?'

'He was tired. He'd just come back from the match. It wasn't unusual. He liked to sit quietly and think about it. Play a video of the game.'

'How did he seem then?'

'I just told you, Matt. He was tired.'

He wondered if that was all it was. Why had Tony wanted to be at home on his own? Why would she stay out so late? He thought about the rumours that had been circulating and wondered if she had been having an affair? If she was, did Tony know about it? Did they have a row? Was that why she had gone on her own? With Tania there was always a façade – you were never quite sure you were getting the whole story.

He wanted to probe further but, sensing an awkward moment, Jane interjected and steered them onto safer ground. 'The police asked her if she had any inkling that he might do it. Well, of course she hadn't. Tony was always able to handle problems.'

Tania nodded. 'I kept telling them I had no idea.' She looked to Matt as if he might have the answers. 'You're his friend, Matt. Why would he do that?'

'I don't know. Do you think he was depressed?'

'Tony?' She dismissed the question with a hollow laugh. 'No. Not Tony.'

'Did he ever say he felt suicidal?'

'No, of course not!'

'The detective kept on asking Tania questions,' said Jane. 'Did he have a life insurance policy? Of course he did!'

'£5 million,' said Tania.

'He'd make sure Tania was looked after,' Jane added with an emphatic nod.

'But what will happen?' Tania said. 'What will happen if they say it's suicide? Will they pay out?'

Matt shrugged his shoulders. 'I don't think so. Not if it was suicide.'

Tania considered his answer in silence. Feeling embarrassed, Jane broke in again.

'Then one of them asked her if Tony had lost money on investments. Well, of course she didn't know!'

'Why did they ask that?'

'Oh, I think they found some correspondence, but I don't know what it was,' said Tania, who had been staring at her palms, as if they might contain the answer.

She looked up at Matt. 'You knew him better than anyone. Why do you think he did it?'

Matt held up his hands. 'Honestly, Tania, I don't know. I just don't know.' He got up, walked to the window, then turned to face Tania. 'Was there anything unusual about his behaviour in the last few weeks, anything that seemed odd?'

'No,' she said, shaking her head and playing with the gold cross that dangled from her neck.

Jane, who appeared bored now, stood up and took the tray out to the kitchen, leaving Matt alone with Tania for the first time. She walked to the window, stared out at the media pack, and then spun round to face Matt.

'It's my fault. If I hadn't gone to that bloody party he'd still be alive.'

Matt froze. What did she mean? What hadn't she told him? He stared at her for a moment, unsure he had heard correctly. She began to cry, quietly at first, until the soft tears turned to sobs. He walked over and put his arm around her shoulder.

'What do you mean?'

'Oh, God!' she moaned.

'Tania, what happened?'

Her face crumbled.

'Were you having an affair?'

She heaved a long drawn out sigh.

'Were you?'

She pulled away from him. 'Of course not!'

CHAPTER FOUR

It was early on Sunday evening when Julia pushed open the engraved glass door of the Prince of Wales and stood peering into the dimly lit bar. The polished dark wood and brass fittings, the cut glass and mirrored bar, the floral banquettes, the smell of furniture polish and the scent of fresh flowers mixed with the beery smell of hops, all suggested a calm and ordered world that had absorbed a thousand secrets. A few regulars gathered round the carved mahogany bar. It seemed to Matt like a good place for a chat.

His sister shook off her wet umbrella, spotted him and waved her arms like windscreen wipers in a downpour. She rushed across the room and hugged him. Sometimes he thought she had hardly changed since they were kids. She was dressed casually in faded blue jeans and a sweater – as she usually was when she was away from the medical practice where she worked as a psychiatrist

They settled into a comfortable bay window seat. Her hair was cut short. She didn't bother with hairdressers or make up, and she rarely wore any jewellery, but her eyes sparkled. It was how he remembered her when she was a teenage girl.

'How are you, Matt? I haven't seen you for ages. You're always so busy. You never call me. How are things with Susie and Callum?'

He shrugged. 'Oh, about the same. I get on okay with Susie. I see Callum whenever I get time. Susie's very good like that.' He paused and looked up at his sister. 'He's a great kid. I feel guilty. I should spend more time with him.'

'Work?'

'Yeah.'

'It must be difficult. How's it going?'

'I've had some good stories, but we've just had more layoffs, so there's more work for the rest of the team. Then there are cutbacks on budgets and, to cap it all, Bill's told me to cut out investigative stories. Can you believe it? They take up too much time! The trouble is he doesn't stand up for himself.' He leaned back in his seat and sighed in frustration.

'Anyway, enough about me. How are things with you?'

'Well, busy of course, and a few serious cases that keep me on call,' she said, pointing at the mobile phone on the table beside her. 'And we're short staffed too. But Tom and I have just planned our summer holiday – a two-week walking tour in the Yorkshire dales.'

'How is Tom?' Matt asked. Her husband was an academic – a lecturer at King's College at the University of London. He was pleasant enough, but usually lost in his own world of microbiology and he didn't have any interest in football. They had never had children, but Tom shared her passion for walking and climbing.

'Oh, he's fine: excited because he's just had a research paper published.'

Matt smiled, finding it difficult to imagine Tom in an excited state about anything. Not like Julia. She always seemed to have enough enthusiasm for the two of them.

'Did you hear about Tony?'

'Yes, I heard it on the radio.' She placed her hand on his. 'I'm sorry, Matt. I know you were close. It must have been a difficult day for you.'

'Yeah, it's been a shock. I've been there all day. The police are treating it as suicide. Bill wants me to get the story.' He screwed up his face. 'Trouble is, Jules, I can't even begin to understand why he would do it.'

'I know,' she said sympathetically. 'It's always hard for those left behind. They want to know why. Know if it was their fault. Know if they could have prevented it.'

He sighed. 'Yeah, I think that's what Tania is thinking.'

'It's much more common than you think.'

'Why? What drives someone to do it?'

'Oh, Matt, it's such a complex subject. There's no easy answer.'

'Jules, just help me to understand it. I need some background for the piece I'm writing.'

'Alright.' She settled back into the seat. 'Look, Matt, I didn't know Tony, so I can't talk about him, but let me try and help.'

Matt nodded and took out his notepad.

'Well, in general terms, suicides can be grouped into two main types: the ones we can help and the "out of the blue" types. The most common cause is depression and that's where we can help. It can be brought on by ill health, marital problems, financial problems or problems at work. They build up until they become too much to bear.'

Matt concentrated on the notes he was making.

'Most people can cope, but some personality types are more vulnerable to depression. They usually provide warnings. Sometimes they even make failed suicide attempts. These are the ones we can help. Counselling and anti-depressants can be quite successful over a long period.'

'Tony never said anything to me. I don't think he was depressed.'

'Well, sometimes it's difficult to tell, especially in people who are naturally outgoing. I often hear people say that. And of course it's worse for people in the public eye. Didn't I see an article recently about a footballer who had the courage to admit he was suffering from depression?'

'Yeah, that's true' said Matt, and told her about a well-known player who had admitted to chronic depression, but only after he had retired. 'And there have been some high-profile cricket players who suffered too.'

'You should know, Matt. They're in the media spotlight every time they play. The pressure is enormous, and players have to accept the brickbats as well as the praise. The trouble is, there's a stigma about admitting depression, especially in a macho world like football. Don't you think the same thing is true for football managers?'

'Yes, I suppose so,' he admitted begrudgingly. 'But they seem remarkably resilient.'

She decided not to pursue it and followed up her earlier point. 'Are you sure there were no warnings? There is usually some history leading up to suicide attempts by depressives.'

'Tania said he had never been suicidal.' He stared into his glass. 'There is one thing though. I think she was having an affair. She might be torturing herself with the thought that he may have found out. Or perhaps he did and they had a row. Could that have caused depression?'

'Well, it could be a contributory factor, but it wouldn't happen overnight. There would be a build up over months. You knew him well. Do you think that's what happened?'

'To be frank, Julia, I think if he knew, he would have had it out with her. He's the last person I can imagine bottling up something like that, or getting depressed.'

'Hmm,' she murmured. 'I don't think you can be quite so sure. Often it's a secret that even close friends would never guess.'

Matt took a sip of his beer and carefully placed the glass on the centre of the coaster.

'You said that suicides divide into two types. So what is the other type?'

'Yes, the "out of the blue" suicides. They rarely show risk factors. Nobody expects it and everyone is shocked. We can't help them because we don't know about them until it's too late.'

'Oh,' said Matt, rubbing his chin. 'Well, I suppose you could say that about Tony.'

'Not necessarily, but you must be the judge of that. We call these types narcissist. They're inward looking, obsessed with themselves and striving for perfection. For them it's all or nothing. They're acutely worried about how others perceive them and would find failure unacceptable. I knew an academic who was given the task of raising £5 million from alumni for an extension to the college chapel. He raised £4.5 million and everyone was delighted. But he was found hanged in the chapel. He committed suicide because he thought he had failed.'

Matt shook his head in disbelief. 'Good God.'

'They're characterised by a dedication to hard work. They have deeply held convictions of conscience and moral principle and they need to do things perfectly. They thrive on accomplishment and set high standards.'

'Well, that certainly applies to Tony. But surely that would be true of anyone at the top of their profession?'

'Yes, you're right,' replied Julia. 'We all have traits of obsessiveness, but most top people have developed ways of coping. They aren't worriers. They've proved to themselves that they can succeed at different levels: at school or university, in sport, or in other positions as they rise up the career ladder. They have protectors like family, social support and religion. What I'm talking about are those on the severe side of the pathological spectrum – the abnormal.'

'Abnormal? What do you mean by abnormal?'

'Do you remember *Les Misérables*?'

Matt nodded. 'Yes. I saw the musical.'

'Well, a good example of suicide by a narcissistic type is the character Javert. Despite being a faithful Christian, he finally jumps from a bridge because he can't cope with the idea that his arch enemy has saved his life. Javert was an obsessive, a perfectionist who bases his life on certain rules. When he finds that he has broken those rules his psychic system can't cope. Suicide is his only "honourable" option.'

'Really?' said Matt, scratching the back of his head. 'I never thought about it like that.'

Julia leaned back in her seat. 'So, what do you think? Was Tony abnormally obsessive?'

He stroked the five-day growth on his chin and considered the question. 'No, I don't think so. All right, I can see that he was obsessed by his job. A football manager has a lot of stress, but he was used to handling that. He had his feet on the ground. He had outside interests. And family, of course.' Matt thought about it for a while then shook his head, rejecting the idea. 'No. I wouldn't say Tony was "abnormally obsessive,"' he said, emphasising the word abnormally.

There was a roar of laughter at the bar from a crowd of regulars. Julia looked across and then back to Matt who was frowning. 'I'm sorry, Matt. I wish I could be more helpful, but I can't tell you why Tony took his life.'

'I know you can't,' he said.

She glanced at her watch and stood up to leave. 'Sorry, Matt, I've got to...' He touched her arm. 'Before you go... there was something else.'

She turned back to look at him, saw the concern etched into his face. 'What? What is it?'

He opened his wallet and carefully took out a faded newspaper cutting and passed it to her. She unfolded it carefully. 'Dad?' she said, and he nodded. Julia sank back in her seat. When she had finished reading, she looked into her brother's eyes. 'Oh, Matt, this has brought it all back, hasn't it?'

'Yes, it has. We never talked about it though, did we? Really talked about it.'

'I'm sorry, Matt.' She reached out and took his hand. 'That was my fault. We were all so shocked.' She sighed. 'I felt I had to go back to university after the funeral.' She inhaled and bit her lip. 'I had exams.' He stared at her. There was a long silence. 'I know, I know. It was selfish: I left you and mum on your own.' She shook her head slowly as if she understood for the first time what he must have been through. 'I'm so sorry, Matt. You were just twelve. I suppose I thought you wouldn't understand. God, I didn't understand it myself back then! None of us did – just tried to deal with it in our own way. And after that... after that I suppose it was just something none of us wanted to talk about.'

He looked at her and nodded slowly, alone with the memories that haunted him.

My chest feels tight and I'm finding it hard to breathe. Sam is whimpering and nuzzling me. Gradually I get my breath back and bang my fist on the concrete floor and scream. No! No! I force myself to get up and look at him again. The rope is looped round his neck and goes up to a beam in the roof. Underneath his feet I notice a stool that must have fallen over. His face looks like he's in pain. I start to cry again. He's wearing his blue club tracksuit and he's got his black trainers on. It can't be true. I think I must be dreaming. I creep forward, stretch out my hands and touch his leg. It's stiff. I push and he just swings a bit. I recoil in shock. He's dead. He's dead! I scream and run to the door. Mummy! Mummy!

His father had been the manager of a League 2 football club. He never set the world alight but was always an honest professional. A man the players respected. Despite his budget being regularly slashed he had kept the club in a league position beyond even the expectations of the town's faithful supporters. Then, out of the blue, the owner of the club had fired him and spread rumours that his manager had taken a bung from a transfer deal. It wasn't true, but it had finished him. He got some work scouting for other clubs – long hours, late nights, driving thousands of miles, and all for a pittance – but he never got another manager's job. A year later he was dead.

When I get to school nobody in the playground speaks to me. They huddle in groups, looking at me and pointing. Even my friends are avoiding me. I suppose they don't know what to say. We drift into the classroom. Everyone is watching me. I sit down at my desk and look up at the blackboard.

MATTHEW NODAD has been written there in large letters. My face is burning. They are all sniggering. Even the girls are laughing behind their hands. I don't care. I look around. Tomkins. He's got this smartass grin on his face. I know it's him. I'm going to get him.

Sir walks into the room and tells everyone to be quiet. He glances behind him at the blackboard. "Who did this?" Now there is silence. He looks around the room. No one answers. Some boys shift in their seats. He shrugs. "This is very childish. Don't let me see anything like this again." He picks up the rubber and wipes it out. That's it. He isn't going to do anything.

As we troop out to the playground at break time, Tomkins and his gang try to get in my way. They circle round me, shouting, grabbing and turning me round.

"Nodad"

"Hangman."

"Nodad."

"Hangman, hangman, hangman."

"Your dad topped himself."

"Loser. Your dad's a loser."

"Your dad got the sack. He's a loser."

"That's why he topped himself."

Tomkins sticks his face in mine. His red hair is plastered down the side of his sweaty head. He spits in my face. "You're a fucking Nodad."

"It was you," I choke. He laughs. I break free of the hands round me and land my fist right on his nose. Blood spurts all over him. He screams, then he's got his hands round my neck. We both roll to the ground. The boys make a circle and shout, "Fight. Fight," and others run over.

He's bigger than me and he's on top, but I push my thumbs in his eyes until he lets go. Then I keep punching him in the face, in the stomach – anywhere I can. He's screaming and there's blood all over him.

The crowd parts and Sir is pulling me off him. He takes us both to the master's room.

"He started it," says Tomkins and starts crying.

"What happened?" he asks me.

I say nothing. He asks me again. Still I say nothing.

Tomkins is dismissed. He picks up a cane and gives me six on each hand. The welts swell up. They bleed and they hurt.

Matt banged his fist on the table, shaking the empty glasses in front of them and held his head in his hands. Julia flinched. 'What is it? Why are you so angry?'

He unclenched his fist and looked up. 'Well, I guess the thing is... the thing is... I think the reason I've never talked about it before is, I'm angry with Dad.'

'Angry with Dad? Why?'

'How could he just give in like that? How could he just accept it? The owner was corrupt. He'd been fiddling the books and he sacked Dad to cover it up. It all came out when he was done for tax fraud a few years later. He was a bully. He was corrupt and he abused his power. Dad let him walk all over him. He didn't fight back. And then he hanged himself.'

'Oh, Matt, I'm so sorry. But you shouldn't be so hard on him. It was another era and you're very different from him.'

Matt sat in silence, not listening. He was back in the school playground, the taunting still stinging his ears.

'But it's made you who you are,' she whispered, leaning over to kiss him.

CHAPTER FIVE

It was nine o'clock on Sunday evening when Matt got home to his flat in Fulham. The shelves were filled with books and CDs. Concert posters of Bowie, Dylan and Mumford and Sons covered one wall. On another wall a glass cabinet displayed football medals. A framed back page showing him holding the FA Cup. Papers were stacked neatly in trays or filed in the cabinet. A cork board on the wall next to his desk displayed notes and reminders of things he was working on. On a table there was a photograph of him with Susie and Callum in the park, all of them happy. There were others of Callum – playing football, on a skateboard and swimming. His black carbon road bike stood in the hall. It was rated by some cycling magazines as the best bike in the world. He had never dared to tell Susie how much it cost. She was always telling him he spent too much. Callum's birthday was coming up. He should buy a bike for Callum – a good one. They could go cycling together.

He had just poured a glass of wine and walked into the kitchen when his phone rang. He glanced at the screen. It was Frankie Warren, one of the network of agents he used to get information about players. Frankie ran things close to the wire. He had begun life working in his father's used car showroom in Dagenham. Now he drove his own Bentley Continental.

'How's things, Frank?'

'Good, Matt, good. I was just thinking you might want to do me a favour.'

He laughed. 'It depends. What is it?'

'I got this player at West Ham, Andersson. He's not very happy.'

'Oh yeah?'

'Well, I thought you might want to do a story on how the boy's not settled. Not happy about being played out of position. Might be considering a move. Know what I mean?'

This was the currency they traded in.

'Why would I want to do that, Frank?'

'I might have some information for you.'

'Yeah?'

'I thought about it when I was watching TV today. Shocking news about Barker.'

'Yeah. I've been there all day.'

'I thought you would.' He paused. 'You know City games were being fixed don't you?'

'What?' Matt's heart was thumping like a jackhammer.

'I was just wondering if that might have anything to do with it.'

'Fixed?'

'Yes.'

'Which games?' Matt waited for an answer that didn't come.

'Did Tony know?'

'I don't know. I should think so. That's what I'm saying, Matt. It might have had something to do with it. Know what I mean?'

'How did you find out?'

'Look, Matt, I can't tell you that, but you know how word gets around. When I heard the news about Barker today, well, it just made me wonder.'

'Yeah, thanks, Frank. Look, when you can tell me any more I'll see what I can do about your boy.'

Matt walked over to the window and looked out. It was dark and mist swirled in from the river like the thoughts in his mind. It could just be rumours; there were always plenty of those. Agents were notoriously unreliable. Stories emerged and then disappeared as quickly as the mist. But agents knew what was going on. Players told them everything. It was possible. Match fixing in the Premier League? Unlikely, but it was possible.

He topped up his glass and paced around the kitchen. If a couple of players had fixed a match and Tony found out, he would have dealt with it. Why would he kill himself – unless he had been involved himself? He exhaled slowly and shook his head. That was ridiculous. But what if Tony was about to uncover something big? He stood staring out at the black night as a torrent of rain lashed against the window. Raindrops slid down the outside, but the thought had lodged in his mind. What if it wasn't suicide?

He looked at his watch. It was five to ten. Not too late to call Julia.

'Matt. Is everything alright?'

'Yes, I'm sorry to ring so late. Something's come up. Look, I haven't said anything to anyone else yet... but I'm wondering... what if it wasn't suicide?'

'What do you mean?'

'Perhaps he was murdered?'

'Murdered? What on earth makes you think that?'

He told her about his call from Frankie Warren.

'But there was no evidence of foul play, Matt. With Barker being who he was the police will have been very thorough.'

'I know, I've been thinking about that. But what if he was murdered and then it was made to look like suicide?'

She didn't answer but he could tell she was thinking about it.

'Do you think that's possible?' he said. 'How can you tell a natural suicide from murder made to look like suicide?'

'Matt, I can see where you're going with this, and I know what you're like when you're chasing a story but honestly, I think you're barking up the wrong tree here. Unexplained suicides are all too common, and loved ones find it hard to accept. But murder disguised as suicide? Don't you think you're letting your imagination run away with you?'

'Come on, Jules,' he snapped. 'My imagination? You know me better than that. Imagination is in my DNA. It's what I do. I keep asking questions. What if... what if... what if... and believing that anything could be possible. And guess what? Sometimes it is!'

'I'm sorry.'

'Then, when I think I've got the story, I'm riddled with anxiety. What if a key witness won't go on the record? What if they've been lying? What if a rival gets there first? What if the editor won't publish the story?'

'Alright, Matt, I'm sorry.' She paused. 'Of course it's possible.'

'Yes, but how could you make it undetectable?'

'I don't know. I'm a clinical psychiatrist, but I can do some research on some medical websites if you like?'

CHAPTER SIX

Matt picked up an early copy of Monday's *Evening Standard* outside Fulham Broadway tube station. The front page headline caught his attention: CHINESE MAN IN MAYFAIR SLAYING. The article reported that a young Chinese man had been found dead at 2 a.m. on Monday morning in an alleyway outside a West End night club. It said that he was young and wearing an expensive suit. Much was made of the brutal nature of the knife wounds and savagery of the attack. Predictably the report stated that the police were following several lines of enquiry, but Matt's eye was drawn to a line buried deep in the article which said that, according to some reports, the man was a frequent visitor to the Blue Note. Matt knew that it was a nightclub some of the City players went to.

Coincidence? Matt didn't believe in coincidence. He pulled out his mobile phone as he walked down the road. 'James, did you see the report in today's *Standard* about the murder in Mayfair?'

'Yes, we're covering it in tomorrow's paper. But it won't get as much space as it did in the *Standard*. It's a London story.'

'Are you doing it?'

'No, but I sit close to the man who is. What do you want to know?'

'Well, the report said that the victim was a frequent visitor to the Blue Note. I've been there. It's an expensive place: a favourite haunt of some of the City lot. I'm wondering who this guy was, and whether he had any links to the players.'

'You think it could be connected to Barker's death?'

'I don't know, but if there was a link between him and the club, two deaths in one day would be suspicious, wouldn't it?'

'Maybe. I'll see what I can find out.'

They agreed to meet at Luigi's, an all-day cafe in Victoria. It wasn't far from Scotland Yard, and Matt supposed it was a place where James met his contacts from the Met. There were no tablecloths on the scrubbed wooden tables and cutlery was collected at the serving counter. The smell of freshly baked bread mingled with frying bacon and coffee. Sounds of sizzling sausages, steaming machines, clanking pans and staff shouting orders streamed from the open kitchen. At eight in the morning Luigi's was doing a roaring trade: a mix of suited commuters arriving for work and blue-collar workers finishing a night shift. The attraction was probably the all-day breakfast. Matt went up to the counter and considered the menu chalked on the blackboard. He ordered a skinny latte and an almond croissant for himself, and a pot of tea and the full English for James. He took the drinks back to a corner table.

James sipped his tea and then flipped open his note pad. 'I've got some stuff on the Blue Note killing for you.'

'Thanks.'

'His name was Zhang Wei. He had a Singapore passport, came here two years ago. No regular employment, but he was loaded. He had been in the Blue Note that night. He went there regularly according to the owner. Left the club on his own, probably around two in the morning, and was attacked just outside. A customer found his body at 2:15 and the manager dialed 999. The police questioned everyone inside, but there were no witnesses, and there hadn't been any trouble. He'd been stabbed and cut. It was a mess. They think the wounds are consistent with Triad killings – a turf war. There's lot of aggro between Asian and Chinese drug gangs in this part of London.'

A waitress brought their breakfast. Matt stared at James's plate of fried eggs, bacon and sausage with two slices of hot buttered toast.

'I thought you told me your doctor said you had to lose weight?'

'Yes, he did, but it's the eighty/twenty rule: it's a treat. Your treat actually, old boy,' he said, wiping butter from his mouth.

Matt smiled. 'Of course. Anyway, did they find anything on him?'

'Yes, his wallet with £1000 in cash, credit cards and a Rolex watch.'

'So it wasn't a robbery. What about his mobile phone?'

'They didn't find one on him, but when they searched a rubbish skip nearby they recovered it. The killers must have tossed it there. It was lucky for you.'

'Why?'

'There were a lot of SMS messages. He was in contact with players at City and other clubs too. He was feeding inside information to contacts in Singapore.'

'What kind of information?'

'Well, it was odd really. The bit you're interested in seems to be just gossip from the training ground – who was injured, the likely team for the next match, players' form, team morale, disputes with the manager: that sort of thing. The police think he was probably working for an Asian gambling syndicate. Giving them information like that edges the odds in their favour.'

'It would. Was he fixing matches?'

'I don't think that figures very high in their enquiry. It's a murder case. He had connections with known drug dealers in town and they think that's why he was killed.'

'Yes, but what if Zhang Wei was fixing matches and Tony found out? He could have killed Tony to silence him.'

James put down his knife and fork and screwed up his face. 'Come on, Matt. Knowing that someone fixed the result of a football match as a motive for murder? Seems a bit unlikely.'

'Why? We don't know how big it was or how deep it went.'

James was sceptical. 'So why was Zhang Wei murdered then?'

'Perhaps someone higher up the chain killed him because he knew too much.'

'Matt, he had contacts with known drug dealers – double crossed them, didn't pay for deliveries, gang wars, you name it – and they took him out. It happens all the time.'

'Did they find any link to Tony?'

'No.'

'Can I see the messages?'

'What! No chance, Matt. The phone's evidence in a murder enquiry.'

'Yes, I know, but can't you get inside information?'

'I already have. Don't push your luck.'

'Did they find his laptop or iPad?'

'No. There was nothing in his flat.'

James pushed his plate away, finished the last piece of toast and looked at his watch.

'One more thing,' said Matt. 'At the press conference the police said they had checked the CCTV and Tony had no visitors on Saturday evening. Could they have missed something? Could the CCTV have been disabled?'

'No, if intruders had disabled it or covered up cameras it would be obvious to the police.'

It wasn't the answer Matt wanted. He screwed up his face.

James smiled. 'But there are people that can hack IP-connected security cameras on unsecured networks.'

'How do they do that?'

'It's not easy, but it can be done by a skilled hacker. They use their laptop to hack into the security system. Then it's a simple cut and paste job. They could cut the section on the video they want to remove. That would leave a time gap so they would go back to the exact same time slot on another day when there was no activity and insert that.'

Matt frowned. 'Wouldn't it be obvious to the police?'

'Only a trained professional would be able to spot the glitch when viewing the footage. It was probably a junior detective constable looking at the video.'

'Can't the system be secured against hacking?'

'Yes, by using point to point closed networks with layer 3 switches. But it's very unlikely that a domestic residence or small business would have this type of infrastructure.'

'So it would have been possible for intruders to get access to the house with nothing showing up on CCTV.'

'Yes.' He looked at his watch again. 'Look, I'm sorry, mate, but I've got to dash.' He pulled on a coat. 'Hope that helps.'

'It does. Thanks, James.'

Matt brushed the crumbs from his jacket and stared out of the window as he waited for the bill. How deeply had Zhang Wei infiltrated the club? Was this what Tony had been investigating?

He pulled out his phone and called Frankie Warren. 'Frankie, did you know that someone was feeding inside information about City to an illegal gambling syndicate in Singapore?'

'I told you City games were being fixed.'

'Looks like the guy is dead now,' said Matt.

'What?'

'He was Chinese, Zhang Wei. Found with his throat cut outside the Blue Note.'

‘Christ! I know the fella. He hangs around some of the players. I told you, Matt.’

‘Which players?’

‘Matt, I can’t tell you that. All I’m saying is there’s shit going down there. You want to look into that. I’m serious. Christ! Barker dead. Now him!’

Matt called the waiter for another cup of coffee and wondered how seriously to take Frankie. He had given him false leads before.

CHAPTER SEVEN

Matt was walking back from Luigi's to the tube station at Victoria when the phone rang. It was Julia.

'Are you sitting down, Matt? I've got some news for you.'

'No, I'm not, hang on a minute.' He stepped into an alley that was sheltered from the bustle of the crowd and traffic noise. 'Okay, I'm listening.'

'I've found something on the internet which I think you'll find interesting. It was done recently by an organisation in Canada called the Laboratoire de Sciences Judiciaires et de Médicine Légale. They're in Montreal. Fortunately, there's an English translation. Let me read it to you.

'The distinction of a suicidal hanging and a simulated hanging following a homicidal strangulation is highly challenging. The present study evaluates the fracture of the cricoid cartilage as a pointer towards homicide. Despite numerous studies on neck fractures this is the first study to concentrate on the cricoid cartilage.'

'Sound interesting so far?' she teased.

'Go on.'

'They looked at neck structure fractures in all cases of suicidal hangings over a six-year period. I'll email you the detailed tables, but in summary, the report says only one broken cricoid cartilage was found in 2,700 suicidal hangings. But in homicidal strangulation it's from five to twenty percent. Let me read you the summary. "It is therefore proposed that the presence of a fracture of the cricoid in an apparent suicide hanging should be considered highly suspicious."'

'Wow. So if the cricoid cartilage in Tony's neck was broken, it could have been murder.'

'That's right.'

'But won't the pathologist see that during the post-mortem?'

'Perhaps, but this research is so new that many pathologists may not even be aware of it.'

'How can you tell if the cricoid cartilage is broken? Is it visible? Can you feel it?'

Julia laughed. 'I've no idea. I'm not that kind of doctor. I think you should find out more about the medical aspects before you go any further.'

'Thanks, Jules.'

'I'll email you the link to the report. And Matt, if Barker was murdered, and I'm not saying he was, be careful. Remember you're a sports writer, not a detective.'

He stood in the alley for a moment, watching the crowd stream by on the pavement, still absorbing what he had been told. The tip from Frankie Warren and Zhang Wei's murder supported the idea that Tony was about to expose a match fixing scandal. Julia's information could prove it was murder. It could be the lucky break that had often proved crucial in a story. He called the *Chronicle's* chief medical correspondent.

'Dr Patterson, it's Matt Riley from the sports desk. Have you been following the Tony Barker story?'

'Of course. It would be hard to miss it.'

'The police have assumed that it's a suicide. I'm not convinced. I've been wondering how you can tell a natural hanging from a simulated hanging.'

'Well, it is difficult. It depends on the circumstances. Why do you ask?'

Matt told him about the Montreal research paper. 'If Barker's cricoid cartilage was broken, I think it means he was murdered. But how easy is it for a pathologist to tell if it's broken?'

'Why don't you send me the link to the research paper first?'

Back at his flat, Matt turned his attention to the Monday newspapers. Acres of forest and gallons of newsprint had been consumed in telling the story of Tony Barker's death. It was a topic that had gripped the country. Matt pored over them. The headlines dominated the front and back pages of every national paper.

MANAGER'S TRAGIC DEATH

TONY BARKER FOUND HANGED

SHOCKING DISCOVERY OF BARKER'S DEATH

TONY BARKER'S DEATH RAISES UNANSWERED QUESTIONS

WAS TONY BARKER SUFFERING FROM DEPRESSION?

His own valedictory piece was given a double page spread and included a triumphant photo of Tony holding the FA Cup aloft, surrounded by team-mates, including a jubilant Matt. He checked his piece on the *Chronicle Online* which included a dozen photographs. Memories of that never-to-be-forgotten day at Wembley flooded back. An hour later his ring tone jolted him back to the present.

'Dr Patterson? Thanks for calling back so quickly.'

'You're welcome. I've read the research paper. It's very interesting.'

'How conclusive do you think these results are?'

'Well, in a natural hanging, damage to the neck is above the larynx. The cricoid cartilage is at the lower end of the larynx, so it's perhaps not surprising that the cricoid wouldn't be damaged in a genuine suicide.'

'But if the cricoid was broken do you agree it would strongly suggest murder?'

'Yes.'

Matt breathed in sharply. 'So how can a pathologist tell if the cricoid cartilage was broken?'

'Well, that depends. What have the police said about the cause of death?'

'They found no suspicious circumstances or evidence of foul play.'

'Well, in that case the autopsy is going to be done by a general pathologist, not a forensic pathologist.'

'Yes,' Matt replied, unable to contain his impatience, 'but why is that important?'

'I'm just about to tell you. A general pathologist couldn't tell if the cricoid had been broken. Not unless they were looking for it. You can only see it when the larynx has been dissected. A general pathologist wouldn't do that if it was a straightforward suicide.'

'Wouldn't there be any clues that would make them suspicious?'

'Well, there could be. Damage to the cricoid occurs when pressure is applied to the front of the neck, pushing the lower part of the larynx backwards, so that the airway is blocked. There could be bruising to the lower larynx and they would probably ask for a second post-mortem. This time it would be done by a forensic pathologist who would carry out a dissection of the larynx.'

'But if there was bruising, and the first pathologist missed it, there could be a broken cricoid and no one would ever know.'

'That's right, but it's unlikely. These are highly skilled people.'

'Yes, but they're human beings, aren't they? What if the pathologist was under pressure, had several autopsies to do, all urgent? Or was interrupted and called away to an emergency? What if the pathologist was a woman who had a phone call to say that her daughter had just been badly hurt in a riding accident?'

'Well, it's possible, I'll grant you that.'

'How can I find out?'

'You're the investigative reporter, not me. See what the coroner's comments are at the opening of the inquest.'

'And what if there was bruising but the pathologist missed it?'

'Well, as I've said, I think that's unlikely, but if Mrs. Barker is not satisfied, she can ask for a second post-mortem by a pathologist of her choice – but it would be at her cost.'

'Who would do that?'

'A forensic pathologist. I can recommend a very good man. If there's anything suspicious, he's going to find it.'

CHAPTER EIGHT

On a cold Tuesday morning, just two days after Tony's body was found, Matt pulled up his collar outside 65 Horseferry Road, the Victorian brick and stone building that was the Westminster Coroner's Court. The rain had turned into a light overnight snowfall, but it had not settled. Matt shivered as he passed though the heavy wooden doors emblazoned with two shields depicting a gold portcullis and stepped into Mr. Matthew Hart's court. The room was warm. It was silent as a library and had a strong smell of furniture polish. The coroner was a tall man with thick silver hair who had a presence that commanded respect, but was softened by a friendly smile. It seemed appropriate for a coroner, thought Matt. Unlike the law courts, the coroner's court of enquiry was more informal. Hart wore a grey suit and sat at a polished wooden table with a member of his staff and a secretary. There was no jury. He announced the opening of the inquest and explained that his duty was to establish the circumstances surrounding the death of Tony Barker including how, when and why the death occurred. He confirmed the identification of the body and that a post-mortem had taken place. The police had found no suspicious circumstances. He registered the death and signed a release slip for the body to be removed for burial.

Four minutes later, Mr. Hart announced that the inquest was adjourned whilst his investigation took place. As he was about to leave, Matt introduced himself as a close friend of the Barkers, asked if he could have a word, and was invited into Hart's office.

'I believe that the autopsy was carried out yesterday. Was there anything in the post-mortem report that might suggest this was not a suicide?'

'No, no indications of anything unusual. Perhaps a high level of alcohol in the body –too high for driving, but not really excessive.'

'Nothing else?'

'No.'

'Can Mrs. Barker request a second post-mortem?'

Hart's thick white eyebrows shot up, signalling his disapproval. 'That's highly unusual. Why does she feel that's necessary?'

'I'd rather not say at this stage, if you don't mind.'

Hart stared at Matt. The friendly demeanour had changed to a glare, challenging him to say more. Not a muscle moved in Matt's face.

'Yes, she can,' he said at last, 'but I'd need a formal request in writing.' He passed his card to Matt. 'She can send her request directly to me.'

Matt sat in his car fingering the thick white card Hart had given him and wondering how Tania would feel about a second post-mortem. Not very happy, he thought, unless she understood why. That would mean explaining his theory that Tony could have been murdered. It would be a shock and he wasn't even sure himself yet. But he had to get her approval, and if he was right – if Tony had been murdered – wouldn't that alleviate her concerns that she could have been, in some way, responsible? Wasn't that better than living with the never-to-be-answered question? Why?

He exited the multi-storey car park and headed for Wimbledon.

Tania was slumped in a chair reading letters of condolence, her eyes still puffy and red. Emma, who had let him in, came back to sit opposite Tania, and picked up her notepad.

'Emma's helping me,' Tania said, pointing at a pile of letters by way of explanation. Matt sat down next to her.

'I've just come from the inquest. It was just a formality. It's been adjourned. But I did speak to the coroner afterwards. Nothing unusual came up in the post-mortem and he confirmed the police view. He's treating it as suicide.'

Tania put down the letter she was reading. 'Oh. Well, that's what we expected, isn't it?' She picked up another letter. 'A lot of these are from football people I don't even know.'

'Tania. Can I talk to you?'

She looked up absent-mindedly from the letter she was reading. 'Yes, well, I'm here.'

'The thing is Tania... it's a bit personal.'

Emma jumped up. 'It's no problem, Matt. I'll pop into the kitchen and make some calls.'

The door closed and Tania turned to Matt. 'She's been so good to me. She's helping with everything. I don't know how I'd manage without her, especially as Jane had to get back to work.'

'Oh. That's a pity. Couldn't she stay longer?'

'She's been here for two days, you know! She can't get away from her job any longer. Anyway, Emma's here.'

Of course,' said Matt, sitting down next to her on the sofa.

'And Mr. Buzinsky says she can spend as much time with me as I need.'

'Really? Well, that is good news.' He hesitated, unsure of how to go on. 'Tania, I've been doing some digging and I'm beginning to think that... perhaps it wasn't suicide.'

Tania's head jerked up. 'Not suicide? What do you mean?'

'I think it's possible that Tony could have been murdered.'

'Murdered?' Tania said, her voice trembling. 'Murdered? Are you sure?'

Matt held her gaze, but did not reply.

'But the police found no evidence of foul play.'

'I know, but it could have been made to look like suicide.'

She shook her head, looking confused. 'I don't understand. Who would want to kill Tony?'

'I don't know.'

There was a long silence. Matt got up and walked to the window, wondering how much to say. 'Look, Tania, there are some things that made me suspicious and I've done some research. Sometimes murder can be made to look like suicide, but I would have to be able prove it. I found a medical report that says that if a cartilage in the neck was broken – it's called the cricoid – then it could prove it was murder.'

'But wouldn't that show up in the post-mortem?'

'No, not unless the pathologist suspected murder. The only way we can find out now is by having a second post-mortem.'

Tania dropped the letter she was holding, frozen in the moment like a startled deer caught in the head lights. 'What!'

Matt hurried over to her, bent down and took both her hands in his. 'I know it's a shock, of course it is, but don't you want to find out what happened?'

'I don't know. I can't bear the idea of him being cut up again. I just want to get the funeral over with.'

'I know. I'm sorry. I'm really sorry to put you through this but, if we don't do it now, how are you ever going to know what really happened? You'll spend your whole life wondering if he'd still be alive if you hadn't gone to that party. You shouldn't have to live with that. Look, Tania, I know this is difficult, but I want you to postpone the funeral, and ask for a second post-mortem.'

Tania stared at her feet, unsure what to say.

'And if he was murdered you would want justice to be done, wouldn't you?'

Tania thought about it. 'And then I would get the insurance money, wouldn't I?'

'Yes, I'm sure you would.'

Christ, he thought. He's only been dead three days and she's thinking about the money. Still. it might make her more amenable to a second post-mortem.

'So what would I have to do?'

'You'll need to write to the coroner and ask for his permission. It's unusual, but it's your right. You can tell him you will be arranging for a forensic pathologist to attend the mortuary. Don't worry. I can make all the arrangements. You'd just have to agree to pay the pathologist's costs.' He handed her the coroner's business card.

She got up and paced around the room. 'I don't know. It all seems so horrible. I just want to get it over with.'

Matt wondered why she seemed so reluctant. He had to admit it would be a sensational story, but it was obviously the right thing for her to do. But then, in fairness to Tania, he had only just broached the idea. It must have been a shock.

At last she turned back to Matt. 'I'm sorry, Matt. Do you mind if I talk to Jane about it tonight?'

'I think you should. It's a big step to take.'

He followed her into the conservatory. Outside, bare black trees were silhouetted in the pale afternoon sun. A light blanket of snow covered the shivering landscape. The mini goalposts that Tony had set up on the lawn looked forlorn and a robin perching on the edge of a black cast iron garden seat was the only sign of life.

'Who could possibly want to murder Tony?' Tania murmured.

'I don't know,' he said, and they stood staring at the bleak mid-winter scene. It was some time before he broke the silence. 'Are you're sure there was nothing unusual in his behaviour?'

'Well,' she said, her brow wrinkling as she searched her memory, 'there was one thing. I was tidying his study a few weeks ago and there was a red briefcase I hadn't seen before. It was the sort that has a catch on each side that you can snap down and lock, but it was open, so just out of curiosity I looked inside. There was a large file and I was just glancing through it when he came in. He flew off the handle. He was really angry and said it was confidential. I was shocked. It wasn't like him at all. He seemed embarrassed and asked if I'd read it. I said, "No, of course not."'

'So you don't know what was in the file.'

'No, not exactly. There were a lot of papers, reports on matches, diagrams, reports on referees, you know the sort of thing. It all looked like the normal stuff he did to me. I can't think why he got so upset.'

'Is it still here?'

'I don't think so. I never saw it again. I suppose he took it to his office at the training ground.'

He took her hand and led her back into the lounge. She went to the window and stood staring at the paparazzi still gathered outside the front of the house. Suddenly she spun around. 'I'm on my own now, Matt. I want Mark and Robert to come home.'

He wondered why she was asking for his approval. 'Of course, they should come home now, if that's what you want.'

'How can they with this mob outside?' she snapped. 'They're only young. It will be horrible. Can't you do something about it?'

Matt shrugged. 'It's difficult. I can't tell them to go away. They've got their job to do.'

'Yes, but haven't I got a right to privacy at a time like this?'

'Of course you do,' Matt mumbled. He thought of all the times he had been part of the baying media pack, hunting down a story, manipulating an interview. It felt different when it had begun to intrude into his own life. 'I know. I'm sorry. It must be hell,' he said.

'Surely you can do something?'

'They might listen to me, but we'd have to give them something to take away. They'll want photographs and quotes. You'd have to come outside with me. Could you do that?'

Tania jerked her head up in surprise. 'Why? Why do you need me?'

'It's the only way I think we can get rid of them.'

'I can't possibly speak to them, Matt.'

'I'll talk to them. You'll just have to read a short statement. I can write it for you. They'll understand.'

'Are you sure?'

'Don't worry. I'll be standing right beside you. They just want photographs and your statement.'

She sighed. 'Alright then. Just give me a minute do my make-up.' She went upstairs to her bedroom while Matt sat down at a table and started making notes.

Matt asked the policeman on duty to open the gates. The media mob surged forward like a swarm of bees, settling below the steps leading to the front door. 'Hi,' Matt said, holding up his hand. The buzz slowly subsided.

'You know what? It feels really weird for me to be standing up here when I should be down there with you.' The ripple of laughter began to settle his nerves. 'The thing is, Tania has asked me to be with her. I think you all know that Tony was a very close friend of mine.' He took a deep breath and stared out at the crowd, sensing a faint murmur of approval. Then again, perhaps he imagined it but there was no turning back now. He looked at Tania, her face pale, pulling her coat around her. 'This is a difficult time for Tania. That's why I'm here.' His eyes searched the crowd, looking for familiar faces. 'Tania needs time alone to grieve. She wants to bring her two boys home. You've got kids of your own. You know what it's like. And I know what you want. I wish I had more to tell you but I'm sorry, I don't. Tania will make a short statement and we will try to answer your questions. You can take photographs, but then can I please appeal to you to leave Tania alone with her family?'

Tania reached into her coat pocket and took out a sheet of paper. Her hand was shaking as she stared out at the crowd, unsettled by the barrage of flashlights and unsure of how to begin. She took a deep breath, put the paper back in her pocket and raised her head.

'You can't begin to understand what it's like to walk into a room early in the morning and see your husband hanging from a rope.' She paused, choking back the tears. 'I know you want to know why he did it. Don't you think I keep asking the same question? I don't know. I just don't know.' She shook her head and brushed back the hair in her face. 'I thought everything was normal. He was the last person I would ever expect to take his own life. We had so much to look forward to. Now I want to bring my two boys home and help them to deal with this. Thank you.'

'Tania, was he under pressure at the club?'

'I don't know. We didn't discuss football at home.'

'Did you have any idea that he was going to do this?'

She shook her head. 'No.'

'Did he have any financial worries?'

'Not that I knew, but he never discussed that with me.'

'Were you both happy?'

She stared at the journalist asking the question. 'He was...' she began to choke up. 'He was planning to... to take me to Venice for our 25th wedding anniversary.' She rubbed the tears from her cheek and Matt stepped in.

'Thanks, everyone. I think that's enough now.'

He put his arm round Tania, who was shivering from the ordeal, and they stepped inside the warmth of the house. Matt took her coat.

'Thanks, Matt. I feel much better now. I want to get the boys back. I need them with me now.'

'I know. Can I go and get them for you?'

'No, Dad wouldn't hear of it. He'll drive. They'll want to help and they can stay until after the funeral. Emma can come around and help me. I've got to get on with things. I've got to make an appointment with our solicitor.'

The next morning, after an early bike ride, Matt was about to take a shower when his phone rang. It was Tania. 'Oh, Matt. I've been worrying about this second post-mortem thing all night. I didn't want to do it, but Jane thinks you're right. Just tell me what I've got to do.'

Dr. Patterson picked Matt's call up after two rings. 'Let me make some calls and get you someone who can do it this week,' he said. 'I'll explain why you want it done and what you're looking for. Then you'll have to ask Mrs. Barker to formally appoint him, and he'll make the arrangements with the coroner. Don't worry. If there is anything that points to murder he'll find it.'

Matt saw that he had a call waiting. 'Thanks, Dr. Patterson. I have to go now.' It was Bill's secretary. 'He can see you at eleven this morning.'

CHAPTER NINE

A passing black cab took Matt to Knightsbridge where IMC – the International Media Corporation that owned the *Daily Chronicle* and its Sunday sister paper was headquartered in a marble and glass edifice. He passed through the new state of the art security system and took one of the lifts to the newsroom floor. The vast open plan office accommodated four hundred journalists. Matt weaved his way through desks grouped by the newspaper's sections until he reached the sports desk at the far end of the room. Despite the drama of daily deadlines there was no sense of panic, no jangling phones, no shouts across the room: only the low hum of a well-oiled machine as writers, glued to their computer screens or phones, researched and wrote their stories.

He was ten minutes early. He picked up a coffee and stood chatting to the journalist on duty at the sports desk. When Bill had finished a long phone call, he heaved his heavy frame out of his chair, opened the glass door and beckoned Matt into his office. Meetings with the sports editor were unusual. Bill ruled here, but his office was neither large nor comfortable. Every work surface was covered in papers, his desk surrounded by monitors. His white shirt was undone at the neck and his sleeves rolled up to his elbows. His lined face was stern.

'I hope this won't take long,' he said. 'I've got a meeting in twenty minutes. What's so important that you can't talk about it on the phone?'

Matt settled into a chair, juggling the cup of coffee and his notepad. There was no point in beating about the bush. He needed Bill's support. He took a deep breath and plunged in. 'I don't think it was suicide. I think Barker might have been murdered.'

Bill swung round in his leather swivel chair, his eyes fixed on Matt in an unforgiving stare. 'Matt, we've been through this before. It was suicide. The police said there was no evidence of foul play. The post-mortem didn't throw up anything suspicious. Nobody in the media, except you, has the slightest doubt about it.'

'Yes, but there are things that I know that they don't.'

Bill's eyes narrowed suspiciously. 'Like what?'

'I think he may have uncovered a match fixing scandal at London City.'

Bill scowled, still sceptical. 'Match fixing in the Premier League? What makes you think that?'

'I had a tip off from an agent.'

'Is that all?'

'No. Did you see that piece about the murder of a Chinese man outside the Blue Note?'

Bill nodded.

'His name was Zhang Wei. He was found with his throat slit.'

'So what?'

'He knew some of the London City players. Wei was working for an illegal gambling syndicate in Singapore.'

'Where did you get this?'

'Piggot-Browne. The police aren't interested in the connection to London City. As far as they're concerned it's a drug turf war and a Triad killing.'

'What do you think?'

'I think Zhang Wei may have been fixing City's matches. Tony found out about it. Zhang Wei killed him to shut him up. Then perhaps Zhang Wei was silenced by someone higher up the chain.'

Bill leaned back in his black leather chair with his hands behind his head. 'It's all very interesting, Matt, but it's just speculation. There's nothing here we can publish.'

'Maybe, but there's more. Tania thinks he was secretly compiling a dossier.'

'A dossier? What sort of dossier? Has she seen it?'

'Yes, as far she could tell it was full of reports on matches.'

'What's so unusual about that?'

'I don't know yet, but what I do know is that Tony was very angry with Tania when he found her looking through it. Don't you think that's odd?'

'Where is it now?'

'She doesn't know. She never saw it again. If he was carrying out an investigation into match fixing inside the club he would have had to be very discreet.'

Bill shook his head. 'Come on, Matt! You don't have a shred of evidence. You need to track down that report if that's what you think.'

'Of course, and I will.'

Bill twirled a pencil between his fingers and thought about it for a while. 'Even if there was match fixing it doesn't mean he was murdered.' Bill shoved his chair back, his arms crossed over his chest.

'Maybe, but I think I can prove he was.'

Bill leaned forward and listened carefully as Matt explained his cricoid cartilage theory.

'What's the source?'

Matt passed the research report to Bill. He put on his glasses and studied it for a few minutes. 'Interesting,' he said when he put it down, 'but nothing showed up on the post-mortem, did it?'

'I know, but it was done by a general pathologist assuming there were no suspicious circumstances. Tania is requesting a second post-mortem by a forensic pathologist. If Tony was murdered, he would find a broken cricoid.'

There was a long pause. Bill fiddled with his pencil. 'Your cricoid idea is interesting. I'll give you that. Obviously if the forensic pathologist says he could have been murdered, that changes everything. But when the editor hears that, it will be a crime story.'

'Maybe, but they'll still need me to work on it. Anyway, if you think I'm barking up the wrong tree, you don't have to tell him yet. If it's about corruption, it's a sports story. I want to stay with it. I've got personal connections with Tania. I have a lot of contacts at the football club. The players know me. I want to follow this story, but I need time.'

Bill smiled. Matt was competitive. He had a good instinct for a story and he hated to be beaten. It was a long shot, but if it came off, it would be sensational.

'Okay,' he said. 'I'm going to stick my neck out. Let me know as soon as the forensic pathologist gives you the run down on the cricoid angle. And for now, we'll keep this between the two of us.'

'And another thing,' Bill said as Matt headed for the door. 'Don't give up on the suicide angle. It's still by far the most likely scenario. I want to know why the wife was out alone at a party until two in the morning. If she was having an affair I want to know about it. That's the story I'm expecting you to come up with.'

'I know, Bill. She denied it when I asked, but I'm going to check it out.'

'Good. Talk to her friends down at the Chelsea Health Club or wherever it is she goes. You'll find a way.'

CHAPTER TEN

Emma had agreed to meet Matt at the Pink Flamingo, a popular cocktail bar in Chelsea, later that day. He arrived early. The modern image was cleverly– and no doubt expensively – created by stone floors, plush black leather seating, chrome and glass tables, and mirrors that made the bar seem much longer. Spotlights on overhead tracks created soft pools of light. Noise levels were rising as more customers arrived, but Matt recognised a Diana Krall song playing in the background. The customers looked young and were sharply dressed. He suspected that most of them worked in advertising, or public relations, or hedge funds, or something smart like that. God, I must be getting old, he thought.

He saw Emma as she walked across the room. As she passed one of the tables a young man turned to watch her. He had to admit she looked good. Funny, he had never really noticed that before. She was medium height and slim; wore a grey business suit and closely fitting white blouse. Her brown hair was shoulder length. She wasn't beautiful, or even pretty, but there was something about her that was very attractive. He thought she was about twenty-eight, with a fresh complexion that required no help from make-up. Matt had spoken to her on the phone often enough, but usually only saw her briefly. Although she was used to protecting her boss from journalists, she always greeted Matt warmly. Tony said she was priceless.

She smiled and thanked Matt as he stood up and pulled out a chair for her. He felt a little awkward, not sure whether a kiss on the cheek or a handshake would be appropriate. She gave him a light kiss on the cheek and they sat down.

'How are you, Matt?'

'Still shell-shocked.'

She nodded. 'I know. When I go into his office I keep thinking I'm going to see him sitting there in his tracksuit.'

Matt shook his head. 'I can't come to terms with it either.' There was an awkward silence.

'What would you like to drink?' he said.

She asked for a vodka cocktail and he ordered the same.

'It was very good of you to spend time with Tania.'

'Oh, Matt, that's nothing. He was such a great guy to work for. It's the least I can do.'

Matt studied the young woman sitting opposite him and wondered how much she would be willing to tell him. Looking at her now, he realised how little he knew about her. Tony had told him she was single and had worked at Adco, an American software company. Adco were the team's shirt sponsors and he had met her at a sponsor's dinner. Two years ago, when his PA had left, she had replied to the advertisement. Tony had been delighted. 'She gets things done,' he had told Matt.

'Tell me, Emma, have you any idea why he did it?'

She took a sip of her cocktail and stared into the glass. 'I honestly don't know. I was probably more shocked than anyone.' She spoke very correctly – posh, his mum would have said, but he could detect the south London accent: Croydon probably, not far from where he grew up.

'Was there anything worrying him? Was he angry or upset about anything?'

She frowned. 'No, I don't think so. Well, nothing more than the hundred and one things a football manager has to worry about every week.'

'What about Buzinsky?' Was there trouble there?'

'No, Tony was fine with Sergei. I know he has this image of being this unapproachable Russian oligarch, but he's not like that really. Obviously, he has to have personal security, not just for him, but for Svetlana and the two children.' She paused. 'Did you know their eldest boy died last year?'

Matt raised his eyebrows in surprise. 'No.'

'Yes, it was tragic. Victor was born with Otahara Syndrome.'

'What's that?'

'A rare form of epilepsy. They kept it very private.'

Matt was surprised she had told him. He wondered how far he could go. She was well connected in the club. She knew everyone. She would have information from his computer and his files. She might be willing to let him see it.

'I know how much Tony relied on you,' he said. 'He must have meant a lot to you.'

She looked up, caught his eye and reached out to touch his hand. 'Thanks, Matt. Yes, he did.'

She left her hand resting on his. He looked down. There was another awkward pause and he put down his glass. 'I was wondering... do you have plans this evening?'

She shook her head. 'No.'

'Would you like to have dinner?'

'I'd love to.'

They went to La Scala. He hadn't booked and it appeared to be full. Waiters in black chinos and red shirts swept between tables with trays held high. The sound of laughter reverberated from the tiled floor of the dining room.

'Nice to see you again, Mr. Riley,' said Giuseppe, glancing at Emma. 'I'm gonna find a nice quiet table for you.'

Giuseppe took them to a corner table at the back of the restaurant. They sat down and a waiter rushed forward to unfold Emma's napkin and give them menus. They studied them quietly for a while.

'You come here regularly, Matt? What's good?'

Matt laughed. 'It's all good, but I like the fish.'

'Ooh yes. I'll have the Dover sole.'

'I'll have the same,' he said to the waiter, and ordered a bottle of Frascati. Emma seemed more relaxed than she had been in the cocktail bar at the Pink Flamingo.

'It can't have been an easy job looking after Tony,' he said when the waiter had poured the wine.

'Oh, he was lovely,' she said. 'The trouble was everybody wanted a piece of him. You know what he was like. He wanted to spend his time with the players and coaching staff at the training ground. I was the gatekeeper. He didn't even like Tania calling him at work. She used to call me to find out what he was doing and pass messages.'

'As a matter of interest, do you think things were okay at home?'

'What?' She looked surprised by the sudden change of subject. 'Why do you ask?'

'Oh, you know; rumours. You must have seen some of the press picked up on Tania being out at a party on her own until two in the morning.'

She thought about it for a while. 'I don't know. He didn't discuss personal things like that with me. It was difficult for Tania. He was away from home such a lot: foreign trips, away matches, dinners. You know what it's like. But she had her own lifestyle. They had become part of a wealthy set in Wimbledon. She met friends at the health club, hairdresser, coffee mornings and trips to the fashion shops in Knightsbridge. They got invited to parties. She's an attractive woman.'

'Do you think she was having an affair?'

She looked up, startled. 'What!'

'Well, was she?'

She avoided his eyes and looked back down at her plate.

'Do you know who it was?' said Matt.

'No.'

'Who was she was going around with?'

Emma thought for a bit, then mentioned a few names. Matt made notes.

'Did Tony know?'

'No.'

'Are you sure?'

'Yes.' She rested her chin in the palm of her hand, staring at Matt as a thought struck her like a slap in the face. 'You don't think that's why he committed suicide?'

'No, I don't.' He swirled the wine in his glass. 'But I think Tania might.'

The waiter poured more wine.

'Did Tony know that someone was passing inside information to an illegal gambling syndicate in the Far East?'

Emma stared at him for some time. 'No. Who told you that?'

'You know I can't reveal sources, Em, but someone at the club was.'

She looked startled. 'A gambling syndicate? I didn't know anything about that. If Tony knew, I'm sure he would have told me. What do you think was going on?'

'I'm not sure yet. But if there are Asian gambling syndicates involved...' He paused, leaving her to draw her own conclusions. The waiter asked if they would like dessert. They both ordered coffee. As the waiter left she said, 'Tania told me there is going to be a second post-mortem. Why?'

'I think the first pathologist missed something.'

Emma leaned in towards him and her brown hair fell across her face. He could smell her perfume. Her eyes narrowed. 'Matt, I know you're a journalist, and it's your job to not believe everything you're told, but the police say there was no suspicion of foul play. What are you suggesting?'

'I'll know more later this week.'

She leaned back, waiting for him to explain, but he took it no further. A slight look of irritation fluttered across her face.

'What about enemies?' he said. 'Did he have enemies that you knew about?'

Emma, who had seemed tense, threw back her head and laughed. 'Enemies? Of course he had enemies. He was a football manager. He had enemies inside the club, among the players, the press, the supporters. It was my job to protect him from all that. I can't imagine that any of them would want to kill him though!'

The waiter brought the coffee and poured it for them. 'Did you know he was keeping a secret dossier?' he said.

'What kind of dossier?'

'I don't know. Tania said she hadn't seen it before.'

Emma paused, as if searching her memory. 'I don't think he ever told me about it, but he did reports on the teams we were due to play all the time, potential transfer targets, stuff like that. They're confidential to the coaching staff, but they're hardly secret. Did she say what it was about?'

'As far as she could tell, it was just reports he had written on matches, players, referees.'

She shrugged her shoulders. 'He does that all the time. Why do you think it seemed unusual?'

'He was very secretive about it when she found it.'

'I'm sure I would have seen it if he brought it to the office.' She leaned forward. 'But he did have a cupboard in the office that he kept locked. I never had a key. Why don't you ask Tania if she can find the key?'

'What was in the cupboard?'

'I have no idea, but it's worth a try.' She leaned forward, touched his hand and he breathed in her perfume. 'Matt, Tony had a lot of respect for you. He talked about you a lot. I want to help you, if you'll let me. I can look through Tony's appointments diary and emails if you like. See if I can find anything that might help.'

He nodded. 'That would be good.' His smile was warm and heartfelt. 'Thanks, Em.'

'That's alright,' she said, smiling and drawing her shoulders together in a gesture that seemed more than just friendly. This was a side of Emma he hadn't seen before.

CHAPTER ELEVEN

Meeting in a mortuary at nine o'clock on a Thursday morning would not have been Matt's choice. Not that he would have welcomed it at any time, but Dr. Andrews had kindly fitted him into his busy schedule. The white tiled floors were spotlessly clean. Stainless steel tables glinted under bright overhead lights and a bank of green storage chambers with stainless steel handles lined a wall at the end of the room. Left luggage lockers for corpses, Matt thought, and shivered. The mortuary was cold. He took a deep breath and tried to put the nauseous feeling out of his mind. Dr. Andrews, the forensic pathologist, came over and introduced himself. He was a tall man, slightly stooped, with grey wispy hair and glasses, and wearing a green scrub suit. He greeted Matt warmly with a vigorous handshake, then turned to introduce the young woman standing next to him. 'And this is Linda Mason, the scene of crime officer.'

Matt thought she looked rather shy, perhaps she was uncomfortable, but then he was feeling pretty queasy himself. She was very young, and he wondered if she had been in a mortuary before.

As they walked over to the first table Dr. Andrews said, 'As you know, I was instructed to carry out a forensic autopsy working from the assumption that the deceased could have been murdered. I was asked to pay particular attention to the possibility that the cricoid cartilage might have been fractured.'

Matt tensed as they reached the table. He knew that the body under the green cover was Tony's. Dr. Andrews noticed and smiled sympathetically. 'He was a close friend, wasn't he?'

'Yes,' said Matt.

'I'm sorry. I'm afraid this is always difficult.'

Matt braced himself for the moment he had been dreading.

'Well, let's have a look, shall we?' said Dr. Andrews, professional again and eager to get down to business. Matt's stomach flipped as the green cover was pulled back to reveal Tony's head and shoulders and then his whole naked body. He looked away, took a deep breath, then stepped forward and stared at his friend. He remembered how he had looked when he last saw him at the training ground, laughing, smiling. Now his face was ashen, his skin as smooth as marble with faint blue veins. Composed. At peace. His mind flashed back to when they had met. Tony: his father figure. 'I love you, Tony,' he whispered to himself. God damn it! How could it have come to this? Tony cut down like a carcass in an abattoir.

'Mr. Riley?'

'Yes, sorry,' said Matt, turning to focus on the pathologist. Dr. Andrews leaned over the body and pointed at a bruised area around the neck.

'As you can see, there is laryngeal trauma. This is caused by the tightening of the ligature around the upper neck, just behind the angle of the jaw here on the right side. But there is no other bruising or mark below the suspension mark. It is consistent with what I would expect in a suicidal hanging.'

Matt frowned.

'However, I dissected the larynx in order to inspect the cricoid cartilage. It takes some time,' he said. Matt felt a tremor of excitement as he watched the pathologist pointing with his scalpel.

'But as you can see, the cricoid cartilage is intact.'

'Intact?'

Matt stared at the body, the blood draining from his face, his world collapsing around him. Intact? It couldn't be. He had been so sure. There had to be some mistake – a misunderstanding.

'Can you be sure?' he said, feeling foolish as soon as he uttered the words.

'Of course,' the pathologist replied patiently. 'Look, you can see it here,' he said, pointing at the cartilage. 'It's perfectly intact.'

Matt gazed at the white, rubbery cartilage. He had to admit that nothing looked broken. He stood stiff and upright, as rigid as the corpse he was staring at.

'And there were no other indications of foul play?' said Matt.

'No, I'm sorry to disappoint you, but I'm afraid not.'

Matt seemed unable to take his eyes off the body. 'So, that's it then,' he said, his shoulders slumped.

'Yes,' said Dr. Andrews. 'But I did find a foreign body.'

Matt's head jerked up.

'What?'

'I found a small slit in the right heel, and some traces of blood. I opened the wound and extracted a small shard of glass. Here it is.'

He picked up the sliver of glass with his tweezers and held it up to the light. 'It's very small, as you can see. Just 10 mm long, 5 mm wide and 2 mm thick.' He turned to Linda Mason. 'Did you find any broken glass at the scene?'

A blotch of red spread over the officer's pale face. 'No,' she replied, so softly that they could hardly hear her.

Andrews looked puzzled. 'Are you sure?'

'Yes.'

'Oh,' said Dr Andrews, as he carefully placed the thin piece of clear glass in a plastic evidence bag. 'Well, I don't know if it has any significance, but that's for you to find out,' he said sealing the bag and handing it to her to counter sign. Then he pulled the green cover back over the body, signifying the end of the meeting.

'I will of course be sending my post-mortem report to the coroner,' he told her. 'He'll sign the paperwork for release of the body for burial.'

The young woman shifted awkwardly from foot to foot, anxious to get away. Looking down at her feet and appearing uncomfortable, she thanked the pathologist for his time, and hurried off with the evidence bag. Matt turned to leave.

'Just hang on a minute, can you?' the pathologist said. Matt looked up, still in a daze. 'Yes. Yes, of course.'

Dr Andrews finished tidying up and they strolled towards the exit. 'Would you like a cup of coffee?' They went into a small staff room. Andrews poured two cups of coffee from a machine and they sat down at a plastic table.

'I can understand how disappointed you are,' said the pathologist, relaxing his formal tone from the meeting with the SOCO, 'but there's something else I think you'd like to know.' He winked at Matt. 'Just between the two of us.'

Matt was fully alert now. Perhaps he had been right about his cricoid theory all along. Perhaps Andrews had kept something back from the police officer.

The pathologist took a sip of the hot coffee and put down his cup. 'When I removed the shard of glass, I took a block of tissue from the affected area, and examined it under the microscope. I found a miniscule fragment of glass: quite invisible to the naked eye. Now I don't know if this has any significance for you or not, but I'm going to send it to the lab for a microscopy examination of the tissue. If there is any sign of inflammatory reaction or healing next to the glass, we will know that the glass had been in place sometime before the death. But if there is no inflammation or scarring, then I can assure you that the glass got into his heel around the time of his death.'

'Around the time of his death?'

'Yes, if there is no inflammation or scarring.'

Matt's mind was in a whirl. 'But... but the SOCO said she found no sign of broken glass at the scene.'

'Yes, she seemed very sure of that, didn't she?'

'So how did it get there?'

He looked Matt in the eye. 'It's not for me to speculate, but I will say this. If it turns out that there is no inflammation,' he paused, twirling the coffee cup in his hands, 'and the scene of the crime officer found no evidence of broken glass, then I would think that's very suspicious.'

Matt stiffened, his heart racing. 'How long will it take?'

'Oh, that's no problem. I can let you know in a couple of days.'

Matt exhaled in relief and held out his hand. Thank you, Doctor. Thank you very much.'

Outside the mortuary Matt leaned against a wall, breathed out slowly and pulled out his phone. 'Good morning, Tania. I've just seen the pathologist.'

'Yes?' she asked hesitantly.

'There was no broken cricoid. He didn't find any evidence of foul play.'

'So, he wasn't murdered?'

'He didn't find any evidence.'

There was a long pause. He wondered if she was thinking about the insurance money again. 'I see,' she said finally.

'Anyway, what I wanted to tell you was that the pathologist is sending his report to the coroner, and you are going to be able to go ahead and make arrangements for the burial now.'

There was a long silence. 'Right.'

She sounded very flat. He didn't tell her about the shard of glass or that he didn't trust the police.

CHAPTER TWELVE

London City's training ground was nestled in a tranquil setting in the Surrey hills. Despite its remote location, and a sign warning that players would not stop to give autographs, there were always fans waiting at the security gate in the hope of sighting a player. Matt showed his press pass and drove down the long road to the administration block and media centre. Familiar faces from other newspapers stood around outside, chatting in small groups, waiting for the club's security staff to escort them to the training session.

The training ground had been Buzinsky's vision, like the new stadium, an investment in the future. It was a state of the art complex that catered not just for the first team squad, but the academy that attracted and nurtured the most talented young players. The facilities matched the best anywhere in Europe, with twelve grass pitches, an outdoor all-weather 3G artificial surface and a full-size indoor pitch. The adjacent modern brick and glass coaching centre housed changing rooms, a gymnasium, treatment room, medical rehab centre, conference rooms, a dining room and a players' recreation room. The manager and all his coaching staff were based there.

The car park glittered with a galaxy of shining cars, Ferraris and Aston Martins, Bentleys and Porsches. Not for the first time, Matt was reminded of how money flooding into the Premier League from television companies had changed football since he had been out of the game. He had missed out on the incredible wealth that players enjoyed now. He was bitter about being robbed of a career as a professional footballer, and he was jealous. He missed pushing himself in training, and the banter of the dressing room. He missed the challenge of playing against some of the best players in the world. But most of all, he missed the indescribable thrill of playing before fifty thousand screaming fans. Nothing would ever beat playing.

The threat of snow earlier in the week had moved on and given way to a bright winter morning and clear blue sky. The group were escorted over to the pitch where they could watch the players training. After the mortuary visit earlier that morning Matt felt good to be out in the fresh air. The session was being taken by the fitness coach, with Dave Wilson, Tony's assistant manager, now caretaker, watching from the side-lines. Matt knew the form: this was no walk in the park. The players had been mentally and physically prepared by the head of sports science to put themselves through the grinder. There would be no holding back. They were just finishing a strength training session, running at speed between red and white poles with frequent changes of direction.

After a short warm down, the players split into two teams – red bibs against blue bibs for one-touch, a practice game that developed fast reactions by only allowing one touch of the ball. The crisp mid-morning silence was shattered by the shouts of players urgently calling for the ball, or warning cries of 'man on', as the game swung rapidly from attack to defence. Dave Wilson moved around the pitch, watching, shouting instructions, and praising smart moves. Matt watched enviously.

When the session wound up, Wilson, track-suited and sweating, walked over to Matt. 'Not as fit as I used to be,' he said, smiling broadly. 'Good to see you again, Stinger. Let's have a chat after the press conference.'

When Tony Barker came to the club he had brought Dave with him as his assistant manager. He had been Tony's number two as he worked his way up the managerial ladder. They were a team. Dave took charge of training when Tony could not be there. He was his conduit to the players.

Today Dave Wilson had the unenviable task of taking the weekly press conference just five days after Tony's death. The purpose-built media room had row upon row of theatre-style chairs, and behind them was a battery of television cameras. On a raised dais at the other end of the room, a covered table bristled with microphones, and behind that a huge screen was covered with sponsors' logos. Wilson entered the room looking as if he was a man heading for the executioner's gallows. He stared out at the cameras and the huddle of waiting journalists, his face grim. The club's press officer made it clear that he was there to talk about the team and Sunday's match against Chelsea, and would not be answering any questions about Tony Barker.

The reporters with the television companies had the first crack at questions. It wasn't live, and it would be edited, but any slip up would be shown on television and repeated endlessly on media websites and YouTube. Managers were guarded in what they said in front of the cameras. Dave Wilson was doubly nervous, not just because he had been thrust into the limelight, but because of the dark cloud that hung over the club since Tony's death. Their questions were mostly focused on injuries, a dip in form from one or two players, and what they could expect when facing Chelsea. When the inevitable question of the vacant manager's position came up, Wilson gave an obviously rehearsed answer.

'It's out of my hands. All I can do is prepare the team to get three points on Sunday.'

The television interview wound up. Cameramen began packing up and the television reporters rushed away. There was an undignified scramble as the press pack pushed forward, placing their phones and digital recorders on the dais in front of Wilson. Not that any of the answers to their questions would be broadcast, but it provided an accurate transcript to check their quotations before they filed their story.

Wilson was more relaxed now, and prepared to talk more frankly in reply to the barrage of questions from football writers he knew. Sniffer Jackson asked if the fact that the next match was against Chelsea on Sunday— the team Barker once played for—created extra pressure.

'Funny innit. Who arranges the fixtures?' Wilson joked, smiling for the first time, rubbing his chin and shaking his head. The journalists laughed. Encouraged by their response he went on. 'I think Tony would have seen the funny side of that.' They laughed again. 'No. No, seriously, I don't think there is any extra pressure for us. They liked Tony over at Chelsea, course they did, and they'll give him a good send off. Don't get me wrong. They want to win and so do we. The best send-off we can give Tony is to get the three points.'

The reporters warmed to him. He was a straight-talking guy, but inevitably towards the end, questions about his own future were fired at him.

'Have you been given the manager's job, Dave?'

'No, I've been asked to be caretaker manager.'

'How long will you do that for? Is it for a fixed number of games?'

'I dunno. No one's spoken to me yet. I'll do it for as long as I'm needed.'

'Are you a candidate for the job?'

'I thought you were going to tell me that,' he quipped.

When the laughter died down he continued. 'Of course it would be an honour to manage this club.'

'Do you know who the other candidates are?'

The press officer interrupted abruptly. 'That's it for today, gentlemen. Thank you.'

A relieved looking Wilson was bustled out of the room.

Afterwards, in the adjoining press room, Matt sat at his laptop along with the others, working out what line they would take, writing their stories, filing them, drinking coffee, chatting, and comparing notes. Few noticed as Emma Griffin walked up to Matt and whispered in his ear, 'Dave would like to see you in his office now.'

'It's a bad business, Matt. Bad business,' Dave said, shaking his head as he flopped into the chair in the privacy of his office. It was very basic; just a desk and a chair for visitors. The trappings of his trade were strewn around: a net full of footballs, bits of kit, a stack of cones, the smell of ointments. There were no photographs or memorabilia of his own career as a player with West Ham. He was in his fifties, but still lean and fit from daily training with the players. Dave was a cockney, down to earth and approachable, and that was what the players liked about him.

'What do you think happened?' Matt asked.

'I dunno, Matt. I dunno. Tony was the last person I'd have expected to do 'imself in. But that's what they say, isn't it? You never know. It's the person you least suspect.'

'Was there anything unusual that was bothering him?'

Dave knitted his eyebrows. 'I dunno. I don't think so. There was pressure though. Always is: you know that. You're as good as your last result. And Buzinsky wants to win! Then there's always rumours your lot put out about whether the manager's job is safe,' he said, rolling his eyes.

Matt smiled. 'Yeah, but Tony wasn't worried about that, was he?'

'No, not Tony. He just got on with the job. The results have been great.'

'Was he having trouble with any of the players?'

'Well, there's always trouble with the prima donnas nowadays. Varta's been a pain in the arse. Tony thought he was brilliant, but you know how temperamental the Argies are. He was telling Tony he wasn't happy and wanted away, but I think that was his agent stirring it up. Agents messing about with a player's head really pissed him off.'

Dave opened a cabinet, took out two glasses, a bottle of red wine, and began pouring.

'It's probably nothing, but...' He put down the bottle, considering whether or not to continue.

'But what?'

'Well, I did think something was bothering him.'

'What?'

Dave stared into space as if he was trying to remember. 'I dunno,' he said eventually, turning back to look at Matt. 'Perhaps it was Mayfield.'

'Mayfield?'

'Well, you know the CEO handles all the contracts.'

'Yeah.'

'Well, I think Tony thought he was a bit too "amenable",' Dave used his fingers to indicate the quote marks, 'with one of the agents.'

'Which one was that, Dave?'

'I don't know.'

'Did he say anything to Mayfield?'

'He may have done. He didn't tell me. He only hinted at it – you know what I mean, the way things just drop out.'

'Hmmm.' Matt paused. 'Did you know that one of your players was passing information to a betting syndicate in the Far East?'

Wilson's jaw dropped. 'You're joking!'

'No, Dave. I'm deadly serious.'

Matt told him what he knew about Zhang Wei. Dave listened without interrupting. Matt thought he seemed genuinely surprised, but wondered if he was keeping something back.

'No, I don't know nothing about that. But you know players. They'd keep that sort of thing close to their chest.'

There was nothing more Matt could get from him. 'If anything comes up, Dave, or you think of anything else, you will give me call, won't you?'

Matt felt sorry for him. He was unlikely to be confirmed as the new manager, and a new man would almost certainly bring in his own backroom team. Meanwhile he had to prepare for the match against Chelsea on Sunday. Matt wished him luck.

CHAPTER THIRTEEN

Callum had asked Matt if he would take him to the Chelsea game. The boy had become Chelsea mad, probably influenced by friends at school. He didn't usually take his son with him when he was working, but the boy was desperate to go, so he phoned the club for permission.

Since he and Susie had split up, they had come to an amicable agreement about how they would share care of their nine-year-old son. Because of Matt's erratic and unsocial working hours, she agreed that he could take Callum out whenever he wanted. Matt's absence had made her life difficult. Working as a teacher, she was at home in the school holidays but, in term time, juggling school runs and after school care was not easy.

Matt collected Callum on Sunday morning from the Victorian terraced house where they had lived together. They walked to Fulham Road, joining the crowd that was already beginning to funnel towards Stamford Bridge. They were early. Matt liked to get to the ground a couple of hours before kick-off. Street vendors were busy selling Chelsea shirts, scarves and hats. The pubs were crowded, and noisy fans spilled onto the pavement. Some of the older ones recognized Matt.

'Oy Stinger! 'ow are yuh?' They came over and he signed some autographs. It was nice to know he wasn't forgotten.

'Dad?'

'Yeah?'

'Why did they call you Stinger?'

'That was my nickname.'

'Yeah, but why?'

He sighed. 'Why do you think?'

The boy looked puzzled. 'Like a bee?'

'Yeah.'

He thought hard about it. 'But why?'

He paused, wondering what to tell him. He didn't want to put the wrong ideas in his head. Still, he would probably find out anyway, and it was time he learned to look after himself.

'Well, when someone fouled me I made sure I always gave it back with interest. You know, when the ref wasn't looking. I made sure they wouldn't mess with me again. '

A look of understanding spread across the boy's face. 'Ah, sting like a bee.' He looked up at his father and grinned. 'Nice one, Stinger.'

Matt clipped him across the ears. 'Don't be so cheeky.'

As they got closer to the stadium the excitement was palpable.

'Who do you think is going to win then?' said Matt.

'Chelsea,' replied the boy, emphatically, then respectfully, 'What do you think?'

Matt gave him a playful punch on the arm. 'City.'

Callum gave him a questioning look. 'City? But you used to play for Chelsea.'

'Yeah, that's right, but it's because of Tony Barker.'

'He just died, didn't he?'

'Yes, he was my friend you know.'

Fans poured onto the concourse in front of the Stamford Bridge Stadium. Well-off supporters made their way into the Millennium Hotel, splashing out on champagne and a three-course lunch. Others hung around outside, devouring hot dogs, and celebrity spotting. Callum held his father's hand as they made their way through the crowd to the east stand and the press room entrance. A security guard scrutinised Matt's press pass and searched the backpack with his laptop and they emerged into the calm of the media room. Journalists sat around in jeans and casual jackets, chatting or checking their phones. A colleague at the *Chronicle* wandered over to Matt and they discussed who would do the match report, player ratings and post-match interviews.

Chelsea provided the press with a substantial hot buffet lunch – not something they got everywhere. Matt made his way over to the buffet with Callum.

'Can I have the fish and chips?' the boy whispered, looking up nervously.

Matt tousled his hair. 'Of course.'

Dozens of television screens around the room were showing matches on the Sky Sports News channel. Callum watched the football while Matt went through his pre-match routine – checking the team sheet and match-day programme notes, hopping online for player statistics, and checking the Twitter accounts he followed.

Callum gasped when they walked from the calm of the media room into the press box outside. The stadium was a seething cauldron – a surging sea of Chelsea blue at one end and a wall of City red shirts at the other. A perfect emerald green pitch still glistened from the morning rain and forty thousand fans sang in unison, their chants cutting the air like a bugle call to war.

'Chelsea! Chelsea!'

The City supporters at the other end fired back, 'City! City!'

Callum looked on in amazement, hypnotised by the high voltage atmosphere.

The press box was low and close to the pitch, placing the press next to the action. It overlooked the home and away dug-outs, giving journalists a close-up of the fist punching antics of the rival managers as they stalked their technical area. Matt plugged his laptop into the electrical socket on the shelf in front of them. 'Wow! Look at this,' Callum shrieked, watching football on a small television screen in front of his seat. 'Will it show the game?'

'You bet. We use it to check the action replays. You know, make sure we get it right.'

Not all clubs were so helpful. In some of the older grounds with more basic facilities, a panicky shout of 'who crossed it?' could still be heard in the press box when a goal was scored.

The chanting of the crowd ebbed away as the referee's whistle marked the beginning of the minute's silence. An intense hush cloaked the stadium as both sets of supporters stood as one, bare headed, alone with their personal memories of a sporting hero. Tony might have been the City manager, but the Chelsea fans had loyal memories of a legend. For one long minute the hairs stood up on the back of Matt's neck as he remembered playing there with Tony. The whistle blew again. Released from their silence, the crowd clapped in unison, letting go their pent-up emotion. Players who had stood shoulder to shoulder, arms linked together, sprinted away to take up their positions. A steady drizzle persisted on a cold January afternoon and Matt bent down to pull up the zip on Callum's jacket.

The shrill blast of the referee's whistle signaled the kick off and the rumble of the crowd built to a crescendo. Callum was mesmerised. City passed the ball back to a midfield player. His long ball out to the right found the winger in acres of space. He sprinted toward the Chelsea goal like a guided missile. Chelsea defenders were racing back but the cross came in. Ricky Varta, City's Argentinian striker, was unmarked. He took the ball on his chest, brought it down and turned to volley the ball past the diving Chelsea keeper. 1-0 to City. The Chelsea fans were shocked into silence. Jubilant City fans chanted, 'You're not singing anymore.' Callum threw himself onto the floor, his head in his hands. Matt smiled. 'Don't worry, Cal. Long way to go yet.'

Chelsea seemed stunned and City were in control for most of the first half. Then two minutes before half time they scored again – a penalty that John Taylor, the City captain, buried in the corner of the goal. City fans went wild, arms outstretched in unison, fingers pointing at the silent Chelsea end, taunting them with their rhythmic chanting. Callum tore at his hair and screwed up his face. Matt thought he was going to cry. 2-0 to City.

But the Blues came out rejuvenated after their half-time team talk, storming the City goal. Ten minutes later their efforts were rewarded when a poor City clearance was headed straight into the path of a Chelsea player only fifteen metres from goal. He controlled the ball with one touch and let fly with a powerful shot that rocketed into the bottom corner of the net. Callum jumped up, punching the air with his fist. 2-1 to City. Reporters looked up and smiled sympathetically at Matt. They had kids too.

But City held out with determined defending as heavy rain swept across Stamford Bridge. Their attacking players came back to shore up the defense. Lung bursting runs and brave tackles held Chelsea at bay. Then, with only ten minutes to go, Fabio Plattini, City's Italian centre-half, lunged in with a late tackle. He already had one yellow card. City fans grimaced and held their breath as the referee ran over to the player. He pulled out a second yellow and then the red card. City were down to ten men. They looked tired. All the momentum was with Chelsea now, spurred on by the roaring crowd. A shot cannoned off the City crossbar. Another shot looked destined for the back of the net, but somehow the City keeper turned the ball round the post with his fingertips. It seemed that City would hold out but, with only five minutes left, a desperate tackle in the penalty area by John Taylor brought down a Chelsea striker. City players clamoured round the referee, protesting. Callum and forty thousand Chelsea fans jumped to their feet, waving their fists in angry protest. The referee pointed to the spot. The noise subsided as the Chelsea player stepped up to take the spot kick, then erupted again in triumph as Chelsea evened the score. 2-2.

With the ninety minutes gone and just four minutes of injury time left, the match looked set for a draw, but still Chelsea surged forward. A shot from a long way out seemed to be well covered by the City keeper who dived to his right, but it struck a defender and was deflected to the keepers left. It hit the inside of the post and agonizingly trickled over the line. 3 – 2 to Chelsea. The crowd went wild. The roar could be heard all the way down the Fulham Road. Callum jumped up and down, hugging Matt. City players trudged from the pitch, mud splattered shirts clung to sweat soaked bodies, heads hung down. Callum looked up at Matt.

'Dad?'

'Yeah?'

'I'm sorry City lost.'

In the post-match press conference, the Chelsea manager was generous in his praise for Dave Wilson and the London City players. When he left the room and Wilson walked in, there was a spontaneous burst of applause. Matt had never seen anything like it. Dave Wilson was clearly overcome with emotion. He took his time, swallowed hard, and dealt with questions like the battle hardened professional he was.

'It's been a difficult week for all of us at the club. But the boys have been brilliant. Tony would have been proud of them. It was just a pity we couldn't get the result he would have wanted.' After he had answered the barrage of questions that followed, he rose to leave, and another round of applause followed him out.

Callum waited patiently, watching football on television while Matt filed his report. City had not played their best – the wave of emotion had affected their concentration. It wasn't surprising. It was still only seven days since Tony Barker had died.

Outside, most of the crowd had drifted away, but as Matt passed the exit from one of the VIP lounges he saw Burak Sahin coming out. The agent was just the wrong side of fifty, short, heavily built and with an olive Mediterranean complexion. He was Turkish, had moved to England as a young man, but professed to still have influential connections in Turkey. His hair was short and thick, and black stubble covered his face. His expensive blue overcoat was unbuttoned, revealing an open neck shirt and a thick gold chain.

'Tragedy about Barker,' said Sahin as they strolled along together.

'Yeah, it's hard to believe,' said Matt. 'Had you seen him recently?'

'No, not for weeks.'

'Really? You're Varta's agent. I heard he was having trouble with Varta. Tony thought you'd been unsettling the boy.'

'Me? No, not me, Matt. The boy's a bit emotional – you know what these Latinos are like.'

'Yeah. By the way, we need to have a chat. I've got something you need to know.'

Sahin touched his nose at the prospects of secrets being exchanged. 'Sure, let's have lunch tomorrow,' and he peeled off towards the car park.

'Who was that man, Daddy?'

'He's an agent, Callum.'

'I didn't like him.'

'Nor do I.'

'Why do you talk to him then?'

Matt smiled. It was a Faustian pact. Agents told journalists what was going on. Players were in their thrall, managers had a love/hate relationship with them, club directors loathed them, and football writers accepted them as a vital link to inside information.

As Callum trotted along beside him they talked about the game. He felt guilty that he didn't see him more often. He knew he should make more effort. He thought the boy had seemed more withdrawn and wondered how much of it was down to him. It was never easy for kids when parents split up. Telling Callum was the hardest thing he had ever had to do. Susie had made him do it. He had gone into his bedroom to read a story, looked at his tousled hair and his crumpled pyjamas and struggled to find the right words. But there were no right words. It had sounded clichéd. The boy had just looked at him in bewilderment – the poor kid was only nine – then tried to be brave and finally burst into tears.

When he and Susie were first married it had been different. They had met at university and fallen in love. It had probably helped that Susie wasn't interested in football or impressed that he had been a professional player. They had married soon after they both graduated and moved to Leeds. Callum was born three years later. As a regional sports writer for the *Daily Express* Matt was not often away from home, but when he moved to London to join the *Chronicle* things had changed. He was ambitious, competitive and eager to make an impression. There had been more days away, late nights, weekend working and trips to Europe. There were always young writers behind him at the *Chronicle* who were waiting to step into his shoes. The sports desk's demand for stories had been unrelenting and Matt had felt insecure if he didn't see a story with his by-line in the paper every other day.

And then there had been temptations with other women. Staying in hotels, travelling abroad, mixing in the glamorous football environment, there were always women around. He had occasionally had one-night stands, but they hadn't meant anything and Susie had never known. It was his insistence that he was unable to change his incessant unsocial work pattern that had made her demand a trial separation.

As they strolled along, he took Callum's hand and squeezed it.

'How's football going at school?'

'Alright,' said the boy, looking straight ahead.

'Are you enjoying it?'

'Yes, but the coach doesn't like me.'

'Doesn't like you? Why do you think that?'

'He doesn't pick me when we play matches.'

'Perhaps other boys are better?'

'No, he doesn't like me.'

'You'll just have to try harder. I'll come and watch when you get in the team.'

The boy looked up at his father. 'Will you?'

'Sure.'

'Dad?'

Hearing the hesitant, questioning tone, Matt glanced down and saw a worried frown.

'Yes.'

'Are you and Mummy going to get back together again?'

He held the boy's hand as they navigated past men working in a hole in the pavement. It gave him a moment to think. 'Well, I'd like to of course, well, I want to, but...'

They stopped and Callum looked up at his father, just an innocent nine-year-old boy struggling to understand a grown-up world.

'But Mummy says I work too hard.' He knew it was an ingenuous answer, but Callum had put him on the spot and it was the first thought that had come into his head.

'Why is that bad?'

'Well, it's not bad, but it means I have to go away from home a lot. You know, Callum: matches in the evenings, working at weekends, traveling abroad. Mummy thinks it's not fair. And she's right. It's not fair on her.'

'But what's going to happen?'

'Nothing, Callum. I'll always be your dad and we'll see each other as much as we can.' The boy still held his hand, but puckered up his mouth as they walked on in silence.

Callum pushed open the front door and ran in. 'Mummy, Mummy, Chelsea won. Daddy bought me a Chelsea scarf.' He held the scarf with arms spread wide above his head and swayed the way the crowd had, then rushed past her into the kitchen.

She snorted and rolled her eyes in a gesture that said, "Kids. What can you do?" She looked good, he had to admit. Her neat figure was accentuated by the snug fitting blue jeans and the tight white T-shirt, her short auburn hair a clue to her strong willed, independent spirit.

'Would you like to stay for a cup of tea?'

'Thanks.'

He was surprised. She did not usually ask him to stay. She went into the kitchen to put the kettle on and make tea for Callum. Left alone, he looked around the sitting room. Nothing had changed since he left six months ago. The same green Chesterfield sofa and button back Victorian chairs, the piano and music stand and her cello standing in one corner. On the pine dresser there were still photographs of the two of them with Callum. He noticed that their wedding photo seemed to have disappeared though. Callum's games and books were scattered around the room. It was homely.

Susie seemed on edge when she came back with a tea tray. He wondered why she had asked him to stay. She poured the tea and sat back. 'Thanks for phoning last Sunday. It must have been a terrible shock.'

'Yeah, then having to report on Tony's death.'

'I read your pieces. You know I didn't like Tania, but it must be terrible for her. Imagine having to tell the children. How is she?'

'Distraught, but coping.'

There was an awkward silence, broken with a chink as Susie put her cup back in the saucer. She leaned forward. 'How did you find Callum today?'

'Okay. Why?'

'I spoke to his teacher at the parents' evening last week. Pity you couldn't come.'

He bit his lips and ignored the sarcasm. 'I'm sorry, Susie. I told you I would be in Munich that night.'

She shrugged her shoulders. 'Anyway, she told me she was concerned about his behavioral problems.'

'What sort of things?'

'Oh, withdrawn. Not concentrating in class...' Matt frowned.

'And fighting in the playground.'

'What? Do you think he's being bullied?'

'I don't know. So how did you find him today?'

'Well, he enjoyed the game, but yes, I did think he was subdued. I thought it was just because he was left alone while I was working.'

'He misses having you at home.'

'It was you that asked me to leave!'

Her cheeks flushed. 'That's rich coming from you. I told you. You can't have your cake and eat it – putting your job first and having us here when it suits you.'

Matt bit his lip and sank back on the sofa. 'I know, I'm sorry.' He sighed. 'There was something else. He asked me if we were going to get back together again.'

She stopped tidying the cushions and looked up sharply. 'What? What did you tell him?'

'Well, he caught me out– it was so out of the blue. I said I'd like to, but it's not fair on you because I work too hard.'

She cocked her head on one side. 'Matt, if you think you can come back, forget it.'

Matt grimaced. 'If only you could try to understand.'

'No, Matt, you have to understand. You could lose your wife and your son.'

He winced. What did she mean? Divorce? He didn't want that. They only argued over the time he spent away from home. Why couldn't she see he was only doing his job? They both cared about Callum. There was no reason why they couldn't go on like they were now: it wasn't as if she was interested in other blokes. Still, he'd have to make more time for Callum.

He took a sip from the tea, but it was lukewarm. 'I was thinking,' he said, 'I was wondering about buying him a really nice bike for his birthday. I could bring my bike over – take him cycling. What do you think?'

She shrugged her shoulders and her face softened into a weak smile. 'Yeah, that's okay.'

'And I told him I'll come and watch when he gets in the team.'

'You should.' She stood up. 'I've got to help him with some homework and get ready for the morning.'

Matt stood up and moved to give her a light kiss on the cheek but she turned away.

'Thanks for the tea. Let me know when he gets picked for the team. I don't want to miss it.'

CHAPTER FOURTEEN

Burak Sahin was in a different league to most agents. Over twenty years he had built a list of clients who were top names in the leading clubs in Europe. His influence with chairmen and CEOs was considerable. He was often hired to bring them players they wanted, and had recently attempted to negotiate the purchase of a Championship club for a foreign buyer. He strolled into the restaurant thirty minutes late. Matt wasn't surprised. He walked over to another table, chatted to an acquaintance and waved across the room to others. The restaurant, which was owned by his cousin, had become popular with the younger Islington set. For Sahin it also had the advantage of only being a short walk to the Emirates Stadium. His cousin rushed up and greeted him with a bear hug. Matt pulled out his phone and pressed the record button.

Sahin strode over and heaved his bulky frame into a chair. 'What are you drinking, Matt? Wine?'

'No thanks. I'll stick with mineral water.'

Sahin ordered the water and a bottle of wine and leaned back in his chair. His blue suit was impeccably cut and his pink button down shirt was handmade. He wore a gold ring on his finger and a diamond Rolex watch on his wrist. 'So, Matt, what did you want to talk to me about?'

'Your boy Molari.'

'Yeah, what about him?'

'Well, Burak, he's been a naughty boy. Goes to a nightclub, gets in a fight over a girl and takes her back to a hotel for the night. Not exactly what the fans expect from a top Premier League player with a wife and two young kids, is it? Shouldn't think his wife will be too pleased either. Then there's his manager. What's he going to do? Oh, and of course there are his sponsors to consider. If they drop him that would cut into your commission wouldn't it?'

Sahin leaned forward, elbows on the table, studying Matt, making calculations. 'Are you publishing it?'

'Well, Burak, you have to admit it's a good story. Definitely front page I'd say.

'"You've got the girl?' said Sahin.

'Yes, she came to us. Photos too. The editor will love it.'

'How much does she want?'

'£25,000.'

'Are you going to pay her?'

'No. You are.'

'Twenty-five grand?'

'No, fifty if you want her to retract the story...'

Sahin gave Matt a knowing, wry smile, then heaved a sigh of relief and eased his frame back into the chair.

'Provided that you tell me everything you know about Mayfield.'

The smile disappeared and Sahin looked confused. 'What do you mean?'

'Mayfield does all the transfer business at City. It seems like an agent has been getting a bit too friendly with him.'

'You think it's me?'

'I didn't say that. I'm just saying. What's Mayfield been up to?'

Sahin rubbed his chin while he thought about it. 'Matt, I can't have you doing a story on this and it getting back to me. There would be too many knives in my back.'

Matt picked up his phone. 'I've only got to press send and the girl's story will be in tomorrow's paper.'

Sahin bit his fingers. 'Is this off the record?'

'It's off the record. That's why I've still got relationships with contacts like you.'

Sahin sighed. 'Alright, Matt. Mayfield's fucking bent. He's got an agent in his pocket.'

'Who's that?' said Matt.

Sahin frowned. 'You're doing a Mayfield story, right?'

Matt nodded his agreement.

'Okay, well let's just call him X for now and I didn't tell you. Okay? So Mayfield tips him the wink on who they like and X pushes the players his way. Mayfield takes half his commission.'

'Cosy.'

'Yeah, and if Mayfield wants a player that is not repped by X, he tells the player X will get him a much better deal.' Sahin drained his glass, picked up the bottle and refilled it. 'And they've got a deal going where X brings him players that can be developed and sold on by X. The club makes a profit. Everybody's happy.'

'So what?'

'X puts a sell on clause in the contract. If City buy for one million and they sell on for an agreed figure, say 20 million, X gets fifty percent of the profit.'

'That's alright if it's in the contract.'

'Yeah, but what's not in the contract is that X gives Mayfield a fifty percent kickback.'

'So where does that leave you with City transfers then?'

'I took a player to Mayfield. Barker wanted him, and the player wanted to go there, but it had to go through X. He tried to offer me five per cent. I told him to fuck off. I could get the player a better deal at another club.'

'So you're pissed off with him.'

'You know,' said Sahin, stretching his large frame back in the chair and lighting a cigar, 'agents have two goals in life: making money and making money. I don't need to get in a war with X. I've got bigger deals than that all over Europe, all the time. It's that cunt Mayfield that gets me – all smooth and sophisticated, well educated, well spoken, like he was so bloody self-righteous.'

'How does Mayfield get the money?'

'Oh, he's smart, not directly of course. He had his own business before he got into football. He set up a company that invoices X for, say, scouting services or commissions, and X pays it into a Swiss bank account.'

'Ahh!' said Matt softly. 'Bribery and money laundering.' Sahin snorted. 'Yeah, and an allowable agent's expense too!'

'Did Tony know?'

Sahin sucked his teeth. 'I don't know. You'd think he would suspect something, wouldn't you? '

Matt finished the grilled fish and pushed his plate to one side.

'Are we done then?' said Sahin. 'You're going to kill the story about Molari?'

'What about Varta?'

'What about him?'

'Tony was having a problem with him. You're his agent. He must talk to you. What was that all about?'

'I don't know.'

'Were matches being fixed at City?

'Match fixing? In the Premier League? I can't see that, Matt.'

Matt looked him in the eye but Sahin didn't flinch. He wondered how anybody ever won any negotiations when he was sitting on the other side of the table.

'Was Varta in trouble?'

The same blank face. 'No.'

Matt felt the phone vibrating in his pocket. He pulled it out, glanced at the screen and stepped outside. 'Yes, Dr. Andrews.'

'Good afternoon, Mr. Riley. I have got the results for you. I think you are going to be pleased. There was no inflammation or scarring in the tissue sample. I can tell you quite definitely that the shard of glass I gave to the police officer entered Mr. Barker's right heel a few minutes before his death.' He paused, 'I will send you the report.'

Matt breathed a sigh of relief. 'Thank you very much. Thank you very much indeed.'

He felt the adrenalin surge through his body as he strode back into the restaurant.

The waiter came with the bill. Matt pushed it across the table, stood up and walked out.

CHAPTER FIFTEEN

A cold north wind swirled around All Saints Church, Wimbledon. The funeral service, just twelve days after Tony Barker's death, was by invitation only: a public memorial service would be held later. It had snowed in the night and half an inch had accumulated on the grass. The mourners, dressed from head to toe in black, stood out in stark relief. Six City players, their faces set like stone and the colour of the ancient church walls, carried the pale oak coffin shoulder high from the black hearse. Walking slowly, and in step, they passed through the church gate where flowers, club scarves and messages of sympathy had been laid by supporters.

The minister met the coffin at the church door, took Tania's hand and walked into the church with her. He welcomed the mourners with words of comfort. 'I am the resurrection and the life. He who believes in me will live, even though he dies, says the Lord.' After a prayer, the congregation stood to sing the first hymn. As the final strains died away – *In life, in death, O Lord, abide with me* – Mark and Robert stepped forward to place their father's FA Cup Final medal on the coffin. The sound of stifled sobbing disturbed the uncomfortable silence.

With a lump in his throat, Matt rose to make his way to the pulpit to pay his tribute. He hit a positive upbeat note, remembering how he had first met Tony, and how Tony had helped young players like himself. He recalled how he had met Tania and the joy of their wedding. He praised Tony as a husband, and as a father, and as a person who always had words of encouragement for his players, and as a manager who always found time to speak to journalists. Matt's humorous anecdotes brought ripples of laughter that lifted the mood. The service ended with the Lord's Prayer before the minister and congregation moved outside for the committal.

The sombre group of mourners gathered around the grave and pulled up the collars of their overcoats as grey clouds scudded overhead and snowflakes fluttered to the ground. The minister intoned his final prayer, commending Tony Barker to God's love and mercy.

'Earth to earth, ashes to ashes, dust to dust,' and the coffin was slowly lowered into the earth.

Tania dropped a white lily onto the coffin and threw a handful of earth into the grave. The wind caught her wide brimmed hat, and as she threw up her hand to catch it, she looked as if she might fall. Sergei Buzinsky, who was standing next to her, jumped forward to support her. The Russian oligarch took Tania's arm and bent over, whispering into her ear.

Matt watched with more than casual interest. He had rarely been this close to the Russian. He had only once met Buzinsky. He wasn't the kind of person that anyone got to know. There was no denying his commanding presence: the unmistakable authority that great wealth and power bring. He had houses in London, New York and Monaco, three super-yachts and a private jet. His trim physique showed no signs of a man living the high life, and at forty-seven years old he looked fit and strong. He reputedly worked out every day in his private gyms, swam in his indoor pools, and skied at Gstaad each winter.

Tania looked up at Buzinsky, smiled and thanked him for his help. The Russian turned to Matt, who was close by. Matt was not sure if the oligarch remembered who he was, but he shook Matt's hand. 'Thank you for your tribute,' he said. 'It's a terrible loss for all of us.'

'Thank you.' He kept his grip on Buzinsky's hand and looked into his eyes. 'I'm sure you understand. It must have been unbearable when you lost your own son.'

The Russian dropped Matt's hand. 'Yes, it was,' he said after a long silence.

'Shocking.' Matt shook his head slowly from side to side. 'Otahara Syndrome. Such a cruel disease.'

Buzinsky's eyes narrowed, looking unsure where Matt was going with this.

'I know someone who suffered. I want to do a story to raise public awareness. Of course, it would get so much more attention if a name like yours was connected to it.'

Buzinsky stared at him. Then, his mind made up, turned and walked away.

A reception had been provided at a nearby hotel. Most of the mourners appeared to be there, even Buzinsky, surrounded by his entourage. Matt noticed Emma talking to Roger Mayfield, the CEO, and Mark Fisher, the head of media communications. Then he spotted Pat McCarthy, who was on his own. He went over to join him.

Pat McCarthy was Tony's agent. He had negotiated Tony's contract with the club. McCarthy was a licensed agent who worked for one of the big international agencies. His players relied on him for everything. He negotiated their contracts, image rights and endorsements. He advised on tax, investments, buying a house, pensions, in fact they hardly made any financial decision without consulting Pat. But it came at a price. He received ten percent of his players' annual salary, twenty percent of endorsement contracts and ten percent of the transfer fee when they moved.

'Did you see this coming, Pat?'

'I'm telling you, I was gobsmacked. I spoke to him the week before. I had no idea this was on the cards.'

'You don't think there was anything on his mind?'

'No.'

A waitress came by and topped up their champagne glasses. Matt leaned closer to Pat.

'Do you think Mayfield is taking a bung?'

Pat shrugged and smiled. 'Mayfield? Probably.'

'Why do you think that?'

'You can judge a man by the company he keeps.'

'Did Tony know?'

'If he did, he didn't talk to me about it.'

Matt said nothing and looked across the room at Mayfield. They both sipped champagne.

'Matt, you're not thinking that had anything to do with Tony's suicide, are you?'

'I don't know. Could be.'

'Come on, Matt, even if Tony knew more about Mayfield's business than I did, it was no reason to take his own life, was it?'

No, thought Matt, but it could give Mayfield a reason to kill him. He looked at Mayfield again. He was in animated conversation with Buzinsky. If Tony had found evidence of bribery, he would take it to

Buzinsky. Mayfield would be finished. He would go to jail unless Buzinsky hushed it up to protect the club. But then Mayfield would be fired and Buzinsky would make sure he didn't work in football again. A motive for murder maybe, but what evidence could Tony have found?

'I don't know, Pat. Perhaps it could have had something to do with it.' They took another drink and looked around the room. 'Did you think that some of City's matches were fixed?'

'What?' McCarthy looked surprised at the switch in conversation. 'Who told you that?'

'Frankie Warren.'

'Warren? Oh really.'

'Yeah, I know, but did you hear anything?'

'Well... I heard rumours, but we hear rumours all the time.'

'Did Tony say anything?'

'No,' said Pat. 'We had a good relationship, but it was just business. You would have been much closer to him than me.' They drained their glasses and picked up two more from a passing waitress. 'Actually, I'm glad I've seen you today, Pat. I wanted to thank you for that tip you gave me on Randall.'

Randall was the chairman of a Midlands club. His manager, Steve Williams, was a client of Pat's. They both knew that Randall was an autocrat and a bully. He had accused his manager of making an unauthorised transfer deal with an agent who had been suspected of giving illegal bungs to managers. He was going to sack him, but they knew it wasn't true.

Matt had never forgotten the corrupt owner who had fired his father. He knew how to deal with men like that.

He had phoned Randall and asked if he had approved the transfer. He point-blank denied it. Then he went to see Steve Williams's lawyer. They went to dinner. He told Matt he had seen a copy of a document signed by Randall authorising the deal. He left the letter on the table and went out to take a phone call. Matt took it to the toilet and photographed it.

Next morning, he called Randall. 'You're a lying bastard,' he said. 'We've got the fucking document with your signature on it and we're doing you in the paper tomorrow.' That finished him. He resigned two days later.

Matt felt a tap on his arm, and turned to see a woman he recognised as one of Sergei Buzinsky's assistants. 'Excuse me, Mr. Riley. Mr. Buzinsky would like to have a word with you. Can you come this way please?'

She led him across the room where Buzinsky sat at a small table. 'Sit down,' he said, gesturing to the empty seat next to him. 'Can I get you something to drink?' Matt declined politely and waited.

'I have to say, Riley, you've got a nerve. But your timing is perfect. My wife and I are launching a foundation to help children suffering from Otahara Syndrome. The foundation will focus on medical research. There is much we can do to help. You can come and see me to discuss the story you were talking about.'

Buzinsky rarely gave interviews. To get close to Buzinsky and find out what he knew about Tony's death. What a scoop! Probably go in the Saturday magazine section. That would keep Bill quiet for a while.

'Thank you,' he said. 'Can I bring a photographer?'

'Yes. My office will be in touch.'

Unable to believe his luck, Matt walked across the room to join the others, but before he reached them Tania came over. She looked pale and drawn.

'I'm going home now, Matt, but I wanted to thank you for what you did today.'

Her face felt like a block of ice as he bent to kiss her cheek.

'I'll call you tomorrow,' he whispered.

An hour later he felt his phone vibrating. It was Tania. 'Matt, I've had burglars.'

He froze. 'Don't do anything. I'm on my way.'

CHAPTER SIXTEEN

Tania opened the door. She looked frightened.

'Are you alright?' said Matt, looking past her into the hall.

'Yes,' she said, 'I'm okay, but it's made me nervous. Come into the sitting room. The boys are with Mum and Dad watching TV in the den.'

'When did it happen?'

'It must have been while we were at the funeral. I saw the mess when I got back.'

'What did they take?'

'Well, that's the funny thing. I don't think anything has been stolen. But there were drawers pulled open: things like that.'

'Did you call the police?'

'Yes, as soon as I got back. They came very quickly, but when I told them nothing had been stolen they seemed to lose interest. Huh!' She snorted. 'I don't know what we pay our council tax for. They just looked around and made a few notes. Told me it wasn't a burglary if nothing had been stolen. Said I should call them if I found anything missing later.'

Matt walked into the sitting room and looked around. Everything seemed to be in place. He looked puzzled.

'The housekeeper has tidied everything up,' said Tania. 'There wasn't really much mess, but I could see that they had rifled through cupboards and drawers.'

'Are you sure nothing has been stolen?'

'Yes. I checked. Well, nothing valuable anyway. My jewellery, silver, antiques, even cash I keep hidden in the bedroom. Everything seems to be there.'

'What about his computer?'

'His laptop wasn't here. The police took it before.'

'What about his study?'

'Oh, that was a mess,' she said.

'Do you mind if I take a look in there?'

She led him into the study that had been Tony's private fiefdom. The split-level room had steps leading up to a gallery surrounded by a wooden balustrade. Bookshelves lined the walls on three sides. The shelves were filled with books on football, the sports sciences and biographies of inspirational leaders. The parquet floor was finished in cherry wood and in the centre of the room a large antique desk sat on a Persian rug. The drawers had been pulled open and papers scattered about.

Matt stood for a while, taking it all in. He shivered at the thought of what had happened there. He felt ill at ease standing next to Tania and wondered what she must be feeling.

'This must be very difficult for you,' he said.

She swallowed and looked down at her feet. 'Yes,' she whispered. 'It is.'

'I'm sorry.'

There was an uncomfortable silence. He looked around the room. 'And nothing's been taken?'

'Not as far as I can tell; well, nothing valuable anyway. I don't know about any of the papers or documents.'

Matt walked across the study to take a closer look at the glass cabinets containing football trophies that recorded the highlights of Tony's career. 'This silver must be worth a bit,' he said. 'They weren't ordinary burglars, were they?'

'What do you think they were looking for?' said Tania.

'I don't know. The dossier perhaps?'

He paused at the glass fronted drinks cabinet, displaying a collection of fine single malt whiskies. He remembered that Tony was a connoisseur. He liked to take his whisky neat, with no ice or water. Next to the drinks cabinet was a taller cabinet displaying glasses.

'Are these the only glasses in the study?'

'Yes, why?'

Matt opened the glass cabinet. Nothing looked disturbed. He examined a set of engraved lead crystal whisky tumblers set in a silver base. It was a set that had been presented to Tony when he retired as a player. Matt had been there on that occasion and he knew they held great sentimental value for Tony. He counted them. There were five.

But there should have been six.

He turned to Tania and held one up. 'Did Tony break one of the engraved whisky glasses?'

'What? No. No, I'm sure he didn't,' she said.

'But there are only five herc.'

She came and stood beside him, staring at the tumblers, puzzled. 'I can't understand it. There were six, of course. If one had got broken I'd have never heard the end of it.

'What about the housekeeper? Would she know?'

'Oh, she's Polish, but she's very reliable. I'll ask her if you like.'

Tania picked up an internal phone. Two minutes later a short well-built woman in her early thirties appeared. 'Danika, this is Mr. Riley.'

'Yes, madam.'

'You know those special whisky tumblers?'

'Yes, Mrs. Barker, the ones with the silver base?'

'That's right. Has one of them been broken?'

'No, ma'am.'

'But there are only five here now.'

Danika stared at the cabinet and shrugged her shoulders. 'Well, I dusted the cabinet last Friday, like I always do, and they were all there then. I would have noticed. There would have been a space like there is now.'

'And you haven't cleared up any broken glass?' Matt asked.

'No, sir,' she said.

When the housekeeper had gone, Tania turned to Matt, seeking an answer. 'What's going on? Why are you so bothered about a missing glass?'

'Dr Andrews, you know, the forensic pathologist, well he found a shard of glass in Tony's heel. I think it could have come from the missing glass.'

Tania looked baffled as she struggled to understand the significance of the missing glass. Matt paced around the study. Why hadn't the SOCO found any broken glass? Of course, the intruders would have cleaned up. The smooth parquet floor would make that easy, but lead crystal shatters into tiny pieces. Surely she should have found some evidence of glass.

'Tania, can you remember what happened when the police were

here on Sunday morning?'

'Of course not! But Jane was here. Why don't you ask her?'

He pulled out his phone. 'Jane, I'm with Tania in the study. There's a whisky glass missing and one or two things don't seem to add up. Can you remember exactly what happened when the police were in the house on Sunday morning?'

'Oh Matt, I don't know. I was with Tania most of the time, and I wasn't paying too much attention, except when they came to ask Tania questions.'

'Who was there?'

'What, in the house?'

'Yes.'

'Well, there was the detective sergeant, of course. I don't remember his name. I didn't like him. He was very bossy. Then there was someone else. I think I heard him say, "This is my detective constable." Then there were uniformed officers outside.'

'But what about the SOCOs?'

'Who?'

'The scene of crime officers; the ones in white overalls. How many were there?'

'Oh, just the one: a young woman. I can't remember her name.'

'Can you remember what she was doing?'

'When I arrived she was in the study taking photographs. I heard the detective say, "You're a bit keen for just a suicide, aren't you?" I thought he was being horrible to her. Anyway, she took no notice, just carried on clicking.'

'What else did she do?'

'I don't know. I wasn't watching her all the time. Anyway, she wasn't there for long.'

'Really?'

'Yes. I heard the detective on the phone. He was saying, "I've got your assistant here now. She's done a good job, but it's only a suicide. If you're short-handed I'm sure she could help you when she's finished here." Then he went back into the study, and I think he said something like, "Linda." That's right, I remember now, that was her name, "Linda, your boss is short-handed on a murder scene in Kingston. He wants you over there now." She left soon after that.'

So, thought Matt, the SOCO officer had been rushed; the scene had not been thoroughly investigated. But now the police had the shard of glass from Tony's heel. If they matched it to one of the five remaining tumblers it would prove that one or more intruders had been in the room – and that they had murdered Tony. Matt walked slowly to the steps leading to the balustrade around the galleried level. Tania had slumped into a chair, watching him.

'Was it here?' he said.

She nodded and Matt shuddered at the thought of Tony's limp body hanging just where he stood.

'What was he wearing?' he said softly

'His pyjamas.'

'Did he have – anything on his feet?'

She screwed up her face as if she tried to remember, then shook her head. 'No. No. He had bare feet. He liked to walk around like that.'

She began to cry and he put his arms round her. 'Oh, Tania, I'm so sorry. Let's go back to the kitchen and have a cup of tea.'

Tony had been murdered. He was sure of that now, but by Mayfield or Zhang Wei? Zhang Wei had been murdered on the same day. Perhaps Tony had found out that Zhang Wei was fixing matches: was about to expose the whole racket. So Zhang Wei had come to the house to silence him. But by then Zhang Wei knew too much. He was expendable, so he was taken out by his bosses.

Matt had to admit that it was a stretch of his imagination. Perhaps Zhang Wei's death was simply a drug turf war killing as the police suspected? But what about the missing dossier? Surely that must have been why Tania had been burgled. If the intruders had searched for it on Saturday night, why had they come back again today? There could only be one reason. On Saturday they didn't know there was a dossier. But where was it? Tania said she hadn't seen it again, and Emma hadn't found it when Tania had given her the key to the locked cupboard at the office.

By the time he left Tania it was seven o'clock. Bill would be busy putting the paper to bed but this couldn't wait. He pulled his phone out of his pocket. 'Bill, I want to break the story. I've found something you're going to want to hear now.'

CHAPTER SEVENTEEN

Knightsbridge underground was still busy at seven o'clock that evening as Matt made his way out of the station and onto Kensington Road. The pavement was surprisingly crowded; probably shoppers still intent on unearthing a bargain at the end of the January sales he thought. As the lift whisked him to the fourth floor of the IMC building he felt increasingly uneasy. Bill had sounded very short tempered when he called.

He didn't feel any better when he walked into the editor's office. Bill slammed down the phone, tie askew, sleeves rolled up, and a face like thunder. And he didn't look in the mood for pleasantries.

'Okay, where have you got to with the story? Did you find out what the wife was up to? Was she screwing someone? Is that why he did it?'

'I checked it out, Bill, I tracked down the man she was with at the party. He was shit scared, terrified his wife would find out – begged me to keep it out of the paper. He admitted he was having an affair with Tania, but it was nothing – just a short-term fling. He asked Tania if Tony knew and she told him there was nothing to worry about – Tony had no idea. Emma confirmed it. Tony didn't know.' Matt paused, 'Anyway, he didn't top himself, Bill. He was murdered.'

Bill's eyebrows shot up in surprise. 'So the second post-mortem showed that the cartilage in the neck was broken?'

'No, the cricoid wasn't broken.'

'What? Well, that blows your theory out of the water then.'

'That's what I thought at first, Bill, but the second post-mortem came up with something else. There was a shard of glass in Barker's heel.'

Bill looked unimpressed. 'So what?'

'It could be significant. Tania showed me Tony's study yesterday and I noticed that one glass was missing from a set of six presentation glasses. There was no sign of any broken glass.' Matt leaned forward to engage Bill's attention. 'I think there was a struggle and the whisky tumbler was broken. Afterwards the intruders cleaned up. But Tony had bare feet. He must have trodden on some broken glass.'

Bill looked unconvinced.

'Can't you see, Bill? It proves that someone else was in the study, someone who murdered him.'

'How do you know that?'

'The forensic pathologist analysed a tissue sample. The shard of glass entered Tony's heel about the time he died.'

'He could have smashed the glass he was drinking from, then trod on it just before he hung himself,' said Bill.

'But the police never found any broken glass. Nor did the housekeeper.'

Bill rubbed his chin and thought about it. 'Do the police know about this?'

'They were at the post-mortem. They've taken away the shard of glass. He was murdered, Bill.'

'Come on, Matt, murder? Even after two post-mortems there is no evidence of foul play!'

'We don't know that yet, but the shard of glass could be the missing link.'

'Hmmm.' Bill leaned back in his chair, crossing his arms. 'Why would someone want to kill Barker?'

'I think he was about to expose a match fixing racket.'

Wickes shook his head. 'You don't really think City matches were fixed, do you?'

'There's plenty to suggest it,' said Matt. 'Zhang Wei was working for a Singapore gambling syndicate. I had information from an agent. Tony was building a secret dossier on it. Tania was burgled by someone who was probably looking for the dossier. It's beginning to add up.'

'Look, Matt, let's be frank: you're clutching at straws. Yes, we know it goes on in Europe. Italy has been plagued by it, but not here in the Premier League.' Matt slumped back in his chair. 'Alright, I'm not saying there's nothing there, Matt. It's possible, but even if you were right, how do you prove match fixing? Look at the DJ Campbell case. The CPS dropped it because there was not enough evidence to provide a realistic prospect of conviction.'

There was an uncomfortable silence. Matt bit his lip, barely able to disguise his frustration. 'There's another possibility.'

'What's that?' said Bill.

'Mayfield was taking a bung and using the agent to launder the money. Tony could have found out and threatened to expose him.'

'He wouldn't be the first to take a bung, but you'll never prove it.'

'I've got the source on tape.'

'Can you corroborate it?'

'Not yet.'

Bill shook his head and sighed. 'I'm not saying this doesn't have the potential to be a big story, but either way it would be hugely damaging to the club. Buzinsky is a powerful man with friends in high places. And he's a ruthless litigator. There's no way this newspaper is going to publish unless we have a watertight case. You know how difficult that is with match fixing and bungs. And as for suggesting that Barker was murdered...' He rolled his eyes. 'I'm sorry, Matt, but I think you've let this get too personal. It's a wild goose chase.'

Matt straightened up, his chest tightening and his breath coming faster. 'With all due respect, Bill, I think that's a mistake. I think the shard of glass will prove that Tony was murdered. I want to break the story.'

Bill banged his fist on the desk. 'And I'm telling you to drop it.'

Matt sighed and tossed his head in the air.

'And don't take that attitude with me. If you still think its murder, go and tell the police your shard of glass poppycock.'

Matt shook his head. What was wrong with Bill? He had a good nose for a story. Alright, he had known Bill spike his stories in the past. There was that time he nailed a famous England player who was having an affair with his au pair. The player denied it and none of the press pack had anything, but he'd got him bang to rights. But Bill just refused to run it – said he was very popular and they would lose readers. And despite the divide between church and state, he knew the paper sometimes shelved stories because a big advertiser might pull out. But this? What was up with him?

There was an awkward pause until Matt changed the subject.

'By the way, Bill, I've set up an interview with Buzinsky. I'm going to his house tomorrow.'

Bill's head jerked up. 'You what?'

'I told him I'm doing a story on children with Otahara Syndrome. His oldest child died from it last year. He and his wife are setting up a foundation.'

'Hmmm.' Bill rubbed his chin. 'Well, that's a turn up.'

'It's a scoop, Bill! Exclusive. What do you think? Interview in the Saturday magazine section?'

He leaned forward. 'Alright, that's good. I'll have a word with the magazine editor. But be careful what you say, Matt. For Christ's sake don't bring up this bloody murder theory of yours with him. I don't want his lawyers coming down on us like a plague of locusts.'

CHAPTER EIGHTEEN

Matt was shown into a lounge in the Buzinsky residence. He took in the opulent surroundings. His eyes were drawn to the modern art on the walls and he recalled that Buzinsky was reputed to have one of the finest collections of modern art in the world. After a few minutes the Russian oligarch entered the room and strode across to Matt, who stood up to greet him. Buzinsky put his left hand on Matt's shoulder and shook his hand in a firm grip. They sat down, the oligarch looking relaxed in black jeans and a black silk shirt. It was the first time that anyone had ever interviewed him in his Knightsbridge home. Matt had no idea what to expect. 'Thank you for the interview,' he said.

The Russian nodded and indicated where he wanted Matt to sit. 'I want to talk to you about the Buzinsky Foundation, but first let's establish some house rules. No photographs of the house, interior or exterior, no photographs of my wife, except one with us together, and no details of our address. Is that understood?'

'Of course.'

A uniformed maid appeared with a tray of coffee and water. 'Would you like coffee?' Buzinsky asked.

'Yes, black please.'

As the maid poured the coffee Matt looked up at a woman who slipped quietly into the room. 'I would like you to meet my wife, Svetlana,' said Buzinsky.

Matt jumped up to offer his hand, hardly able to believe his luck. Buzinsky's wife was rarely seen in public and had never been interviewed. He looked at her for as long as seemed polite. She was an attractive woman – tall, supermodel slim, with jet black shoulder length hair. About forty-five, he thought. She was wearing a plain white dress and although he knew nothing about designer fashion, he could see it was classy. She sat next to her husband, reached out and held his hand.

'Svetlana and I are endowing one hundred million pounds to help children with Otahara Syndrome.' Matt blinked and whistled under his breath. 'You are a journalist, we know, and I liked the way you supported Tania. If your story is going to help to build awareness for Otahara Syndrome, we are happy to be interviewed. You don't need me to tell you the consequences for the *Chronicle* if we, or our foundation, are misrepresented.'

'I understand,' said Matt. 'Is it alright if I record this?' Buzinsky nodded his agreement. Matt reached into his bag and pulled out his phone and a notebook. 'Can you tell me more about the Foundation and its goals?'

Buzinsky's face softened in a way that Matt had not expected. 'It's a rare epileptic condition that occurs in very young children. It's usually diagnosed at three months, but the first signs are often seen in the first ten days of life.' He exhaled.

Matt sucked his lips. 'That's awful. What causes it?'

'Usually brain malformation, or metabolic disorder, or genetic mutations. But we have much to learn.'

'What are the prospects for children who have been affected?'

'The outlook is bleak. Hope relies on medical research – understanding more about the causes and what treatment may work. That's where we can help,' he said, looking into his wife's eyes and squeezing her hand. She dabbed her eyes.

''Victor was our first child,' Svetlana said. 'We were so excited, but in a few days I knew something was wrong. We went to specialists. They did endless tests, but in the end they just tell you...' she welled up and Buzinsky put his arm around her.

'It was very difficult for Svetlana,' he said. 'As time went by, he needed twenty-four hour care. We had a nurse, of course, but Svetlana wanted to try to do everything herself.'

'He was such a lovely boy,' she said. 'He was beautiful. I was so proud of him. When he smiled it broke my heart. I knew I was going to lose him.' She paused to take a deep breath. 'Sergei was wonderful. He had his business and the football club, but every morning he spent time with me and Victor. He was always so positive. It breaks some marriages, but it made ours stronger.' He hugged her again. 'When Victor died he was five. Our world fell apart. But Sergei was strong.'

'We will never get over it,' he said, 'but we have two other children, both healthy and happy. We are grateful for that. Now that we have had time to grieve we want to do something to help. Not just with medical research, but to help other parents. We had the means for round the clock care and teaching. Most don't. We can help with that.' Two young children skipped into the room, laughing, and rushed to their mother, chattering in Russian. Svetlana smiled and listened, then looked up at Matt.

'Will you excuse me?'

'Of course,' said Matt and turned to Buzinsky. 'Can I ask my photographer to come in now? We would like a picture of you with your wife?' Buzinsky indicated his approval with a slight drop of his chin. 'Can we include the children?' said Matt. Buzinsky looked at Svetlana. She smiled warmly. 'Of course.'

The photographer walked round the room, looking at the family group posed on the sofa, checking shots with his camera. 'I was thinking,' he said, 'it's a bit formal. What about something more natural? Maybe Mum reading a story to the kids?'

Buzinsky thought about it for a while, unsure, pursing his lips.

'You are very private people, but I think it would help tell the story you want the world to see,' said Matt.

Buzinsky, still hesitant, turned to his wife again. 'Svetlana?'

'Okay,' she said, her pale white hand brushing back her jet-black hair.

After Svetlana and the girls had left, and the photographer had finished packing up his equipment, Matt and Buzinsky sat alone together.

'I had no idea,' said Matt. 'Has it helped you having the football club during this difficult time?' The look on the Russian's face told Matt he had touched a nerve.

'Actually, yes. It has. It has given me a place to channel my energy, something else to focus on. Building the new stadium, the new training complex – it was a huge project. I was very involved and I enjoyed it. It's been very successful.'

'Canary Wharf seems to have been an inspired decision,' said Matt.

'Yes. I had options on the site. With West Ham moving to the London Stadium, there was a gap. There is a lot of wealthy support in the City and from the residential development in the east of the City.'

'You've won the Premier League. What are your ambitions now?'

'Champions League. I want us to be as big as Real Madrid and Barcelona.'

'Have you always been passionate about football?'

'Oh yes.' His eyes glazed over. 'I was crazy about football as a boy: always playing football. I was a striker. I liked to score goals, but I was too small. I didn't make it past the youth team.'

'Did it bring back memories when you and Tony watched the players training?'

'Oh yeah, I enjoyed that,' he said smiling.

'It must be a blow, losing Tony. What do you think happened?'

A shadow wiped the smile from the oligarch's face. He frowned and shook his head. 'I'm not going to talk about that.'

As he walked into the street Matt switched on his phone. He had missed two calls and a text from Susie. **Callum picked to play on Saturday 9 am**. He replied immediately. **Great! I'll pick him up**.

Both the missed calls were from Tania. He touched her number.

'Oh Matt, I'm so glad you called back.'

'Why? What's the matter?'

'I went to see our solicitor yesterday afternoon. He gave me a sealed envelope. It was from Tony, "only to be given to me in the event of his death."'

Matt stopped in his tracks. 'What was in it?'

'The keys and password to a security deposit box in a City bank. I thought it might be to do with... you know.'

Matt felt a shiver of excitement. It must be the dossier!

'Tania, this is really important. You mustn't go on your own. I'll come with you.'

CHAPTER NINETEEN

Matt was waiting outside the bank in Threadneedle Street at eleven o'clock on Tuesday morning. A car drew up and dropped Tania off. She was wearing a fur coat, and appropriately dressed for a meeting with a private bank. He kissed her on the cheek. 'How are you?'

She took a deep breath. 'Nervous.'

He took her arm. 'Don't worry. Let's go in.'

The elegantly attired gentleman rose from his seat in the wood paneled office.

'Welcome to Rutherfords,' he said, shaking hands. 'My name is Jonathan Price, I'm a vice-president of the bank.' Tania introduced Matt and they sat down at a coffee table by the window with views over the City. 'I was so very sorry to hear about your husband's death, Mrs. Barker. He was a valued client and I knew him personally. He was a gentleman. In fact, he sometimes sent me tickets for matches.'

Coffee was brought in and they exchanged pleasantries. Price put down his cup and paused, carefully judging the right moment to bring up the matter in hand.

'Tell me, how can we help you today?'

'My husband had a security deposit box here. I would like to open it please.'

'Certainly, Mrs. Barker. You have the security code and the key I assume?'

'Yes, of course.'

'I'm afraid I have to ask to see some form of identity.'

Tania reached into her bag and handed him her passport. He scrutinised it, then passed it back to her.

'Thank you. Mrs. Middleton is responsible for the security deposit boxes. She will escort you and Mr. Riley to the vaults.'

He pressed a button on his phone and a middle-aged woman in a dark suit joined them. She acknowledged Tania with a friendly smile. 'If you will come with me please, madam.'

They followed her along the hall to the lifts. 'Access is back down through the reception area,' she said. 'A secure lift there goes directly to the vaults.' In reception she swiped a security card that called the lift, and took them down one floor to the vaults. The low ceiling, subdued lighting and wall to wall thick pile carpet created a claustrophobic atmosphere.

'It's incredibly quiet,' said Matt.

'Yes, the walls are two metres thick.'

At the end of the corridor they reached a door which their escort unlocked by punching numbers into a keypad. Stepping inside the room, they were surrounded by rows of grey metal drawers, the largest at the bottom and the smallest at the top. They sat at an antique table, inlaid with leather. The only item on the table was a computer. Tania looked around the room, somewhat overawed.

'Now, Mrs. Barker, can you please tell me your security deposit box number?' She typed in Tony Barker's name on the computer and tapped in the number Tania had given her. Satisfied, she took them both over to Tony's box.

'Have you got your key ready?' she asked Tania.

Tania looked in her bag and held up the small brass key.

'Good. You need that to open the drawer to your box. Then I will use my key, because the drawer will only open when both keys are used together.'

Tania stepped forward, her hand shaking as she turned the key. When the second key was turned the drawer sprung open and Mrs. Middleton slid out a large black box and handed it to Tania.

'You can open your box in the privacy of one of these rooms,' she said, pointing to four small private rooms. 'I will be standing outside the vault. When you have taken what you want just knock on the door. I will come back in and we'll put your box back and lock it.' She closed the door and they were left alone inside the vault. The air conditioning had been set low. The room was cold and still. Tania set the box down on a green felt cloth covering a table and shivered. For a moment they both sat silently staring at it.

'Open it then,' said Matt.

Tania carefully lifted the lid, took out a large file and placed it on the table.

Matt picked it up and flicked through the pages, his heart pounding against his ribs. 'This is it! I'm sure this is it. It's the dossier.'

'But what's in it? What's in it that's so secret?'

'I don't know yet. I need time to read it. I think it's going to tell us why Tony was killed. Look, I want to take it to the *Chronicle's* office. It'll be safer there. Is that okay with you?'

'Yes.'

'You had a driver to bring you here?'

'Yes.'

'Is he waiting?'

'No.'

'Oh.' He thought about it. 'I don't want you to leave here on your own. Come with me to the office and then I'll take you home.'

Matt clicked open the strong metal case he had brought. The dossier fitted perfectly. He snapped it closed and locked it using a number combination.

They stepped out of the small room into the vault and knocked on the closed door. Mrs. Middleton, who was waiting discreetly outside, came in and together they put the box back in its place and locked the drawer.

'Is there anything else?' she said.

'Yes please. Can we have a taxi to pick us up?' said Matt.

'Of course, that's no problem.' She picked up one of the phones, spoke quietly, then turned back to Matt and smiled. 'There should be one here in a couple of minutes.'

They took the lift up to reception, thanked her and signed out. The security guard opened the door and they stepped outside. The pavement was crowded with workers coming out for their lunchtime break. It was busy with cars parked on each side of the road. Matt looked up and down. 'Can you see the cab?'

Tania studied the parked cars. 'No, is it a black cab?'

'I don't know. I suppose so.'

A white van was in his way and Matt took a few steps further to get a better view. He was studying the road, the pavement was crowded, and he didn't notice the man with a dog coming towards him. Too late he saw a flash of black and brown. The German shepherd jumped up on Matt who jerked back to fend off the heavy animal. A well-dressed gentleman pulled the dog back on his lead. 'Oh, I'm terribly sorry,' he said. 'I can't think what made him do that. He's normally very good. Oh no, look! He's put dirty paw marks all over you.' He began rubbing mud off Matt's coat. 'I'm so sorry.'

'Don't worry,' said Matt, brushing himself off. 'It's nothing.'

Tania, who had been staring at the dog, suddenly turned to look behind them.

'Matt! Matt! Behind you!'

He spun round just in time to see a man in jeans and leather jacket, the silver case in his hand, jumping into a waiting Mercedes. Matt sprinted to the car but it had already pulled out and was accelerating away. He turned back to grab the man with the dog, but he had already vanished into the crowd. His heart thumping, he rushed back into the bank and grabbed the security guard. 'Did you see that?'

'What, sir?'

'I was mugged as I left the bank. They took my case and got away in a black Mercedes.'

'I'm sorry, sir, I didn't see it. Are you both okay?'

'Yes.' He looked up at cameras in the foyer. 'What about CCTV?'

'Yes, sir. Where exactly were you when it happened?'

Matt took him outside to the spot where he was attacked. The security man looked around.

'Sorry, sir. You were too far away from the entrance. There are no cameras covering where you are now. Did you get the number?'

Matt shook his head and sighed in frustration. 'No. It all happened so quickly.'

'I'll make a report, sir, if you will give me the details. You will notify the police, won't you?'

Matt knew there was no point. He didn't trust the police.

Matt was on his bike early, pushing himself hard down Kings Road and over Putney Bridge. He passed through Roehampton Gate into Richmond Park. It was a crisp dry morning, and the sun had just risen. The road circuit round the edge of the park was already beginning to get busy and at Robin Hood Gate he cut across past the central Pen Ponds and White Lodge towards the Sheen Gate. A herd of red deer ambled across the road in front of him. He hardly noticed. His mind was focused on yesterday's events. He was still angry about the attack. Could it have been a mugging? The silver metal case did look exactly like the kind that someone might use if they were withdrawing large amounts of cash. A professional mugger could have been lying in wait for a target. It wouldn't be the first time.

But after the attempted burglary at Tania's home just four days ago it seemed too much of a coincidence. It was the dossier they were after. Now they had got hold of the evidence that would have revealed what Tony was investigating. Evidence they didn't know about, or couldn't find, when they murdered Tony.

He began to put the pieces together. Now that he had noticed the missing whisky glass he was sure that the shard of glass that Dr. Andrews discovered was crucial. He had proved that it had entered Tony's heel at the time of death.

He imagined the scenario. Tony had been alone in his study, drinking his favourite malt whisky – the first post-mortem showed a large amount of alcohol in his system– probably watching a replay of the match. Intruders got into the house. There was no sign of forced entry, so it seemed likely that he knew them. There was nothing on CCTV but he knew from James that it could have been remotely disabled. There would have had to be more than one intruder to overpower Tony without causing any sign of physical harm. They must have come prepared, maybe gagged him with chloroform. Tony struggled and the whisky glass he'd been drinking from was knocked to the floor and smashed. He had bare feet and stepped on some broken glass. When he was unconscious, they put the noose round his neck, carried him over to the gallery level, stood him on a chair, tied the rope to the top of the balustrade and kicked the chair away. He just hung there, asphyxiated, until he was dead. Then they cleaned up the broken glass, and any other signs of a struggle, and left through the front door.

It was neat, but it was still just a theory until he could prove that the shard of glass came from the missing whisky tumbler. Why hadn't the police carried out a proper search at the time?

CHAPTER TWENTY

James looked up as Matt approached, put down a doughnut, and wiped jam from his mouth with a paper napkin. Matt set down his coffee and slumped in the chair. The coffee shop was busy with shoppers, but James had found a quiet table.

'You look fed up, old chap,' said James.

Matt told him about the attack outside the bank and the stolen dossier.

'Well, it could have been a mugging, Matt. A metal security case like that would be a dead giveaway for a withdrawal of a hundred grand in cash. I've reported robberies like this outside a bank before.'

'I know, I thought of that, but I think it's unlikely.'

'What has Bill said?'

'I haven't told him about it. He told me to drop the story.' James looked surprised. 'Really? Why?'

'I think Tony was murdered but he's not buying it. He told me to drop the story or go to the police.'

'You really think Barker was murdered?'

'Yes. Look, James, a lot has happened since I saw you two weeks ago.' He paused and took a sip of his coffee, wondering how much to tell him. 'I think the police are covering it up.'

'Why don't you start by telling me why you think Barker was murdered?'

Matt told him about the shard of glass and the missing whisky glass.

'Hmmm, interesting theory, Matt, but you don't know that the glass was broken on Saturday night.'

'I do, James. The forensic pathologist took a tissue sample from the injury. It proves that the shard of glass entered Tony's heel around the same time that he died.'

'Wow.' James ran his hand though his thick mop of unruly snow-white hair. Deep creases lined his forehead. 'But it doesn't prove that there was someone else in the room, does it? He could have broken it himself just before he died.'

Matt shook his head from side to side emphatically. 'No. If he had, Tania or the housekeeper would have found broken glass. But they didn't. And what's more, the police didn't find any broken glass either. The intruders cleaned it up.'

'So why don't you want to tell all this to the police?'

'That's why I wanted to talk to you. I don't trust them. They rushed the inspection of the study. Why didn't they find any evidence of broken glass? The young SOCO woman seemed pretty embarrassed about it when I saw her at the mortuary.'

'She took the shard of glass back with her?'

'Yes, the pathologist gave it to her in an evidence bag that she signed for.'

James sat back in his seat rubbing his chin. 'The missing whisky glass is interesting, I'll grant you that. When the police know that, they will have to do a forensic investigation to see if the shard of glass matches the remaining glasses. That will be the proof you need. Then you can do the story.'

Matt shook his head. 'No. I can't go to the police.'

'Look, Matt, I know the police aren't perfect. We all know about corruption and cover ups in the Met, but you don't know it's happening here. Anyway, you've got no choice. The police have the shard of glass from Barker's heel, and only they can match it to the original set. You need to tell D.S. Maclean about the missing glass.'

Matt looked unconvinced.

'Trouble is though, I'm not sure that he'd want to talk to a sports writer,' continued James. 'They hate the press unless it's someone they trust. Maclean's an old sweat with a reputation for being a hard man, but he knows me. Why don't we go together?'

The next day they walked into Wimbledon police station. It looked modern and welcoming from the outside, but the austere interior and utilitarian furniture were showing the wear and tear of the 24/7 fight against crime. At the front desk a large woman with long, greasy, black hair was screaming at the desk sergeant.

'I want to see my 'usband. I know me rights. You can't stop me talking to 'im.' The sergeant asked her to sit down and said someone would be out to see her shortly. The woman flounced off to the seats in the waiting area to join six others.

James told the sergeant they had an appointment with D.S. Maclean. The officer picked up his phone. 'D.S. Maclean will be with you shortly, sir. Would you like a cup of tea?' James thanked him, and they sat down as far away from the simmering woman as they could.

The two men nursed their plastic cups of machine-made tea for fifteen minutes. James checked his watch. At last an older female officer came to escort them to Maclean's office. Andrew Maclean stood up, and gestured for them to take the two seats in front of his desk. He spoke with a strong Glaswegian accent which was tough and uncompromising, an impression reinforced by his barrel chest and short, steel grey hair. The office was furnished in regulation fashion, with no signs of Maclean's personal taste. There were no family photographs and no personal possessions, other than a photograph of a young Maclean, hands raised in victory in a boxing ring.

After introducing them both, and judging that Maclean was in no mood for small talk, James got straight to the point. 'We are covering Tony Barker's death for the *Chronicle.* Mr. Riley knew Barker very well, and he has information which could be important. I suggested he came to see you.'

Maclean listened impassively, waiting for James to continue.

'As you know, Mrs. Barker requested a second post-mortem.'

'Yes, of course,' Maclean interrupted abruptly. If he wanted to give the impression that their visit was an unwanted irritant he had succeeded. 'Why was that?'

'Well, I'm not sure. No doubt Mrs. Barker has her reasons, but she didn't want to be there and asked Mr. Riley to attend on her behalf.'

'Why did she ask you?' Maclean asked Matt suspiciously.

'As James said, I'm a close friend of the family.'

Maclean looked unimpressed. 'My SOCO was at the second post-mortem. What is there that we don't already know?'

'Well,' said Matt, 'although nothing new came out of the post-mortem, the pathologist found a shard of glass which he extracted from Barker's heel.'

'I know that,' Maclean snapped. 'It was in her report.'

Matt paused, locking his eyes on Maclean's glare. 'Like you,' he continued, 'I've been wondering if it could have anything to do with Barker's death. So afterwards I went back to Tania's house and had a look round his study. I found that one whisky glass was missing from a set of six.'

Maclean's eyes narrowed. 'So?'

'Naturally, I wondered if the shard of glass in Barker's heel had come from the missing whisky tumbler.'

Maclean shook his head. 'If there was a glass missing it could have been broken days before.'

'I think that's unlikely,' replied Matt. 'It was part of a set that was of sentimental value to him. Tania would have known about it. You have the shard of glass. If you match it to another glass from that set, you can see if it came from the missing tumbler.'

'Of course we can, but what does that prove?'

'That someone else was in the study.'

'No it doesn't,' barked Maclean. 'He could have accidentally broken the glass at any time when he was on his own, then cleared up and disposed of the broken glass.'

It was obvious that Maclean was not interested in considering the possibilities that the missing glass presented. Matt had no intention of telling him about the tissue sample or explaining his theories.

'We are obviously wasting your time,' said Matt.

'No,' Maclean said, his tone more conciliatory now. 'The missing glass could be interesting, but all the evidence and two post-mortems point to suicide. We have no doubt about that, but of course the coroner will be carrying out a full investigation.'

He pushed his chair back and stood up, indicating that the interview was over.

'So, what do you think?' Matt asked as they walked away from the police station.

'As far as they're concerned it's still a clear-cut suicide. '

'Come on, James! What about the missing glass?'

'Yeah, that's embarrassing. Now that you've pointed it out they'll have to match the shard to the existing set. When they do it will be a murder investigation.'

'Huh. We'll see.' said Matt. 'I don't trust that fucking Maclean.'

'Don't worry. I'll keep my nose to the ground,' James said as he disappeared into the Wimbledon Underground. Matt walked on to the car park alone. His phone buzzed and he pulled it out of his pocket.

'Is that Mr. Riley?'

'Speaking.'

There was a long pause.

'Barker's death is not being investigated according to police procedures.'

CHAPTER TWENTY ONE

Matt stopped in the street, pressing the phone closer to his ear. 'Sorry, traffic noise, what did you say your name was?'

'I can't tell you that. I'm calling from a public phone. This has to be anonymous.'

'Of course,' said Matt, anxious to keep the whistleblower talking and desperate not to scare him off. 'Don't worry. We never reveal our sources. It's a journalist's golden rule. How did you get my number?'

'I've been following your stories about Barker in the *Chronicle*. I rang the sports desk. They gave it to me.'

'Good. You're talking to the right person.' He paused. 'You said Barker's death is not being investigated according to police procedures.'

The caller hesitated. 'Yes.'

'Do you have evidence of that?'

'Yes.'

'Can we meet?' said Matt.

'No. I don't want anyone to know I'm talking to the press.'

Matt guessed he was a police officer, probably young and certainly very nervous. He could lose him at any minute. 'Look, I know how you feel. You're doing the right thing. You said you have evidence?'

'Yeah.'

'What sort of evidence?'

'Photographs.'

Matt's heart missed a beat. 'Of what?'

'The rope that hanged Barker.'

'What about it?'

'There were signs that the knot had been professionally tied. The officer in charge should have consulted a forensic rope knot expert. It could have established whether the death was a homicide.'

'Yeah. That's good. Can you send me the photos?'

The caller hesitated. 'No. No, I can't. It could be traced back to my phone.'

'There's no story unless I have evidence to back it up.'

There was a long pause. 'Look, you don't realise how serious this is. It would wreck my career.'

'No, I understand, I do, really.'

'Sorry, I'm going to have to go.'

Matt's mind was spinning. 'No, hang on. I've got an idea. You know that cemetery next to Stamford Bridge?'

'Yeah.'

'It's called the Brompton Cemetery. Go in by the first gate past Stamford Bridge. On your right there's a bench with a rubbish bin next to it. Can you go there tonight at eight o clock and leave the photos in the bin?'

'I suppose so.'

'When you do you'll find a bubble-wrap envelope. Take it. Inside will be a burner phone. I don't know your name and I don't want to know. But if there's bad stuff going down at your station I do want to know. Use the code name Mercury. That way you can contact me again and nobody can trace it. When we're done, just dispose of it.'

Matt ended the call. There was a message from Susie. **Don't forget Callum's match on Saturday**. He took it as a rebuke. **I know. I said I will take him. OK?** He pressed send and then bit his lip, regretting it.

After dark he collected the envelope as arranged with his mystery informant. Back home he laid out the photographs on his desk. A blue rope was tied in a noose, with close ups from different angles. He studied them for a while but they meant nothing to him. He pulled out his phone and called James.

'You're a yachtsman, aren't you?' said Matt.

'Yes, I've got a half-share in a thirty-eight footer. Why?'

'I'm looking at photographs of the rope that hanged Tony. I need your help.'

'Good God. How did you get them?'

Matt told him about his whistleblower. 'He said police procedures were not being followed. He thinks the rope could show if Tony was murdered.'

'You've got a "just cause" officer, Matt.'

'A what?'

'It's how a copper justifies grassing on his mates. Just cause. It's not uncommon in a station where there are bent coppers. What did he tell you?'

'Come round and I'll show you the photographs.'

Thirty minutes later they sat at Matt's kitchen table where the photographs were spread out. James picked up each one carefully, examining them before he spoke.

'Well, the first thing is the rope. It's dark blue with green flecks woven into the material. It looks like 1/4" braided polyester. It's a type that is commonly used on small boats. You can buy it in any yacht chandlers.'

Matt was intrigued. 'What about the knot?'

'I was coming to that. The rope has been doubled, and the noose formed by making a half hitch with a left twist, and then a further half hitch with a right twist. It's a common enough knot for anyone with boating experience. We use it all the time for stowing small ropes on a rail.'

'But complex if you don't know anything about boats?'

'Well, you couldn't do it by accident. The choice of knot, and the method of tying it, tells us that this was a person with experience of boats and knowledge of knots. Was Barker a sailor?'

Matt shook his head. 'Absolutely not. He had a fear of water. You'd never get him on a boat in a month of Sundays.'

'Well, if he didn't tie this knot it certainly proves your point, but you're going to need more than that.'

'I know. But now I've got someone on the inside. I think there's a lot more to come.'

CHAPTER TWENTY TWO

The Blue Legume was a new Chiswick neighborhood bistro that had become very popular. The outside tables were bare, and a cold wind whistled up the street. He saw Emma sitting at a table inside and made his way through the busy restaurant. She was wearing figure hugging jeans and a dark blue jacket.

'You look great,' he said.

She stood up and gave him a warm kiss on the cheek, and he breathed in her delicate fragrance. 'I've ordered a bottle of chardonnay. Is that okay for you?' she asked as they sat down.

'Absolutely. Would you like to eat?'

'Yes, I'm famished. I haven't eaten all day.

'Good, me too.'

'Matt, after we met I looked through Tony's diary. I didn't find anything that seemed odd, but I studied it again yesterday. I think I may have found some things that might interest you.'

He took a sip from his glass. 'What kind of things?'

'Well, for instance, there was an appointment with Roger Mayfield back in November. It struck me as unusual because he wanted Tony to come to his office to discuss a problem with a player. The chief executive wouldn't normally have anything to do with players, except when a contract was signed. When Tony came back he was livid. I thought about it again when you told me about a player giving information to an Asian gambling syndicate.'

'I didn't say it was a player.'

'Oh, I assumed it was.'

'Do you know what happened at the meeting?'

'Yes. Tony said Roger had a visit from a uniformed police officer, someone very senior I think. It was all very hush-hush. Anyway, the police officer told Roger that there was a contract out on the player's life.'

'Really?'

'Yes. Apparently he'd racked up huge gambling debts and couldn't pay. The officer told Roger that if the debt wasn't settled by the end of the week a contract killer would be looking for the player.'

'That's hard to believe.'

'Yeah, Roger didn't believe it at first either. "This is the heart of London," he said, "not the back streets of Hong Kong." Then the officer asked him if he knew how much it would cost to hire a contract killer in London. When Roger suggested £50,000, he just laughed and told him it was £5000 if you want it done in a hurry or £1000 if you can wait six weeks.'

Matt whistled under his breath. 'Bloody Hell!'

'Roger asked Tony to sort it out. He didn't want the player dead! And nor did Tony!'

'How was Tony going to do that?'

'By getting the player to pay up immediately, I suppose. Or if he couldn't do that, the club would loan him the money.'

'What happened?'

'I never heard any more about it, so I assume Tony sorted it.'

'Who was the player?'

She shook her head. 'Tony never told me. I'm sorry, I honestly don't know.'

Matt waited, hoping she would say more, but either she didn't know or she wasn't going to say.

'How did Tony get on with Mayfield?'

She looked surprised. 'Fine. He didn't have that much to do with him. Roger dealt with the business side and he didn't interfere on the playing side. They only really had contact when it came to player transfers.'

'Did you know that Mayfield was taking bungs?'

She pulled away from him. 'What?'

'He was getting a slice of commissions from an agent.'

'Are you sure?' she said, her eyebrows knitting together. 'He wouldn't dare! Not with an owner like Buzinsky.'

'He wouldn't be the first,' said Matt. 'Did Tony ever say anything to you about it?'

'No.'

'Do you think he would have challenged Mayfield with it? It's serious stuff, Emma. It would have given Mayfield a motive for murder.'

She thought about it before she looked up. 'I don't know, Matt.'

Matt stared at her. 'Do you think you can find out where Mayfield was from ten until midnight on the evening that Tony was killed?'

She hesitated. 'Yes, I expect so.'

The mood had changed. She seemed deep in thought as she stared into the wine glass that she was twirling in her hand. She looked up. 'I think I've got something else that will help you. I made a copy of Tony's diary for the last six months. Would you like to see it?'

Emma's flat was on the tenth floor of a modern luxury apartment block in Chiswick. The large, open plan living room had white walls, wooden floors, and recessed spotlights. It was expensively furnished and the brightly coloured cushions, the flowers, the soft lighting were all unmistakable feminine touches. There were copies of *Hello, Cosmopolitan* and *Tatler* on the glass table. An enormous flat screen television dominated one wall. He wondered how she could afford it. He looked around whilst she disappeared into the kitchen to make coffee. There were photographs on a side table. He picked up one of Emma sitting in a white Mercedes sports car with an older man.

'Nice flat,' he said, as she walked into the room carrying a tray of coffee.

'Thanks. I bought it in 2009 just after the crash. It was a steal.'

She put down the tray and undid the top button of her cream silk blouse. A pile of papers sat on the coffee table. 'Would you like a brandy with your coffee?' she said.

'Hmmm... I think I would. Thanks.'

They sat next to each other on the sofa, poring over the pages of Barker's diary. She explained the background to interesting entries and he made notes. They paused at the entry when Barker had met Mayfield to talk about a contract on a player's life. 'Do you think the player had something to do with Tony's death?' she said.

Matt thought about Zhang Wei. 'Someone was passing information to a gambling syndicate so it could have been this player. Tony got him out of trouble. Perhaps that's how he found out that matches were being fixed.'

'You think our matches were being fixed?'

'It's possible.'

'And you really think Tony was murdered?' she whispered. Matt nodded.

'Have you told the police?'

'Yes. They're not interested.'

There was an awkward silence. 'Another cognac?' she said at last.

He nodded and she poured a large slug into his glass. It was warm and smooth and her scent was intoxicating. Matt settled back on the sofa and sipped the cognac. 'Is that your father I saw in the photograph?'

Her hollow laugh dismissed his question. 'Hardly. My father is a bank clerk living in a semi-detached in south Croydon. The nearest he'd ever come to a Mercedes is if one was parked next to his Ford Fiesta in the garden centre car park.'

'You don't get on with your parents then?'

'No. My mother phones, "Just to see how you are, dear,"' she said, mimicking her mother's south London accent.

'Who's the girl with you in the wedding photo?'

'Oh, that's my elder sister, Charlotte. She's the clever one – always studying. Daddy's favourite. She's a lawyer now.'

'And what about you?' he said.

'I was the opposite: hated school. I left home at eighteen and went to work in marketing at Adco. I did well. I was highly thought of and got the job as product manager for Europe. That's how I met Jeremy. '

Matt looked puzzled. 'The man in the Mercedes,' she said. 'He's the marketing director at Adco.'

He looked much older than her. Probably married, he thought. She seemed to have intuitively read his mind.

'I'm not seeing him anymore. We both needed to make a change. I was lucky to get the job with Tony.'

'Wasn't it a step down though, to take a job as Tony's PA?'

She bristled. 'I'm not a secretary, you know!'

'No. I was just saying.'

'I don't think you understand my role at the club. Tony wanted to be with the players and the coaching staff. As time went by he left me to deal with the business side of his job. I went to meetings with all the senior management for him – including Sergei. They trust me.'

She leaned forward to refill his cup. 'More coffee?'

'Please.'

She was silent for a while, her chin resting in her hands. 'Tony was great. He made me feel I was one of the team at the top.' She shook her head as if dragging herself back to the present. 'Anyway, enough about me. You haven't told me anything about yourself.'

'Oh, boring really. Married to my job, I suppose. When I had to accept that I couldn't play again I wanted to be the best in investigative journalism.'

'I know. Tony really respected you for that. Are you married?'

'I was, but the unsocial hours play hell with a marriage. Susie and I are separated. She doesn't seem to understand that the late nights, weekend working and overseas travel are part of the job. I suppose it's partly my fault. I know I can be bloody difficult.' He shrugged his shoulders. 'But she knew that when she married me.'

'Oh, Matt, I am sorry. Do you have children?'

'One boy, Callum. I get to see him whenever I can.' He pulled out his phone and showed her photographs.

'How old is he?'

'Nine. He's a great kid. I've got to try to make more time for him.'

'Does he like football?'

'Oh yes. Loves it.'

'You should bring him to City. I'm sure we could arrange something special. You know, meet the players.'

'He'd like that,' said Matt.

'What about work? I see your by-lines in the *Chronicle* all the time.'

'Yes, but it's very competitive, all of us pushing to get our story in, looking for the big exclusive.'

'What does your editor think about this story?'

'Well, to be honest, I'm disappointed in Bill. I thought he had a nose for a story: that he'd be backing me on this, but he isn't convinced yet. He wants more evidence before he'll consider publishing anything.'

'Oh, Matt, it must be so difficult.' She slipped an arm around his shoulder, pulled him towards her and kissed him. He hadn't expected it but he lingered over the aroma of cognac, perfume and the sweet taste of her lips for a moment, then pulled away. He shook his head.

'I'm sorry, Em. I can't stay.'

For a moment he thought he saw a flash of anger, but she just raised her eyebrows in an unspoken question.

'Sorry,' he said again, biting his lip, 'I can't stay. I've got to catch an early flight tomorrow.' He stood up, kissed her again and made for the door. 'I'll be in touch when I get back.'

CHAPTER TWENTY THREE

Victoria Station was crowded with commuters. They flowed from the arrival platforms, streaming onto the station concourse before disappearing into the depths of the London Underground. Others queued for buses and taxis or drifted out into the greater reaches of Victoria. Pushing his way against the incoming human tide, Matt turned right and emerged into the calm backwaters of the Gatwick Express platforms. As he took his credit card out of the ticket machine he saw the doors of the next train about to close. He rushed for the barrier but the train was already pulling out.

'Too late, mate,' said the attendant.

'What time is the next one?'

'Fifteen minutes.'

He sat on a bench and pulled out his phone and called the sports desk at the *Chronicle*. A familiar voice answered.

'Oh good. It's you, Charlie. I'm just calling in to say I'm away for a few days. I've got myself on a private trip with some of the City players.'

'Sounds good, Matt. When will you be back?'

'Not sure. A few days.'

'Okay. I'll let Bill know.'

'Thanks, Charlie.'

Matt grimaced as he thought about the next call he had to make.

'Susie, I'm really, really sorry, but I'm not going to be able to make it to watch Callum on Saturday.'

'Matt! You promised him! It's a school match.'

He winced. 'I know, I know. I was looking forward to it too. Something's come up.'

'What's that?'

'A trip. I'm on my way to the airport now.'

'Where?'

'I can't say now.'

She slammed down the phone.

Matt settled back in a section of the carriage where there was no one else around. He gazed out on the drab, rain soaked streets of Battersea and Clapham, thinking about what Emma had told him. The connection between Mayfield and a player threatened with a contract on his life was interesting. Still, she hadn't given anything away when he asked her if Mayfield was taking bungs. He decided to call Mayfield. To his surprise, he reached him on the first attempt.

'Roger, is it true that one of your players was threatened with a contract on his life?'

'I can't comment on that.'

'And is it true that you asked Tony to sort it out?'

'No comment.'

'Can you tell me the name of the player?'

'Don't be ridiculous, Matt.'

He knew that the CEO would be livid, his mind still spinning with the revelation. He waited just long enough for his next question to catch Mayfield off guard.

'And Roger, would you care to comment on allegations that you were taking bungs from an agent?'

There was a long silence. Then Mayfield's tone changed from dismissive to threatening.

'How dare you! There is no truth whatsoever in that and if you publish anything, anything like that, I promise I will sue the ass off you.'

Matt was left listening to a dialing tone. Clubs often chose not to tell the press the amount a player had been sold for, but he had checked with a contact at the FA. The transfer payment Sahin had told him about was recorded as £15 million by the seller and the buyer. But it meant nothing. The agent could have taken £750,000 from his commission of £1.5 million and paid it into a Swiss bank account for Mayfield. Tony could have known about it but would he have had any proof? And if Mayfield was bent could he also be a killer?

Emma's tip about a player being blackmailed made sense though. At least one of the players had been involved in fixing matches with

Zhang Wei and he knew Zhang Wei was working for an Asian illegal gambling syndicate. The player must have refused to play ball and Zhang Wei told him he would be forced to pay up his gambling debt. Perhaps Tony became involved and made the player spill the beans in return for clearing the debt. Zhang Wei could have found out that Tony knew too much so he had to be silenced. But who was the player? And who was pulling Zhang Wei's strings?

The train pulled into Gatwick Airport station with ten minutes to spare. He found his way to the terminal for private jet passengers. The car park was filled with Mercedes, BMWs, Audis and more exotic marques, and for once the players' cars did not look out of place. Matt showed his passport at the reception desk in the VIP lounge, and that was it. No tickets, no check-in, no boarding pass, no queues, just a fast security scan on his bag and then a glass of champagne. I could get used to this, he thought. He saw the players over in a corner or, to be more precise, he heard them. They were in high spirits and the decibel levels were rising.

Well-heeled businessmen were watching, some interested in the celebrity footballers, others disapproving of the noise. John Taylor, who was standing with the players, spotted him.

'Hey, Matt, over here.'

He walked over and they shook hands. When he had told the City captain that he wanted to feature him in a story about how players' lives had changed in the last twenty years, and they needed to spend time together, Taylor had suggested he come along.

'Thanks for including me, John. Where are we going?'

He winked at Matt. 'Shh, nobody knows yet.

'Alright lads, quiet please. Quiet!' he shouted. The noise gradually subsided and there was a tremor of anticipation. 'Do you want to know where we're going?' A barrage of indecent suggestions followed. He waited for them to calm down again. 'No, it's not Ibiza.'

There was a chorus of, 'Shame.'

He strung out the pause. 'Any other ideas?' he teased.

'Marbella,' came back the answer.

'No, not Marbella,' he said to more groans. Shouts of, 'Get on with it,' came from the back.

'It's Las Vegas!' announced Taylor.

A riotous chorus of, 'Yeah!' shattered the calm in the lounge. Players punched the air and jostled round, clapping John on the back. Matt looked surprised. 'Don't worry, the party's on us,' said John. 'I know a football hack's wages don't run to this,' he said, digging Matt in the ribs. He silently breathed a sigh of relief.

'Thanks, John. I appreciate it.'

It was a crisp, bright morning as they strolled out to the Gulfstream 550 that stood gleaming in the morning sunshine. Hannah, their flight attendant, welcomed everyone on board with a glass of champagne. Her slim figure, pale blue uniform and white blouse, drew looks of admiration. The players' cheeky banter was rebuffed with a friendly smile.

Matt took in his surroundings. The cabin was fitted out with sixteen white leather seats with pale wood trim armrests. The interior walls and cabinets were all in white oak. Head linings were in a soft white material. His shoes sank into the deep-pile fitted grey carpet and he inhaled the rich smell of natural leather and expensive upholstery. His fingers ran over the warm cherry wood table in front of him. Looking forward he could see that there was a full galley equipped, no doubt, to prepare five star meals with the appropriate wines and champagne. This was not just any executive jet. The G550 was a mini-airliner with a top speed of 500 mph and a range of over 5000 miles. Matt wondered how much it had cost to charter.

He took the seat opposite John and they settled back in the soft, leather seats, sipping champagne as they waited for take-off. Matt raised his glass. 'Thanks, John. I could get used to this.'

'Yeah, not a bad life is it?' he said with a grin.

Once they had reached cruising height Hannah brought fresh glasses of champagne. John took a sip and put his glass back on the table between them. 'So, Matt, what did you want to talk about?'

Matt explained what he needed for the story. They discussed the material benefits and lifestyle of the modern player, changes in coaching methods, training schedules and the importance of sports sciences and the role played by psychologists. John asked Matt what it was like in his day.

'They used to call you Stinger when you played for Chelsea, didn't they?' said John. 'Stinger Riley.'

Matt smiled. 'That's right. I did get a bit of a reputation at Chelsea and it doesn't ever go away, does it? I wasn't shy about giving it back when someone had a go at me. Knew when to choose my moments. Made sure they would think twice before they tried it on again.'

'Good for you, Matt. Some things don't change, do they?'

An hour later they were still chatting when Hannah brought a tray with a lobster salad appetiser. Their animated conversation continued through the main course of chateaubriand steak. Wine flowed freely. After lunch, when most of the players were asleep, Matt glanced at John. He had drunk much more than him. Hannah cleared the trays and brought coffee.

'You must have been shocked when you heard about Tony,' said Matt.

'We was all gutted. I still can't believe it,' John said, shaking his head.

'Do you have any idea why he did it?'

'Honestly, Matt, I've no idea.'

Hannah brought coffee refills, and Matt waited until she had gone. 'Tony told me that he was having a problem with one of the players. A serious gambling problem, wasn't it?'

'You mean Varta? Well, we all did a bit: you know, football, horses. But Ricky was seriously into it.'

'Did you know he was in trouble?'

John sighed. 'Yeah, Ricky was moody. His head was messed up and it was affecting his game. I had a chat with him one day after training. He told me he was in debt to a bookie – big time. He was worried, didn't know what to do.'

'Did he tell you who the bookie was?'

'No. But I think it must have been that Chinese guy that hangs around. You know; the one that got done in the other day.'

'Yeah. I know the one you mean.' Matt looked out of the window at an endless blue sea. John had drunk a lot of wine. He thought he could push him further. He turned back, sucking his teeth.

'Did you ever think some of your games were fixed?'

John, who had almost dozed off, jerked forward, almost upsetting his coffee cup.

'Fixed? Why do you say that?'

'Tony thought some of your matches were fixed.'

'Did he?'

'That's what I heard.'

'I've often wondered. You hear a lot of talk about it in the dressing room, especially about some European teams.' Matt had to lean across to hear what he was saying. 'There was a Champions League game in Turkey before Christmas what we won when I thought we was lucky. They missed a sitter, let us in with a dodgy back pass. Refereeing decisions went our way. You know how it is, Matt, these things happen. But I had a funny feeling about that game. I'll be honest with you. I did. But nobody said nothing in the dressing room afterwards.' He put his head back and was soon asleep.

As the Gulfstream made the final approaches to McCarran Airport the excitement on board was palpable. The sun burned down from a clear blue sky as the aircraft dropped down over a crumpled brown desert and then, as if by magic, Vegas appeared, sparkling in the sunshine. The aircraft came in on the north-south approach, giving them a panoramic view of downtown Vegas. Players crowded round the windows like children, pointing out the names of the iconic landmarks: the Wynn, the Venetian, Caesar's Palace and the MGM Grand. They were speeded though immigration with minimal delay and three stretch limos whisked them from the VIP terminal to the Venetian.

Next morning Matt made his way down to the poolside restaurant for breakfast. The five diamond hotel and resort complex was spectacular, even by Vegas standards. The thirty-six storey hotel tower dwarfed a replica of the tower of St. Mark's Campanile, which itself overlooked a replica of the city of Venice. Gondoliers in black and white striped shirts steered their craft along canals that ran through the hotel and out into the "Grand Canal". The Venetian's facilities included the casino, a Parisian opera house, an Asian inspired nightclub and an opulent rooftop beach club. The hotel had cost $1.5 billion to build in 1999, and it wasn't hard to understand why.

The pool was surrounded by palms, lush grass and swathes of red and yellow hibiscus, magically conjured out of the harsh Nevada desert by an expensive irrigation system. Matt strolled into the restaurant. Most of the players who had made the trip were lounging around and discussing their plans for the day.

'I fancy one of them pool parties,' said Gary.

'Yeah, I seen it on TV – loads of talent!' added Wayne, with shouts of approval from the others.

'What about when Prince Harry got done by the *Sun*? There was photos of him naked, playing billiards after a pool party,' said Danny.

'Good on yer, 'Arry,' bawled Gary and everyone fell about laughing.

'John, get yer man over 'ere,' shouted Danny to John Taylor. 'What do you call 'im? A sorter? Well, get him to sort out a pool party for us.' Everyone cheered.

John called Chuck over. The man he had hired wore a white suit, black open neck shirt, and slick, black hair. His chiselled face was tanned. It was a scene plucked from *The Godfather*, thought Matt. The players called him a 'sorter' but he was a special concierge provided by the hotel. He told them he knew everyone in Vegas and could get them in anywhere with seats at the best tables – for a price, of course.

'You boys want the best pool party in Vegas?' said Chuck.

'Too fucking right,' they shouted.

'Okay. I'm gonna take you to Rehab. Get you the best cabana at the poolside.'

'What about women?' one of the boys shouted.

'Don't worry. I'll fix it. They're gonna be beautiful!'

And they weren't disappointed. At $10,000 a day the cabana was probably the most expensive in Vegas, but with these players – who cared? With three pools to choose from the place was jumping with beautiful people. It was one big party, everyone hanging out in the pool in the most suggestive swimwear possible.

John stood by the side of a pool with Matt with cold drinks, watching nymphs wearing outrageous bikinis.

'They're like kids in a candy store, aren't they?' said Matt, pointing at three of the players drooling over a group of hot babes.

A cute blonde sidled up to Matt. 'Hi, my name's Patti,' she said, cuddling up to him, her breasts pressed up against his chest so hard he could feel her nipples.

'You from round here?' Matt asked.

'No, ah'm from North Carolina,' she drawled. 'Ah'm competin' in the Rehab bikini invitational competition.'

'Do you think you'll win?'

'Well ah'd sure like to. There's $100, 000 in prizes, but there's a whole lotta competition.'

'Yeah, I see what you mean,' said Matt as a girl walked by in the briefest polka dot bikini he had ever seen. Two more followed with a matching pair of yellow and blue bikinis, one with SWE and one with DEN printed on their tops. Matt gave her a cuddle. 'Good luck.'

He strolled back to their cabana with John. Some of the girls Chuck had 'sorted' lay sprawled on cushions, soaking up the rays. Trays of Screwdrivers and Bloody Marys were brought by white liveried waiters. Matt nursed an ice-cold Pepsi. Up on the stage a dreadlocked DJ ramped up the atmosphere.

There were shrieks from the pool. He looked up. Manuel, Fabio, Sergio, Wayne and Gary had been joined by girls in a water balloon fight. One of the girls had lost her bikini top which was being passed around by the boys as she chased after it. A friend threw her a T-shirt.

'Wet T-shirt competition!' yelled Wayne, as they chased the screaming girls and tried to pull off their bikini tops. Girls at the poolside tossed in more T-shirts. It was insane, but nobody seemed to mind. It was a place where there was nothing a person couldn't have, as long as they had the money to pay for it.

As the bright Nevada afternoon sun faded into evening, some of the players disappeared to their rooms with girls to party. Matt had been watching for an opportunity to talk to Ricky Varta all afternoon, but the handsome Argentinian always seemed to have a girl at his side. Now he was on his own but, as Matt walked over, he beckoned to a dark, tanned girl with hair down to her waist. She wrapped her arms around him. Damn it, thought Matt, and turned back to wait for another opportunity.

'Welcome to the Pacific Rim,' said Chuck as they entered the exclusive TAO nightclub and strolled into the lounge with its lush velvets and silks, clattering waterfalls and aged wood and stone. Matt stared up at a tall, hand-carved Buddha rising from an infinity pool teeming with Japanese koi. Marco nudged Matt in the ribs, leering at a naked oriental model lying immersed in a bath, covered only by rose petals.

'She's all right!' he sniggered.

After cocktails in the lounge Chuck introduced Signor Cottorini. The manager bowed, shook hands with the players and took them to one of the best tables overlooking the dance floor. It came with a minimum spend of $5000. Not that that was a concern to anyone.

'It's real exclusive,' said Chuck. 'I've seen Madonna, Jay Z, Usher, Rihanna and Kim Kardashian in here.'

'Yeah, well now you can tell your clients you've seen Fabio Plattorini, Manuel Hernandez and Jake Thomson in here,' quipped Gary.

'Sure. I told Signor Cottorini who you were,' replied Chuck, not quite getting the footballers' dressing room banter.

Cottorini raised his arm, clicked his fingers, and a line of women appeared, looking like Miss World finalists. 'Just tell me which ones you like and I'll send them over,' he said. Mario and Wayne jumped up, pointing and shouting. Matt winced at their crass approach. Chuck noticed his expression. 'Don't worry,' he whispered in his ear, 'these girls earn thousands of dollars a night. And that's just for providing their company at your table – anything else is extra!'

The party on the next table were from an Italian football club, and they recognised some of the City players. One of them stood up and raised his glass. 'Champagne war?' he taunted.

Gary jumped to his feet and looked round the table. 'You lot up for it then? Cristal champagne?'

'Yeah, send them a jeroboam,' urged Danny.

The waiter brought the jeroboam and opened it with a flourish at the next table. The Italians responded by sending back three litres of Cristal champagne plus fifteen tequila shots.

Already drunk from the champagne and tequila, John stood up and suggested a game where players had to sing a song or recite a poem. If they refused they had to pay a forfeit. Matt grimaced when John suggested he should start first, but there was no dodging it.

'American Pie?' he suggested. He had sung it when he was a player and still trotted it out for karaoke sometimes. He thought he could remember all the verses. He needn't have worried. They were so drunk he could have made the words up and they wouldn't have noticed. But they all joined in the chorus.

Gary was up for another round in the champagne war. 'Let's blow them out the fucking water,' he bellowed, urged on by the others.

'Okay,' said Chuck, 'here's what we can do. For clients like you the club can "fly" bottles of champagne to any table on wires. If you like, the DJ will play your song as the bottles fly in. It's awesome.'

'Yeah', said Gary, 'let's do it. Send six jeroboams. Can he play "*We Are The Champions*?"'

'Sure.'

With Queen blasting out their anthem they all stood, glasses in hand, singing and swaying to the music. Spotlights had picked out the jeroboams as they flew over the heads of the guests on a wire.

Players were getting wrecked – jackets off, ties askew, hair tousled, faces red. Some had girls draped over their laps. Fabio stood up to sing an operatic aria and Gary stealthily pulled his chair away. When Fabio finished, and tried to sit down, he fell and rolled backwards on the floor. Everyone collapsed with laughter. At last the final six jeroboams came back empty with a white flag hanging from each one.

Matt looked up as the waiter presented him with a black folder. He looked inside: it was the bill. The total came to $150,000, excluding gratuities. He stared at it. The players roared with laughter.

'Do you need a hand with that, Matt?'

He grinned. 'You bastards!'

He was no angel: had seen his fair share of players' parties, drinking, practical jokes, and girls of course, but this was over the top. He was sickened by how little regard these players had for money, how the huge amounts they earned had changed them. He had been earning £200,000 a year when he was forced to give up playing, but now, only twenty years later, these players were earning more like £100,000 a week. It made the $150,000 bill for this machismo behaviour seem like small change.

Matt went to the bathroom, used the toilet and winced at his craggy face in the mirror. The old scar on his forehead stood out like a white welt and there were dark lines under his eyes. They looked puffy. He didn't have the stamina for this high octane boozing anymore. He filled the basin with cold water and splashed it over his face. Out on the terrace, with its spectacular view over the city skyline, there was a breeze and he filled his lungs with fresh air. It felt good. The bright lights of the city lit the sky. It would be dawn soon, but it would make no difference. This was a city that never slept. In the casinos, the high rollers would not know if it was night or day.

Back in the club, most of the players were dancing with the girls on the floor below. Celebrity DJs generated a supercharged atmosphere. Beautiful bodies pulsated to the music.

Ricky Varta sat alone at the table, his head in his hands, tie loosened, his hair disheveled. There were stains from spilled champagne on his white shirt. His eyes drooped and his face was drawn. He was very drunk. Matt sat down next to him and put an arm round his shoulder.

'What's up, Ricky? Would you like a coffee?'

Varta nodded and Matt asked the waiter to bring two large cups of black coffee.

'You don't seem too happy.'

The waiter set the coffee down in front of them. Varta stared morosely into the depths of the cup, head resting in his hands.

'You were lucky that Tony got the bookies off your back.'

Varta looked up sharply. 'Whatchoo mean?'

'I know all about it, Ricky. Tony told me he saved your life. How much was it you were in for?'

'Two mill' hic 'illion,' mumbled Varta.

Matt tried to disguise a sharp intake of breath. He had no idea that it could have been so much. 'That's right. Who were you betting with?'

'A Chinese guy we knew.'

'Zhang Wei?'

Varta nodded.

'And Tony paid off two million?'

'If he hadn't they would have killed me,' Varta whined.

'How did it get to that?'

'Zhang used to hang round the club. We got friendly. I was betting a lot and I was winning. The bookies din't like it. They gave me a limit. We used to talk about it. I wanned to make bets on matches that I din't want traced back to me. "We can take care of that," he said, "there's no limit with us." So I started betting bigger. Then, when I lost, I had to bet even more bigger to get it all back.'

'So they had a hold on you.'

Varta lowered his face and nodded.

'And you were feeding them inside information.'

'What else could I do?' he whimpered.

'Did you bet on fixed matches?'

Varta put his head in his hands. 'Sometimes they would tell me the results of games before a ball was kicked.'

'Did they ask you to fix matches?'

He sat crumpled over the table and looked up at Matt defiantly. 'No.'

Matt didn't believe him for a moment. 'Were City's games fixed?'

Varta wouldn't look him in the eye. Beads of sweat dripped down his face. His red eyes twitched and he chewed his fingernails.

'What you mean?' he finally replied.

'Well, you must have known.'

Varta shrugged.

'Which one?'

'In Turkey, a Champions League game.'

'Did Tony know about it?'

'The boss said he would help me, but I had to tell him everything. They would've killed me.'

'What happened in that game?'

I was just told that we would win by two clear goals. All we had to do was not mess it up. An' 'at's what happened, we won 3-1.'

'What about other games?'

He wouldn't answer.

'Who murdered Tony Barker?'

'Barker, murdered? Fuck no! I don't know nothing 'bout that. But I'm telling you: you don't fuck with these people. They killed Zhang Wei, din't they?'

'Who did?'

Varta lifted the glass in his hand and smashed it down on the table. He opened his fist and blood oozed though his fingers onto the white tablecloth. 'I don't fucking know. Just leave me 'lone,' he said, and threw up at the table. Two waiters hurried over and helped Matt drag him to the bathroom.

CHAPTER TWENTY FOUR

Darkness was drawing in and mist was creeping up from the river when Matt arrived home, a day earlier than he expected, feeling physically and mentally drained. He reached into his pocket, pulled out a couple of tenners, paid off the cab and dragged his case to the lift. There was nobody around on the fourth floor. He pushed his key into the lock, but the pressure he applied caused it to open slightly before he could turn the key. He was certain he had locked it when he left. He stood still for a moment, his heart missing a beat. Someone had been into his flat. Then, with a sharp stab, came the thought that they could still be in there. His fingers trembled as he eased the door open, hoping the hinges would not make a sound.

He stepped into the hall and stood still, the silence roaring in his ears. The apartment was almost dark and only a faint orange glow from the outside streetlights provided any illumination. On the left was his bedroom. He stepped inside, his nerves as finely tuned as a violin, and stood motionless until his eyes became accustomed to the dark. There was nobody there. He crept into the living room, wondering if the thumping of his heart could be heard. He wasn't frightened now and a wave of anger washed over him. He looked for a weapon and picked up a heavy glass vase that was standing on the table, gripping it tightly in his right hand. In the glow of the streetlights he could see that the room was undisturbed.

Behind him there was a clunk from the kitchen. He jumped, but it was only the central heating clicking in. He exhaled silently. A shadow moving to his right caught his attention, and as he turned back, something hard and cold struck the back of his head, knocking him to the ground. His head exploded with pain but a surge of adrenalin shot through his body, fuelling his anger. As his assailant stepped over him, Matt caught his leg, pulled him down and rolled on top of him, grabbing his throat and squeezing it hard with both hands. He sat astride him, pinning him down, but the man was kicking hard and his flailing arms thrashed against Matt's side. Matt heard him croak as the breath was being squeezed out of him. His eye were bulging. But then, in a final desperate effort, the intruder jerked up, twisted, and jammed his knee into Matt's balls. Matt gasped for breath and released his grip on the man's throat. His attacker rolled over and smashed his fist into Matt's face. He drifted into darkness. He could have only been unconscious for seconds but when he opened his eyes the man had gone.

Dragging himself to the kitchen window he saw a tall figure with a shaved head, dressed in black, jump into a black Mercedes. The car was parked underneath a streetlight, but he was too far away to make out the license plate as it sped away.

Matt hobbled into his study, switched on the light and stopped dead in his tracks. It had been turned upside down. Drawers and cupboards had been opened and the contents strewn over the floor. He had left the rope photographs that the whistle-blower had given him in a locked drawer in the centre of his desk. The drawer had been forced open. They were gone. He clenched and unclenched his fists, blinded by fury at this violation of his personal space. He pulled out his phone, but then thrust it back into his pocket. What was the point of calling the police? This was no ordinary burglar.

Every bone in his body ached. The back of his head was drumming as if a woodpecker was trying to bore a hole in it. He put his hand there. It felt sticky and his fingers traced a lump. He pulled his hand back and saw that his fingers were covered in blood. When he washed the wound in the bathroom the bleeding stopped and he applied some antiseptic cream. It hurt, but it was probably not a deep wound. Peering into the mirror he could see that his face was a mess. His right eye was already bruised red and the swelling was closing the eye.

He poured himself a glass of brandy, swallowed two Aspirin, and sat down. Whoever it was knew he was investigating Tony's death, knew where he lived, knew he was away. Matt had never feared anyone. He knew he could take care of himself, but for a moment an image of Zhang Wei lying dead in an alley with a slashed throat flashed into his mind. For the first time in his life he wondered if he might have taken on more than he could handle. He wiped the cold sweat from his brow.

His ring tone jolted him back to the present. He looked at the screen. It was Susie.

'I wanted to remind you about Callum's birthday,' she said. 'It's next week.'

He rubbed the back of his head and groaned. 'Oh Susie, I know that. I'm not going to forget his birthday, am I?'

'Like you did with his football match on Saturday you mean? Where were you anyway?'

'Las Vegas.'

She snorted. 'Jesus. Las Vegas! How irresponsible is that! You're living the high life and you can't bother to come to your son's football match. Gambling, were you? How much did you lose?'

'No, I wasn't. Look, Susie, I know what you think but it wasn't like that. Can we meet? I want to explain.'

'I don't know.' She hesitated. 'When?'

He nursed the back of his head again. 'Not tonight. How about tomorrow?'

There was a long silence. 'Why do you want to meet?'

'Because I want to say sorry.'

He heard her sigh and waited. 'Alright,' she said reluctantly. 'Let's meet at the wine bar we went to last time, you know, the Grapevine. Eight o'clock tomorrow.'

CHAPTER TWENTY FIVE

The Grapevine was busy when Matt arrived but he found a table for two where they could talk. The waitress brought a chilled bottle of chardonnay in a bucket and two glasses. The place was buzzing with conversation, ripples of laughter and the chink of glasses. David Bowie's *Space Oddity* was playing in the background. Waitresses in green aprons with a Grapevine logo ferried back and forth to the long, polished wooden bar, holding trays above their heads. Everybody seemed happy except Matt. At the next table a young black girl with a warm smile was in animated conversation with a tousle-haired unshaven man in jeans and T-shirt. From time to time she collapsed into peals of laughter. The Grapevine was a good choice. He hoped it would improve Susie's mood.

She was ten minutes late when she pushed the door open and strode across the wine bar towards him. She was wearing an attractive olive green dress and matching jacket he hadn't seen before, but her curly auburn hair framed a grim white face.

'You look nice,' he said, wincing with pain as he stood up to kiss her on the cheek. He breathed in a familiar perfume that reminded him of happier times. He picked up the bottle, filled her wine glass and slid it across the table to her.

Susie stared at him as she sat down. 'Good God! What happened to you?'

'It's a long story. I'll tell you later,' he said, sliding a large package across the table.

'What's that?'

'A present for Callum.'

She raised her eyebrows. 'What is it?'

'Can't you guess?' he said with a weak grin.

She put down her glass and felt the package carefully, turning it around in her hands.

She shook her head. 'No.'

‘It’s a cowboy hat.’

She smiled. He hoped it was an early sign of a thaw in their relationship which was currently at zero degrees.

‘Susie, I wanted to tell you how gutted I am at missing Callum’s match. I’m really sorry. The truth is that I was invited to Vegas with some of the City players. I had to go.’

She snorted and leaned back.

‘No, listen. One of the players was involved with an Asian gambling syndicate. He was being blackmailed. Tony knew about it. I wanted to find out how much he knew. It could explain why he was killed.’

Her jaw dropped. ‘Killed? You mean murdered?’ She stared at Matt. ‘But if you think it was murder what about the police? Aren’t they investigating it?’

‘It’s a cover up.’

She shook her head slowly as if nothing surprised her anymore.

‘So this is your big story now. Bit out of your depth, aren’t you?’

He frowned at her sarcastic tone. ‘It’s huge. You can see that, can’t you?’

‘And what about the swollen nose and black eye?’ she said. As he told her about the intruder in his flat her demeanour changed from critical to that of genuine concern. ‘Matt, what the hell are you getting yourself into? You may be a lousy father but you’re the only one Callum’s got.’

‘I’ll be alright. Nobody’s going to try to kill a journalist.’

‘Don’t be stupid, Matt. Journalists are killed and kidnapped all the time. It’s dangerous and you know it is. Who else knows what you’re doing?’

‘Well, Bill of course, and James Piggot-Browne from the crime desk. Then there’s Tania and Emma.’

‘Who is Emma?’

‘She was Tony’s PA. She’s a primary source. She’s been very helpful.’ Susie’s cynical smile and gentle nodding suggested that she had not taken his explanation at face value. He wondered how much she had known about his previous dalliances and if he had given away any indication of his relationship with Emma.

He shrugged his shoulders. ‘I talk to a lot of people. That’s my job.’

She folded her arms across her chest, angry again, and looked into his eyes. 'I hope you know what you're doing.'

He broke away from her penetrating stare and picked up his glass.

'I'm sorry, Susie, I'm not giving up on a story like this. I can take care of myself.'

She was about to reply but had second thoughts, pushed her chair back, picked up the package and stood up to leave. 'You are so selfish, Matt. Don't think you can go on having access to Callum whenever it suits you. And if you don't want to completely mess things up with your son, make sure you are not late for his party.'

She swung around and marched out of the bar, leaving Matt chewing his lip and looking at two glasses of wine and an unfinished bottle.

CHAPTER TWENTY-SIX

'Dad, what happened to your face?' The swelling had gone down over the last four days but the bruise was a purple red colour. It hurt like hell but he wasn't going to let Callum see that.

'Just an accident. I banged into a door, nothing to worry about. Now, I want you to take off your shoes and stand against the wall.' Callum slouched against the wall in Matt's flat.

'No, not like that! Stand up straight with your back against the wall.'

'What are we doing?' said the boy.

'Measuring you,' said Matt as he placed a book on Callum's head and marked the spot with a pencil. Then he slid the book between the boy's knees. 'Pull it up tight between your legs.' Matt marked the spot between the boy's legs.

'Why? Is it for my birthday? It's not for new clothes, is it?' he said, pouting.

Matt laughed as he measured the distance from the floor to the two marks on the wall.

'No, it's not for new clothes. You'll be getting presents at your party this afternoon, but this is something special, something you can't unwrap at the party.'

The bike shop was an Aladdin's Cave of bicycles. They stood on floor racks and hung from the ceiling in a dazzling display of colours. The place had a smell of new rubber, paint and oil. It was still early on Saturday morning and the shop was not yet busy. The owner was an older man with a shiny bald head and grey hair that curled round the sides. He wore a thick green woolen cardigan with brown buttons down the front. He knew Matt from the cycling club and pumped Callum's hand as if they were old friends.

'So, who's going to be a lucky boy today, then?' he said with a twinkle in his eye as he looked the boy up and down. 'You've got the measurements, Matt?' Matt handed him a piece of paper. 'Good,' he said inspecting it. 'Yes, 24-inch I think. Cranks not too long; about 140-150 mm? Let's go and have a look.' They strolled over to the section of the store where there were dozens of children's bikes of different sizes. They inspected two or three models. Callum ran his hands over them. Then they came to the Isla bikes.

'Isla tick all the boxes,' the owner said to Matt. 'This is the Beinn 24. See the gears? The eight-speed cassette gives you a range of low, wide gears that help kids become intuitive about gear changing.' Callum put his hands on the handlebars. 'Feel the grip-shift, Callum,' he said. 'It makes changing gear fun and easy.' He turned to Matt. 'In my experience, children only get confused by a full front derailleur. The bike invariably ends up with the chain on the smallest sprocket.' He shook his head with disapproval. 'Noisy and inefficient.' Callum looked confused, but Matt nodded his approval.

'Lightweight alloy wheels?' said Matt.

'Yes, with quick release levers – easy to remove for car journeys or changing inner tubes,' said the owner. 'What do you think about tyres?' Callum pointed to the off-road tyres on the bike next to the Beinn 24. The owner laughed. 'I knew you'd like those. Kids like the off-road treads,' he said to Matt, 'but I think a set of semi-slicks might be a better compromise.'

'That's right, Callum,' said Matt, 'and they'd be better for the road work when we're out riding together. Go on, sit on it and see how it feels.'

Matt held the bike and Callum swung his leg over the saddle, a broad grin on his face.

'Yeah, right size,' said Matt. 'Let me adjust the saddle. That's better.' He turned to the owner. 'How much is it?'

'Four hundred and nineteen pounds, but I can do a five percent discount for cycling club members.'

Callum looked up, alarmed. 'Four hundred and nineteen pounds!'

Matt put his arm round his son's shoulder. 'It's alright, Callum. Cheap bikes don't last. They break down and get abandoned. With this one you'll have more fun. Anyway, when you outgrow the bike it will still have a good second-hand value.' Callum looked unsure and Matt tousled his hair. 'Don't worry. I can afford it.'

'You sure, Dad?'

'Yes. Now, what colour would you like? They do it in red, green and teal.' The boy looked at his father, still unsure. 'Can I have the red one?'

Matt looked over at the owner. He nodded. 'Yup, we've got that size in stock in red.'

Callum jumped in the air, ran over and gave Matt a long, loving hug.

Matt watched with amusement as eight children ran up the stairs into the ten-pin bowling alley, screaming with excitement. Some of them stopped at the game machines. Others just chased each other. Susie checked in their party at the desk and took the cake and gifts the children had brought to the private room that had been assigned to them. Matt gradually restored order and took them to try on bowling shoes. Callum's friend Martin looked as if he was about to cry because he couldn't find the right shoes.

'It's alright, let me help,' said Matt as he sat down next to the boy. When they were all happy that they had shoes that fitted, and after repeated requests to put their own shoes in the locker provided, Matt took them to the lanes Susie had booked.

'Right, listen everybody,' said Matt. 'We've got lanes nine and ten, so that's four in each lane, so get yourselves into teams of two.' There was a scramble with a great deal of pushing and protests until they were finally paired up.

'Okay, calm down', said Matt, raising his arm in the air for attention. 'Callum, you and Violet will play against Martin and David.' Matt sat down at the console and entered their names. Susie and one of her friends did the same thing in the lane next to them. The children looked up expectantly at the screen.

'Callum, it's your turn first.' said Matt. With the rails up, the pins went down and they were soon getting decent scores. Every so often there were shouts of 'spare,' and then, as they got better, 'strike' as the children jumped in the air, screaming.

An hour later boys and girls, still full of endless energy, gathered for tea and presents. Cakes and sandwiches disappeared like snow in a fast thaw. Callum's eyes were on the large birthday cake with ten candles and his name on it. Matt took out his iPhone to capture the moment as Callum puffed out his cheeks to blow. As he put the phone back in his pocket it rang. He stepped to the side of the room to take the call. It was the burner. The voice was hushed.

'It's Mercury.'

'Yes.'

'I think we should meet.'

Matt held his breath. If Mercury wanted to meet he was throwing caution to the wind, something big must have come up.

'Of course. When?'

'Now. I haven't got long.'

'OK. Do you know the Starbucks at Clapham Junction?'

'Yes.'

'Meet me there in half an hour.'

Susie had noticed and watched warily as he walked over. 'I'm really sorry,' he whispered in her ear, 'but something's come up. I have to leave now. I'll just slip away without anyone noticing.'

She shook her head in disbelief. 'You are unbelievable.'

He pushed a plastic bag into her hands. 'Take this. It's leaving presents for the kids.' She took the bag of playing cards he had brought from Las Vegas but she turned away without speaking as he walked out.

Matt took the train across the river to Clapham Junction and turned right outside to cross into St. Johns Road. He approached Starbucks with a mounting sense of apprehension and excitement. Mercury had sounded nervous.

He was sitting alone at an inside corner table. He was well away from the window and had positioned himself so that he could see anyone coming in. He was younger than Matt expected: fresh face, cheeks flushed from the cold outside, short blond hair neatly brushed. About twenty-five, he thought. Even in jeans and a sweater it wasn't hard to see he was a copper.

'Mercury?'

'Yes.'

'Can I get you a coffee?'

'Thanks. A large cappuccino.'

Matt went to the counter and ordered the cappuccino and a double espresso for himself. He stared at the tip jar as the barista prepared the coffees. It was a glass bowl with only a few coins in it. He was deep in his thoughts when a sharp voice from behind startled him.

'You really should tip, they don't make very much,' the woman shrilled. Matt turned around. 'I beg your pardon?'

'I said you should put some money in the tip jar.'

Matt glared at her, then turned back to pick up the two coffees. He paid and left the counter without putting anything in the tip jar. Still angry, he took the drinks back to their table. As he sat down the woman came across the room towards him.

'Huh,' she snorted as she walked past. 'They don't make much, you know.'

'So you said,' Matt fired back, his response laced with sarcasm.

The woman, who was walking away, turned back and looked him up and down in his black designer jeans and Patagonia jacket. 'Really?' she said. 'Well, in that case you shouldn't be drinking coffee in here.' Matt watched her go, his eyes cold and hard.

'Jesus!' he said, barely able to suppress his anger. 'Who speaks to a stranger like that!'

Mercury, who had been looking very serious up to that point, burst out laughing.

'Sorry. She really pissed me off,' said Matt. He looked at the young man, shrugged his shoulders and smiled sheepishly. He took a sip of his coffee. Mercury was quiet again, fidgeting with a paper napkin.

'What did you want to tell me?' said Matt.

The officer leaned forward. 'You won't believe this.'

'What is it?'

'You remember the young girl, the junior SOCO? You saw her at the second post-mortem.'

'Yeah, I remember her. What's happened?'

'Well, her name's Linda. Linda Mason. We're quite good friends actually.'

Matt let the statement hang in the air.

‘Well I was the... Look, this is all off the record isn’t it? You agreed total anonymity.’

‘Absolutely.’

‘Well, I was the D.C. at the scene. Linda was the SOCO. We’ve become good friends.’

Matt smiled to reassure the young police officer that he understood.

‘She came to see me yesterday. She was in tears.’

Matt frowned. ‘Why?’

‘She brought back the shard of glass that was found in Barker’s heel. It was properly bagged and filed in the evidence store.’

‘I know. I discovered that one of Barker’s whisky glasses was missing. The shard has to be matched against the other whisky glasses.’

‘Well, it’s missing! Maclean is blaming her for losing it.’

Matt grimaced. ‘Missing? How can that happen?’

‘That’s just it. It shouldn’t. Linda put it in the evidence cupboard, locked it, and signed the evidence book. Maclean says she’s lying. It can only mean one thing.’

‘He’s destroyed it,’ said Matt

‘Exactly.’

‘So the matching analysis of the glass shard hasn’t been done?’

‘No.’

‘Bloody Hell!’

They sat and stared at each other for a moment. The young officer looked at his watch. ‘I’ve got to go now.’

Matt shook his hand. ‘Thanks. You’ve done well.’

Matt waited until he had gone before getting up. He passed the tip jar and dropped in a pound coin. Outside, he checked that he was not being followed and walked to Clapham Junction.

He caught the train back to Imperial Wharf and walked east along the embankment. He needed time to think. The path was almost deserted. A woman, well wrapped up, walking her miniature dog, passed in the other direction and said good evening, but he barely noticed. He sat on a bench, staring at the ebbing tide. It was a clear, still evening with only a cat’s whisper of breeze ruffling the dirty grey surface of the river. Gulls picked around on the mud flats becoming exposed at the edges. A barge made its way upstream. Matt sat alone with his thoughts. There was no doubt in his mind that the police were covering up a murder. It was time to break the story but he was worried about Bill. He wasn't sure what his problem was but with proof that the police had destroyed evidence — well, surely he would listen now.

Bill's assistant answered the phone. Davina was young, single and fun. Matt rather fancied her.

'Hello, Davina. Is Bill free?'

'Oh, hi, Matt. No, he's on another call. Can you hang on for a minute? I don't think he'll be long.'

'Is he in a good mood?'

'No, he's a bit grumpy: argument with the editor-in-chief over space.'

'Never mind, I'll wait.'

After a couple of minutes she said, 'He's free now. I'm putting you through.'

'Bill, there have been some important developments. I want to break the Barker story.'

'I thought I told you to drop it?'

'Yes, but right out of the blue I got a breakthrough.'

'What?'

'I've got a "just cause" officer inside the Met.'

He paused, expecting a positive reaction, but there was only a long silence before Bill's curt reply.

'I think you'd better tell me everything that's going on. Meet me for lunch tomorrow.'

CHAPTER TWENTY SEVEN

Walking down Sloane Street from Knightsbridge tube station on Monday morning, Matt wondered if he had made a mistake by calling Bill. He might want to dismiss his ideas again now that the shard of glass was missing. But it was obvious to Matt that the police were covering up. He was bound to pick up on that, and the theft of the rope photographs. A sudden thought flashed through his mind: a thought that wracked him with anxiety. What if he did believe that Tony was murdered, but then decided to hand the story over to the crime desk?

His editor was already seated at his favourite table in the Knightsbridge restaurant. A perfunctory nod instructed Matt to sit down opposite him.

Bill didn't open the menu. 'I'll have the rib, rare,' he told the waiter. Matt consulted the menu before ordering the grilled sea bass.

There was an awkward silence. Bill took a sip of his mineral water. 'I think you'd better tell me exactly what happened.'

'I went to the police, as you suggested. James Piggott-Browne and I saw D.S. Maclean, the officer in charge at Wimbledon. I told him that I'd discovered one of Tony's whisky tumblers was missing, but he didn't seem very interested. Then I suggested he match the shard the SOCO brought back to the remaining whisky tumblers.'

'And has he?'

'No. He can't now because it's gone missing.'

'How do you know?'

'My whistle-blower told me.'

Bill looked sceptical. 'Do you think he's telling the truth?'

'I'm absolutely sure of it. He works in that station. He was the D.C. with Maclean at the scene. He knows that Linda Mason, that's the SOCO officer, locked the evidence bag in the designated evidence cupboard. Then she was accused of having lost it.'

'Well, if she had lost it she could be lying to Maclean to cover her ass.'

'No, Bill. This is a source I trust.'

The waiter arrived with their food. Bill tucked a large white napkin into his shirt collar. As he sliced into the beef, blood ran onto the plate. 'We've been through all this before,' he said finally. 'It's still just speculation. You can't prove it was murder.'

Matt leaned forward. 'Look, the missing shard of glass is a setback. But I know something that Maclean doesn't. I didn't tell him the glass in Tony's heel entered his body right around the time of his death. Matching the shard of glass to the rest of the set is the missing link. It was murder. The fact that it's gone missing just proves the police are covering it up. And I can prove it wasn't suicide.'

Bill looked up. 'What do you mean?'

'The whistleblower showed me photographs of the rope that was used to hang Tony. It was a type of rope that almost certainly came from a yacht chandler, and the knot used could only have been tied by an experienced sailor.' He paused, 'There is no way Tony could have tied that knot.'

Bill banged his fist down on the table. 'You've gone far enough. You could be getting us into serious legal difficulties. I warned you to drop it but you took absolutely no notice. You've got personally involved because Barker was a friend. Now I'm telling you for the last time, either drop this investigation or you're out.'

Matt's mouth dropped in astonishment. His fork paused in mid-air.

'You're going to fire me?'

'Not if you are going to drop the story.'

Matt rocked back in his chair. It beggared belief that Bill was not prepared to even listen. He was an editor that fought for exclusive stories that broke new ground. He had backed Matt's instincts in the past and been rewarded with a back page splash and stories that ran for weeks. Matt scrutinised the man sitting opposite him. How much did he know? Was somebody upstairs leaning on him to suppress the story?

'I can't believe it, Bill. I'm so close to getting you the most sensational story you've had for years. If I can just find another shard of glass... '

'Yeah, if. Well, you're treading on some pretty important toes and you just can't see it.'

So that was it. Matt locked eyes with his editor in an accusatory stare. There was a long awkward silence. Finally Matt pushed his chin forward. 'Is someone putting pressure on you to spike this story?'

'Don't be so bloody insolent,' snapped Bill. He sighed deeply and looked around the room, then turned back to face Matt. 'Look, I'm sorry it had to come to this. It's your choice. Are you going to drop it?'

Matt stood up and flung down his napkin, knocking over a glass which fell to the floor and smashed. Other diners turned to look. 'I'm about to break the biggest story of my life and you want me to drop it?'

Bill glared at him, glanced around the room, and said in a hushed tone. 'I like you, Matt, but let me give you a word of advice. Keep your mouth shut or you will never work in Fleet Street again.'

Matt spun round on his heel and walked out.

CHAPTER TWENTY EIGHT

Matt came back from his second visit to the toilet and sat down at the bar. The Devonshire Arms was on the corner of an elegant white three story Edwardian terrace. It had been tastefully renovated to offer rustic character and vintage style. He knew James liked it because it was close to Kensington High Street and they offered a choice of real ales.

Since he had walked out on Bill his stomach had been churning. Now he felt sick. He wanted to tell Bill to stuff his job, but it was a good job. He'd worked hard for it, climbed the ranks to be chief sports reporter. Now Bill's words were ringing in his head. If he was fired, Bill would put the word out on the street and badmouth him. He was sure of that. Would he be able to get another job on Fleet Street? There were financial considerations too. What about Susie and Callum? He was still paying the mortgage. He ordered a brandy to settle his stomach. His mind kept going back to Bill's stubborn resistance to run the story, or even let him continue to investigate. *'You're treading on some pretty important toes,'* he had said. Matt wondered if the *Chronicle* was under pressure from the police. The editor-in-chief would never put himself in that position, would he? He had a reputation as a crusading and fearless editor. It seemed unlikely but then, what did he know about the relationship between the media and the police? James would know though.

Ten minutes later James strolled in, tweed jacket undone, running his hand though his bushy snow-white hair. 'Christ, you look terrible Matt. What's up?'

'I've just had lunch with Bill. I've been fired!'

'Fired? Christ! What happened?'

'Bill said drop the investigation or you're fired.'

'Bloody Hell!' James shook his head and ordered a pint of London Pride from the waiter. 'Well, I'm sorry, Matt. What are you going to do?'

Matt shrugged. 'I'm not going to drop it, not now. I'll go freelance.

It's better in some ways. I'll be free to pursue the story any way I want.'

'Yes, but what about money? Not just the loss of your salary, I'm sure that's pretty good, but you'll run up some big expenses on an investigation like this.'

'I've got a case for unfair dismissal. I'll be entitled to a severance payment. I'll take legal advice from the NUJ and negotiate a settlement. The union are hot on things like this. The *Chronicle* won't want it blown up into a big fight that could escalate. Bill's threatening to badmouth me on Fleet Street, but when the lawyers get involved they'll want to hush it up.'

'What if that isn't enough to keep you going?'

'I'm alright. I made some good investments when I finished playing. And I'm negotiating a retainer with the *Telegraph*.'

'Matt, you need to think carefully before you rush into a decision like this.'

'I know. That's why I wanted to talk to you.'

James put down his pint. 'Okay. How can I help?' he said, his tone one of genuine concern.

'I just don't understand why he isn't listening to me,' said Matt. 'He's got a nose for a story. It's not like him.' He picked up a drinks coaster and rolled it round in his fingers. 'Do you think the police could be leaning on the editor to suppress the story, and he's told Bill to fall in line?'

'I don't know. It's possible.'

'Have you heard anything?' Matt asked.

'No. The news desk always believed it was a straightforward suicide. We were told not to spend any more time on it.'

'Do you think that was from police pressure?'

'I'm not sure. The police have very close relations with the press at a senior level. Scotland Yard want to control the media. "Keeping the media on message" is what their spin doctors call it. There are discreet visits from the Met Commissioner to key media bosses. Then they have this grubby lobby system of authorised correspondents. I expect you know who ours is. Most of them don't want to bite the hand that feeds them stories, especially the "sexy" crime stories the news desk want, so they toe the Yard's line.'

'Didn't that come up in the Leveson Enquiry?'

'Yes. The report suggested there was a cosy relationship between certain top cops and some journalists to the exclusion of other reporters.'

'So what do you think happened here?'

'Powerful men protect powerful men. If what you say is true, someone with a lot of clout has told the police at a senior level that Barker's death is a clear cut suicide – they shouldn't waste any time or resources on it. Now you've shown your hand to the police they know you are on the track of evidence that points to Barker's murder. So they want to shut you up. Someone at the Yard could be threatening the editor.'

'How would they do that?'

'They've got far-reaching legal powers. There could have been verbal threats or they may have written a letter. And don't forget the quid pro quo of police co-operation we just talked about. That could be withdrawn. I don't think you'll ever find out what it was.'

'Why not? It can't be that difficult. Why don't we work on it together?'

'Matt, I admire your enthusiasm. You're young, you're ambitious and you're passionate, but count me out. Perhaps I was a bit like that myself, once. What I saw in Northern Ireland with the SIB changed me. I can't even begin to tell you some of the things we had to deal with.' He looked up, staring into the distance, his face blank. Matt looked into the dark pools of his eyes, imagining the horrors James had seen; guessing at risks he must have taken with his own life. But he said nothing and waited for James to continue.

'Sorry, Matt. Anyway, after that I opted for an easy life. Now I just want to keep my head down. I'm only a few years off early retirement when I can claim my pension. I don't want to mess that up. I'm looking forward to getting out of all this and spending time messing about on my boat.'

He finished his pint and sat back. 'You're on your own, Matt, and I warn you, you've got everything against you. You don't have the backing of the *Chronicle*. Your police informer is off the record. You've lost the dossier. The shard of glass has gone missing. Alright, the knot photographs make suicide look unlikely, but let's face it, Matt, even if you do find evidence that Barker was murdered, what can you do? You can't go to the police. They stick together tighter than a clam.'

Matt's head dropped and he stared down at the floor, biting his nails. James could see that he had knocked the wind out of his sails. 'Look, Matt, I'll help you if I can, but to be honest, I think you should drop the murder investigation. You're out of your depth. Stick with the *Chronicle.* You can still work on the match fixing angle. It looks as if you're on to a good story there. I'm sorry, old chap. I've got to get back to the office. You know. Deadlines.' He clapped Matt on the shoulder and was gone.

Matt sat for a while staring into his brandy glass. James was right. He was out of his depth. Perhaps that's what he should do. Give it up. It was just a story he would be walking away from.

But it wasn't. It was a friend. Tony was about to uncover corruption and he had been murdered. Swirling the amber liquid around in the glass he saw shadows of boys in the playground. Saw Tomkins's raw-boned face inches from his. Tomkins's spit stinging his face. Their voices taunting him. *'Your dad's topped himself. Your dad's a fucking loser.'* He felt his cheeks burn. He remembered the shame. His father gave in when he faced corruption.

His mind was made up. He emptied the glass with one swallow and made his way home.

CHAPTER TWENTY NINE

Matt sat at the desk in his flat and thought about it. He wasn't going to drop the story. Surely the paper wouldn't want a battle with the union. He had called the NUJ and spoken to a lawyer for an hour. She was very supportive and thought the chances of negotiating a substantial severance package were extremely good. She warned Matt about the arguments the paper would put up. They would want confidentiality and non-compete agreements, but that was all negotiable. When he put the phone down Matt had felt much better.

His mind kept coming back to the missing evidence. The police had "lost" the shard of glass, and without it his theory didn't stand up. He had to find some other way to prove that someone else was in the study that night. Linda Mason hadn't been able to finish her search, so perhaps there could still be fragments of glass left behind in the study? It seemed like a long shot, but it was surely a possibility.

Matt opened his laptop and did a Google search. It threw up several companies who could provide the service he was looking for. He chose Oxford Forensics. Their website looked impressive. They were independent of the police, highly professional, and had a team of experts specialising in different forensic areas. He contacted the company and made an appointment for three o'clock the following afternoon.

Oxford Forensics was based in a high-tech business park on the outskirts of the 'City of Dreaming Spires'. The two-storey building was brick with large dark glass windows that reflected the last of the afternoon's wintry sun. There were around thirty vehicles in the car park. Matt parked his BMW in one of the five spaces reserved for visitors and walked into the reception area.

The managing director, Roger Johnson, came out to meet him. He was in his late thirties or early forties, with short cropped blond hair and rimless glasses. His piercing arctic blue eyes gave the appearance of a man who missed nothing: a man who ran a tight ship. They sat down in Johnson's comfortable office and he asked his secretary to bring them tea.

'Let me tell you something about Oxford Forensics while we're waiting,' he said. 'We were founded in 1982 by Dr Stephen Langton, a highly-qualified Home Office forensic scientist, to provide an independent service to defence lawyers and a better balance of forensic science expertise at court. Now we are one of the largest independents in the country, with a team of highly experienced scientists and our own custom designed laboratories. Our commitment to quality is paramount and we guarantee total security and confidentiality.'

'Impressive,' said Matt

'Well, now you've had the sales pitch, I'm sure what you really want to know is how we can help you.'

His secretary brought in the tea. Matt waited until she left before he replied.

'Tell me more about your assurance of confidentiality?'

'Of course. That's fundamental here. All our staff are security cleared. We use secure email systems and our premises are secured to a level required by the Home Office.'

Matt nodded. 'That's good because this is very sensitive. As you know, I'm a journalist. I'm investigating the recent death of the football manager, Tony Barker.'

'Ah yes, I read about it. Terrible,' he said shaking his head. 'I'm a City supporter myself, actually.'

'Well then, you'll know that the police are treating it as suicide, but I think he was murdered. The police have "lost" vital evidence. I suspect it's part of a police cover up. They were in possession of a shard of glass which a forensic pathologist found in Barker's heel. I believe it came from an engraved lead crystal whisky tumbler that was part of a set of six in Barker's study, but now it's missing. If it had been matched to another glass from the same set it could prove that Barker was murdered. No glass was found at the scene—it was probably cleaned up—but the SOCO officer who was present was taken away from the crime scene before she was finished, so there may still be glass fragments left. The room has been cleaned since then, but do you think your experts could still find any glass?'

'Yes, if the glass was broken in a struggle, and the SOCO's search was incomplete, I think it is quite possible that our forensic examiners will find fragments.'

'And if you do, can you scientifically match them against another whisky glass from the same set?'

'Oh yes. We don't do that in our own laboratories, but we work with specialists. The one I would use in this case is in Sheffield. They are experts in glass analysis: the best in the country.'

'Do you think they will be able to match it?'

'Normally it would be very difficult, but in this case, because it comes from an engraved set of lead crystal glasses, it's possible.'

CHAPTER THIRTY

At 6.30 the next morning Matt wheeled his bike out into a cold, chill wind funneling down the river from the east. Ten minutes later he had worked up a sweat as he pushed himself hard. Cycling cleared his mind of trivialities and helped him to work out his frustrations. It was good thinking time. His mind kept turning over the events in Vegas. Varta must have known more than he had admitted – much more – but getting him to talk was another thing.

At the end of his workout Matt unlocked the door to his apartment, parked the bike in the hall, took a soft cloth and wiped it dry. Then he dropped his sweaty shorts and jersey in the washing machine and stepped into the shower. He rubbed himself dry and checked his watch. He hadn't seen Emma since he left for Vegas and he wanted to see her again. He picked up the phone.

'Hi, Em. How are you?'

'Matt! How lovely to hear from you. I was wondering if you were going to call. I heard about your trip to Vegas.'

'Oh, don't believe what you hear from the players.'

'Hmmmm.'

'Em, I was wondering if you would like to have dinner tonight?'

'Ooh yes. I would love to.'

'Great. Shall we say 7.30 at the Blue Legume again then?'

'Sure.'

'By the way, Em, can you do me a favour?'

'That depends, Matt.'

'Can you give me Varta's contact details?'

Her tongue clicked in mock disapproval. 'You know we're not supposed to do that, Matt, but as it's you...'

He smiled, imagining her curled up with the phone tucked under her chin. 'Thanks, Em.'

'But not now, I'll text you when I'm in the office.' She paused. 'I have some information for you about Mayfield.'

'Yes?'

'Not on the phone, Matt. Tonight?'

Emma texted Varta's contact details later that morning but he knew the player would not be back from training until the afternoon. When he called, the Argentinian answered his phone with a grunt.

'Who's this?'

'Hello, Ricky, it's Matt. You didn't tell me the truth in Vegas, did you?' There was no response. 'I want to know what you told Tony.'

'I told you before,' he snapped.

'No, you didn't, but you're going to this time. You forget I'm a journalist, Ricky. What I know about you and your gambling history is a guaranteed back page splash. It's a great story for me but it will mean a long ban from the FA for you. That would be a pity, wouldn't it? A career like yours cut off in its prime.'

There was a long pause. Varta cleared his throat. 'What do you want?'

'I want to meet you, Ricky, and you're going to tell me everything that happened. I mean *everything*.' Varta had no choice. He agreed to meet Matt at a cafe in the Kings Road the next day.

Matt stood up as Emma walked into the Blue Legume. She was wearing a short, clinging black dress that accentuated her figure. He gave her a hug and felt the soft curve of her body.

'I missed you,' he said softly.

After they had ordered, they talked about Vegas. Emma chatted about gossip at the club and who the new manager was going to be. When their food was served, and the waiter had topped up their glasses, Matt said, 'So, you were going to tell me about Mayfield?'

'Yes.' She swirled the wine in her glass before looking up. 'He was at a PFA black tie dinner at the Connaught that night. There must have been two hundred people there.'

'Did you speak to anyone who actually saw him there?'

'Yes.'

Matt frowned. 'Could he have slipped away early?'

'I don't know. The speeches went on until after midnight.'

Matt thought about it. Tony could have known about the bungs, and he could have challenged Mayfield. But murder?

'What's he like, Mayfield?'

'Roger's okay. Firm, efficient. Some people think he's a bit stuck up: public school and all that. You know he has a business background outside football?' She mentioned the company name and he made a note. 'He handles the players' contracts.'

'How does he get on with Buzinsky?' said Matt.

'Very well. Sergei is interested in the business side of things. He always wants to know about transfer business.'

Matt noticed that she seemed to be on first name terms with all the senior management, even Buzinsky. He wondered how close she was to them. If Tony had as little as possible to do with the business side, she could have even more inside information than he had hoped.

'What do you know about Mayfield's lifestyle? Does he look as though he spends more than he earns?'

She shrugged. 'I don't know. He doesn't flash it about if that's what you mean. He has a very nice house in Esher, a second home in France, wife at home. They seem to be happy. Four children at public schools, top of the line BMW. No more than you would expect from a chief executive.'

'Does he gamble?'

'Not that I know of. He doesn't seem that type to me.' She paused and looked Matt in the eyes. 'You don't really think he was taking bungs, do you? I can't believe he could dare to under the nose of Sergei and his people.'

Matt spread his hands. 'I don't have any evidence, just sources, so I can't do a story. But I always think something suspicious is possible until I can rule it out. Do you think you can check on all the meetings he had with these agents in the last three months?' He wrote names on a sheet of paper, tore it from his pad and passed it to her. 'You know, dates, times, places. Maybe check if anyone saw him at the Connaught around midnight.'

She slipped the paper into her bag and they went on to talk about Buzinsky and how they were all seeing much more of him since Tony's death. 'He has this public image of being very remote but he's very different when you get to know him. That's why he did that interview with you.'

Matt sat in the Café del Sol in the Kings Road waiting for Varta. He looked at his watch again, then called the waitress over for a second cup of coffee and checked his phone. Nothing. No messages. *The bastard! He's going to blow me off,* he thought. He waited another fifteen minutes, silently cursing footballers' bad time keeping habits. The cafe was quiet, as he knew it would be, a few women chatting about their shopping, some Middle Eastern young men in jeans and leather jackets drinking coffee and laughing. It occurred to him that Varta might have suspected a trap – thought that he might be waiting with a pap.

He tried calling him, but there was no reply. He left a message and then texted. Nothing. He waited another half an hour. Finally he walked round to the Chelsea Harbour address Emma had given him. It was only ten minutes away. Perhaps Varta was sleeping or had plain just forgotten. As he turned right into Lots Road a police car swept past him, blue lights flashing and siren screaming. He quickened his step past the auction rooms, the fine art college and the chic designer shops. The police car he had seen was slewed across the centre of the concourse in front of the Chelsea Harbour Hotel. A small group of policemen stood talking into their radios. Matt ran around the buildings that led to the marina and the luxury tower where Varta lived. As he turned the corner into the marina he could see more police cars and an ambulance. Uniformed emergency workers in high visibility jackets hurried to and fro and a small crowd had gathered on the embankment by the marina lock. The gnawing in his gut grew stronger and a sixth sense told him told him this was not news he wanted to hear. He began to run, but as he got closer his way was blocked by blue crime scene tape and a police officer barred his way.

Matt pulled out his press card. 'What's . . ?' He gathered his breath. 'What's happened?'

The officer glanced at the card and looked surprised. 'You were quick.'

Matt looked across at the body covered by a blanket. 'Is he...?'

The officer gave him a patronising glance and craned his neck to look up at the balcony. 'Eighteenth floor. What do you think?'

Matt's instinct told him the answer to his next question, but he asked anyway. 'Have you identified the body?'

'Young white male, about twenty-five.'

'A name?'

'Yes, but I can't tell you that yet.'

'Ricky Varta?'

The officer nodded.

'What happened?'

'He fell from the balcony of his apartment on the eighteenth floor. Looks like he jumped but we don't know yet. You're going to have to wait for the post-mortem.'

He moved away and pulled out his phone. 'James, it's Matt.'

'Oh, Matt. I'm glad you called. I was going to call you. They have just made the official announcement of your resignation—very low key. Did you sort out a severance package?'

'Almost, the lawyers are tying up loose ends. The money's good, but I've had to make non-disclosure concessions—not revealing anything about my arguments with Bill — and I can't be employed by another paper for a year. The good news is I'll be able to follow the story as a freelance.'

'That's good, Matt.'

'Listen, that's not why I called, I've got a tip-off for you. Varta's dead. "Fell" from his eighteenth-floor balcony in Chelsea Harbour. Get down here now. Meet me at the Riverside.' He walked along the embankment to the pub and ordered a large brandy, his hand still shaking with shock. It was beyond coincidence that Varta had died just before he was about to spill the beans. He had been murdered. He had no doubt about that.

James joined him at the Riverside an hour later. 'What a mess. When did you last speak to him?'

'Yesterday. We arranged to meet. When he didn't turn up I tried calling again and left a message.'

'You'd better expect a call from the police. They'll have your calls on his phone records. And they'll find your message on his voicemail.

You'd better get your story straight.'

'I've got nothing to hide. I was just meeting him to do an interview.'

'Come on, Matt. Just an interview?'

'OK, I was threatening to do him in the paper. Expose his gambling debts if he didn't tell me everything. He agreed to meet me in the Kings Road but he didn't turn up. He was about to spill the beans, James. And he fell to his death from the balcony?' Matt shook his head. 'Come on. He was murdered.'

'Not necessarily,' said James. 'It could be suicide. What I'm hearing is that there are drugs involved.'

Matt raised his eyebrows in contempt. 'Well, they would say that, wouldn't they?'

'Here's something else for you to think about, Matt. He may have been so frightened about what you were going to get out of him that he jumped. He probably thought that, once he coughed, he was a dead man anyway.'

Matt shook his head vehemently. 'No way, James. He knew what happened to Tony. He was murdered to shut him up.'

They stared out over the river, watching a barge pushing its way upstream against the ebbing tide. Matt banged his fist on the table. 'Jesus, I was so close!' An empty glass fell to the floor and smashed. A dog sitting close to them jumped and ran away.

CHAPTER THIRTY ONE

James left Matt staring into the murky waters of the river, the surface whipped up by the clattering rotor blades of a chopper landing at the London Heliport. Matt's phone rang and he clamped it to his ear.

'Mr. Riley?'

'Yes.'

'This is Roger Johnson from Oxford Forensics. Can you talk now?' Matt's heartbeat quickened. 'Yes, of course.'

'I have some good news. We got your job done much more quickly than I expected. We were lucky; the lab in Sheffield was not busy.' Matt listened patiently, hardly daring to breathe, hoping he would come to the point. 'Thank you for making the arrangements with Mrs. Barker. She was very helpful. We were able to make an appointment and give our technicians access the next day. I think you will be pleased.'

Oh God, please get on with it, thought Matt.

'The housekeeper had cleaned the study quite thoroughly, but they found another small shard of glass embedded in the Persian carpet. We sent it to Sheffield, along with one of the remaining whisky tumblers.'

Matt held his breath.

'It's a perfect match. The shard of glass we found in the rug came from the missing whisky glass in the collection.'

Matt breathed a long sigh of relief. 'There's no doubt about it?'

'Absolutely none.'

'That's fantastic!'

Matt thanked him and ended the call with a light-headed feeling. This was the breakthrough he had been waiting for. Sometimes that was all it took to crack a story open. He gazed out across the river considering how this had changed things. Now there could be no doubt Tony had been murdered. The shard of glass in the carpet came from the missing whisky glass. Neither Tania nor the housekeeper could account for the missing glass. Dr. Andrews had already proved that the fragment of glass he found entered Tony's right heel only a few minutes before he died. Someone else had been in the room and the glass was broken in a struggle.

He didn't need Bill's approval to run the story anymore. He had his retainer with the *Telegraph*. They would bite his hand off to take the story. But, he thought, if he did that the story would be out in the open. The rest of the media would pick it up. It wouldn't be his exclusive anymore. And it would tell the killer what he knew.

He had to find out who it was.

Mayfield had a strong motive if he was taking bungs from an agent. But he only had Burak Sahin's word for it. Sahin could be inventing the story because he had been double crossed by the agent. And Mayfield had an alibi that put him at the PFA dinner that night.

But Varta's death had changed things. Varta was being blackmailed by Zhang Wei. Zhang Wei had been murdered and now so had Varta. The link was an illegal Singapore gambling syndicate.

James called when Matt was at home poring over the entries in Tony's diary again. 'I've seen the result of Varta's post-mortem. Toxicity tests showed a high level of drugs in the body. There were no signs of a struggle. The police think a high balcony rail appears to rule out an accident. They are confident that the coroner will find a verdict of suicide.'

'No surprises there, then,' said Matt.

'And, by the way, I have been doing some digging of my own. You were right. The editor has been heavily leaned on by a senior Scotland Yard officer.'

'How do you know?'

'I have seen a letter from the Yard.'

'Really?'

'Yes. I had to go and see the editor, but then he was called away. His secretary left the office and I saw the letter on her desk. It warned him of the legal consequences if he was to publish the story. You really are on your own now.'

Matt turned the pages of Tony's diary yet again, looking for a name that stood out. Someone Tony might have met who could have given him information that had put his life in danger. Already he had noted dozens of entries and followed them up, but none of them had led anywhere.

Most of the names were familiar, but this time one sprang out that he had not noticed before – Jurg Hartmann. Underneath the name Tony had written a Swiss telephone number. Matt remembered the name. Hartmann had been a top executive at FIFA who had accused the president of being involved in corrupt practices in relation to World Cup bids. The president denied that he had broken any rules. He was a powerful man, had sought the backing of his executive committee, and Hartmann was forced to resign. But why would Tony have been to see him?

He called Emma. 'Em, I'm going through Tony's diary again. Do you know why Tony went to see Jurg Hartmann in Geneva?'

She thought for a while. 'Hartmann? Yes, I do remember him going to Switzerland.'

'What was it about?'

'I don't know. Why?'

'That's what I'm going to find out.'

CHAPTER THIRTY TWO

From thirty thousand feet the Alps glinted in the winter sunshine like crumpled, shiny, silver paper. As Matt entered the airport building the sun glared off the snow covering the surrounding mountains. The endless bank of advertisements along the moving walkway to the immigration booths reminded him that he was in Geneva – they all seemed to be for expensive Swiss watches or private Swiss banks.

The airport arrivals hall connected directly with the train station. He followed the signs and took the train to Geneva Central. Outside the station Matt pulled his overcoat around his neck as a harsh winter wind whistled up the street. There was no snow, but winter had kept its icy grip on the city.

He strolled down the Rue de Mont Blanc, an elegant tree lined avenue: a respectable façade for diplomats during the day but where, at night, the side streets were home to the city's infamous red light district. Crossing over the Pont du Mont Blanc, the flags of the United Nations crackled in the stiff breeze. The iconic Jet d'Eau spewed its column of water high into the clear blue sky. Matt paused on the bridge, gazing down at the surging torrent of the Rhone that flowed through the lake fed endlessly by mountain snow. Turning into the Quai Général Guisan, Le Jardin Anglais was on his left, and he soon found the offices of Hartmann & Associates. The glass doors were embossed with the company name. In contrast to the traditional stone exterior, the interior of the building had a modern design finished in light oak and glass. He stepped into an elevator that whisked him to the third floor where Jurg Hartmann welcomed him politely, shaking hands and offering coffee.

He was about fifty years old, tall and slim, with neatly cut short black hair which was greying at the temples. He was dressed in a grey suit, white shirt and blue tie. His desk was tidy and clear of any papers. Bookcases were filled with legal tomes and there were paintings of Swiss mountain scenes on the walls. It was what Matt had expected from a Swiss lawyer.

'Mr. Riley, tell me, why are you here?'

'I'm a journalist. I'm investigating the death of Tony Barker.'

'Yes, it was very sad. But it was suicide. Why do you think I can help?'

'He was murdered.'

Hartmann gasped. 'My God!' He stared at Matt. 'What have the police said?'

'They're saying it's suicide. It's a cover up.'

Hartmann fell back in his chair, rubbing his forehead. 'Are you sure?'

'Yes. I can prove it. I have the evidence.'

Hartmann stared at Matt in disbelief. 'This is shocking. Why do you think I can help?'

'Tony came to see you late last year.'

'Yes, that's right.'

'What did he want to talk about?'

The lawyer leaned back, rubbing his chin, as if wondering how much he should say to the intense young man sitting opposite him. At last he seemed to have reached a decision. He leaned forward. 'He thought the results of some of his matches were being fixed.'

Matt stiffened.

'He knew that I had been exposing corruption in FIFA. He thought that perhaps I could tell him how it was being done.'

'And were you able to help him?'

'Yes, I think so. When I was at FIFA I wrote a report on the corruption of referees. It was shocking but, of course, it was all hushed up. I told Mr. Barker about it.'

'Can you tell me?'

He slowly nodded his assent, a wry smile creasing the side of his lips. 'It begins subtly with small gifts but then it escalates. It's a fine line between an acceptable gift or hospitality and bribery. The people behind this – the Asian gambling syndicates – are clever. They have connections in Europe, and they make it their business to find out about referees' personal affairs – their personal weaknesses. One may like to show off with a Rolex watch. Some have financial problems. They need cash. Others have wives who like expensive clothes. Another may have a sick child and want help with medical bills.'

Matt rolled his eyes. 'Every man has his price?'

'I'm afraid so, but those are extreme examples. Sex is the most common temptation. It usually starts when a referee is overseas. I was at a tournament where fixers sent women up to the referees' rooms. Often it would be the translator, usually young and pretty of course, but then she would be friendly and say she could stay. It's quite subtle to begin with. The next morning a mysterious man would come up and say, "If you are not sympathetic to our cause, we will let people know what you were doing last night." Once you are on the slippery slope you are a marked man. The threat of exposure is always there if you don't do what they want.'

Hartmann refilled their cups from the coffee pot on the tray.

'Of course, here in Geneva there are many high-class prostitutes. We have the United Nations, our Swiss banks, many corporate headquarters. These diplomats and bankers have healthy appetites and lavish expense accounts. They require the very best when it comes to women. Some of these girls are flown to the major European cities before important football matches. They're paid 2000 francs a night to sleep with referees, often more.'

'What about the other three match officials though?' Matt asked.

'No problem: they send up three girls. At some tournaments it would get so bad that the referees would be sitting chatting at a bar in the hotel, and one would look at his watch and say to the others, "It's six o'clock. The girls will be here soon."'

'Jesus,' Matt said. 'I knew about Robert Hoyzer in Germany, but I had no idea it was so bad. Do you think this is what was happening in City's games?'

'I don't know, but Mr. Barker asked a lot of questions.'

'What sort of questions?'

'About the referees who were in charge of the games he was suspicious about.'

'Did you know them?'

'Yes. I told him that at least two of them had probably been corrupted.'

'Who were they?'

Hartmann gave him two names.

Matt gave a low whistle and shook his head in disbelief.

'But the referees are the pawns. I told him it was almost certainly being organised by one of the powerful illegal gambling syndicates in South East Asia. They are the puppet masters. They pull the strings. They are the brains and money behind match fixing. They have influential contacts in Europe – people who are known to players and referees. Players and referees do what they tell them.'

'Did you tell Tony which syndicate controlled the referees he suspected?'

Hartmann nodded. 'I wasn't sure. I thought it might be a syndicate in Singapore.'

Matt made a note. 'Thank you.'

'Matt, let me warn you. These people are impossible to find. They are well protected and it will be extremely dangerous.'

Matt said nothing. Hartmann smiled, took a sip of his coffee then placed the cup carefully back in the saucer. 'Do you know how much Barker found out?'

Matt, still deep in thought, looked up. 'Enough to get himself killed.'

CHAPTER THIRTY THREE

Matt had been round the road circuit in Richmond Park twice already. The anti-clockwise twenty-five minute circuit had been busy with other cyclists, but he hardly noticed them. His mind was buzzing with Hartmann's revelations the day before. He had pushed himself hard for the last fifty minutes, but as he reached Roehampton Gate he decided to make another circuit. The road climbed up Sawyers Hill to Richmond Gate before flattening out along Kingston Hill. He thought about Singapore. Was Hartmann right? Was he prepared to go halfway round the world to find out? And if he did, how would he track down the gambling syndicate that Tony had been on to? Hartmann had said it would be impossible. He focused on the road as he negotiated the descent down Broomfield Hill. At Roehampton Gate he left the park with the satisfying feeling of a good workout, but no clear idea of how to use Hartmann's information.

On Roehampton Lane the morning traffic had built up. He had space inside the line of cars and buses and maintained his speed. But he was wary. Motorists were often blissfully unaware of cyclists and sometimes downright aggressive. It was the usual convoy of single occupant cars, drivers resigned to the mindless boredom of their daily commute and anaesthetised by the car radio. He looked across at a woman in a silver Mercedes estate car being distracted by three children. A red double decker bus followed the Mercedes.

Something had happened up ahead. Cars were forced to slow down. There was nothing unusual about the tracksuited jogger running towards him. Joggers could often be seen making their way to the park. The traffic started to move again. The Mercedes estate caught up and accelerated past him. The jogger was a fast approaching blur on the periphery of Matt's vision. In the split second before impact, Matt saw him step into the road and lunge towards him. A fist rammed against his shoulder, he lost his balance and toppled into the path of the bus. The driver reacted instinctively, braking hard and swerving to the right. The bus shuddered to a halt inches from where Matt lay sprawled in the road. His bike's rear wheel was crushed by the nearside front tyre of the bus.

It all seemed to happen in slow motion, the final moment frozen in Matt's mind. He heard the cab door of the bus slam shut. An ashen-faced driver bent over and peered into his face.

'Are you alright, mate?'

Matt groaned. A bystander rushed to his aid, phone in hand. 'Call 999,' said the driver. The traffic in both directions had stopped. Some bus passengers began to disembark. Others were injured, holding their heads and moaning.

Helped by the driver and the bystander, Matt stood up and gingerly walked to the pavement. His shoulder and hip were sore, probably badly grazed, but at least he could stand. The bystander lifted his twisted bike onto the pavement. The bus driver, still shaking, turned to Matt. 'You looked dazed. You must be in shock. Are you sure you're okay?'

Matt moved his arms and legs carefully; took off his bike helmet and ran his fingers through his hair. He inspected his fingers. There was no blood, but his head ached. 'Yes, I think so. He came out of nowhere.' He paused and looked up at the driver. 'You saved my life.'

'I've never seen anything like it. Not in thirty years. Thank God you're alright.'

'Yes, thanks to you.' Matt moved closer and gave him an awkward man hug.

'I just can't believe it.' said the driver. 'Did you see it?' he said, turning to the bystander.

The man looked around as if he might still see the jogger. 'He just pushed him into the path of the bus – the jogger.' The driver shook his head in disbelief and walked back to attend to his passengers and await the ambulance.

'Did you see what he looked like?' said Matt.

'Not really. I was behind him, about ten metres away: blue tracksuit, male, tall, woolen hat. I didn't see him after he pushed you. I just rushed over to see if you were alright. Then when I looked up he had gone.'

The police and ambulance arrived. The police quizzed Matt, spoke to witnesses and took statements, but no one had anything to add, and no one came forward with any phone footage. The ambulance crew insisted on taking Matt to hospital for a check-up, but he was home in the afternoon with instructions to rest. Only the deep grazes remained to remind him that someone had tried to kill him.

CHAPTER THIRTY FOUR

James took off his jacket, settled back in his seat in the Devonshire and picked up his pint. 'So, what did you want to talk to me about?'

'Someone tried to kill me.'

'What?' James slammed his pint down on the table.

'I was on my bike. A jogger pushed me under a bus.'

'Bloody Hell!' He scrutinised Matt. 'Were you hurt?'

'No, I was lucky – this time. I know too much, James.'

James took a sip of his beer. 'What are you going to do now?'

'I've got no choice, James. I have to find them before they kill me.'

James thought about it. 'How are you going to do that? You're a journalist, Matt, not a cop.'

'I know. That's why I want to talk to you. I want to infiltrate the syndicate — go undercover.'

James shook his head. 'You're dealing with dangerous people, Matt.'

'I know. So how am I going to do it?'

James sat back and took a long draught from his pint. 'I don't know.' He swirled the beer in his glass and peered into it as if it might contain the answer. 'I was thinking, you know, that thing the police say – it takes one to catch one.'

'What do you mean?'

'What about you being one of them: a professional gambler?'

Matt screwed up his face. 'A professional gambler?'

'Why not?'

'Me? You're joking. I never win anything,' said Matt. 'You should have seen me in Vegas.'

'Well, I might be able to help. Do you know about the professional gambling syndicates here?'

Matt shook his head.

'I did a story about professional gamblers last year. These people make a living from betting on sport – especially football. It's big business. They're hot on research and statistics and they get wealthy investors to back them. I met one chap who made hundreds of millions. That could be your cover: working for a UK gambling syndicate.'

Matt ran his hands through his hair. 'I don't know...'

'You would have to change your identity of course.'

Matt grimaced.

'Don't worry. I know where you can get these things done.'

Matt looked doubtful.

'It's not too bad. You'll need a false passport of course, maybe a hair colour change and glasses. And you will have to cut off all your connections to Matt Riley.'

Matt mulled it over. It was alright for James, with one foot in the police world and the other in the criminal underworld. James understood what was involved, but what did he know about it? He thought of the mafia movie he had seen last year. What was it called – *Donnie Brasco*? Sometimes it took a couple of years to become embedded and trusted by a criminal gang. How could he do it? Christ, just the thought sent a chill down his spine.

He tried to imagine how he would adopt a new persona. What background did a professional gambler have? How would he dress? Christ, he didn't even understand gambling, let alone feel confident to pass himself off as an expert. How the Hell was he going to be able to convince an organised crime gang in Southeast Asia? The dark waters of the Malay Straits flashed though his mind. He shuddered. The more he thought about it the more it seemed impossible. But James persisted. He phoned back the next day.

'You've had a lucky break. I did a follow up on that UK gambling story. The company I interviewed is thinking about doing business in Asia. I told them I know someone with an inside track in football who is looking at that market. I said I would give you his number. Call him.'

Matt hesitated. 'I don't know anything about gambling.'

'I can help. I did a lot of research on this business. I can brief you.'

Making an appointment had turned out to be easy. The CEO saw him two days later. The offices of Precision Betting were on the South Bank. Matt caught the District Line to Blackfriars, walked over the bridge, and crossed the busy junction with Southwark and Stamford Streets, before finding the road he was looking for. One side consisted of older, white, three-storey terraced properties. On the other side there was an inner London school. It was break time, and the playground reverberated with the shouts of boys playing football. They were about eleven years old. As he stood and watched, the playground of his childhood returned to haunt him, the brutal taunting ringing in his ears. *'Your Dad's a fucking loser.'* He breathed in sharply, shook his head to dispel the vision, and strode on.

Some of the white buildings had flaking paint. Number 44, the one he was looking for, had recently been renovated. A shiny brass plate told him he had found Precision Betting. He pressed the security button, gave his name (he had decided to stick to his own identity and see what happened) and a female voice told him to enter. The door clicked, he pushed it open and stepped into a bright reception area with fresh flowers on the table. A middle-aged woman, smartly dressed in a pinstriped business suit, welcomed him. He followed her up the stairs, where she swiped a card that gave them entry through a glass door into the main office.

The whole floor was open plan. Some twenty men and women were studying large computer screens. Each one had two or three screens, populated with data. The thick carpeted floor blotted out sound, but the office seemed to hum with an air of harnessed energy. The woman – he assumed she was a personal assistant – opened the door to a glass fronted office on a side wall.

The man who rose from his desk to greet him was in his early forties. He was wearing designer jeans and a white open-neck shirt. His designer stubble, short, silver hair, penetrating eyes and confident demeanor gave the impression of a man who was used to getting what he wanted. James had told him that Sean Masterson was a Cambridge graduate with a first in mathematics, who had moved on to a successful career as a city trader with an international bank. Then he had left suddenly. There were rumours about insider trading, but nothing had ever been proved. Just before the financial crash of 2008 he had set up Precision Betting using the fortune he had accumulated in the city and backing from a small group of wealthy investors. Now he had multiplied his fortune many times over. Unlike most of the betting public, emotion played no part in his decisions. He bet on football, but rarely watched a game. His success was based on detailed research, sophisticated statistical analysis, and scrutiny of the changes on the betting lines during the build-up to a game. The twenty four employees of Precision Betting were young, well qualified and extremely well paid.

Masterson leaned back, hands clasped behind his head and one leg crossed over his knee. 'I gather you are interested in working for us?'

'Well, yes.' Matt tried to look confident, but he knew he was going to have to wing it. 'I think I might be able to help you with research in Southeast Asia.'

'I've already got plenty of researchers. What makes you different?'

Matt told him about his work as an investigative journalist.

'Well, that's an unusual background for us. So what are you suggesting?'

'I want to infiltrate the illegal gambling syndicates in Southeast Asia.'

Masterson looked interested.

'Of course, there's no such thing as certainty, but the illegal gambling syndicates in Southeast Asia are shading the odds in their favour. But you know all about that,' Matt said, waving his hand in the direction of the computer screens in the outer office.

Masterson's eyes narrowed. 'Are you suggesting you can fix games?'

'No, but they can.'

Masterson leaned forward. 'Perhaps you might be able to help us. UK bookmakers don't like us. They don't like to lose. They watch us carefully and a line of credit could be switched off in a heartbeat. I want to find ways of placing large bets that don't attract attention. The gambling market in Southeast Asia is so large that the syndicates can place big bets without being noticed. Perhaps you could help us with that?'

'What size bets are you talking about?' said Matt.

Masterson mentioned a figure and Matt tried not to look surprised.

'Let me be frank with you, Matt. This is a pretty unusual situation. You haven't told me why you want to work for us.'

Matt breathed out and decided that with this man anything untrue was going to be ferreted out. 'The fact is, I was fired by the *Chroni-*

cle. My editor told me to drop the investigation into match fixing I was working on. I refused, so I'm working freelance now. That doesn't bring in much. I'm separated, but I'm still supporting my family and I need to start earning serious money again…'

'Yeah, but that's not what it's about is it? You're still working on the story.'

Matt hesitated for a split second. This wasn't a good time to get caught out. 'Of course. I'm going to infiltrate an illegal match fixing syndicate. It's a big story.' He paused. 'Look, I know this is unusual but I think this can work for both of us.'

Masterson smiled, nodding his head gently as he scrutinised Matt. Half an hour later they had agreed how the arrangement would work and how he would be paid. Somehow he had convinced Masterson, but he was far from sure that he could carry it off. He tried not to think about what might happen if he was exposed.

He booked the next flight to Singapore, flicking through his new passport, taking time to get used to his new name, Simon Jackson, and staring at the photograph of a man with heavy, black-rimmed glasses.

The last thing he did before leaving was to send messages to Susie, Emma, Tania and James telling them that he was going away and would be out of touch for a while.

CHAPTER THIRTY FIVE

Passengers arriving at Changi Airport on Singapore Airline's flight 407 from London joined other arrivals in a stream flowing down a long escalator and into the immigration hall two floors below. The cavernous space that enclosed the immigration hall might have been a Pharaoh's ante-chamber with its vast marble walls covered by giant tropical trailing plants. But what struck Matt most was the silence. Thousands of passengers were arriving and departing, but he hardly heard a sound. He held his nose and blew, wondering if he was still affected by a change in air pressure. But he was not deceived. The acoustics were astonishing.

He was relieved to find all the immigration booths manned and, with short lines, he passed through without any questions in under ten minutes. He collected his bag, strolled through the green customs channel and emerged into the arrivals hall. A group of liveried chauffeurs held up cards with the names of passengers. Tourists were weary and overawed, wives hugged returning husbands, an older man kissed his granddaughter and businessmen and women marched for the exits. Matt scanned the crowd looking for anyone taking an interest in him. One man did not appear to be meeting anyone. He was Chinese, smartly dressed and wearing aviator sunglasses. He glanced at Matt, pressed his phone to his ear, and walked away. Matt wondered if he was becoming paranoid.

The dispatcher expertly marshalled the cabs that swallowed the long line of passengers. The driver took Matt's bags and he flopped into the backseat of the air-conditioned Renault. As they drove off, the driver turned around and beamed at Matt.

'You first time Singapore, lah?'

'That's right. What's it like?'

'Very nice. Very clean. Nice homes. Government provide HDBs.'

'HDBs?'

'Housing Development Board. Tower blocks, lah? All nationalities live together in HDB – Chinese, Indian, Malay. Everyone have good jobs. Thanks to Lee Kuan Yew. His son now prime minister.'

The taxi swung into the outside lane, overtaking slower vehicles as they sped down a multi-lane highway with a landscaped central reservation towards downtown Singapore. Huge rain trees lined the verges, the grass was neatly cut and a profusion of red, yellow and purple bougainvillea covered the pedestrian overpasses.

The driver watched him in the rear-view mirror. 'Nice gardens, lah?'

'Yes,' replied Matt. 'In England these bridges would be covered in graffiti.'

He chuckled. 'Can't happen in Singapore. Against law. You come Singapore on business?'

'Yes.'

'What you do?'

'Sports industry.'

'You follow English Premier League?'

'Sure.'

'Premier League damn shiok.'

'Shit?' said Matt.

The driver roared with laughter. 'No, no no. Damn shiok mean damn good! Not like S League in Singapore.'

'What's wrong with S League?'

'Kelong. S League kelong, lah. Everyone betting, but matches fixed.'

'How do you know that?'

'Ya lah, everybody know it. Sometimes CPIB catch player but nothing change, lah.'

'CPIB?'

'Ya, Corrupt Practices Investigation Bureau. Player gets caught. Big fuss in newspaper, but nothing change. Never get big boss.'

'But you still gamble?'

'Ya, lah – know it, ah. Bet on S League. Try to beat bookies. Everybody bet on Premier League. Watch on TV. Man U, Liverpool, Man City, Chelsea, Arsenal, London City. Good teams, lah?'

The taxi pulled up outside his hotel off Orchard Road. The driver handed the bags to the bell boy and bowed as Matt gave him a generous tip.

'Thank you, lah. This week I got Man U to win home to Tottenham. Two ball. What you think?'

'You could be on the money.'

The driver's face broke into a wide grin.

The next morning a persistent, intrusive, jangling sound broke a dream in which he was being chased down a dark alley. He awoke in a cold sweat and fumbled for the bedside phone.

'Is that Matt?'

'Who is this?'

'It's Lee.'

'Oh, Lee, I'm sorry.'

'Did I wake you?'

'No, that's alright. Thanks for calling.'

'No problem. Welcome to Singapore. Did you have a good flight?'

'Well, it was long, but it all went smoothly enough.'

'Good. Look, I was thinking. Why don't I pick you up this morning? Give you a little tour of the city and then take you for lunch. It's Saturday. I've got the day off.'

Lee Parker was a journalist with the Singapore Times. They had become friends when they were on the same journalism course in London and, although Lee went back to Singapore when they graduated, they had often swapped notes on international stories. When Matt had told him about his investigation into Tony Barker's death he was pleased to help.

Matt was waiting in the hotel lobby when Lee strode though the revolving glass doors. Lee was his own age, with pale brown skin and short dark hair. His father was English and his mother Chinese. Lee slapped him on the back and shook his hand enthusiastically. He stood back, looking puzzled. 'You've changed.'

Matt laughed and took off his glasses. 'I'll tell you about that later. How's Sooky?'

'She's fine. We've just had another baby. How about you?'

Matt screwed up his face. 'Not very good. Susie and I began a trial separation six months ago.'

'Oh, I'm sorry, Matt. How is Callum?'

‘He’s okay. It’s difficult with me being away so much.’

‘That’s a shame. Look, we want you to come to dinner with us one evening, but let’s start by showing you the city, and then we’ll go and have lunch.’

Walking out of the hotel was like stepping into a giant oven. It was a relief to climb into the cool of Lee’s air-conditioned car. The roads were perfectly paved and traffic flowed smoothly. Every other car seemed to be a Mercedes, BMW or Audi. Only the Chinese signs above shop fronts and offices reminded him that he was in Singapore. The signs of Lee Kuan Yew’s modern economic miracle were everywhere and the traditional areas like Change Alley and Bugis Street were long gone. Matt gazed up at the towering forest of steel and glass.

‘That’s the Central Business District,’ said Lee. ‘Land was reclaimed to make space for the Singapore Eye and the Botanic Park. The Formula One race track is over there,’ he said pointing. The iconic Marina Bay Sands Hotel, with its three towers, dominated the skyline. It was the world’s most expensive building – symbolic of Singapore’s ambition to be bigger and better than the world’s other great cities.

‘It’s not just a hotel, is it?’ said Matt.

‘Hardly! It’s euphemistically known as an “integrated resort.” It’s a giant casino catering for Asia’s lust for gambling.’

They drove past the legendary Raffles Hotel – transformed by a $160 million investment into one of the world’s most modern luxury hotels – and made their way down to the Singapore River.

‘This is Boat Quay,’ said Lee. ‘where shophouses and godowns used to line the banks of the river. Hundreds of traditional wooden boats – they call them tongkangs and twakows – would be ferrying freight. Hundreds of coolies would be loading cargo onto boats and ox-drawn carts. Now we have the restaurants and bars of Boat Quay. It’s a tourist hot spot, but locals come here too. Remember Nick Leeson? It was a favourite haunt of his. You must see it. Let’s stop here for lunch.’

They sat at a table by the side of the river, and Lee ordered cold beers. He lifted a glistening glass and chinked it with Matt’s. ‘Cheers.’ He took a long swig. ‘So you think Barker’s murder is linked to a match fixing syndicate in Singapore?’

‘I’m sure it is. ’ said Matt, putting down his glass.

‘I’m not surprised. Singapore is a hotbed of match fixing.’

'So how does it work?'

'You have to understand that the gambling syndicate is not the fixer,' said Lee. 'It's a small group of wealthy gamblers. Sometimes they are euphemistically called "investors". They are very secretive, so no one knows who they are. They want to improve their chances of winning, so they form a loose knit association with a successful match fixer. They put up the money for him to make the fix, which can be quite substantial. Of course, only he knows how much he spends on fixing, and how much goes in his back pocket. If he asks them for $100,000 to fix a game he might spend $60,000 and use the other $40,000 to bet on the game himself. Anyway, the fixer will usually choose a big game he is confident he can fix, and ask his "investors" for the money to do it. If he gets results they come back for more. If not, they go elsewhere.'

'So, is the fixer employed by the syndicate?'

'No. These guys are wheeler dealers. They make money any way they can. Sometimes the fixer may not even be acting for his own gambling syndicate. He could be approached by someone who wants a game arranged and he'll name his price. It's a murky business, and there are no rules and no tax returns. Nobody really knows how much they make, but it's millions.'

'How are they actually fixing games?'

'It's a long story, Matt. Look, I'm hungry. Do you fancy trying the local food?' Matt stared at the menu. 'I've no idea. What do you suggest?'

'Why don't you try Wanton Mee? It's a Singapore speciality – wanton noodles with slices of pork and dumplings, all covered in a light sweet sauce. And you get a small bowl of soup on the side.'

The waiter took their order and asked if they wanted spicy or not. Matt looked doubtful.

Lee chuckled. 'It's alright; spicy just means they mix some chilli into the noodles.'

Matt shrugged. 'Okay then, in for a penny in for a pound.'

As soon as the waiter had taken their order and was out of earshot Matt turned back to Lee. 'You were going to tell me how they fix matches.'

'Well, the big fixers would never be directly involved. For a start, fixers don't meet with the players: that would immediately create suspicion. They use go-betweens, they call them runners: someone already well known to the players.'

Like Zhang Wei, Matt thought.

'Usually it's someone who hangs around the club. Someone who can get access to the players or their hotel. Often it's an ex-player.'

'What about referees?'

'Yes, of course. It goes on here all the time. I know for a fact that a referee for an Asia Cup game in Singapore picked up the newspaper that had been delivered to his hotel room and found $10,000 in cash wrapped inside. At breakfast a fixer came up to him and told him what score he was expecting.'

'How would they do that in Europe?'

'The fixer would have high level contacts: people in Europe who had built up a relationship with referees and had them in their pocket.'

The waiter set a bowl of steaming noodles in front of them. The smell of the sweet sauce wafted up and Matt tucked in. 'Mmm, good.' He put down his chopsticks. 'I think one of the runners at City was a man called Zhang Wei. He was found with his throat cut the day after Tony Barker died.'

'Well, it might not be connected to Barker's death at all. It's a duplicitous business. He could have been working for two paymasters and double-crossed one. It happens all the time.' He took a mouthful of food. 'How do you like the wanton noodles?'

Matt grunted, dropping a pork dumpling and splashing sauce on his shirt. 'The police must know what's going on.'

Lee laughed. 'The police? They're in it up to their necks.'

Matt shook his head and wiped his mouth with a napkin. 'Why am I not surprised?'

'Two months ago,' Lee continued, 'a man representing a Malaysian gambling syndicate came here. He expected to be met at the arrivals hall, but not by a police officer as he stepped off the plane. He thought he was in trouble, but the officer whisked him straight through customs and immigration. His bags were the first onto the carousel, and they were escorted into town by three motorcycle outriders. After his meeting with the boss of one of the syndicates they went to dinner, where they were joined by the chief of police.'

'Jesus,' said Matt, shaking his head in disbelief.

'It gives you an idea of what you're up against.'

Matt sat with his chin resting in in his hands.

'Don't worry. You'll get used to it. It's just different here. Let's get the bill and take a walk along Boat Quay.'

They strolled along by the river, passing dozens of restaurants and bars in older traditional buildings. Somehow Boat Quay had retained some essential elements of the city's charm and history, but there were no tongkangs and twakows plying their trade. Now traditionally designed bum boats – water taxis and tour boats – streamed up and down beneath the spectacular skyline of the Central Business District. Along the promenade sculpted bronze figures depicted life as it was – Chinese men with pigtails in long robes, an ox pulling a cart, and naked boys jumping into the water.

Matt found himself staring once again at the mesmeric Marina Bay Sands Hotel. 'You said that the integrated resorts are really giant casinos. But gambling is illegal here, isn't it?'

'Yes, it is, but gambling is endemic. Punters have the Singapore Pools, which is government run, and the regulated casinos at integrated resorts like the Marina Bay Sands Hotel, but that's mostly for the wealthy and tourists. The ordinary man in the street still likes to bet with the bookie. They call it betting on the outside: the odds are better than the Singapore Pools.'

'And by the way, you'd better remember that the bookies here don't like to be called bookies. They're agents and super-agents. They probably account for up to eighty percent of all football gambling. It's a huge market, probably worth tens of billions of dollars. And it's all controlled by twenty-five major bookmaking organisations in Southeast Asia. They have a pyramid of networks that go right down to street level.'

'But if gambling is illegal, how do they get away with it?'

'Matt, you've got to understand that corruption is rife here. These super-agents are rich and powerful. They have the money and contacts to make sure they are well protected. And don't forget the government wants to maintain the squeaky-clean image of Singapore. So corruption cases are seen as isolated incidents. Oh, there are token cases sometimes, to make a show. Players are fined or suspended. There are a few raids on bookies, but the big men behind it are never touched.'

They sat down on a park bench. A small group of young children were kicking a football. Two older men ambled by in deep conversation, their dogs trailing dutifully behind them. Matt, who had been watching them, turned to Lee with a deep frown on his brow. 'So, let me get this straight. The fixers, or their syndicates, place their bets with the bookies, sorry, super-agents.'

'Yes, that's right.'

'So, it's the super-agents that are being cheated?'

'Yes.'

'But don't they want to cut that out?'

'Of course, and they would if they could trace the bets. But they can't. It just doesn't show up in the huge market they are operating in. And don't forget, the fixers are criminals, and they're clever about how they put their bets on.'

They strolled back to where Lee had parked his car. Lee was about to open the door but he paused. 'Matt, are you really sure you want to do this?'

'It's the biggest story of my life. You think I'm going to stop now?'

Lee shook his head, his face full of concern. 'Matt, I don't think you realise how dangerous this could be. It's not London, and don't be fooled by the low crime Singapore Government image. Men like this will do anything to protect their turf. Violence is second nature to them. They'll stop at nothing. I know. I've reported the stories. Men get beaten up, carved up, shot. But mostly you don't see it because the bodies are never found. They just go missing.'

Matt took a deep breath and felt the muscles in his stomach tighten as they did before he ran out in front of forty thousand screaming fans at Chelsea. 'Of course I'm nervous, Lee. I wouldn't be human if I wasn't, but I'm a journalist like you. It's not a story I can walk away from.'

'I thought you'd say that, but don't say I didn't warn you. And another piece of advice: don't tell anyone you're a journalist. Think of something else as a cover.'

'Yeah, that's what I wanted to tell you. I'm not Matt Riley here. I'm Simon Jackson. I'm representing a UK gambling syndicate. They want to make an alliance to get into the Asian market.'

Lee smiled and nodded his approval. 'That's good. Look, Matt, I can see you're serious. I think I'm going to be able to help you more than you think. I'm working on a story about corruption inside the Asian Football Confederation.'

'Really? The AFC?'

'Yeah, it's a swamp.'

'How did it get so big?'

'Oh, it was always big in Southeast Asia. It's the Chinese obsession with gambling. At first it was contained within local leagues. Then satellite television brought live coverage of top European games. They loved it. They were cynical about games in the S league, which they knew were kelong, but English Premier League games were clean. And now they've got the internet they can bet on live games in Europe. So what do you think the fixers did?'

'Fixed games in Europe?'

'Exactly,' said Lee. 'They couldn't believe how easy it was. The police over there often know who they are, but when they try to bring them back to Europe to face charges they're blocked because they have no extradition treaty with Singapore or Malaysia.'

'And the AFC?'

'They just want to shove it under the carpet. They don't want to admit to wide scale corruption. It would jeopardise television income and scare off sponsors. Okay, they crack down on a few players locally, but that's just a PR exercise. They never go after the big operators. When they're challenged with a case in Europe they just say it's out of our jurisdiction.'

They got into the car. Lee turned the ignition key and looked at Matt. 'One more thing. Get yourself a driver. Not just to take you around. Someone who knows the ropes: someone who can look after you.'

CHAPTER THIRTY SIX

Matt towelled himself down after a heavy two-hour session in the hotel gym, dressed and went down to the lobby to meet his driver. Sami bounded up to him like a lightweight boxer, sparring. He was short, well-muscled, and full of energy. They shook hands and then sat down, chatting over a cup of coffee.

'Do you like to gamble on football, Sami?'

'Ya, lah. Everybody here gamble.'

'It's illegal though, isn't it? How do you put your bets on?'

Sami grinned at him. 'Easy, lah. With agent.'

'Can you show me?'

'Sure. In my house everybody crazy about gambling. Love English Premier League. You want meet my friends?'

'Yes, I would. That would be great. Thanks.'

Sami jumped up and marched his client out to his new red Honda Civic in the hotel car park. He looked around before he opened the car door. Matt felt he was in safe hands.

Dusk was falling fast as they drove out through the suburbs, past pink houses, shopping malls, gas stations, strip malls and car lots illuminated by red, yellow and blue neon signs. Sami lived in an ordinary single story brick house, memorable only for a giant satellite dish in the back garden.

As they walked up the path the door was opened by a man in his thirties, casually dressed in blue jeans and a blue open-neck shirt. His thick black hair was brushed back and he had an irrepressible grin on his face.

'Hi, Lex,' said Sami. 'I like you meet my client, Mr. Jackson.'

Lex beamed and pumped Matt's hand. Another, younger man came out wearing a dove grey suit and blue button-down shirt. 'This is Lawrence,' said Sami, completing the introductions. 'Mr. Jackson wants to know how to bet on football in Singapore.'

They all laughed. 'Oh, very good. Tonight we got Arsenal v Liverpool.'

Matt glanced at his watch. That was in one hour's time: a 3 p.m. kick off at the Emirates. 'You stay up late to watch games?'

'When they have evening kick-off we get up at four in morning. Watch game before we go to work, lah.' Lex and Lawrence laughed as if it was the most normal thing in the world.

They sat down on a sofa in the living room in front of a giant television screen showing football. Lawrence worked as an accountant. Lex was in shipping. They were obsessed with Premier League football and Matt worried that they might remember him from his time at Chelsea twenty years ago, but with their age and his name change, they made no connection.

Lex turned to Lawrence. 'You took Arsenal, two ball. Why crazy?'

'No way, lah. You don't know what you're talking about. Arsenal in good run of form now. Take the odds, lah.'

'Hang on,' said Matt, 'what's a two ball?'

Lex explained that, amongst the many betting lines available, the Asian handicap – which was like spread betting in Europe – was the most popular. This was a bet, not on which team won or lost, but on the favourite winning by a certain number of goals. So in a two ball, the score could be 2-0, or 4-2, or any other combination of a two-goal margin to pay out.

Matt immediately saw the advantages for a match fixer. Fixing a match was not just about one team throwing a game. If the fixer wanted a two-ball result, and Team A were at home and strong favourites to win, he wouldn't ask the Team A players to lose: he'd just ask them not to win by more than two goals. Then he would tell the Team B players not to spoil it by losing by only one goal. That way there would be no surprises, and no reason for suspicion.

It was quite subtle because the players involved might feel that it was something they could live with. The Team B goalkeeper might think: what's the difference between losing 2-1 and 3-1. It was not like being asked to throw a game you expected to win. It made fixing games in the Premier League or the Champions League a much more likely scenario. And the Asian handicap was where the serious betting money was.

'Tell me, Lex,' said Matt, 'you don't have betting shops on every high street like we do in England, do you? So how do you place your bets?'

They both laughed. 'Easy, lah,' he replied. 'Local agent has a runner – runner has maybe fifteen or a hundred clients – he takes bets to the agent. Agent just covers a small neighbourhood: takes all his bets to regional counting centre. Regional agent is big man, totals up all bets and sends them off to national agent.'

Matt remembered his father telling him when he was a kid that off course betting on horse racing was illegal in England until 1960. Every street had a runner who would take your bet in the local pub and put it on with a bookie. It was an open secret but no one ever got arrested.

'Do you use a runner?'

'No. No. That's for cash betting. We have an account. We used the phone. Now it is all on the internet. Agents have software from India.'

'But it's an illegal bookmaking operation,' said Matt. 'Aren't they worried about police raids?'

They bent double with uncontrolled laughing. 'I think there is supposed to be a button they can press which will erase all the files if there is a raid,' said Lex when he recovered, 'but they don't worry about that. Sometimes the agents will give the police a place to raid. Just for show, lah! Keeps the system turning. Not make anyone look too bad.'

CHAPTER THIRTY SEVEN

Lee had called to ask Matt if he would like to go to an S-League game. 'The Tigers are at home to the Chargers. I expect it will be a bit of a culture shock for you, and the football's not great, but you might meet some people who could help you.'

'Great. Thanks, Lee.'

'OK, I'll meet you outside the ground and have a press pass for you.'

On the way Sami chatted away about clubs in the S League.

'Who do you support?' said Matt.

'Tigers,' replied Sami. 'I think they win today. I got a two ball.'

There was plenty of space in the car park. Grey puddles still lay about from the torrential rain that seemed to wash Singapore every afternoon. The temperature was still over 30 C and the heat radiated up from the asphalt. Lee came over, handed Matt a press pass, and they strolled towards the VIP entrance. The stadium was something of a shock in this modern city: it was barely up to the English Conference standards. The press shared the hospitality room used by the directors, sponsors and club officials. VIPs from government, showbiz and business mingled. Lee pointed out the owner of the club, a big property tycoon who was in a huddle with some government ministers. Matt was introduced to other journalists, some television people and agents as Simon Jackson —a representative of a London gambling syndicate. The talk was all about the game and the likely score. Tigers were top of the league and expected to beat a mid-table Chargers team. Many of the guests were on their mobile phones.

'They're placing bets,' Lee observed drily.

They took their seats in the press box ten minutes before the kick-off. It was no more than a small section of the main stand with barriers to keep it private. There were no television monitors for instant replays, but there were sockets for laptops. The floodlights intensified the lush green pitch, fresh from the afternoon downpour, and there was an air of expectancy from the crowd that had swelled to over four thousand. Small groups of Tigers supporters made up for their lack of numbers with boisterous singing. Chants of 'Tigers, Tigers,' rang round the ground as their team attacked, but they were soon silenced when a sloppy back pass led to a shock early goal from the Chargers. Tigers came back into the game, but just before half time the Chargers scored again. The crowd fell silent, worried that their bets were going down the drain, but to their delight the Tigers refused to lie down and stormed back to score four goals in the second half.

After the game Matt stood alone in the VIP reception area where guests were having drinks and a buffet supper. Lee was in a corner with other journalists, hunched over his laptop. Matt looked around the room. It felt very different to England where he could count on knowing everyone in the press box. He was about to join a nearby group when he noticed a player's agent he had met earlier coming towards him. He was wearing a shiny lightweight suit. The top of his head was thinning and bald patches gleamed under the lights. The grey hair on the sides was slicked back. He was very thin and the brown skin on his face and hands was heavily lined. His name was Jimmy Wong.

'What did you think of the game?' he asked Matt in a bored, matter of fact way.

'Great fight back by the Tigers. Six goals. It was exciting.'

Wong shook his head at Matt's apparent naivete.

Matt looked at him quizzically. 'Was it kelong?'

Wong raised his eyebrows and smiled in a non-committal way. 'I don't know but I put a $1000 on a Tigers two ball,' he said, making it sound as if it was small change.

'Wish you'd given me the tip.'

Wong looked Matt up and down, not sure yet what to make of him. 'So what are you doing in Singapore?'

'I'm with a UK gambling syndicate. We want to do business here.' Matt saw a flicker of interest flash across Wong's face. Lee came over from the other side of the room and joined them. 'Some of the players are going to a KTV lounge. It's over on Baliester Road. Do you want to come?'

'Sure,' Matt replied.

Outside the club a liveried doorman nodded a greeting to Lee.

'This is a friend of mine, Okay. We're joining the Tigers. '

'Wah, all very happy. Score four goals right. I play six goals. Damn shiok. I play Singapore pools and also play outside, so collect double!'

The KTV lounge was dimly lit and reeked of whisky and over-ripe fruit. It had been divided into dozens of glass partitioned rooms. In each room middle-aged Chinese men, jackets off and ties loosened, were gyrating with a microphone, singing karaoke, and surrounded by friends egging them on. Most had beautiful girls with them; some were sprawled on their laps. Lee walked on through until he found the Tigers' party. Players lounged in chairs watching one of the team belting out Michael Jackson's "*Billie Jean*" and cheering at his passable attempt at the Moonwalk. Girls reclined with arms round the players' necks. The table was covered with glasses of whisky, bottles of beer and bowls of fruit. The players waved at Lee. A Chinese girl with long black hair and dressed in a tight blue cheongsam glided up, smiled invitingly, and asked them what they wanted to drink.

'I'll have a beer,' said Lee.

'And I'll have the same,' added Matt, mesmerised by her swaying hips as she walked away. 'What's with the fruit bowls?' he said, looking puzzled.

'Well, if you want a girl to sit with you it's free, but you have to pay for the fruit. A bowl of fruit costs a hundred dollars. Main course is extra.'

'I don't think I'm hungry yet,' quipped Matt.

The beige carpet had large stain blotches and the cheap furniture was worn. 'This place is pretty seedy, isn't it? Why do the players come here?' said Matt.

'It's owned by one of the football club's sponsors. He likes having the players here. It's good for business and he gives them free drinks.'

Lee introduced him to the players. They had more beers. The singing grew louder. Matt whispered into Lee's ear. 'See that bloke sitting over there? After the game he gave me the impression it was kelong.'

'That's Jimmy Wong. He's an agent. '

'Who's that big fellow with blond hair sitting next to him?'

'That's Dennis. He's English. They call him Dennis the Destroyer:

Singapore's answer to Vinnie Jones. Well, he was. He's injured now, and he's over the top. Word is he may have to retire at the end of the season. If anybody was fixing games at this club it would be those two.'

Matt raised his eyebrows in expectation.

'Don't get too excited, Matt. Wong may be a fixer, but he's small time.'

Lee pulled his phone from his pocket. He mouthed 'sorry' to Matt and jammed the phone to his ear. It was a short conversation. 'Matt, I've got to go. I'm meeting a contact. It's my AFC story. Could be interesting. I'll call you tomorrow.'

The players ribbed Matt when he had gone. 'Come on, Ang Moh. Now you got to sing for us,' they chanted.

Reluctantly he shuffled up onto the karaoke platform. 'Okay you guys. Do you like Queen? Bohemian Rhapsody?'

'We like, we like,' came back the chorus.

Matt strutted his Freddie Mercury stuff and they loved it. They slapped him on the back and poured him more beer. He flopped down exhausted and knocked back the beer. When he looked up, Jimmy Wong was sitting next to him, eyeing him suspiciously.

'You want to do business in Singapore?'

Matt sat up straight and collected his thoughts. He took another swig of his beer and wiped his mouth. Wong could be a lead. Or he could just be small time as Lee had warned. Or he could be letting himself in for a heap of trouble. He decided to take a chance.

'I'm looking for a syndicate we can work with.' Jimmy Wong leaned back in his chair, tilting his head to one side and weighing Matt up. 'What are you looking for?'

'We want to invest in games where we know the odds are in our favour.'

The music blasted out and there were screams of laughter. Wong moved in closer and spoke quietly. 'I think I might be able to help you.' He looked at Matt's empty beer glass.

'You don't want any more of that stuff. You want a proper drink. Johnny Walker Blue Label.'

Wong clicked his fingers and the girl in a blue cheongsam shimmied over. He hardly glanced at her as he ordered the bottle of whisky, but Matt watched as she padded away. Wong noticed. 'Nice arse, eh?'

Matt nodded.

'Do you want to take her home?'

He was a little drunk, and he thought he would have liked to, but not so drunk that he wanted to put himself in a position where Wong could call in a favour. He shook his head.

'Did you think that game tonight was kelong?' asked Wong.

'I couldn't tell.'

'That's good because it was.'

Matt's eyebrows shot up. 'How do you know?'

The girl brought a silver tray with the bottle of Johnny Walker, two glasses and a bucket of ice. She set it down on the table, bowed her head and left.

'How do you think?' said Wong, as he poured out two slugs of whisky.

Matt considered this. 'Yes,' he paused, 'perhaps you could help me.' He took a sip of his drink and studied Wong. He might only be a minor player able to fix S League games, but perhaps it would lead him to the syndicate fixing City games.

It was hot and stuffy in the club. Sweat was oozing from the pores in Wong's wrinkled brown face. Matt could see that he had taken the bait. Wong refilled their glasses and looked up at Matt. 'I know the right man.'

'Can he deliver big games?'

Wong put his hand on Matt's arm. 'You don't need to worry, my friend. He is top man.'

'Good. Who is it?'

Wong pulled out a large handkerchief and mopped his brow. 'I can't tell you that yet. First I will ask him if he wants to meet you.'

'Okay, I understand. Take my number.' Wong punched it into his phone. 'Call me when you've spoken to him.'

'What is the name of the company you represent?' said Wong.

'I'll tell your man when I meet him.'

Matt made his way unsteadily out of the club. The fresh air outside felt like nectar after the rotten smell inside the club. As he paused to take a deep breath a man coming out of the club bumped into him. 'Sorry, sorry' he said, patting Matt on the back. As the man walked away down the street Matt subconsciously felt for his wallet. It was gone. 'You bastard,' he shouted.

The mugger turned, saw Matt sprinting towards him and began to run. Sami, who had been parked further up the street, got out to block the mugger's path. The assailant stopped, looking confused, then ran into a narrow cul-de-sac. Matt caught up and grabbed him round the neck, spinning him round and punching him hard in the face. The mugger screamed and broke away, his hands clutching his face. Matt punched him again, this time in the stomach and he crumpled to the ground. Matt bent down and ripped his wallet from the man's pocket, then kicked him in the ribs. The man screamed and Matt kicked him again, and then again and again until Sami caught up, panting. 'Enough, enough boss,' he gasped, pulling Matt away.

Sami looked down at the mugger's blood-splattered face. 'Jesus,' he whispered. Matt, grim-faced and breathing heavily, sucked the blood from his knuckles as Sami led him back to the car.

CHAPTER THIRTY EIGHT

The KFC that Wong had told him to go to was not busy. Twelve customers sat at the tables. He ordered extra crispy tenders and a cup of the Colonel's iced tea and sat down at a table facing the street. Sami came in a few minutes later and sat further back in the restaurant, watching the door and Matt's back. He appeared to be absorbed in his newspaper. Matt played with his food. His stomach was burning from too much drink the night before, and he wasn't hungry. The thought of fried chicken made him want to run to the bathroom. A woman came in with two young children. He looked at his watch. It was ten past six. Ten minutes after the agreed time. Perhaps Wong was all piss and wind.

Matt waited another ten minutes. He was about to leave when Wong walked in.

'Sorry,' he said. 'Traffic.' He called the waitress over. 'I'll have a coke.'

He turned to Matt. 'I've spoken to my partner.'

'Yeah?'

'I think we can do business.'

'But you can't fix matches in Europe.'

'No, but he can.'

'What's his name?'

'I can't tell you that. He is a very secret man. You have to work through me.'

What's your deal then?'

'I bring in the investors. That's how it works. He has many investors in his syndicate. He fixes the matches and I take a split of the profit.'

Matt screwed up his empty cup, tossed it onto his tray and leaned back. 'Let me tell you something. We are big investors and there is no way we are doing this unless I meet the organ grinder.'

'The what?"

'Mr. Big.'

There was a thin film of sweat on Wong's bald head. He twisted the gold ring on his finger. He shook his head. 'No. Nobody gets to meet him. We don't know who you are.'

'If he wants to do long term business with us he'll see me. Here are my details. Check the company out.' He passed a card across the table. Matt stood up. 'When you have done that, call me.'

He turned and walked out. Sami followed behind. Wong stared at the card.

Back at his hotel Matt lay on the bed, worrying about whether he had overplayed his hand with Wong. It could just be bullshit, and even if he had a big fixer for a syndicate, he had no idea if he was fixing City games.

His phone rang. It was Lee. 'I've had a call from a whistleblower at the AFC.'

Matt sprung up and sat on the edge of the bed. 'Bloody hell. That's brilliant.'

'He called from an untraceable phone, but he's inside the AFC. I'm sure of that. He used the code name Raven. He knows who I am from the stories I've been doing. I've got him to agree to a meeting.'

'He's going to come in?'

'No. I'm going to meet him in Kuala Lumpur. I think you should come.'

'Thanks, Lee. Do you know what he wants to tell you?'

'He didn't say. He's very nervous and it's off the record for now. I'm looking at a lot of angles. Match fixing maybe? The syndicates may have got their tentacles in there. I'll say we're working together.'

CHAPTER THIRTY NINE

A taxi took them from Kuala Lumpur's international airport to the Peninsula Hotel. Matt paid off the cab as another taxi pulled in behind them. He stood watching as the taxi drove off with its passenger still inside. He ran to catch up with Lee, feeling an uneasy quiver in his stomach.

'Did you see that? The taxi behind was following us. It pulled up but nobody got out. Then it drove off.'

Lee looked back, smiled and clapped Matt on the back. 'You're getting paranoid. The passenger must have changed his mind. Come on. Let's go in.'

Matt joined Lee in his bedroom. Lee ordered a bottle of Johnny Walker and paced the room, checking his watch and looking out of the window. At six exactly the phone rang. Lee grabbed it, giving Matt the thumbs up. Five minutes later there was a tap on the door.

The man was a Chinese Malaysian in his mid-fifties, dressed in a crisp lightweight suit, white shirt and blue tie with the AFC logo. He looked down the corridor, checked that no one was there, and then slipped into the room. Lee shook his hand and gestured towards a chair. The man ran his eyes over the room. He stiffened when he saw Matt sitting in a chair by the window.

'Who's this?' he snapped, blinking rapidly and jerking his head towards Matt.

'Simon Jackson. A colleague of mine,' said Lee. 'We're working together on this story. Do you mind if he sits in?'

The man stared at Matt, and then turned to Lee. 'You trust him?'

'Absolutely,' said Lee.

'You are certain?'

'With my life,' replied Lee.

The man opened the bathroom door and looked inside. He walked over to the desk and picked up the phone, checked it for bugs and did the same with the extension by the bedside table. Finally, he turned to face them both.

'Do I have your word that my name will never be used?'

'Of course. This is off the record.'

The man flopped in a chair with a sigh. 'I don't think you realise how dangerous life is here.'

'Is that why you contacted me and not the Malaysian press?'

'I can't trust the newspapers here. People in high places know owners and editors. I'd be exposed in hours.'

'Would you like a drink?' asked Matt.

'Thanks.'

Matt gestured towards the bottle of scotch. 'Whisky?'

'Please.'

Matt filled a glass with ice, poured a generous measure, handed it to the visitor and poured two more for Lee and himself. Raven took a slug of his drink, loosened his tie and undid the top button of his shirt. He began to relax but took his time, as if still wondering how much to say. He took another sip from his glass and finally looked Lee in the eye.

'I'm a senior executive with the Asian Football Federation. I've been with them for twenty years. My whole career has been in football. I've been a player and a referee and I've always been straight. What I see now – it's a cancer. It's eating the game from the inside out.'

'Inside the AFC?'

'Yes!' he said, wringing his hands together. Beads of sweat glistened on his forehead and he pulled out a large white handkerchief to mop his brow. He glanced nervously at the door. Matt was worried that he might suddenly change his mind and decide to bolt. The man was as jumpy as a kitten.

'How high does it go?' pressed Lee.

Raven raised his eyes to the ceiling.

'You mean the president?'

Raven nodded emphatically.

Khalid Al Muhammed, president of the AFC, was an Arab sheik from Qatar. He was a powerful and wealthy man, often seen on television, white robes flowing behind him as he marched into a summit meeting. His high cheekbones, black eyes and hawk-like nose reflected his arrogant demeanor. He was a man no one dared to argue with.

Raven crumpled in his chair. The poor man was torn between a desire to tell them everything and the need to protect his family. He picked up his glass and swallowed more whisky, put the glass down and shrugged his shoulders. 'Where to begin?' he whimpered.

'Just tell us what you want. Don't worry. It's not going to be traced back to you. We all want the game cleaned up, don't we?'

'It starts at the top and works its way down.' Raven sighed deeply as if it was a relief to finally get the weight off his shoulders. 'The president controls companies that have AFC contracts. They take a slice for TV rights, merchandising and ticket sales. He has siphoned off hundreds of millions of dollars. He bribed AFC members to vote for him to become President of the AFC. Now he wants to be the next president of FIFA, so he has expanded his power base across the world. And he accepts bribes himself. Where he sees corruption, he can be paid off with money or favours. The gambling industry in Asia is worth billions and, with so many on board, nobody wants to rock the boat. Corruption and match fixing are covered up because everyone is being paid off.'

Lee and Matt looked at each other. The story would be dynamite, but it wasn't exactly a surprise. Rumours about Khalid Al Muhammed had been circulating for years, but nothing could ever be proved. He had an iron grip on his web of contacts and the AFC Board. He was smart and he had clever lawyers. Matt knew it was one thing to make contact with a disaffected employee, but a completely different thing to acquire written evidence or a witness that would stand up in court.

Lee smiled at Raven sympathetically. 'It doesn't surprise me. It's destroying football. We'll back the investigation with whatever resources are needed, but my editor will want facts. Have you got evidence of these allegations?'

There was a long pause. 'No, but I have seen things.'

Raven looked around. They waited for him to continue. Lee picked up the scotch and poured him another drink.

'What have you seen?' asked Lee.

'Emails. I have a friend in the IT department. He is very clever. He can see everything. And he hates Al Muhammed.'

'Can you let us have copies?'

'Yes. I'll talk to him.'

'What else have you seen?'

'Invoices.'

'You have a contact in the accounts department?'

'Yes.'

'That's good. That's very good. Look, I don't want you to worry. We will work out a way for you to get this information to us. It will be completely secure. I will let you know a system we can use to communicate with each other. From today we will only ever use your code name. It will be safe.'

Raven sagged in his chair with a weary sigh, relieved to have taken the first step. It was some time before anyone spoke. Lee looked at Matt and nodded imperceptibly.

'Do you think Al Muhammed had anything to do with Tony Barker's death?' said Matt. Raven looked puzzled. 'Barker? Yes, I read about it of course, but it was suicide, wasn't it?'

'He was murdered.'

There was a long silence. Matt wasn't sure if it was because Raven was shocked to learn that Barker had been murdered, or because he knew but had been taken by surprise.

'And you think Khalid Al Muhammed had something to do with it?' said Raven.

'I don't know. City's Champions League matches were being fixed in Singapore,' Matt said. 'When Barker was about to expose it, he was silenced.'

Raven's eyes widened. 'How do you know that?'

'One of Barker's players was gambling heavily on matches through a fixer in a Singapore gambling syndicate. He built up a massive debt and was being blackmailed into giving the fixer inside information and helping to fix matches. The player had begun telling me about it, but he was murdered before I could get the whole story.'

Raven's head jerked back. 'Good God,' he gasped.

Raven asked Lee for another drink. 'I am sorry about Tony Barker,' he said at last. 'That's terrible. I met him once.' He shook his head. 'You're sure he was murdered?'

'He was hanged. It was made to look like suicide, but it was murder,' said Matt. Raven's head tilted as he weighed up the possibilities. 'Aren't the English police investigating?'

'They're covering it up.'

Raven shook his head in disbelief. 'It's shocking." He pursed his lips, concentrating as he thought about it. 'I don't think that Al Muhammed would have anything to do with it. He flies at much higher altitudes.'

Raven looked from Lee to Matt and leaned forward. 'I'll be honest with you though, I heard rumours.'

'Rumours?' said Matt.

'Yes, but I put it out of my mind. At the AFC we hear rumours all the time. They're almost always false. We get used to ignoring them.'

'What rumours?'

'About a European match fixing operation that involved London City.'

Matt leaned forward like a hound following the scent. 'Do you know who was fixing it?'

The only sound was the muffled hum of traffic outside. Matt hardly dared to breathe. Raven was wringing his hands together, his chin pressed into his chest. After what seemed to Matt like minutes he looked up.

'It was Henry Tan.'

Matt exhaled slowly, hardly moving, anxious not to break the spell that had filled the room. 'Tell me about Tan.'

'His tentacles reach every part of Europe. He began as a loan shark and now he is probably the most powerful fixer in South East Asia. He has a network of contacts in Europe who can fix games.'

'And no one can touch him?'

Raven shook his head. 'He pays off everyone – the police, the Corrupt Practices Investigation Bureau, politicians who protect him from criminal charges in Europe – he's got them all in his pocket, and if that doesn't work he can make people feel very frightened.'

'But what about the AFC? Can't you act?'

'You don't get it, do you? What I just told you. Tan pays people off.'

'Do you think Tan murdered Barker?'

Raven thought about it for some time. 'I'm not saying that. He could have. He has a vicious temper. He has a violent organisation behind his loan shark business.' He paused while he gave it more thought. 'I don't think he'd need to get involved in something like that over there. He has contacts in Europe who would take care of that.' He turned to Lee spreading his arms in frustration. 'Why don't you concentrate on what I've told you about the AFC?'

Raven stood up as if to leave. Lee stepped over and put an arm around his shoulders. 'Don't worry about that. This is a huge story. My paper will put all its resources behind investigating it. Have no doubt about that.'

They took the next flight back to Singapore. At the airport Lee spent an hour on the phone. When he finished he smiled at Matt. 'I've put a name to our whistleblower. Raven is Michael Chang. The editor's all over it. It's a scoop, Matt! I'm getting a lot of back up.' Sami greeted them in Singapore with his usual cheerful smile and led them to the car park.

'Where to, boss?'

'We need a drink to celebrate. Penny Black, Boat Quay.'

They were stuck in a line of cars trying to leave the airport: a typical Singapore torrential downpour had slowed down the traffic. Joining the highway into the city the tailback started to move freely again. Sami, who had been watching his rear-view mirror while they talked, groaned. The car behind them switched on its flashing blue light and Sami pulled over into the side of the road.

'Oh shit,' said Matt.

'No worry, boss. Leave it to me'

One police officer stayed in the vehicle whilst his colleague swaggered up to the car. Sami lowered the window. The officer's digital radio crackled as he began speaking. Matt strained to hear what he was saying but he couldn't make it out. He noticed the hand gun strapped to the man's belt. The officer checked Sami's license and then turned back and asked Matt for ID. He produced his passport.

'Why are you in Singapore?' the officer asked.

'I'm visiting my friend here on business.'

Lee leaned over and showed his driving license.

‘What were you doing in Kuala Lumpur?’ the officer asked Lee.

‘Meeting contacts.’

The policeman stared at them for a while and then made a show of flicking though the pages of Matt’s passport before handing it back to him and wishing him goodnight. Matt slumped back in his seat and exhaled slowly. ‘How did he know we had been in Kuala Lumpur?’

Lee shrugged. ‘They’re always watching journalists. They want to know where we go and what we do.’

CHAPTER FORTY

Matt was sitting by the hotel pool with a cup of coffee reading the *Singapore Times* when his ring tone disturbed the tranquil setting. He snatched the phone from the table. It was Wong.

'Jackson?'

'Yes.'

'We can do business.'

Matt laughed. 'So you checked me out then?'

'We can arrange a European game next week. But we need the money up front.'

'No. That's not going to happen. Not for the first deal. We don't know if you can deliver. If we are getting into a long-term relationship with your syndicate, with million dollar bets, I want to know who I'm dealing with.'

There was no answer. Matt bit his lip. Had he overplayed his hand? Or was Wong setting him up for a sting? He wondered if the line had dropped. 'Wong?'

'No,' Wong replied at last. 'I can't tell you that.'

'All bets are off then,' said Matt.

There was a grunt followed by a long silence, then finally a sigh of exasperation. 'I want $50,000 cash up front by Friday.'

Matt paced around the pool, his phone clamped to his ear. At this time of the morning there were only a few guests lounging in the shade of the poolside gardens. The only sound Matt could hear was the thumping of his heart. He had no idea how he was going to get Masterson to give him $50,000 without knowing anything about the match to be fixed.

'I can't get the cash unless I know who it is.'

'You can get the $50,000?'

'Yes, if I know the name. We're not doing business unless I know the name of the man I am dealing with.'

There was long silence, then a heavy sigh before Wong whispered the name. 'It's Henry Tan.' Then more urgently, 'You're sure you can get the cash?'

'Yes.'

'Okay. I'll call you later today and tell you which match, and how you will hand over the cash.'

Matt held his breath, hardly able to believe his luck. He had the name. Now he had two days to get $50,000.

It had taken several phone calls before Masterson agreed to wire Matt the money. He had asked a lot of questions. There was more risk than he would have liked, but the upside was exciting. Finally convinced, he called Matt and made arrangements to wire $50,000 dollars.

Mindful of his experience in London, he asked Sami to drive him to the Singapore National Bank on Orchard Road. As they pulled up outside he asked Sami to wait in the car.

'No boss. No parking here,' he said, pointing to the signs. 'Police will move me on.'

'Okay. Wait around the corner. I'll phone you when I'm about to come out.'

Matt announced himself at reception and within minutes the assistant manager asked him into his office. They chatted and drank the coffee that had been brought. With formalities over, he inspected Matt's passport, checked it carefully and scrutinised his face. Satisfied at last, he asked a teller to bring the money. Matt had never seen so much cash: stacks of green bills that had the unmistakable smell of freshly minted bank notes. The teller counted it for him and he signed a receipt. His hand was shaking as he placed the package in thc case he had brought with him. He took out the handcuffs, clipping one end onto his wrist and the other on the handle of the case. Then he phoned Sami. He looked out onto the street. Nothing seemed unusual. Sami's Honda pulled up and he jumped into the car.

Back in his hotel Matt put the cash in the safe in his room and waited for Wong to call. By Friday evening he heard nothing. The thought that Wong could be setting up a sting still troubled him. But if he was, why hadn't he called? He had a headache and picked up a glass of water to swallow two aspirin when his phone rang.

'Have you got the cash?'

Matt steeled himself for the crunch. 'Yes, I've got the cash. But the deal is only on if I hand it over to Tan myself.'

'I can't do that.'

'Well, you can forget it then.'

Matt heard a sigh of exasperation. 'Okay. Give me an hour.'

Matt knew that Wong could smell the money. He knew he would agree. An hour later he called again and they made the final arrangements.

They left the city behind, passed though suburban developments with their HDB tower blocks and headed out into the country. After half an hour they turned off the road onto a dirt track, finally arriving at a narrow peninsula with views out over the Straits where scores of tankers and container ships were anchored. They pulled up on a patch of bare earth which had been used for car parking but was deserted now. Nearby there were empty wooden trestle picnic tables. Bloody Point was a popular spot at weekends. It was hard to see why, but the litter bins were full, evidence that some people enjoyed this godforsaken spot. There were only a few straggling trees and low bush. A narrow path led down to a pebble beach that was polluted by tar and littered with plastic bottles and bags. Crows pecked around the trash and the sun bore down from a clear blue sky. Large black birds circling endlessly. Probably vultures, Matt thought.

In the distance a low dust cloud was moving towards them as a car approached, travelling at speed. The large black Range Rover screeched to a halt about fifteen metres away. Two men got out and began walking towards them. They were both Chinese, dressed in loose black linen jackets, black trousers and black shirts. The younger one was of medium height and well-muscled. The older one was taller and distinguished by a long scar down his cheek. He jerked his head towards Wong.

'Get out.'

Wong hesitated, scowling at the scar-faced man, then pushed the door open and climbed out into the glaring sun.

'Step away from the car,' said Scarface.

'Look, what's going on . . ?' The words froze in his mouth as Scarface pulled a gun out of his jacket pocket. Wong began to whimper and sweat dripped down his fat cheeks. The sharp retort from the gun startled the crows. The sound of their cawing shattered the silence as Wong crumpled and sank to the ground.

Matt's mouth dropped open. He was hardly able to believe what he was watching. His fists were tightly clenched and he could feel his nails biting into the palms of his hands. He looked down and saw they were smeared with blood.

The two men stood over Wong as he lay face down in the sand. The short one used his boot to turn the body over. Blood had turned the sand dark red. Satisfied, Scarface turned away and walked up to Matt, gesturing for him get out of the car. He patted him down and took a small can of pepper spray out of Matt's pocket. 'You not needing that,' he said, 'or this,' removing Matt's phone. He smiled, 'Okay, I keep, but you have phone back later,' and he signaled for Matt to follow him. When they reached the Range Rover a third man got out with a long white scarf in his hands.

'Where we are taking you secret, lah,' he said as he tied the scarf over Matt's eyes and then eased him into the back seat. The car smelled of leather, tobacco smoke, body odour and a dog. The sensation of being driven blindfold was disorienting. There was very little conversation between the men, and when they received a phone call they were brief. Matt assumed they were reporting that they had collected their visitor and were on their way.

After about twenty minutes the road traffic noise disappeared, the road surface becoming rough, and he guessed they were going up a long private road. The car stopped and he was told to get out and escorted into a building. Once inside, the scarf was removed and Matt staggered slightly as his eyes adjusted to the brightness. He appeared to be standing in a large hall. There was no natural light, but from the dim glimmer he could see that it was furnished with heavy wooden furniture on white marble floor tiles. Ceiling fans whirred softly in the background.

Scarface took him down a corridor and stopped outside an ornately carved double door. Matt's mind was racing. Wong's killing had shocked him. But Wong had been bullshitting him. He hadn't been a partner. He was just an opportunist, a small time player who got out of his depth and outlived his purpose when he delivered Matt. Tan had taken the bait. He wanted a big-time investor. The question was, could he carry it off? If Tan saw through his cover he had no doubt what the outcome would be. The door opened, he was pushed into the room and the door closed behind him with a heavy clunk.

What he saw next surprised him. He had expected a tough, mafia-style gang leader, but the man sitting at the large mahogany desk in the centre of the room looked younger than he had imagined, almost boyish. He was wearing a clean white T-shirt and blue jeans. His thick black hair was parted in the centre and cut short on the sides so that it did not cover his ears. A mop of hair flopped down over one eye and he brushed it away. He was not overweight, but his cheeks were chubby and it was perhaps this that contributed to his boyish looks. But the feature that caught Matt's attention was his eyes. They were deep brown and had an intense quality that gave him an air of authority that suggested unequivocally that this was a man not to be crossed.

'Ah, Mr. Jackson.' His manner was surprisingly welcoming. 'Please have a seat.' Matt took the chair offered opposite Tan and looked around. A large fish tank with brightly coloured tropical fish dominated one end of the room. At the other end, French windows opened out into a courtyard with an ornamental fountain. White muslin curtains fluttered gently in the breeze. A beautiful Asian girl in a long silk dress was draped over a settee watching a game show on television with the sound turned down low. Tan's minder sat in a chair by the door, a large German shepherd dog at his side.

'I'm sorry about the unfortunate incident back there. I'm sure you understand that, in our business, we can't be crossed. I hope the journey didn't inconvenience you too much.' He smiled at Matt as if they were discussing traffic congestion.

Tan spoke perfect English. Matt was encouraged that he had used the word 'our'. He hoped it meant that Tan accepted his cover. He faced him confidently. 'Of course. I would have been suspicious if you hadn't taken precautions.'

'So, Mr. Jackson, you want to do business with us.'

Leaning back in his chair with his arms crossed Matt hoped he was projecting the confident character he had created. 'We are a syndicate of wealthy professional gamblers in Britain. But UK bookmakers don't like us. We win too often. We want to find other ways to channel our bets.'

Tan raised his eyebrows. Matt could see he had piqued his interest.

'We are talking millions,' said Matt, watching Tan's face closely. 'Multi-millions.' Although it was almost unreadable he saw the flicker of greed in his eyes. 'But we are not satisfied with our returns,' he continued. 'I want to know if you can fix games for us.'

Matt looked into his eyes – so dark brown they were almost black– and felt them drilling into him, reaching right down into his deepest thoughts. He began to feel sweat trickling down his back and clinging to his shirt. It was impossible to tell if Tan had swallowed his story. Terrible thoughts crept into his mind, as he imagined what might happen if Tan was to quiz him and reveal him as an imposter. He was alone. No one knew where he was or would be able to trace him. He had no phone.

Tan continued to hold Matt in his laser gaze. Then he said quietly, 'Yes, I can arrange the results of matches.'

Disguising a sigh of relief Matt leaned forward. 'Yes, that's what I heard, but we need to know if it's true.'

Tan jerked upright, affronted by the insinuation. 'If it's true? You doubt it?' His eyes narrowed and bored into Matt. 'Do you know who I am?'

Matt returned Tan's stare without flinching, but sweat dripped down the back of his neck and his hands were clammy.

'I'm sorry, Mr. Tan, but as you've just said yourself, we all have to be careful. I have to be able to prove it to my people.' Matt kept his eyes firmly fixed on Tan. 'Or we can forget it.'

Tan glared at him. 'You have the $50,000?'

Matt nodded.

'Well, that's easy. This week I fixed a game in Germany. Bundesliga. Give me the $50,000 as your share of the fix. Then I will give you the information you need to place the bet.'

Matt felt the adrenaline coursing through his veins. This was the moment of truth. There was no turning back now. He pushed the case containing the cash over the desk.

Tan opened it, inspected the cash, and nodded in satisfaction. He reached for a notepad, began writing, then tore off the sheet and handed it to Matt. 'Hanover are playing Kaiserslauten tonight. Hanover will win by at least two clear goals.'

Matt stared at the paper. As if reading his thoughts, Tan pushed a mobile phone across the desk. 'You can use that.'

He had no choice. His heart was racing as he dialed Masterson's personal cell phone. What if he didn't answer? What if he didn't agree to make a substantial bet?

When Masterson answered after six rings he silently breathed a sigh of relief.

'We have our first deal,' said Matt and gave Masterson the details he needed to place the bet.

'Let me check the odds,' said Masterson. Matt waited, hardly daring to breathe. 'Okay 4-1. Not bad. Our first time with them so I'm going to do a quarter of a mill.' The line went dead. Tan looked at him, eyebrows raised. Matt pushed the phone back. 'It's done. Quarter of a million. You had better be right.'

Tan grunted. 'You'll see.' He checked another phone with the latest scores in European matches. 'Kick off in ten minutes,' he said.

'Is it true that you've fixed games in the World Cup?' said Matt.

'Yes, Ghana against Italy.'

'How did you do that'? '

'I know people in the Ghana FA'

'Who?'

'The Under-17 coach. He knows everyone. I paid $550,000. I had to find new investors for that one, but they were very happy. Ghana lost 2-0 so we beat the spread.'

'But Ghana have some great players. They beat the Czech team and the USA. The whole country was backing them. They were on win bonuses. Why would they agree to lose a game like that?'

Tan's withering look suggested that this was a question that didn't deserve an answer. Matt wondered if he was pushing him too far. Tan snorted, shook his head, but then continued. 'The win bonus from the Ghana FA was $20,000 and believe me, a win is not guaranteed. From me they get $50,000 for one game if they want to take it. When they see the money, they take it. I had enough players helping me and I had the referee.'

Tan checked the score in the Hanover game and passed the phone over to Matt. He frowned. '2-2 at half time?'

Tan grinned. 'You'll see.'

'Yeah, as you said, getting the referee – that's good. Not so easy in Europe though.'

Tan lifted one shoulder, dismissing the suggestion. 'I get to know their weakness. It takes time. I paid for university education for a referee's daughter. It got me results in the Champions League.' Matt thought back to his conversation with Hartmann.

'Okay, Africa, Italy, Eastern Europe, I can understand all that,' said Matt, 'but what about English clubs? Can you do that?'

Tan tilted his head back and laughed. 'Of course I can. It depends which team, who they are playing, who the players are, who the referee is. I have contacts there.'

'But players in the Premier League are earning so much. Why would they be tempted?'

'Perhaps some won't, but others will. We have other ways to encourage them.'

'Other ways?'

'Yeah, players are stupid. They get into trouble. You know – gambling debts, alcohol, drugs, sex.' He shrugged his shoulders. 'We can help them keep it quiet. We wouldn't want to see their careers ruined.'

Varta! He must be talking about Varta. It had to be Tan's syndicate that was blackmailing Varta.

Tan's phone pinged, and a look of smug satisfaction spread across his face as he read the text. He looked up. 'Hanover just beat Kaiserslautern by 5-2.' Tan clicked his thumbs over the key-pad, found the web site with the latest scores and passed the phone to Matt. He glanced at the screen and there it was: Hanover 5, Kaiserslautern 2. If he wanted proof in real time, this was it. Hanover had won by two clear goals.

Matt handed the phone back. 'Okay. You can fix games.'

'Yeah, and you just made a million dollars.'

Look, let's not beat about the bush. We want to do business. Can you take bets of over a million dollars?'

Tan was scornful. 'Of course. How do you think I could work with my investors if I couldn't do that?'

'Good. We want to fix a Champions League match.'

Tan shook his head from side to side, smiling at the naiveté of the demand. 'They don't get done to order. It depends on the game. I'll let you know.'

Matt shook his head in agreement.

'And you need to know that a big game needs big money up front to make the fix. I'll need $300,000 for the fix. '

'That can be arranged,' said Matt.

They blindfolded him again, took him to Bloody Point where a car was waiting to take him back to the city. They gave him back his phone. There were a lot of missed calls, five of them from Lee. It had to be urgent. He tried to call him, but by then the weak signal had disappeared altogether.

CHAPTER FORTY ONE

Within five minutes he had three bars up and called Lee.

'Hey, man, where have you been? I called five times trying to get you.'

'Yeah, I know, sorry. No signal. What's up?'

'Raven is dead,' said Lee.

Matt's mind flashed back to the Kuala Lumpur hotel room where they had met him.

'Raven is dead?' he repeated in disbelief.

'It was a boating accident. He had one of these big sport fishing boats – you know, the ones with the high-flying decks for spotting fish. Well, he was out with his family at the weekend. There was some sort of problem with the engine exhaust and the boat started taking in water. Then a following wave came over the back of the boat. It tipped over and sank.'

'What happened to Raven?'

'He had been up on the flying deck steering, but his wife was down below in a cabin with her sister who had a young baby. Apparently he swam down into the cabin to try to bring them out. They didn't make it. They were all drowned.'

'Oh, Jesus,' Matt choked, 'I can't believe it.' There was a long pause as he slumped in his seat and tried to collect his thoughts. The countryside passed by in a blur.

'And he's dead?' he repeated.

'Yes, and his wife. The rescue people recovered all the bodies.'

'God! The children too?'

'No, they were lucky. They were on the flying deck with Raven. When the boat tipped over they were flung into the water. Another boat that was nearby came to the rescue and managed to recover the children.'

Slowly, Matt's brain began to function again. The meeting only four days ago, and he recalled Chang's nervous behaviour, searching the room for bugging devices, his fear of reprisals. He felt a hollow feeling in his stomach as a terrible thought struck him. Had they been responsible for Chang's death?

He cleared his throat. 'Was it an accident?'

'Well, there's no police investigation or suggestion of a suspicious death, but there will be a civil enquiry into the cause of the accident. There's talk about some mechanical malfunction: that the boat manufacturer might be responsible. It's early days.'

'But what do you think?'

'What do I think? I think it's bloody suspicious. He dies in a boating accident four days after we meet him? That's more than coincidence. And do you know what's worse?'

'No, tell me.'

'It means someone else may know that it was us that Chang met at the hotel.'

CHAPTER FORTY TWO

Two days later Matt was sitting with Lee in a Hawker Centre where restaurants catered for every imaginable Asian taste. Matt's phone rang. It was Tan.

'FC Olympic v London City. Champions League semi-final, second leg in Athens. I can buy this game.'

All around him young Chinese men and women were enjoying their lunch. The food court was alive with the buzz of chatter and peals of laughter. Lee was watching him closely. He mouthed, 'Tan?'

'That's great,' said Matt. 'We like that. What score?'

'City to win 2-0.'

'Really?'

'I want one million dollars up front to fix this.'

'What! A million? You said $300,000.'

'Yes, but then I didn't know I could get this game. And this score. You know Olympic won the first leg 2-1 at City? That's why the odds are 25-1. You'll make a killing.'

'But how sure are you? Who is fixing it?'

There was a pregnant pause. Finally, Tan replied. His voice had a chilling edge.

'Why are you asking that?'

'We want to know that you've got it sewn up.'

There was another long pause from Tan. 'You don't need to know that. You've met me. You've seen that I can deliver.'

'Yeah, yeah, okay.' Matt sucked his lips. 'But I don't think we can go over $500,000 for our first big deal.'

There was a long silence. Matt could see it all going down the drain if he couldn't get the cash from Masterson. Even $500,000 was probably pushing it. He bit his lip and waited. A bead of sweat began to drip down his face. He looked at Lee and rolled his eyes upwards. Lee smiled back encouragingly.

'Okay. I have been making some calculations. I think I may be able to do it for $700,000,' said Tan.

Matt's hands were clammy and his tongue felt like a stone in a dry riverbed. At last he heard himself croak, 'I think I can push them up to $600,000 up front for the fix. That's double what I first told them.'

After a pause Tan relented. 'Okay. Today is Monday. Nothing will happen unless I get the cash by midday on Friday. I will call you and tell you where to take it.' The phone clicked off.

Lee, who had been listening, raised his eyebrows. 'Sounds like you're in business?'

'I can't believe what I've just agreed to do. I've got to get $600,000 by Friday. I don't know if they'll risk that much.'

'I hope you're convincing.'

'Yeah, so do I, but that's not the only problem.'

'You mean you've got a bigger problem than coming up with $600,000 in four days?'

'Yes. Tan won't tell me who is doing the fix.'

'I'm not surprised. What are you going to do?'

'I don't know.' He stared at his unfinished food, then pushed the plate away. 'I was wondering about hacking Tan's phone.'

'Yes, you could do that. It's illegal, of course. What if he doesn't use the phone to set up the fix?'

'I could hack his computer.'

'You would be getting in deep trouble here. I'm sorry, Matt. I couldn't get involved in anything like that. The penalties here are draconian. It would be jail and the end of my career.'

'No, I understand that. But it could be done?'

'Of course. We have some of the best brains in the cybercrime business in Singapore.'

'I just need a name.'

Lee hesitated. 'I don't know. I told you, I can't have anything that connects it to me.'

'Look, Lee, you're a mate. This is my story and I'm going to find out who killed Tony.'

'I don't know Matt. . .'

'Lee,' Matt's voice took on a hard edge. 'Just point me in the right direction.'

Lee finished his drink and examined the bottom of the glass. 'I'll make some enquiries and someone will be in touch with you.'

'Thanks, Lee, but I need it now.'

CHAPTER FORTY THREE

Masterson asked a lot of questions. The odds were very attractive, but he wanted to be sure that they would accept such a large bet – much larger than he could place with a UK bookmaker. Now that had been confirmed, but there was still more risk than he would have liked, even fixers could not guarantee the result. He had checked the stats and a 2-0 away win for City was most unlikely. Still, the odds made it very tempting. A million dollar bet would bring in $25 million. And, if the arrangement worked, there would be much more to come. Finally convinced, he called Matt and made arrangements to wire the $600,000 dollars cash to make the fix.

Having collected the cash from the Orchard Street branch he had used before, Matt waited for Tan to call with instructions for the handover. When his phone rang he grabbed it and wrote down the details of the handover.

He felt a hard knot in his stomach as he walked up the steps of the prestigious Straits Hotel. The sleeve of his jacket covered the handcuff clipped to the case, but the hard metal bit into his wrist. The thought of six hundred thousand dollars made the case feel unnaturally heavy. His shirt was clammy with sweat. A doorman opened the engraved glass doors. He couldn't shake off the uneasy feeling that he was being watched as he stepped into the cool of the air conditioned lobby.

He sat and waited, scanning the lobby for the handover. Sami sat ten feet behind him, reading a newspaper. A waiter arrived. Matt ordered a glass of mineral water. A business man in a blue suit sat down next to him, talking on his mobile phone. Damn it, Matt thought. The contact won't approach me while he is so close. A few minutes later a woman arrived, shook hands with the man and walked off.

As he watched them go he felt a tap on his shoulder and spun round. A young man with an open neck white shirt stood smiling at him.

'Are you an Arsenal fan?' he asked.

'No, I have always supported Tottenham Hotspur.'

Both men relaxed at the exchange of code words and the contact sat down opposite him. Matt unlocked the handcuffs on his wrist and slid the case across the glass table. The man opened the case, checked the bundles of money and walked away with $600,000.

Matt watched him go with an uneasy feeling that he could have been duped into giving the cash to an imposter. His right hand now seemed oddly light and he rubbed the marks made by the handcuffs. As he stood up to stretch his phone rang.

'Hi, Matt. My name is Cheng Li. You need some help with your computer, lah?' Matt breathed in sharply. 'Yes.'

'Can you meet me in your hotel room in one hour?'

Matt beckoned to Sami. 'Back to the hotel. Now!'

CHAPTER FORTY FOUR

Matt studied the man who sat opposite him. Well, he was just a boy really, probably no more than twenty. He was skinny, wearing torn jeans and a yellow T-shirt. His hair was black, and his skin a light olive colour. Behind his John Lennon style glasses his eyes sparkled. What Matt most noticed was his boyish enthusiasm as he explained the methods he could use to get into Tan's phone and his email. 'No problem, lah.'

Matt didn't understand a word of it, but he was in no doubt that the boy could do everything he said he could. He passed over an envelope containing a thousand dollars. The boy looked inside and smiled.

'Double that when you deliver,' said Matt.

Days went by and Matt was unable to sleep. Three weeks in Singapore had taken a toll. He felt drained by the constant anxiety of working undercover: tense and ever fearful that he would make a silly slip that would give him away. The closer he got to finding who was fixing City games, and who killed Tony, the more nervous he got. Tan had told him that he had the cash and the fix was on. Time was moving ahead. It was only two weeks before the City game in Greece and he still knew nothing. He had again pressed Tan for details. Who was arranging the fix? Was the referee involved? Which players were being approached? Tan had given him blunt, evasive answers. Told him not to worry: his people were working on it.

But he did worry. He drifted in and out of sleep. What if Cheng Li was unable to find the evidence he wanted? How good was this computer geek anyway? And how discreet would he be? What if Tan somehow became suspicious that he was being hacked or, even worse, found out? He didn't want to think about it. He was in uncharted waters and they were deep: deeper than he had ever expected. Singapore seemed a very lonely place.

The corridor was impenetrably black. He stumbled forward, holding one hand over his head, overwhelmed by a sensation that the ceiling was pressing down on him. His other hand flailed to one side, expecting to touch a wall, but felt only space. Drumming footsteps behind him became louder. Somebody was chasing him, and they were coming closer. A large dog with red fangs jumped out to his right, snarled in his face and disappeared. He tried to run, but his feet felt glued to the ground. He stumbled and fell. A giant Chinese figure towered over him, brandishing a broad silver sword. It slashed past his ear and clattered to the floor.

He grabbed the sword but he hardly seemed to have the strength to lift it. With a supreme effort he raised the silver blade above his shoulders and sliced into the naked body. He cut and hacked until it was in pieces. But then, as he stared at the pieces, they reformed like coagulating blobs of blood. The jelly-like body rose up in front of him again, a ghastly smile on the aggressor's face. He slashed at it again and again, the blade crashing on hard rock. Each time the pieces he cut came together to form the figure that tormented him. He knew he couldn't win. It was going to kill him.

He woke up in a cold sweat, his phone ringing insistently. He fumbled for the bedside lamp and its warm glow revealed familiar items; the desk, the painting of the old Singapore waterfront, a chair with his clothes flung over it. He threw off the bed clothes and picked up the phone, glancing at the bedside clock. It was midnight.

'Cheng Li?'

The boy sounded very excited. 'I cracked it. Working on it now. Ready in the morning. You be very pleased, lah.'

Matt stumbled into the bathroom for a glass of water, wide awake now, his mind in turmoil, trying to make sense of the chain of events he had set in motion, impatient to find out what Cheng Li had uncovered.

The house that Cheng Li had told him to come to was in Woodlands, an old part of the city that had seen better days. The houses were large and multi-tenanted with concrete paths and playing areas for children. The children stopped kicking their football and stared at the angh moh. The concrete radiated the stifling 30-degree heat and 90 per cent humidity of equatorial Singapore. He wiped away the sweat that trickled down his face as he searched for Cheng Li's name on the list of tenants. He pressed the button for number 18 and the door opened.

The steps to the third floor were tiled and chipped. The walls were peeling and needed repainting. He paused at the door, trying not to expect too much. But Cheng Li had been very excited when he called. 'You be very pleased, lah.'

The room was dark. What little natural light there was had been shut out by blinds that had been closed. The only sound came from the whirring of a large fan. Cheng Li went into the kitchen to make coffee. Gradually Matt's eyes became accustomed to the half-light as he looked around. Computer screens covered tables. Grey boxes with electrical wires sprouting in all directions filled one corner. On the table in front of him a pizza box lay open. An empty coffee cup was next to an ashtray overflowing with cigarette stubs. Cheng Li placed the coffee in front of him and apologetically gathered up the debris.

'Sorry about mess. Working late last night,' he said with a grin.

Matt took a good look at him. He was unshaven, and the body odour suggested he hadn't showered either. His yellow T-shirt was crumpled, and he blinked like an owl. Matt thought he'd probably lost track of whether it was night or day.

'Bloody Hell,' said Matt looking around. 'This is quite a set-up you have here. How many clients do you have?'

'Enough to keep me busy.'

'Who do you work for?'

'Ah, you be surprise,' Cheng Li said, grinning. 'Many people want to know secrets. Businessmen and women, journalists, showbiz celebrity, politicians, jealous husbands... everyone. You be very surprise.'

'So, what have you got for me?'

The young man smiled and took him across the room to a desk with a large computer screen. He pulled up a small wooden chair for Matt, and sat down at his own high back, worn, leather chair. His fingers began to fly over the keyboard. Screens appeared and disappeared as Cheng Li clicked away. Codes were entered. At last Matt saw a screen he recognized. They were looking at emails in Tan's Outlook inbox.

'Christ, how do you do this?' he gasped.

Matt scrolled down. Mostly the names still seemed to be Chinese, Malaysian or African, but one shone like a beacon.

Burak Sahin. Re: London City

Matt stared at the screen for a moment and let out a long, low whistle as he scrolled down to the beginning of the email trail.

From: Henry Tan

To: Burak Sahin

Can you do the City game in Greece?

From: Burak Sahin

To: Henry Tan

Yes probably. Let me see who the referee is.

From: Henry Tan

To: Burak Sahin

I want this one.

From: Burak Sahin

To: Henry Tan

Have you got the money? This one is going to cost.

From: Henry Tan

To: Burak Sahin

Don't worry about that. I got a new investor.

From: Burak Sahin

To: Henry Tan

Just checked the referee. It's Milanovic. Serbian. No problem. I own that fucker.

From: Henry Tan

To: Burak Sahin

What about the players?

From: Burak Sahin

To: Henry Tan

Don't worry. I know FC Olympic. I've bought the goalkeeper and two others before. What score do you want?'

From: Henry Tan

To: Burak Sahin

2-0 City win.

From: Burak Sahin

To: Henry Tan

2-0! That may be difficult. Olympic won 2-1 in London in the first leg. City has to win 2-0 to reach the final. The odds will be great though! I'll work on it and let you know.

Matt looked at Cheng Li and shook his head in astonishment. 'I can't believe he can be so bloody indiscreet.'

Cheng Li smiled. 'They all think email private. Some people take precautions. Make my life very difficult. But guys like this so fucking stupid.'

'Let's see what else you've got. ' Matt did a search for Burak Sahin on all mail items. He wasn't disappointed. There were dozens of messages and attachments with documents. He felt a lightness in his chest and a broad grin creased his face.

'Jesus. Look at this!' His eyes widened with an incredulous stare. 'It's unbelievable. They've been fixing matches all over Europe.' Each revelation brought a sharp intake of breath from Matt.

'Top teams. I can't believe some of these names.' He looked up at Cheng Li. 'This is dynamite. Can you download all this on a hard drive for me?'

'No problem, boss.'

Matt handed over an envelope containing $2000 and the boy grinned again. It was the best $2000 I ever spent, thought Matt.

CHAPTER FORTY FIVE

The Singapore Airlines flight touched down at Heathrow at ten to five on Friday morning. A heavy April shower had drenched the early promise of spring. Pools of water had formed on the black tarmac and driving rain was illuminated in the yellow lights. By the time Matt had passed through immigration and collected his bags he was dead beat. It had been difficult to sleep on the plane: his mind was too active. He glanced at his watch. It was six thirty in the morning. He took the Heathrow Express into London, eager to get home for a shower and change of clothes.

An hour later he crashed out on his bed at home. He hadn't meant to. There was so much he wanted to get on with. When he awoke it was nearly eleven. He showered, made a cup of espresso and sat down in the kitchen and opened his laptop for the first time in three weeks. He had three hundred and fifty emails. He phoned Susie. It was a difficult conversation, but she agreed that he could come round to see Callum on Saturday and take him to watch Chelsea. Emma had sent him a string of messages saying she needed to see him urgently when he got back. He felt an urge to be with her again. He picked up his phone.

'Matt, how good to hear from you. Where have you been? I missed you and I've got things to tell you. When can we meet?'

'I don't know. I just got back this morning. I'll call you later today.'

'Tell you what, Matt. Why don't you come to mine tonight? I've got some news for you. I'll cook dinner. How's that?'

It sounded good, he thought.

His next call was to James. 'I've just got back. A lot's happened. Can we meet?'

'Sure – tomorrow? A long Saturday lunch?'

'No, I can't do that. I'm taking Callum to Chelsea. Can you make it today? It's urgent.'

There was a momentary silence. 'Okay. I can rearrange things. How about lunch at the Devonshire?'

The pub was busy but the waitress found them a quiet table in an alcove with blue buttoned upholstery. Behind the seating, a red brick wall was adorned with rustic watercolour paintings and brass lights.

'Well, old chap, buy me a pint and tell me all about it then,' said James. They both ordered London Pride and steak and kidney pie. An hour later, Matt pushed his empty plate forward and drained the last of his beer.

'So, you see, Sahin was fixing games for Tan all over Europe. Tony must have finally worked out what he was up to.' He paused. 'Or perhaps Varta told him.' Matt leaned his head on one side, still thinking. 'Or maybe Sahin just found out what Tony knew and had him eliminated.'

James sat chewing his lips. 'I don't know. Even if he was fixing City matches you have no evidence that he murdered Barker.'

'Come on, James. I've got the emails.'

'It's good stuff, Matt, but it doesn't prove he murdered Barker. Only that he might have a motive. In any case, the computer and phone hacking evidence was obtained illegally. It's inadmissible in court.'

'I know that!'

'Apart from anything else it's a criminal offence. You could be in serious trouble yourself. And just to cheer you up even more, if Sahin finds out, you are a dead man walking.'

'I know.'

'Do you think Tan has talked about you to Sahin?' said James.

Matt's face tightened as he concentrated. 'I don't think so. Cheng Li hacked his emails and his phone, but my name, Simon Jackson that is, never came up. Tan keeps his contacts close to his chest. These guys are double crossing bastards. I don't think he would trust anyone. He wouldn't reveal his European fixer to me, and that wasn't out of loyalty. It was greed and self-preservation.'

'So what are you going to do now?' asked James.

Matt stared into his empty glass as if the solution might be hidden there. 'I was thinking about meeting Sahin and wearing a wire.'

James pursed his lips as he thought about it. 'I don't think so. It could be useful to the police in a prosecution, but it's fraught with legal problems. It's not the movies, Matt. In any case, he's a hardened criminal. He's not going to cough up a confession just because you know stuff, un-provable stuff, about him. And if you still need convincing, you've shown your hand and you're a dead man. Forget it.'

Matt banged his fist down on the table, shaking the cutlery and glasses. 'Jesus.'

'Calm down, Matt. Let me think about it. I've got an idea. I have a few favours I can call in.'

CHAPTER FORTY SIX

Matt pressed the buzzer outside Emma's apartment block clutching a bunch of roses rather awkwardly in one hand. 'Come on up,' she said. He took the lift and opened the door to no. 14. She was standing at the open plan island kitchen preparing dinner. Seeing him enter she waved, put down the knife she was using, wiped her hands on a towel and stepped out to meet him. She was wearing a blue and white striped apron that covered her from neck to knees.

'Are those for me? They're lovely. How sweet,' she said, taking the flowers and putting them down on a chair beside her. She put her arms round Matt and kissed him on the lips – a long lingering kiss. He felt her soft brown hair brush against him and breathed in her fragrance. 'Thank you,' she said at last, leaning back to look at him. He drew her close again, his hands on her bare back, then slid them down her body, past the apron string tied in a bow at the back, exploring further and feeling the soft smooth skin of her bare buttocks. She pulled herself up closer and he could feel her firm breasts pressed against him. His chest was tight and his mouth dry as the excitement rose up inside him. He took hold of the bow to untie the apron strings but she pulled his hand away, smiling. 'What's the hurry? Don't you want a drink? I put champagne in the fridge to welcome you back.'

He breathed in deeply, forcing a degree of self-control as blood pulsed through his veins. 'Thanks.'

They moved away to the sofa where two champagne flutes were waiting. She brought the bottle over from the fridge, handing it to Matt. He popped the cork and they chinked glasses.

'Welcome home. Where have you been? Why the mystery?'

He sighed. 'It's complicated.'

'But why didn't you ever call me?'

'Sorry, Em. I can't say.'

'Why?'

'Because... because it would have endangered you and other people. I don't want you to get involved. Let's not talk about that now. Let's talk about you.'

'Okay,' she said finally and picked up her glass. They talked about the club and the excitement building up for the second leg of the Champions League semi-final in Greece.

'We see a lot more of Sergei these days,' she said. 'I think that story you did about him made a lot of people see him in a different light – the foundation has had a lot of publicity. He's much more involved at the club. People like him. We've got a new manager now, of course, Enrico. Sergei is doing everything he can to see he settles in quickly, making sure that it all goes smoothly. Of course, it doesn't help that Enrico's English is so bad. He brought a Spanish PA to help the communications with the players and the media. She speaks perfect English, so that's good, and she's very nice.'

He frowned. 'Where does that leave you?'

'I've had a bump up. Sergei wants me to broaden my experience at the club. I'm working as the media relations executive.'

'Hey, that's great! Congratulations.'

He leaned over and kissed her, a long passionate kiss, and she caressed the back of his neck. Then she stood up and took him by the hand. 'Come on then. Dinner will have to wait,' she said, her eyes twinkling.

She led him into the bedroom, reached behind her back, untied the bow and dropped the apron to the floor. He breathed in sharply and stood rooted to the spot. She laughed and flung herself on the bed, reclining on one elbow as she watched him undress. He could not take his eyes off her. She was petite, with her neck, arms, hands, legs and ankles all perfectly proportioned. Her flat stomach accentuated her firm pale breasts, the pink nipples small and hard. She was, he thought, like a white rosebud ready to bloom.

Later, they lay relaxing on the bed with glasses of champagne. She snuggled up to him. 'You know you asked me to find out if Roger could have left the Connaught early?'

'Yes,' he said, sitting up.

'Well, he did. He slipped away before the speeches began.' Matt stared at her. 'What?'

'I talked to one of our players. He saw him leave the room at about

9.30 when dinner finished, and he didn't come back.'

Matt leaned back on the headboard, his eyes narrowed. 'Are you sure?'

'Yes, another player told me the same thing. But that's not all, Matt. After what you told me I had a discreet word with the CFO. He has been making enquiries about transfer irregularities. It looks like you were right. Not for publication yet, but I'll make sure you get an exclusive when we are ready.'

Matt was stunned. Mayfield's alibi had been shot. He had the motive, the means and the opportunity. He would have been able to get access to the house: Tony would have opened the door to let him in. He would have needed help and someone to fix the CCTV, but he would have had contacts for that. But was he a killer?

Matt stared at the wall and shook his ahead. 'No. It can't be Mayfield.'

It was her turn to look surprised. 'Not Mayfield? What do you mean?'

'I mean he didn't kill Tony.'

'What!'

'Burak Sahin did.'

'Sahin?'

'Yeah. He was fixing City games. I'm that close,' he said, holding his thumb and forefinger an inch apart. 'I know he murdered Tony.' He sighed with exasperation. 'I just can't prove it yet.'

'So what are you going to do now?'

Matt bit his lip. 'I don't know yet. I'm going to see what happens at the match. I've got an early afternoon Easy Jet flight to Athens on Sunday morning. I'll be there two days early. Sniff around. Talk to players, the referee, Sahin. Maybe I can challenge him and record it.' He bit his nails. 'Trouble is, he knows me. He wouldn't admit anything. Unless he lost his temper maybe.'

'I could do it,' she said slowly.

'Em! Why would you do something like that?'

She drew closer. 'I said I wanted to help you Matt. I would do it for you.'

He shook his head slowly. 'But how could you do it?'

'I know him. He finds me attractive. When he used to come and see Tony he was always looking at me. He'll meet me in a hotel if I ask him. Maybe I can plant a bug. You can listen in and perhaps I can get him to say something you can use.'

'Plant a bug? What do you know about planting bugs?'

'Not a lot,' she conceded, 'but it can't be that difficult, can it? I've seen websites advertising all kinds of covert surveillance devices. They're tiny. All kinds of people use them – even jealous husbands!' She laughed nervously, trying to make light of the situation.

'No, Em, I can't let you do it. It's out of the question.'

'I think you underestimate me,' she said, reaching across to kiss him lightly on the lips. 'Shall we see if we can rescue the dinner now?'

CHAPTER FORTY SEVEN

Matt drove up West Hill from Putney and joined the A3 heading south for Gatwick. He knew where the speed cameras were and kept his speed under the limit. He had plenty of time for the flight to Athens. Pulling out to pass a large truck, he noticed a black 4 x 4 behind him.

His mind drifted back to his meeting with Susie. When he went to collect Callum to take him to the Chelsea match they had rowed. She wanted to know what he had been doing in Asia and he refused to tell her. And that made her even madder. She said he couldn't take Callum, but the boy had been listening upstairs and came down in floods of tears. In the end she had reluctantly yielded to Callum's pleas and they went. But it had been an ugly scene.

He wondered how much he would glean from the entourage of press, agents and hangers-on at the team hotel. It was the perfect place to pick up gossip. He might meet Sahin. A blast on the horn from a truck behind startled him. He had been dawdling in the slow lane, dreaming. He picked up speed and raised his hand in apology to the truck driver.

At the Hook Underpass he took the slip road off the A3 onto the A243 to Leatherhead and Dorking. He glanced in his mirror and a black Porsche Cayenne took the same exit, its understated lines concealing its powerful V6 turbo engine. Nice car, he thought.

His mind wandered back to Emma and her suggestion. For a moment he had been tempted to let her meet Sahin, but he had quickly dropped the idea. It was touching that she had offered, but it was out of the question. It was something he had to sort out for himself.

Joining the M25, he touched the accelerator and his BMW responded effortlessly, surging past the trucks and slower cars in the two inside lanes and into the fast lane. The black clouds that had been threatening finally burst, and in seconds the motorway was awash from the downpour. Spray from the car ahead was thrown onto his windscreen and the wipers struggled to keep up. He slowed right down, checked his rear-view mirror and noticed a black Porsche Cayenne. Was it the one he had seen before? It was hard to tell in this deluge, but when he looked again it was gone.

The cloudburst had turned into a steady drizzle as he neared the turn off for the M23 to Gatwick. He checked his rearview mirror again and there it was—the Porsche Cayenne. Was he being followed? He tried to stay calm. You're getting paranoid he thought. Plenty of people could be driving to Gatwick Airport in a Porsche Cayenne. They were expensive, but not that uncommon in this part of England.

He slowed to fifty and it was still there. He accelerated to eighty and it followed. He dropped back to seventy and it was still behind him. No, he wasn't being paranoid. His heart was beating faster. He decided to try to drop the tail. Spotting a gap in the traffic ahead, he accelerated, crossed the middle lane and forged into the fast lane. In four seconds the BMW surged effortlessly to 100 m.p.h. He glanced back. The Porsche had cut up a blue saloon in the middle lane in an effort to catch him. A red Ford ahead of him in the fast lane was probably doing the regulation seventy but Matt came up on it so fast it seemed to be stationary. He swerved into the middle lane to pass the Ford, then pulled back out into the fast lane. The startled Ford driver pulled into the middle lane, blocking the Porsche as it tried to follow Matt. It looked as if the Porsche would rear-end the Ford, but the driver of the Porsche braked hard and, with tyres squealing in protest, wrenched the steering wheel over to pass the Ford.

Up ahead, a block of slow-moving traffic had filled all three lanes. Matt could see no way through. He checked the mirror again. The Porsche was racing up behind him. Suddenly it swerved into the middle lane. The driver was trying to overtake him on the inside. Matt had nowhere to go. The Porsche swung violently towards him and Matt reacted instinctively, pulling the wheel to the right. His front wheel hit the central barrier at ninety and the BMW spun round, facing the oncoming traffic as it careered across the motorway. The steady hum of traffic was shattered by the sound of screeching tyres and tearing metal. Cars and trucks slammed violently into each other, and then, just for a moment, there was a deathly silence.

Matt's car spun across the lanes, hitting glancing blows on two following cars. It crossed the hard shoulder, ploughed through a hedge and into a field, rolled over, and came to rest upside down. The only sound was steam hissing from the engine.

He must have passed out. When he came to he tried to move his arms, but he felt nothing. He tried to move his legs, but he couldn't. He passed out again. The high-pitched whine of a powerful saw cutting though metal penetrated his brain and slowly the mist in his head cleared. Firemen in their orange protective gear and yellow helmets cut him free. Ambulance men gently lifted him onto a stretcher with words of comfort and he drifted into darkness again.

CHAPTER FORTY EIGHT

Matt lay motionless in a hospital bed. One eye was swollen and shut. Wires taped to parts of his body disappeared into the equipment that surrounded him. He tried to open his eyes, but could only see out of one. He groaned and closed his one good eye.

A nurse sat watching him. 'Hello,' she said. 'It's good to have you back with us.' He tried to sit up, winced and sank back on the pillows. 'You're doing well, Mr. Riley,' she said, tucking in a covering sheet and plumping up the pillow. 'Are you Irish?' He smiled weakly and shook his head. 'I'm Mary. Don't bother yourself now. I'll get the doctor to come by and see you shortly.' She checked his vital information and filled in a chart at the bottom of the bed. 'I'll be back in no time at all,' she said as she bustled out of the room.

Matt lay there, wondering where he was. What had happened? It hurt to even think about it. He heard footsteps and the door opening. He opened one eye and saw a man in a white coat. Was he the doctor? He looked so young. Matt saw that he was smiling. He took that as a good sign.

'You've had a rough time, but you've been very lucky.'

Matt managed a sickly grin. 'You think this is lucky?' he choked.

'How are you feeling?'

'Like I've been under a steamroller,' he whispered.

'Yes, I'm not surprised.' he said sympathetically.' Can you remember what happened?'

Matt searched his mind. It was a blank space. He felt frightened.

'No. No, I can't.'

'You've been in a car accident. Do you remember anything about it?'

'I remember leaving home.'

'Where were you going?'

Matt hesitated, his eyebrows knitted as he thought about it. 'Gatwick,' and then more confidently, 'Gatwick Airport.'

'You don't remember anything about the accident?'

'No.'

The doctor smiled reassuringly. 'Don't worry. Temporary amnesia is very common.'

But Matt did worry. What had he done? Had he caused an accident? A terrible thought clouded his mind. Had he killed anyone?

He leaned forward, feeling nauseous, anxiously looking for a bowl. 'I think I'm going to be sick,' he muttered. The nurse hurried forward with a receptacle and he vomited. 'I'm sorry,' he said, as she wiped his mouth with a towel.

'Don't worry,' said the doctor, 'morphine often has that affect. How does your chest feel?'

'It hurts.'

'Yes, it would. You have a small pneumothorax, but it should resolve itself in time. Ribs badly bruised but not broken. And we are keeping a close eye on your abdomen.' He laughed when he saw Matt's wrinkled brow. 'Don't worry; there are no signs of any serious organ damage.'

'What about my eye? I can only see out of one eye.'

'Yes, that's interesting. It's a hyphaema.'

Matt looked alarmed. 'A what?'

The doctor smiled at him. 'It's alright. It's a bleed in the front of your eye. You probably had a hand up in front of your face when the air bag went off.'

'Will I get my sight back?' he asked.

'Of course. Don't look so worried,' said the doctor. 'If you keep still in bed for a few days it should settle.'

'But when will I be able to leave?'

'I don't want you to rush it. You've got off very lightly but you're going to need a lot of rest.' Matt slumped back on the pillows. The doctor gave him a pat on the shoulder. 'With any luck we'll have you on your way in a couple of weeks.'

'A couple of weeks!'

'Yes. You need rest. Now, try drinking a little water and we may be able to take the drip out later. You probably won't feel like eating for a day or two though.'

Matt lay back on the pillows, defeated by the pain, and dropped off to sleep.

He woke with a start a few hours later when the nurse breezed in. 'Well, the police are here to see you. The doctor said they can only stay for a few minutes.'

Matt looked up at her and blinked rapidly. 'What time is it?'

'Two in the afternoon.'

Matt looked around the room. 'When did I get here?'

'You came in here this time yesterday.'

She stepped aside and a uniformed police officer took the seat next to the bed. He was a big man, about his own age, with a warm, friendly smile. 'How are you, Mr. Riley?'

'Been better.'

He nodded. 'I can see that. I'm Constable Baker. Do you mind if I ask you a few questions about the accident?'

'No, go ahead.'

'We are investigating the traffic accident you were involved in. Can you tell me what happened?'

'I was on my way to Gatwick.'

'You were the driver of a silver BMW 325?'

'Yes.'

'What do you remember about the accident?'

Matt closed his eye, trying to concentrate, then shook his head. 'Sorry, I can't seem to remember anything.' He paused, struggling to sit up. 'What happened? Did I cause the accident? Did I kill anyone? Is that why you are here?'

The policeman rested a hand on Matt's shoulder. 'It's alright, sir. We are just making enquiries. Witnesses say that a black Porsche Cayenne seemed to lose control and hit you. Do you remember that?'

Matt thought about it. 'No.'

'It appears that you were in the outside lane and the Porsche was on the inside. He swerved to the right and hit you a glancing blow. You swerved to the right, hit the central barrier, took glancing blows from two other cars then spun off the motorway. Does that bring anything back?'

'No, nothing. Is the Porsche driver okay?'

The officer pursed his lips. 'We have not been able to trace the Porsche driver or the vehicle.'

'Oh?'

'Looks like a hit and run sir. He caused the accident and fled the scene. Could have been on the phone, loss of concentration, alcohol... we don't know. Naturally we are very anxious to trace the driver.'

The nurse came back in and shook her head at the officer, firmly suggesting that enough was enough. 'All right, sir,' he said, 'we won't trouble you anymore. You don't need to worry. It was not your fault. But if you remember anything at all, anything, you will give me a call, won't you?' he said, handing over a card.

The nurse plumped up his pillows and Matt lay back in his bed, unsettled. However hard he tried he could not remember what happened. Had it been an accident? An uneasy feeling gnawed in the pit of his stomach. He reached over to the bedside table, took a sip of water and breathed in deeply. Had someone tried to run him off the road? Had Tan seen through his cover? Had Sahin found out how close he was to exposing him? But the police thought it was an accident. Perhaps he was getting carried away. He thought about it and decided not to tell anyone his suspicions. Not even James.

He looked out of the window. There was a wonderful show of daffodils and a cherry tree was in blossom. A gardener was weeding a flower bed, then covering it with mulch from a wheelbarrow. Everything outside seemed perfectly normal.

Emma called him that evening. 'Matt, are you alright? I heard rumours at the club and then I saw it on Twitter. Is it true? Are you okay?'

He told her what the police had said about the accident. 'Anyway, it's not serious and the doctor says I should be out soon.'

'Thank God for that! Oh, Matt, I'm sorry. How awful. I want to come now but I'm on my way to Athens for the match. I'll come and see you as soon as I get back.'

He thought about Callum and knew he should call Susie, but didn't feel up for it. He could guess what she would say. She might even try to prevent him from seeing Callum. But if it was on social media he had to call her. When he did call he made light of the accident and she promised to come as soon as he was allowed visitors.

Tania called. She had heard about the accident from Emma. She was obviously upset and seemed genuinely concerned. After he had reassured her that he was not badly hurt she asked if he was any closer to finding out who killed Tony. He had phoned her several times since the dossier had been stolen two months ago, but had been reticent to reveal too much. He had simply assured her that he was going to get the killer. She had wanted to come to the hospital but he had discouraged her. He didn't want to be in a situation where he might appear to be evasive or have to tell her more than he wanted. He didn't know who else she talked to. She was dissuaded but next day a huge bunch of spring flowers arrived from her.

CHAPTER FORTY NINE

Matt was beginning to feel better, but he felt stabbing pains as he reached for the TV remote. The stirring music of Handel's *Zadok the Priest* heralded the beginning of the Champions League TV coverage. Images of Heineken bottles disappeared from the screen, and cameras panned in on the players lining up on the pitch. The duty nurse came in to check on Matt, but he waved her away. FC Olympic started brightly, drawing two good saves from the City keeper. If anything, it looked as if City was the team trying not to win. They appeared to be happy to contain Olympic and their attacking ambitions were limited to a couple of long shots that sailed high over the bar. At half time the score was still 0-0. Olympic had won 2-1 in London, scoring two crucial away goals. City had to win by two clear goals to go through.

Nothing Matt had seen yet suggested that Olympic were a team that wanted to lose. But five minutes after the break a controversial referee's decision saw the Greek team down to ten men. A key midfield player was sent off for a high boot in his opponent's face. Matt watched the replays intently. It looked as if the Olympic player was trying to bring the ball down with his foot fairly and the City man ran into him. The referee had no doubt in his mind. He reached in his pocket and pulled out a straight red. With Olympic down to ten men the balance swung in City's favour. They surged forward with attack after attack, but found it hard to break down a packed Olympic defence.

And then, with only ten minutes to go, everything changed. Under pressure from repeated City attacks the Olympic centre-back made a weak back pass that failed to reach his goalkeeper. City's athletic Italian, Fabio Plattorini, dashed in, controlled the ball, turned, dummied the keeper, and slotted it into the net. 1-0. The ecstatic City players raced to Fabio to join a group hug. The aggregate score was 2-2, but if it stayed as it was, Olympic would go through on the away goals rule.

With only five minutes left John Taylor burst through on goal. A

Greek defender lunged to make a last-minute tackle and Taylor was left sprawling, and appealing for a penalty. The referee did not hesitate. The Olympic players rushed to surround him, protesting angrily. He waved them away, collected the ball and put it on the spot. The crowd was in uproar. Flares were set off around the stadium and thrown onto the pitch.

The TV commentator raised a concern that the game might have to be abandoned. The replay of the incident was shown several times from different angles, and the studio team gave their verdicts. The question was, did the Olympic defender get enough of his foot on the ball before bringing down Taylor in the tackle? It was an appeal that most referees would have waved away. But the decision stood. Order was finally restored and John Taylor stepped up to take the kick. The whistling from the Greek crowd was deafening as Taylor ran forward and then, decisively, slotted the ball in the right hand corner of the goal. 2-0! He turned, ecstatic, punching the air with his fist, before he was buried under an avalanche of his team mates. City kept possession to see out the last four minutes, and they were through to the final.

Matt muted the sound on the television and called Masterson. He picked up after three rings.

'Well, you got your result,' said Matt.

'Riley? Yes, I even watched it, which is unusual for me. I've got to hand it to you. I had my doubts, but you really delivered.'

'You made a killing.'

'Yes, we got a million on at 22-1.'

'I'm glad, because I'm going to have to end our relationship there.'

'Oh, why is that?'

'I can't say anymore now, but I think you would be wise to avoid further contact with that source.'

Masterson was silent for a while. 'Yes, I understand. Thank you.'

'I want to thank you too.'

'It's okay. We're all square. But Riley...'

'Yes.'

'You'll be getting a bonus in the final settlement.'

On Thursday the doctor seemed to be pleased with the progress he was making. He was still badly bruised, but the swelling around his face was going down and he could see out of both eyes. It was the day after the match and he had been reading all the reports on his iPad. Nowhere was there any suggestion that the result was suspicious. Most writers agreed that City had pulled off a surprise win and had their share of good luck.

The nurse opened the door and Emma rushed forward. She paused at his bedside. 'Oh Matt! You look terrible,' she exclaimed and kissed him gently on the lips. 'I came straight from the airport. How are you feeling?'

'Not too bad – getting much better actually.'

'Thank goodness. What happened?'

He told her what the police had said.

'And you haven't heard any more from the police?'

'No.'

'That's awful. I hope they get him. How long do you think you will be here?'

'The doctor says I should be able to go home next week.'

'Good, because I have got a surprise for you!'

'Oh? What's that?'

'I've been invited to a party on Sergei's yacht and I want you to come as my partner. It could be just the rest and relaxation break you need.'

'Really? When is it?'

'Ten days' time. In Monaco. Do you think you'll be able to make it?'

'Of course I will. But what will Buzinsky think, you inviting a journalist?'

'It's alright; I asked him, of course. He seems to quite like you anyway since you did that piece on him.'

She leaned over, took his hand looked into his eyes. 'Matt, have you thought any more about Sahin?'

'Hardly! But something will open up. It usually does.'

'Well, you know I'll help if I can.'

He squeezed her hand. 'I know. Thanks'

'I've got to dash: press conference.'

As she left the nurse appeared again. 'My goodness, you're popular today. You've got another visitor.' Susie walked in.

He turned quickly and felt the pain in his chest and winced. The nurse pulled a face. 'Take it easy now. Not too much excitement in one day.'

Susie pushed past the nurse and sat down on the bedside chair.

'Who was that I saw leaving as I came in?'

Matt's eyelids flickered. 'Oh, that, that was Emma. You know, she was Tony's PA. She's been helping me.'

'Hmm,' she muttered, rolling her eyes.

'Thanks for coming, Susie. Where's Callum?'

'He's in school. I didn't want to bring him until I found out how you were.' She inspected him more carefully. 'How do you feel?'

'Actually, it looks a lot worse than it is according to the doctor. He says I could be out next week.'

'What happened?'

'That's just it. I don't remember. The police came to see me, but I wasn't able to tell them anything. According to witnesses a black Porsche Cayenne hit me.'

'What do you mean, hit you?'

'What I said,' he snapped back. 'It hit me.'

'But was it an accident?'

He returned her stare. 'That's what they think. I expect they'll tell me if they know any more.'

'What is going on, Matt? You never tell me anything.'

'I was driving to Gatwick: flying to Athens for the City match.'

'What happened? You're hiding something.'

'No, of course I'm not.'

'This is all about your bloody story, isn't it? You knew it was dangerous, but you didn't care. You're so stubborn. You don't think about us.' She took a deep breath and ran her fingers through her auburn hair. 'Alright, you think Tony was murdered, but why couldn't you just hand it over to the police? You couldn't leave it alone, could you? You got yourself fired from one of the best newspaper jobs in the country. Disappear for weeks. What are you after – a Pulitzer Prize? All you care about is yourself and your bloody story. Why can't you just drop it?'

'I'm sorry, Susie. I can't do that. I just can't. I'm so close. I can't let it go now. Just give me a couple of months and then I can spend more time with you both. '

She jumped out of the chair, her chest heaving. 'A couple of months and then it'll be alright! I don't think so!' She strode across the room to the window and stood looking out over the gardens, then spun round, glaring at him. 'I wasn't going to tell you this now, Matt, but I think you should know that I'm seeing somebody else.'

Matt blinked rapidly. 'What?'

'I didn't want to talk about it now, but you... '

'What about Callum?'

'He doesn't know.'

'So who is it?'

But the door had already slammed behind her.

CHAPTER FIFTY

'You look cool in your dinner jacket,' Emma said, as she stood back and appraised Matt in the lobby of their Monaco hotel. 'No signs of damage. How are you feeling?'

He smiled. 'A bit tender but I made it, didn't I?'

The truth was that he was feeling much better. Ten days' rest had worked wonders. He had thought a lot about the accident, hoping that he would remember what happened. He felt sure someone had tried to kill him. It wasn't the first time. Or was he becoming paranoid? There was no evidence that someone had forced him off the road and he had heard nothing more from the police. Unable to trace the car or the driver, they were treating it as an accident. But he wasn't buying that. Now his life depended on finding Tony's killer.

The glass door of the hotel was opened for them and they strolled hand in hand past the casino and down the hill leading to the yacht club. As they turned a corner the view opened up. The harbour was packed with luxury yachts. 'So, which one is Lady Ellana?' asked Matt.

'Over there, the largest one,' said Emma, pointing.

'They all look large to me,' he said.

'Oh, Matt. Over there, docked next to that cruise ship. The white one with all the lights blazing.'

Ten years ago, she had been one of the largest in the world, but since then a flood of petro-dollars had led to an Arab frenzy to own the world's largest yacht.

He stood next to Emma on the dock, gazing up at this huge vessel. The yacht had six decks and, at 138 meters, Lady Ellana was longer than a football pitch. She required a crew of sixty to run the ship and look after the needs of up to fifty guests. Two swimming pools, a massage pool, gym, disco, cinema, hair and manicure salon and dining rooms catered for their every need. Two helipads were available and Buzinsky's own helicopter was always on hand, his pilot in a state of readiness to whisk him away to meetings anywhere at any time of the day or night. The yacht even had its own submarine that allowed the owner and his friends to explore the wonders of the deep.

'Christ, Em, it's amazing.'

'I know. Just wait till you go on board. One of the decks is partitioned and opens out to a ballroom that runs the length of the yacht. Then there's the stern garage. It's where he keeps the four tenders that take guests to and from the shore. There are ski boats, jet skis... oh, and the Ferrari and Range Rovers, of course!'

'You seem to know a lot about it.'

'I helped to organise the party, Matt.'

This was no ordinary yacht, and Buzinsky was no ordinary man. It epitomised the power, wealth, privilege and secrecy that went with being one of the world's wealthiest men. The Russian oligarch was a man who was protected wherever he went. The vessel was built with bullet proof glass and armour plating. It was even reputed to have its own German-built missile defence system.

They passed through a security check at the dockside, walked up the gangway and stepped onto the pale teak deck. The cultured sounds of a string quartet floated on the air and a hostess stepped forward to offer them a slender fluted glass of Dom Perignon. Another followed with a selection of caviar on a silver platter.

'Hmm, I could get used to this,' murmured Matt, as he sipped the champagne.

They leaned on a rail, watching as guests began to arrive: men in white tuxedos and women in long evening gowns. The yacht gleamed in the evening light, her polished white hull reflected in the dappled water. Stainless steel fittings sparkled in the spotlights that lit the decks.

It was a clear, warm, night and small groups gathered on the aft deck. Matt was used to meeting celebrities, but this was definitely A list. They moved from group to group, chatting to some of the world-famous football legends. Emma kept nudging him when they saw big name movie stars and rock musicians. He had to admit he was impressed.

He watched Buzinsky, who was moving freely amongst his guests, and saw him walk over to a beautiful blonde woman in a long black dress. He whispered into her ear in a way that suggested a certain intimacy.

'Who's the woman with Buzinsky?' he asked Emma.

'I've no idea,' she replied with a toss of her head. 'Come on; let me show you the main stateroom.'

The sliding glass doors were open, and they strolled into the master stateroom. A wide circular staircase rose from the centre of the room to the decks above and below. It was entirely made of glass.

'Impressive, isn't it?' said Emma.

An orchestra was playing as Emma led him in to dinner. A magnificent swan ice sculpture dominated the centre of the room, and tables were decorated with exotic flowers. Chefs in white uniform manned individual serving stations. Others shuttled in and out, bringing steaming dishes. Still more were carving roast joints and slicing chateaubriand steak. Waiters flitted from table to table, bringing buckets of champagne and fine wines.

They sat together at a table where Matt spoke to two big-time agents. Emma introduced him to one of the club's sponsors, an online gambling company. All the talk was about a big player that Buzinsky was rumoured to be about to sign. There was speculation about whether the signing would take place on the yacht that night, with Buzinsky producing the player like a rabbit out of a hat. Burak Sahin was the player's agent, but he was nowhere to be seen. It would be a good story, but with agents you never knew. Sometimes talk was all it was. Matt asked questions about the game in Athens, but it seemed that no one suspected anything. Most of them seemed to think that City had a very good chance of winning the final. 'Do you think the party is an early celebration?' one of them joked.

A Russian woman came over to Emma and whispered in her ear. Emma nodded and turned to Matt. 'I'm sorry, Matt, I've been called away. There are one or two problems I've got to help sort out. I'm not sure how long I'll be. Will you be alright?'

He laughed. 'Don't worry. It would be hard not to enjoy myself here.' After a while he excused himself from the table, took a stroll on the deck outside, and found himself leaning on the rail next to a tall young man in white uniform. He introduced himself as the yacht's first officer. He seemed happy to answer Matt's questions and invited Matt to see the bridge. An array of screens ran from one side of the bridge to the other. Matt walked across to the large steering wheel and ran his fingers over the hard, smooth surface of the carved mahogany wheel.

'So, this is where you steer then?'

'No, actually, it isn't,' replied the officer, 'that's mostly for show. We use this,' he said, and to Matt's surprise pointed to a two-inch joystick on a control panel. 'Of course that's just when we're manoeuvring. When we're underway we use the autopilot all the time.' The first officer walked to the side of the bridge. 'And when we are docking we use this.' He ushered Matt out onto a wing that butted out from the bridge. 'From here the captain has a clear view down the side of the ship and all the controls.' He pointed to the steering joystick, the bow and stern thrusters and the engine controls.

Matt shook his head in disbelief. 'It's amazing.'

On his way back down from the bridge a saloon door opened and the elegant woman in the long black dress he had seen with Buzinsky stepped out. She saw Matt, but turned and walked in the other direction. She didn't look back. Matt made his way forward to the door she had come from. Peering through shuttered blinds he saw what appeared to be a board room. Two men sat at a long, polished table. Despite the dim light he had no trouble recognising one of them. It was Burak Sahin.

Matt moved away from the door and went to see if he could find Emma. He went into the main stateroom where a small crowd had gathered to listen to a band playing. He looked around but she was nowhere to be seen. The gig was almost at an end and Matt drifted back outside, this time on the other side of the yacht, and climbed the steps to the deck above.

Passing a dimly lit lounge he peered through a port hole. At first he thought there was no one in the room. And then he saw her again: the blonde girl in the black dress. She sat alone in a corner, her long dress clinging to her slim body, exposing only her pale arms. Her fine blonde hair was cut short and sculpted, accentuating her elegant curved neck and sparkling drop earrings. He opened the door and stepped into what must be the library. The woman looked up and her piercing blue eyes met his for a moment. He walked across the empty saloon.

'May I join you?' he asked.

'If you like,' she said, cocking her head towards the empty chair next to her. As he sat down he breathed in her musky scent.

'Are you waiting for somebody?' he asked.

'Oh no. I'm here alone,' she said in a heavy Russian accent. 'And you?'

'I was invited by a friend,' he said, looking around as if he might see Emma. 'She's helping with the party.' He paused. 'My name's Matt by the way,' he said, leaning across and offering his hand. Like a pedigree cat, she watched his every movement, then slowly extended her slender bare arm. He shook her hand. It was soft and smooth. The nail varnish on her perfectly manicured fingers was a deep red and she wore no rings.

'Anna Malatova,' she said. 'So, Matt, tell me, are you enjoying yourself?'

'Well, yes, it's a wonderful party, but it's not what I'm used to.'

'Oh, and what are you used to?' she said.

'Something a little less luxurious than this. Normally the closest I get to people like these is an interview in a hotel.'

'An interview?'

'Yes, I'm a journalist.'

She looked surprised. 'I didn't know the press were here?'

'No, of course they're not. Emma works for London City Football Club. She invited me as her partner.'

'Ahh, I see.' She looked into his eyes. 'So, which paper do you work for?'

'I was at the *Chronicle*. I'm freelance now.'

'And what do you write about?'

'Corruption.'

She sat up and stretched her lithe body, looking interested for the first time. 'So, who do you investigate, Matt?'

He shrugged. 'Oh, just the usual: people who are misbehaving. You know, drugs, sex, gambling, and corruption in high places – that sort of thing.' He took a sip of the champagne that the waiter had brought. 'What about you?'

'I'm in the hospitality business.'

He looked surprised. 'What? You mean organising events like this?'

'No,' she said, giggling. She leaned in and whispered, 'I work for an escort agency.'

She sat back to watch his reaction.

'Ahhh, I see,' said Matt. 'Perhaps we sometimes meet the same people?'

She laughed again – a soft tinkling sound that put him at ease. 'Yes, quite possibly.'

He studied her more carefully – her fashionable dress, sparkling jewellery, expensive shoes. 'Well, you're obviously very good at it.'

She laughed again, louder now, a coquettish laugh but still friendly. She took a long sip of wine and stretched effortlessly.

'I like you, Matt.' She paused, crossed her long legs as she studied him.

'Tell me about your work,' said Matt. 'You must meet interesting people.'

'Nyet.' She stiffened and the smile dropped from her face. 'I'm breaking all the rules already.'

Matt held up both hands in apology.

She began to relax again. 'I want to know more about you.'

It appeared that she knew Sahin. He had just seen her come out of the saloon he was in, and there were only two men in the room. Perhaps Sahain was a client? As a high class escort she was unlikely to be his friend. But she might know a lot about Sahin. He felt the thrill of the chase.

'Well,' he said, 'some journalists dig the dirt, but I don't. I like to find out what the big shots have been covering up.'

'Big shots? Who do you mean?'

'Men who have pushed their way to the top without caring who they trample on.'

'Like who?'

His mind flashed back to the football club owner who had ruined his father. But he didn't talk about that to anyone. 'Have you heard of Khun Sumiri?'

'Isn't he the owner of an English football club?'

'Well, he was. He's a wealthy Asian who took over the club with money he had obtained fraudulently. He made promises of loans to the club, then began siphoning the club's money back to his own companies. He nearly bankrupted them. He was extradited to his own country, tried, found guilty and jailed. Now the fans have got their club back.'

'And you exposed him?'

'Yes. I worked on that story for a year.'

'Isn't it dangerous?'

'Not usually.'

'But why do you do it? Is it for the money?'

He gave her a wry smile. 'No, that's not what motivates me. I do it because I want to expose the bad guys.'

She curled up in her chair in a feline gesture that expressed beauty, charm and grace. Like a Siamese cat, she was sleek and playful. Matt was mesmerised. At last he broke the silence. 'So, tell me about you.'

She smiled wryly. 'Matt, you don't really want to know, do you?'

The truth was, he did. He was fascinated by her – her feline face, high cheekbones, vivid blue eyes, perfect blonde hair and her soft, slim body hidden tantalisingly beneath the clinging black dress. There was an aura about Anna.

He spoke quietly. 'Oh, but I do.'

'You know, Matt,' she said, twirling the champagne flute in her hands, 'a girl like me does not just go with any man, only a man who can pay the very high prices the agency charge.' She watched him carefully. 'My services are reserved for "special clients".'

He flushed with embarrassment, thinking that she had assumed he was trying to pick her up. He cleared his throat. 'I'm sorry, I meant... umm, I'd just like to know you better.'

'You really want to know about me?'

He nodded and she seemed to be thinking about it for some time. 'Well... I came from a poor farming family in Siberia,' she said finally. 'I was ambitious; I did not want to be like other girls – married to a tractor driver who is drunk on vodka in the day, and raping her at night. I won a competition to go to Moscow to try for a career as a model. I met a recruiter who made it seem so easy. I was young. I was stupid. He took me to Geneva. It seemed wonderful at first, but then I was working as a prostitute in a night club. But the money was good. I sent money back to my mother each month. Told her I was a model. I opened a bank saving account. I wanted to do better for myself. I learned French and I read books. Not love stories. No! Books about history, art, music. Then I was lucky. An escort agency in Geneva, one of the most exclusive, heard about me. My life became better. I was introduced to some of the agency's very special clients. There are just a few, and some I don't see very often, but I have to be available when they ask for me. These men are very rich. I make a lot of money. Soon I was the highest earner in the agency.'

'Well, I can't say I'm surprised, but what are you like as a person?'

She threw back her head and laughed. 'What am I like? Well, Matt, it depends on the client. What they want me to be. I can be Innocent Girl looking into his eyes, pretending to be impressed by his tales of glory and power. Or I can be Femme Fatale, pouncing on men who are insecure, taking charge of the situation, relieving them of responsibility and guilt so they don't have to worry about anything. And then there are others that want me to be Understanding Mother, the woman who listens sympathetically to their stories and gives them her advice.'

He wondered why she was being so frank. Perhaps she liked him. Perhaps it was because he was different. 'They tell you everything?' he said.

'Of course. Believe me, they all have their insecurities. I'm their therapist and their confessor.'

'You must know a lot of secrets then?' he teased.

Her eyes narrowed and the faintest, tantalising smile, spread across her face.

'Matt, these are things I can't tell you.'

'Of course. I'm sorry.'

There was an awkward silence.

'What are your dreams?' said Matt, putting down his glass.

'What do you mean?'

'Well, it's a glamourous life, but you can't live it forever,' he said softly.

'No. Every girl knows that.'

'So, what will you do?'

She looked at him for a while, deciding how she would reply. She sighed. 'I want to make enough money to go back to Russia. Have my own fashion business. Design and manufacture women's clothes.'

'Why don't you?'

'It's not so easy for me. They wouldn't just let me walk away.'

'Who?'

'Clients.'

'But you'd like to?'

She surprised him, smiling like a demure young girl, not the beautiful, sophisticated woman she was. 'Don't laugh, Matt. I'd like to be married and have children and grandchildren.' She bit her lip. 'But it's just a dream.'

A couple walked into the room, appearing to be slightly drunk. The man stared at Anna, then quickly looked away.

'Shall we go out on deck and get some fresh air?' Matt suggested. She nodded. The outside deck on the upper level was deserted. They leaned on the rail, gazing at the casino and the skyline that towered above the harbour. Although it was two in the morning, it was a blaze of lights. Matt felt the familiar thrill of taking risks that had cracked stories in the past.

'Do you know Burak Sahin?'

She looked up, surprised. 'Yes.'

'Is he a friend?'

'No. Why do you ask?'

'Would you protect him?'

'From what?'

'From me.'

'Ahhh,' she said, her raised eyebrows signaling a flash of understanding. 'I think perhaps we might have something to trade.'

CHAPTER FIFTY ONE

The British Airways Airbus 320 climbed to its cruising height on the short flight back to London. Matt and Emma accepted a glass of champagne from the flight attendant in business class. Emma leaned over and held his hand. 'Did you enjoy it?'

'The party or back at the hotel afterwards?' She slapped his wrist. 'Matt!'

'Both, actually,' he said. 'It was lovely. Thank you for inviting me.'

'Who was the tall blonde girl I saw you with?'

'Which one was that?'

'Matt! You know who I mean. The girl in the black dress. You seemed to spend ages with her.'

'I didn't know you were watching that closely. Not jealous, are we?' he said, nudging her shoulder.

'Of course not.' She paused, 'Matt, I'm sorry I was called away from the party last night.'

'Yes, it's okay.'

'Well, you know I promised to give you the story?'

Matt turned to stare at her.

'I was going to tell you last night, but you got in late and then... you know...'

'Well?'

'It's Mayfield. He is going to be fired in the next few days.'

Matt twisted in his seat to look her in the eye. 'What?'

'Our investigation is complete now. It was what you said. He was getting kickbacks from agents for putting transfer business their way.' Matt nodded. 'There was some debate about whether he would just be forced to resign to keep it quiet, but Sergei was so livid he is going to fire him. It will probably lead to a prosecution. He's talking to our lawyers now and the police will be called in soon.'

Matt grinned. 'We got the bastard then. Is it exclusive?'

'Yes, I promised you.'

‘Can I check some details?’

‘Sure,’ she said. He pulled out his pad and began making notes. When they had finished he gave her a hug. ‘Thanks, Em.’

‘You deserve it, Matt. We would have known nothing about it if it wasn’t for you.’

After clearing immigration at Heathrow and collecting their bags they checked their phones. Emma looked up. ‘Sorry, Matt, I’ve got to dash.’ She gave him a peck on the cheek and ran for a taxi.

Matt stood there, a nagging worm of doubt turning in his mind. Mayfield had the perfect motive. Matt screwed up his face. No. Mayfield wasn’t a killer. He pulled out his phone and called his contact at the *Daily Telegraph*. ‘I’ve got a scoop. I’ll file the story in an hour.’ He walked past the crowd greeting arrivals and sat down in the nearby coffee shop to write his story.

CHAPTER FIFTY TWO

On his way to the Heathrow Express he picked up a text from James that stopped him in his tracks.

URGENT. NEW LEAD. CALL ME.

Two hours after leaving Terminal 5, he sat down with James in a Kensington coffee shop. James tipped two heaped spoonfuls of sugar into his cup and stirred slowly.

'Two spoons?' said Matt. 'What happened to the healthy diet?'

'At my age, I need the energy.'

Matt shook his head. 'So, you've got a new lead?'

James took a sip and put down his cup. 'You remember I said I'd put some feelers out?'

'Yeah.'

'Well, I did. Apparently someone else is after Sahin.'

Matt looked up, surprised. 'Someone else?'

'Yes. I've had a tip off from a friend, a journalist with *Le Monde*. It seems that Sahin is under investigation by a French investigating magistrate – a juge d'instruction they call it.'

'What's the investigation about?'

'Apparently Sahin is involved in a serious corruption case involving a top French football club.'

Matt pushed his cup away and leaned forward, elbows on the table, chin cupped in his hand. 'Tell me more.'

'I think it's going to be big. You know, Matt, I think it would make a lot of sense for you to collaborate with him.'

'A magistrate? In France?'

'Don't let the title put you off. It's not like an English magistrate. A juge d'instruction is a very senior judge. They have far reaching powers. In France they operate under an inquisitorial system. It's not like our adversarial justice system.'

'How is it different?'

'It's very different. Look, I don't want to bog you down with legal detail. It doesn't matter. What does matter is that it's usually only used in serious and complex cases, and there's a much better chance of getting a conviction. The investigating judge has the authority to arrest, detain for long periods, search and summons in the course of his enquiry. By the time a case reaches court there is a greater presumption of guilt than in our system where we assume the accused is innocent until proven guilty.'

Matt hadn't taken his eyes off James.

'You've got information that he almost certainly won't have, like your penetration of the Singapore gambling syndicate.'

James paused, seeing that Matt was looking doubtful.

'Yeah, I suppose so,' said Matt, biting his lip, 'but it doesn't get me any closer to nailing Sahin for Barker's murder, does it?'

'No, probably not. But let's be frank Matt, you've reached a dead end. You have got nothing to connect Sahin to Barker's murder. The police are covering up for someone, so that route is closed. Alright, you've got him on match fixing, but your evidence is inadmissible.'

Matt slumped back in his chair.

'Cheer up, old chap. Go and see Pierre at *Le Monde* and find out what this investigation is about. Collaborating with the juge d'instruction is probably your best chance of bringing Sahin to justice. It may not be murder, but the charges would still be very serious. He'd go away for a long time. And you never know what might come out of the woodwork.'

Matt's chin moved up and down slightly as he thought about it. 'Yeah, I suppose you're right.'

'Shall I call him now?'

'Yes.'

Ten minutes later Matt had arranged to meet Pierre in Paris the following day.

CHAPTER FIFTY THREE

They sat in the spring sunshine, drinking coffee at a café just off the Avenue des Champs-Élysées. Parisians had left their winter coats behind. Girls walked by with short skirts and light jackets. Matt stretched out his arms and took a long, deep breath. 'Ah, April in Paris!'

Pierre smiled. 'Yes, of course. It is a good time to be here. Now tell me, what is your interest in Burak Sahin?'

Matt explained how Tony Barker was murdered, how Sahin's match fixing was connected to Tan's gambling syndicate in Singapore and why he had not been running the story. When he had finished he sat back. 'How did you get your story?'

Pierre ran his hands through the thick mop of black hair that flopped over his eyes. 'I heard about the juge d'instruction's enquiry from contacts. At first it related to one French football club. It came to light because a large amount of taxpayers' money was being put in to support the club, and there were allegations of serious fraud. Sahin had persuaded the owner that he could bring him success on the pitch and he began to fix matches for him. Most of the time it worked very well. They created two sets of books – a legitimate account that was submitted to the tax authorities, and a secret account. The secret account was to provide the money they needed to bribe players and officials – big money! What they were doing was manipulating the transfer fees paid for players. Sahin was the agent responsible for many of the transfers at the club, buying and selling, so he was in a unique position to make the financial arrangements. If they publicly stated that a player had cost ten million euros, but the real cost was much less, say seven million, they would take three million off the books. Some of it went into a secret slush fund that was used to fix matches.'

Matt smiled. 'Sounds familiar, but will it stand up in court?'

'Yes, absolutely. M. Quentel is the juge d'instruction. He has the power to trace bank accounts and access phone records. He can tap phones, seize computers and access email records. His job is to gather all the evidence and make a recommendation to the trial judge. He has to be very sure they can get a conviction.'

Matt nodded with satisfaction. 'Is there any evidence of Sahin being connected to violent crime?'

'No, I don't think so.'

Matt poured some more coffee. 'Pierre, you are a long way down the road with the Sahin story. Why don't we work together on it?' He took a sip and put down his cup. 'Perhaps Quentel's investigation will expose what I'm looking for – evidence that Sahin killed Barker.'

Pierre nodded. 'Yes, we can do that. You should go to see Quentel. Tell him what you know.'

It had not been easy to make an appointment with the judge. He was a busy man and had a deep suspicion of journalists, but Matt had told him enough to capture his interest and a week later he sat opposite Monsieur Quentel in his office. He was a man of around sixty, short and stocky with stiff grey hair that was cropped short. He looked as if he had been a front row rugby player and his large frame filled the chair, but his dark blue suit and crisp white shirt reflected the formality of his position. Papers were spread over the polished mahogany meeting room table. He pushed back his chair and stepped forward to greet Matt, who made a clumsy attempt to introduce himself in French.

'Don't worry, Mr. Riley,' he said, extending his hand and smiling. 'We can conduct the meeting in English.' Matt – who was, unusually for him, wearing a suit and tie – breathed a sigh of relief and sat down facing the judge across the table. M. Quentel shuffled his papers together, put them to one side, and poured coffee from a cafetière that had been set on a tray with china cups. 'Sugar and milk?' he asked.

'No, just black, please.'

'Of course,' he said, handing the cup to Matt and stretching back in his chair, studying his visitor with curiosity. 'So, you're a journalist, aren't you? Now tell me, why are you here?'

'I think you might be interested in information I have about Burak Sahin.' The judge nodded politely. 'Perhaps. What can you tell me?'

'I've been conducting an investigation into Sahin myself. Perhaps there are ways we can work together?'

The judge scowled. 'That's out of the question,' he snapped, then paused and took another look at his visitor. 'So, what is your interest in Sahin?'

Matt had thought about how much he would say, but finally decided to tell the whole story. He explained the circumstances of Barker's death and his own conviction that he was murdered by Sahin because he was about to uncover a match fixing scandal.

Quentel raised his bushy eyebrows in surprise. 'How can you be sure he was murdered?'

Matt told him about the shard of glass from the missing whisky tumbler, how he had matched it, and the tissue sample analysis which had proved that the glass entered Barker's heel at the time of his death.

'Why didn't you inform the police?'

'I did. I gave them the shard of glass, but then the evidence conveniently went missing.'

'Ahhh, I see.' Quentel nodded and pressed the tips of his fingers together and smiled, as if it was a story he had heard before.

Matt went on to tell him about Sahin's involvement with Henry Tan's illegal gambling syndicate. 'So you see, Sahin was fixing games all over Europe. He was getting paid by the syndicate and betting large sums on the games he had fixed.'

The judge, who had listened without interrupting, finally said, 'You have evidence of this?'

'No. Not written evidence. If I had, I would have run the story.'

The judge stared at Matt, his head cocked on one side, as if he was wondering how seriously he should take this intense English journalist. 'You realise that I have no jurisdiction over any crime that may have been committed in England?'

'Of course.'

Quentel put his elbows on the table and pressed his fingers together. 'Mr. Riley, what you have told me is interesting, but you cannot show me any evidence.'

Matt returned his stare. 'No, Monsieur Quentel, but I understand that you have the power to search bank records, phones and computers?'

The judge nodded.

'I can tell you where to look.'

CHAPTER FIFTY FOUR

Matt decided to walk down Park Lane to the Dorchester. Approaching the hotel, he glanced back, then stepped into a doorway and watched who walked past. When he was sure he was not being followed he took up a position near the hotel entrance where he could observe guests arriving. The black cab pulled up outside at four in the afternoon: precisely the time that Anna had asked him to come. He watched as she walked into the hotel, but she was not being followed.

It had taken persistence. He had called her twice since their meeting on Buzinsky's yacht two weeks ago. She had been friendly, but not friendly enough to answer any questions or meet him again. Then she had suddenly changed her mind and invited him to the Dorchester.

He strolled into the opulent setting of the Dorchester's Promenade where afternoon tea was being served. Anna had chosen a quiet table away from the area where well dressed women were taking a break from shopping. She stood to greet him, offering a pale cheek to kiss. He inhaled her perfume.

'Mmmm–reminds me of lilac.'

Her blue eyes sparkled. 'That's nice, Matt. I'm never fully dressed without perfume!'

For a while they drank tea, ate cake, and talked about London and how unusually warm it was for April. She told him that she often came to London for a client. He wondered why she had changed her mind and agreed to see him now.

'Matt,' she said, 'I was wondering... when we met on the Lady Ellana you told me you were investigating a story.'

'Yes.'

'What were you investigating?'

He paused and put down his cup. 'The murder of Tony Barker.'

She did not blink an eyelid and her face gave nothing away.

'Why are you asking?' he said.

She looked around the room. There was nobody nearby. She leaned forward, her face deadly serious now. 'Matt, you have to appreciate that girls like me are in a very difficult position.'

'I understand that.'

'I don't think you do.'

There was a long silence. Matt sat quite still, eyes fixed on Anna, and waited. She looked around again before continuing. 'We hear and see things we shouldn't.' He nodded, encouraging her to continue. 'Our profession is based on secrecy.' She studied Matt for some time and he was afraid that she would not go on.

'Of course,' he whispered.

'Let me ask you a question, Matt. Let's say there was a girl. A girl who had a secret: a secret that could put her life at risk. But she had a reason why she wanted to expose the truth. How could a girl like that be protected? I mean, be really safe?'

Matt felt a shiver of excitement run down his spine. He swallowed and cleared his throat.

'I can help with that.'

'Are you sure?'

'It can be arranged.'

He poured more tea for them both. 'Tell me about Sahin.'

'Sahin? Burak Sahin is a shit. Always full of himself and his multi-million dollar deals. He would sell his own grandmother to the Arabs if the price was right.'

'You know him well, then?'

'Buzinsky introduced me to him. He asked me to do what Sahin wanted. He didn't want to have sex with me – I think he has other interests – but he sometimes asked me to find girls who would sleep with referees when there was an important match. I arranged the girls and he bought them flights to London or Athens or Rome or whichever city the game was in.'

'Do you have dates and names?'

'Yes, I keep a diary.'

'Can you give me the details?'

She sighed and slumped back in her chair, her hand trembling slightly as she picked up a glass of water. She took a sip and placed the glass back on the table.

'No', she said softly. 'First you tell me how I can keep my friend safe.'

Two hours later Matt met James in the Devonshire. He came back from the bar with two pints of London Pride.

He looked around. The pub was busy. 'Let's go out to the beer garden,' he said.

James had settled in a high-backed upholstered chair. 'Do we have to?'

'Come on, James. There's nobody out there and it's a warm spring day.'

They sat at a wooden table outside sipping their beer. Matt put down his glass. 'I have a new source.'

James looked up in surprise. 'Well?'

'I think she has a secret she wants to tell me, a secret that could put her life at risk.'

'Why does she want to do that?'

'She wouldn't say.'

'Why wouldn't she go to the police?'

'For a lot of reasons. She trusts me, James.'

'So, what do you think it's about?'

'I think she knows that Sahin killed Tony, but she's too frightened to tell me.'

'How does she know? Does she have any evidence?'

'I don't know, James. She won't tell me. She wants protection. She's really frightened. She won't say anything unless she is guaranteed witness protection. That's why I wanted to talk to you. You know about that, don't you? How does it work?'

'Yes, I know a bit,' said James, 'I had to protect informants when I was in Northern Ireland. It's not simple.' He took a long drink and put his pint back on the table. 'Now, assuming that she is a witness that could convict a murderer, there are only two ways she could be protected. The first is witness anonymity. No one will know who the witness is. The statement will use a false name. It could be male or female – Lesley Smith for example. The statement the defence see will be heavily redacted to remove anything that could give a clue to the witness's identity. The defence hate it! The witness will be present at the trial through a video link, and have to answer questions from the prosecution and defence, but only the judge will be able to see her face.'

'Won't the defendant recognise her voice?' said Matt.

'No. Voices are modulated. You know, like a computer voice. You can't even tell if it's male or female.'

That won't work, thought Matt. Once Sahin hears the evidence, if it is Sahin, he is bound to guess who the witness is. With his money and contacts she could never be safe.

'Okay. And what's the second option?' said Matt.

'The witness protection program. This is really serious stuff, Matt. From the moment she enters the program she will have no more contact with anyone she knows. And that includes you. She will be given a new look, a new identity, a new passport and a new life in a new country. She will simply disappear.'

As soon as James left, Matt called Anna with the news he thought she wanted to hear, but her mood had changed. She seemed reluctant to talk about it.

'I don't know, Matt. Let me think about it,' was all she said.

CHAPTER FIFTY FIVE

Arriving home later that evening, Matt picked up a stack of letters. He shuffled through the pile of junk mail, pausing only when he recognised Susie's neat handwriting. He tore the envelope open.

Dear Matt,

I've been doing a lot of thinking since I saw you in hospital. Nothing has changed, has it? As I said then, I have met someone else. I am very fond of him and I know he cares a great deal for me. I know you didn't want to believe this when I spoke of it before, but it's true. We have been seeing each other for a while now. Gerard is single, and he wants to get married and have children. He has asked me if I would consider getting divorced so we can marry.

Matt, I'm sorry it has come to this. I warned you but you didn't listen. You are selfish and your family comes second. The truth is, you're married to your job. Gerard is not in a rush for us to be married, but he wants to know if we have a future. I hope you will understand that this is what I want. I have spoken to a solicitor and I hope we can soon have an amicable discussion about the plans for a divorce.

I know you have been seeing more of Callum lately, and you want to be a good father, so I hope we will be able to agree access arrangements that work for us all.

With love,

Susie

Matt screwed up the letter and hurled it into a waste bin. He went to the cabinet and took out a bottle of brandy. His hand was shaking as he poured it into a large balloon glass. He sat down, swirled the golden liquid around, and raised the glass to his nose. He breathed in deeply, inhaling the fiery fragrance before tipping it back. The warm glow in his chest eased the bitterness in his heart. Callum having another father! The thought was unbearable. Who was this Gerard? What did he look like? How old was he? Probably some bearded, leftie, *Guardian* reader she had met in the orchestra. He poured himself another slug, slumped into a chair and fell asleep.

CHAPTER FIFTY SIX

Through May and June, Matt and Pierre pursued the story relentlessly. They spoke on the phone weekly, sometimes daily, following leads that would give them more insights. Pierre's contacts and his backing at *Le Monde* kept him informed on the progress of Quentel's investigation. They had kept the story under wraps, confident that no one else would get a whiff of it until they were ready to break the news of Sahin's arrest.

It became clear that Sahin would plead guilty to some charges of fraud in return for exposing the wider European match fixing network. More serious charges of money laundering and corruption would be dropped.

Things were moving much faster than they expected, but Pierre kept the agreement with his contact that they would not break the story before the arrest was made. Finally Matt got the call he was waiting for. 'The arrest will be at 5 a.m. tomorrow.'

The next morning, Matt had a front page splash in the *Daily Telegraph.*

MATCH FIXING NETWORK SMASHED. INTERNATIONAL AGENT ARRESTED IN DAWN RAID

Burak Sahin had been arrested at five in the morning and dragged from his hotel room. It had been a scoop, but nothing in Quentel's investigation had connected Sahin to Barker's murder.

The story was headline news on every TV station and newspaper in Europe and Matt had the inside story. He was in demand for TV interviews and newspaper columns, explaining how match fixing worked and how deep the cancer had penetrated.

At the trial, Sahin's daily revelations shook the world of football as he exposed the European network of corruption. No country emerged unscathed and many famous clubs were caught up in the scandal.

Having just returned from a TV interview in Germany, Matt had flopped out in a chair with a glass of whisky when his phone rang. He guessed it was another TV channel wanting an interview, but to his surprise he heard an unmistakable female Russian accent.

'I've just been watching you on TV.'

'Anna? Anna, are you OK? I've been worried about you. I tried phoning but you never returned my calls.'

She hesitated. 'So your investigation brought down Sahin. Now he is going to jail. Matt... do you think that Sahin killed Barker?'

'Yes, of course.'

'He didn't.'

'What?' Matt felt like a drowning man swept away on a tsunami. 'But I thought that was what you were trying to tell me at the Dorchester – that Sahin killed Barker — but you were too frightened to admit it.'

'You thought what you wanted to think, Matt.'

He paused. 'But how can you be sure it wasn't Sahin?'

'Because I know who did it.'

Matt felt a flush of adrenaline surge through his body. She began to cry. 'Matt, I'm frightened.'

'Where are you?'

She told him. 'Stay where you are. I'll be on the next flight.'

CHAPTER FIFTY SEVEN

They met in the Hotel du Lac. It was a well-appointed period building on the shores of Lake Geneva: small, discreet, tastefully furnished and very expensive. The gravel drive led past well-manicured lawns to the main entrance, where Mercedes and BMWs were parked. Matt had given the taxi driver fifty euros to watch for a tail and drop him at the tradesman's entrance at the back. He stepped into the hotel, then looked back through a window with a view of the drive. There was nobody following. He watched for a few minutes before making his way through corridors that led to the lobby area.

He made straight for the lift. Anna had told him which room she was in. When he knocked, the door opened a crack. She let him in, quickly slammed it shut and put on the chain. She collapsed into a chair, holding her head in her hands. 'I need a drink, Matt. There's champagne in the fridge.' He poured the wine for them both. Her hand was trembling when he gave her the flute.

He sat close to her on the sofa and put his arm round her shoulder. 'What's happened?'

'I'm frightened, Matt.' She took a long drink.

'Why?'

She averted his gaze and looked down at her shoes.

'Tell me about it,' he whispered.

She stood up, walked to the other side of the room, turned and sighed. 'You remember that, when we met on Lady Ellana, I told you that I have a few very special clients?'

'Yes. Yes, I do.'

'Well, one of these men is Sergei Buzinsky.'

She dropped the name like a stone into a pool and the ripples began to spread. So this must be who she came to see in London, he thought. She raised the glass to her lips, draining half the champagne, and came back to sit next to him. 'I was seeing a lot of Sergei. In the bedroom, of course.' Her hollow laugh reverberated around the room.

'He would always take important calls, even when he was in the bedroom. I began to hear conversations that I shouldn't. He was in trouble with Putin. Putin was trying to take back ownership of some of his businesses. Sergei was bribing people in Russia to falsify documents and make false statements in court. Then the Kremlin began to realise what he was doing. Someone was leaking information. I don't know how they found out, but I think he began to suspect it might be me. It was true that I knew a lot of what he had been doing. And he knew it too. I began to get frightened. That's when I took out insurance.'

'Insurance? What do you mean?'

'It was a few months ago. We were in bed, but he took a phone call and went to the bathroom. The door was left open. When I heard what he was talking about I pressed record on my phone.'

She stared past Matt into the bathroom as if she was reliving the moment. Matt waited, hardly daring to breathe. When she turned to look at Matt again something had changed. She was calm. Her hands rested in her lap, and her blue eyes had a glint of cold steel.

'I heard him order Barker's killing.'

'Buzinsky! Oh, sweet Jesus. Buzinsky!'

For a second his brain struggled to come to terms with what he had heard. Then it seemed blindingly obvious. It was never about match fixing and gambling syndicates. Buzinsky wanted to win the Champions League. He knew Sahin could fix matches and paid him to ensure that City would win when he wanted. If Tony had exposed it, the scandal would have been a disaster for the club. Buzinsky would be finished in football and facing criminal charges.

'Why didn't you say anything before?' said Matt. 'Why did you let me go on thinking it was Sahin?'

'I'm sorry, Matt.' She closed her eyes and swallowed. 'I was too frightened. Buzinsky was getting more and more suspicious that I'd leaked secrets to the Russian government. I was sure I was being followed. Then Natasha …' Her words died away. She was twisting her hands together.

'Natasha?' he prompted.

'Natasha,' she repeated, staring into space. 'She's my best friend. She works at the agency.'

'What happened to her?'

'She was beaten up two weeks ago. Her face is badly disfigured. She'll never work again.' Anna swallowed hard and dabbed her eyes. 'It was Sergei. He wanted to know who I was seeing. What I had told her.'

'Good God.'

'He was mad because she told him nothing.' She got up, paced round the room, stopped, and spun round.

'I think he is going to kill me, Matt. The recording is my insurance. If I give it to you, can you keep me safe?'

'Anna, he's going to jail for life.'

'But a man like Buzinsky; with his contacts? He can still come after me.'

'It's alright, Anna. I told you before. If you testify you'll get witness protection. They can make you disappear. You can start a new life.'

'Are you sure, Matt? I'm so frightened. Hold me.'

He took both her hands, lifted her out of the chair and took her in his arms. Her warm body trembled like a wild bird.

CHAPTER FIFTY EIGHT

They sat together at Geneva airport next morning, waiting for the first flight to London to be called. Anna had given him her phone and told him to go. He couldn't do that. At first she had protested when he asked her to come, but then she had slipped away from the hotel with him, bringing just those possessions she had with her. Now she sat on the edge of her seat in the departure lounge, her head swiveling to scrutinise each passenger. Matt was checking his phone when it rang. It was Emma.

'Matt, can I see you?'

'Sorry, Em, I'm not in England right now.'

A loud announcement came over the public address system.

'Where are you? I can hardly hear you.'

'I'm on my way back to London. I can't say anything now.' He looked around, then whispered, 'I've had a breakthrough.'

'What? What did you say, Matt? You're breaking up, I can't hear you.'

'Sorry, Em. I can't talk here.'

'When can I see you?'

'I've got a meeting in the City tonight. If it really is urgent I could see you after that.'

'Okay. Where is your meeting?'

'On Bishopsgate. McKenzie, Scott and Warburton.'

'That's Tony's solicitors.' she said, her tone questioning. 'David Marshall? Why are you going to see him?'

The PA system announced that the last call for their flight. 'I can't tell you now. Sorry, I've got to go, Em,'

'I can meet you in the City after that.'

'Okay, my meeting is at five, so let's say about six. Do you know the All Bar One in Bishopsgate Arcade?'

'Yes. I'll see you there then, Matt. Take care.'

Matt had booked a London chauffeur service he trusted. They had only a short wait at immigration and no checked luggage. As they emerged from the terminal at Heathrow, Matt saw his driver waiting at the kerb with the engine running. He bundled Anna into the back seat and looked around before jumping in beside her. Following Matt's instructions, the driver deviated from the route twice, taking side streets to see if they were being followed. He assured Matt they were not.

When he phoned his sister he asked if she was alone. She responded without questioning him when he told her he was on his way with a friend. If she was surprised to see Anna standing next to Matt on the doorstep she didn't show it. She gave Matt a hug, kissed Anna on both cheeks, took their coats, and ushered them into the lounge. Finally, when they had settled down, and she had brought them tea, she sat back and smiled at Matt, looking him squarely in the eye.

'So, what's this all about then, Matt?'

When he had finished telling her the story she shook her head in disbelief. 'You poor girl. How terrible.' She stood up and walked over to Anna. 'Let me give you a hug.' She turned to Matt, 'Of course I'll look after her.'

'I'm sorry to involve you in this, Jules, but it all happened so quickly. I couldn't think what else to do. It's just for tonight. A day or two at the most, until I can get a safe house organised. But be careful. Don't tell anyone, and she mustn't go out at all.'

'It's alright, Matt. I'm on my own. Tom is away at a conference all week. Don't worry. Off you go to your meeting.'

Matt put Anna's phone in his pocket and walked the short distance to Fulham Broadway. He took the District line train to Notting Hill Gate, then changed to the eastbound Central line, watching to see if anyone had followed him. At St. Paul's he got out of the carriage, but then waited on the platform, pretending to check his phone. As the train was about to leave he jumped back inside. No one else had tried to board again. He emerged two stations later at Liverpool Street, turned right and walked down Bishopsgate, his backpack slung over his shoulder.

It was a hot summer evening and the streets were busy. Office workers had begun to make their way home, pouring into the pubs and spilling over onto the pavement outside. He checked his watch. It was ten minutes to five. He was in good time for his appointment with Tony's lawyer. His mind kept turning over how he was going to get Anna into a safe house, and fast. Absorbed in his thoughts, he hardly noticed the man who came up to him as he approached the plate glass doors of the law firm's prestigious offices.

'Mr. Riley?'

'Yes.' Matt glanced up in time to see a tall eastern European looking man with a shaved head. The stranger pulled a hand out of his pocket and a glint of steel flashed in the late afternoon sunlight. Instinctively Matt turned away, raising his arm and shoulder to protect himself. He heard the knife slice into his backpack and felt a searing pain in his back. As his attacker tried to withdraw the knife, the backpack fell to the ground and Matt smashed his fist into the man's face. He crumpled and Matt hit him hard in the solar plexus. He fell to the ground gasping for breath. In the left field of Matt's vision he became aware of a second man who darted in and picked up his backpack. As he straightened up, Matt thrust his knee into the second attacker's groin. He staggered back, groaning. The street was busy and already a few onlookers had rushed forward to help. The two assailants pushed past them, knocking over a woman, and jumped into a black Porsche Cayenne waiting at the kerbside, its engine running. Matt collapsed on the pavement, watching the Porsche speed away. A dark red patch began to spread on the side of his shirt. Two men bent over him. 'Don't move him,' one of them said. 'Call an ambulance.'

The uniformed security guard inside the firm's office rushed out. He bent over Matt to assess his condition. 'Take this,' Matt wheezed, pulling Anna's phone out of his pocket and thrusting it into the security man's hands. 'Take this to David Marshall.' He screwed up his face as the pain racked his body. He tried to breathe slowly and steadily. 'Tell him...' he groaned... 'tell him to lock it in a safe.'

Five minutes later the ambulance arrived and Matt was lifted onto a stretcher. The vehicle sped off to nearby Saint Bartholomew's hospital, sirens blaring, scattering the rush hour traffic.

Matt was rushed through A & E and into the operating theatre. The next thing he remembered was a blur of lights and figures in green scrubs moving around, speaking in hushed tones. He focused on one of the figures who was peering into his face.

'How are you feeling?'

'I'm fine.'

'You've lost a lot of blood, but no real damage. It's all stitched up now. You'll be out soon.' The surgeon turned on his heels and strode off to his next patient.

The surgeon's words had struck a chord somewhere. "*Stitched up*." Matt kept replaying the attack in his mind. Realisations rolled up one after another and caught him like a succession of blows. The black Porsche Cayenne getaway car outside the solicitor's office today. The black Porsche Cayenne driving to Gatwick. The attack outside the Rutherford's bank in the city.

His heart was pounding as his mind made the connections until he came to the inescapable conclusion. Emma. Only Emma knew where he was going each time. He had a sensation of losing his balance and fell back on the pillows, staring at the ceiling.

Emma! Emma! But perhaps he was still confused from the anesthetic. Perhaps today had just been a mugging outside the solicitor's office. But it couldn't have been. They knew who he was. They had spoken his name. He gripped the metal rail on the side of his bed, his knuckles white and let out a long, low moan. Oh, Emma! He turned over and flinched at the sharp stab of pain. 'You bitch.'

He stared out of the window at the London skyline. They had tried to kill him. Now Anna would be next. He reached for his phone.

'Jules, is everything okay?'

'Yes, fine. Why?'

'Are you sure? No phone calls, no visitors?'

'No, everything's fine. What's the matter?'

He told her what had happened. 'They knew where I would be. They may be watching me. Don't go outside. Keep doors and windows locked. I'm going to get her to a safe house as soon as I can.'

James rushed in. 'I got your text. What happened?' Matt tried to sit up and moaned.

'I've been stabbed.' He winced as the pain shot through his side.

'It's okay. I've been stitched up.' Matt beckoned for James to come closer. He pulled his chair up next to Matt and leaned forward. 'Two thugs tried to kill me. I need to get my source into a safe house.' A nurse walked by, looking at Matt disapprovingly. He waited until she had moved on.

'The thing is, James, now I know who killed Tony.'

James chin jerked up. 'What?'

'Sergei Buzinsky.'

'Good God!' James let out a long low whistle. 'Are you certain?'

'Yes. My source gave me the evidence. She needs to go into witness protection. I need to get her into a safe house.'

'Where is she now?'

He paused. He wasn't sure he should tell anyone that. 'In London.'

'It's not that simple, Matt. The police will want a lot of information before they begin a process like that. If she goes into the witness protection program she will have to disappear.'

'Disappear?'

'Yes. The police will want absolute control over your contact. They will want a signed agreement that she agrees to their terms. She'll be assigned a handler. Only the handler will know where she is and she will have no contact with the outside world, and that includes you, Matt. No phone calls. Nothing! Like I said before, this is really serious stuff. The police are only going to go for it if they are really convinced the case won't collapse.'

Matt cut in. 'What do you mean? With her as a witness, and the evidence she has, they can put Buzinsky away, can't they?'

'I don't know. You are going to have to tell me a lot more if I am going to be able to help you. What is this evidence you have got?'

Matt sucked his lips.

'Sorry, mate, but you are going to have to tell me if you want me to help.'

Matt told him about the phone and what had been recorded.

'Where is the phone now?'

'With a lawyer.'

'That's good. But the problem is you are relying on one piece of evidence. The CPS will be thinking how the defence can attack it. The police will interview your source. Several times probably. What is her background? Is she a credible witness? What is her motive? Then there's the evidence. Can it be supported? Is it beyond any doubt that it is the killer's voice? Can the police prove the killer made the call from his phone records? Can they prove he was in the hotel with her at that time?

'And you are going to be interrogated, Matt. Who are you? Are you telling the whole truth? They'll be doing research on you to corroborate what you tell them.'

'You don't understand, James. They tried to kill me! My source is in immediate danger. I have to get her into a safe house. Now.'

James played with his fingers and thought about it for what seemed like minutes. At last he looked at Matt and nodded. 'Yes, I think I can help. I have a contact that will get me in front of a very senior officer at Scotland Yard. It's time they knew everything. He will go straight to the commissioner.'

'It's urgent, James.'

'I know.' He squeezed Matt's hand as he hurried to leave. 'Don't worry.'

Matt felt reassured. He settled back on the heap of pillows, picked up his phone and saw that he had two missed calls from Emma. He bit the inside of his lip. He didn't want her to know that he had seen through her betrayal. He wasn't sure how, but he thought he might be able to use her. He touched the missed call.

'Matt, what happened? You didn't turn up?'

'I was mugged.'

'Oh my God! Are you alright?'

'Yes, someone tried to stab me. They took my backpack but I'm fine. I'll be out tomorrow.'

'Oh, Matt, that's terrible. Still, I'm glad you're okay.' She hesitated. 'Matt, do you know who did it?'

'Yes.' He paused. 'Look, I'm sorry, Em. I can't tell you now.'

'When can I see you?'

'I'm not sure. I'll call you as soon as I can.'

CHAPTER FIFTY NINE

Later that day, Matt was taken into a private room in the hospital where he met Commander John Allen and Detective Chief Inspector Nigel Watkinson from Scotland Yard. Within hours Anna was moved into a police safe house. When Matt explained how Barker had been murdered, the first question Watkinson asked was why he had not come to the police before. His face muscles stiffened when Matt told them about the police corruption and disappearance of evidence. They listened without interrupting as he told them his suspicions about the murder of Zhang Wei, which remained unsolved, and the death of Ricardo Varta.

At the end of the first debriefing, which had taken all morning, Commander Allen thanked Matt and warned him how serious the situation had become. 'We're going to put plainclothes officers at your disposal round the clock. When you leave here, go somewhere safe. You can't stay in your flat—they know where it is. You're in even more danger now. Check into a hotel and don't tell anyone where you are. You must have minimal contact with the outside world.'

Their first interview with Anna – now in a safe house with her handler – had been satisfactory, but they remained concerned that the case hinged on the evidence of the recording on her phone. They had taken it from the office of David Marshall at McKenzie, Scott and Warburton. The quality was not great. The recording was done in a bedroom when Buzinsky was speaking in the bathroom, and there were extraneous noises. It was in Russian and a linguistic expert had given them a transcript that had been translated.

Commander Allen sent DCI Watkinson to the FBI in Quantico, Virginia, where they had the finest sound equipment in the world, and the recording was cleaned up. He had engaged an audio linguistic expert who would testify that comparisons proved that the voice on the recording was indeed Sergei Buzinsky. He knew that the defence would have their own expert. He thought they would probably go to

Dr. Goodwin, and he was good. If anyone could pick out a flaw and put doubt in the minds of the jury, he could.

Matt had been discharged from hospital after two days, his ribs heavily bandaged. Now, a week after his first debriefing, he met the Scotland Yard officers in a hotel in Bloomsbury. Commander Allen expressed his worries about whether he could convince the CPS that they had a rock-solid case that could justify the expense of a witness protection program.

'There's another option,' said Matt. Commander Allen cocked his head up, looking intrigued. 'What's that?'

'Let me go in and get a full confession.'

The two detectives looked at each other. Watkinson raised his eyebrows in surprise and shot a questioning glance at the Commander, who responded with a short negative head shake. 'Too risky,' said Watkinson.

'You don't know how Buzinsky did it or who else was involved,' said Matt, 'and with all due respect, Commander, you've got two unsolved deaths on your hands – Zhang Wei and Ricardo Varta. You've got no leads and Buzinsky was probably responsible for both murders. There's a lot more we don't know yet. What part did Emma play? How much did Sahin know? These are questions only Buzinsky can answer.' He looked round, hoping to see signs of support, but their stony faces were not encouraging.

'I agree, but that's our job,' said Commander Allen. He pursed his lips as he considered the possibilities of Matt's suggestion. 'What makes you think Buzinsky would give you a confession?'

'He doesn't know about the recording on the phone. Neither does Emma. When I play it, he'll go ballistic, but he'll know he's got me trapped. He'll have me and the recording. He's powerful enough to believe he can get away with it.'

The two officers looked unconvinced. 'Why would he agree to meet you?' said Watkinson.

'I can persuade Emma to tell Buzinsky I know who the killer is. They don't realise I know it's him. They probably think I still suspect Sahin, but Buzinsky will want to find out how much I know. After I've played the recording I can goad him into bragging how smart he's been. I'll be wearing a wire and you'll hear the whole thing. It's your best chance of getting the answers.'

Despite the lateness of the hour and the length of the briefing session, the adrenalin pumped though Matt's veins the way that it did when he was waiting to run out on the pitch in front of forty thousand screaming fans. 'Can you set up an operation that can pull me out as soon as you've got what you want?'

Commander Allen shook his head. 'Have you any idea how dangerous this is?'

'Of course I do. He's tried to have me killed three times. I want to make sure you nail the bastard!' Commander Allen glanced at his colleague, but said nothing. Matt looked from one to the other, hoping for approval, but finding none. 'I've been investigating Tony Barker's death from the beginning. I'm not pulling out now.'

The two officers looked at each other, silently signalling that, however unusual and risky this idea was, it was a possibility they should consider. 'Matt, give us a few minutes please,' said Commander Allen. 'We need to take a break to talk about a couple of things.'

The two officers returned fifteen minutes later and Matt searched their faces for clues. There were none. They all sat round the table again. Commander Allen cleared his throat.

'Matt, this is an unusual and high risk situation, but we think it has merit. It would have to be approved by the deputy commissioner. I'm going to have to do a full risk assessment for him.'

Matt's initial excitement at the Commander's response was curbed by his terse tone and the unknown implications of a risk assessment.

'The first thing you've got to understand is that this is not your investigation,' said Commander Allen. 'I control this investigation and it will be run by DCI Watkinson. For security reasons, it is highly confidential and we will be the only two police officers involved.'

'Okay, I understand,' said Matt

'Let's be clear about this Matt. Part of the assessment is about you. I have to know that I have total control over you and every aspect of the planning and execution. I have to know that I can trust you: that you will follow orders. If I have any doubts, it will be in my risk assessment and the operation will not go ahead. Do you understand?'

'Yes, of course.'

'Okay. Let's begin by asking you why you want to do this – put your life at risk unnecessarily. Why?'

'I can give you three reasons,' said Matt without hesitation.

'First, Tony Barker was a good friend. He was a father figure to me. Tania, his wife, has lived with the shame of suicide that has stained his reputation. She wants closure for herself and her two boys. She wants justice.

'Second, it's my job. I'm an investigative reporter. I investigate corruption in sport. I don't give up when things get tough.

'Third, I want to make certain that Anna Malatova is safe for the rest of her life.'

Commander Allen had nodded his head with approval when Matt had mentioned closure for the family. 'Okay, let's talk about the operation. How are you going to get access to Buzinsky?'

'Emma – she's my way in. She doesn't realise that I know she's his mole. The obvious place to do it is in his office in Canary Wharf. Nowhere public. He'll feel totally secure there and she could arrange that.'

The detectives looked at each other and nodded. 'You can't wear a wire though,' said DCI Watkinson. 'Technology has moved on.' Commander Allen looked at DCI Watkinson and nodded. 'What do you suggest, Nigel?'

The DCI turned to Matt. 'We usually use a special phone app for undercover operations now. It records conversations and transmits them. The signal goes to a hardware box that talks to your smartphone and decodes it. Our team wait in the wings, listening to the audio as it's being recorded, so they can judge if and when to intervene.'

'But once I produce Anna's phone and play the recording he'll immediately be suspicious of phones. He'll take my phone away, won't he?'

'Yes, you're right, but he won't know it has the app embedded and it goes on transmitting wherever it is.'

Matt took his time thinking about it. 'I like that. I like it, but...' Matt leaned his elbows on the table and rubbed his forehead. 'He knows I'm an investigative journalist and he'll expect me to be wearing a wire to record the whole thing. Why don't I wear one anyway? Let him find it, think he's safe. Think he can say whatever he wants.'

Commander Allen leaned back in his chair and spread his hands behind his head.

‘He’s got a good point, Nigel.’

The Inspector rubbed his chin. ‘Yes, I agree. I think what might work best here, then, is a belt transmitter.’

Matt leaned forward, listening carefully.

‘You can wear a trouser belt that looks perfectly normal: quite smart actually. A body wire is concealed behind the buckle. You can activate it by an unobtrusive micro switch. It has an imbedded antenna which takes up a good length of the belt, and creates the extended transmission radius we’re going to want. He’ll see it if they rip it off you.’

‘Sounds good,’ said Matt.

Commander Allen looked thoughtful. ‘It is good, but it’s not fool proof. We will be relying on the phone if he takes the belt. I think we should try to plant a bug a few days before you go in.’

Matt’s eyebrows shot up with surprise. ‘Can you do that?’

‘We’ll get blueprints of the building. Check out the plans for the systems – heating, air conditioning, electrical, plumbing – see what works best. Then we’ll put a man into one of the maintenance firms. He’ll be able to tell us about the layout in Buzinsky’s office and plant one or more bugs. We need the approval of the assistant commissioner, but that shouldn’t be a problem. We’ve got to be certain we hear everything, so if we think you are in danger the armed response team will crash in and get you out.’

‘We’ll have undercover officers planted in the building. Outside we’ll have tactical support teams waiting to move in. If we can put snipers on another building with a view into his office, we will. We’ll get you out, Matt, and we’ll arrest him, but we’ll have back up plans.’

In the week that followed, Commander Allen completed his risk assessment, got authorisation for the intrusive covert operation and, after a long and difficult meeting with the Deputy Commissioner, received approval from the CPS. After a tense few days Matt was called to a final briefing.

‘We’ve already seen plans of the building and had men inside,’ said Watkinson, ‘so we know the layout. We want you to go there in a black cab, only it will be our driver. We’ll have the boys in unmarked cars watching and we'll have someone undercover in the building. When you've been taken up to Buzinsky's penthouse office suite we'll bring forward the armed response teams. They'll enter immediately if they think the situation demands it.' Matt clenched and unclenched his right hand. 'Don't worry,' said DCI Watkinson. 'You're going to have a crack team behind you. We'll collar Buzinsky in his office but, in the remote possibility that he tries to get away, we'll have every road blocked off and a chopper on standby.'

'Let's do it,' said Matt.

Okay,' said Watkinson. 'Just let me know when you've fixed the meeting with the target using the secure line.'

CHAPTER SIXTY

Matt had been stalling Emma. He would have to be careful. His plan depended on her not knowing he had seen through her betrayal.

They sat in the Flamingo, the bar where he had first taken her, and ordered vodka cocktails. 'Matt, what's wrong?' she said. 'Why can't you tell me who did it?'

He breathed in, held his breath, then exhaled slowly. 'Sorry, Em. It's been difficult.' He leaned across the table, took her hand and looked into her eyes. 'Em, you remember you said you would do anything for me?'

She squeezed his hand. 'Yes, of course, but you've been so distant lately.'

'I know, and I'm sorry, but now you really can help. I want you to arrange a meeting with Buzinsky.'

Her eyes narrowed. 'Buzinsky?' She stared at him. 'Why? What for?'

'I think he will want to be the first to know. I'll show him the evidence.'

'What evidence?'

'I can't say now.'

'You can't tell me?'

'Sorry, Em, it's for your own safety. It might put your own life in danger. But I want you to come to the meeting.'

She thought about it for a while, unsure what was going on. 'Alright,' she said finally, 'what am I going to tell him?'

'What I said. I know who did it. I've got the evidence.'

'Where do you want to meet him?'

'I'll come to his office at Canary Wharf.'

She phoned back two hours later. 'He's out of town. He wants to see you at five tomorrow afternoon.'

The offices of the Kopec Corporation were in a new glass tower building in Canary Wharf. It was from here that Sergei Buzinsky ran his vast business empire. The black cab pulled up outside. Matt was tense. He took deep breaths as they walked up the steps, through the glass doors, and up to the reception desk. A uniformed girl asked for ID and smiled at Matt as she handed it back and issued passes. A stony faced security guard checked their bags and took them to an electronic gate, which opened when they touched the pad with their passes, and escorted them to the elevator. Neither of them spoke as they were whisked to the top floor. A tall, tough looking Russian with a shaved head met them and they were ushered into Buzinsky's opulent office suite.

The oligarch was standing with his back to them, staring out of the floor-to-ceiling windows overlooking the river. He turned to face them, immaculate in a perfectly cut blue suit, crisp white shirt and blue tie. He looked fresh and fit and slightly flushed as if he had just showered and come from the gym. He prowled across the room to his polished antique desk, not taking his eyes off Matt. Emma strolled over to an L shaped lounge area with sofas and a coffee table and stretched out on a sofa in a familiar way that suggested that she had been there before.

'Sit down,' Buzinsky commanded, indicating the chair that Matt should take in front of his desk. He glanced at his watch. 'What is it you want to tell me?'

'I thought we'd have a little chat,' said Matt.

The Russian stared at him, pricked by his insolence, but impatient to find out what this man knew. 'Well, what is it?'

Matt pulled Anna's phone out of his pocket, held it up, and pressed play. Buzinsky stopped drumming his fingers on the desk and his body stiffened as he listened to the recording. His eyes were cold and flinty and he was breathing heavily. 'Where did you get this?'

'That's my business,' said Matt.

Buzinsky turned to Emma, whose face was ashen. 'Did you know about this?'

'No, of course not, Sergei.'

Buzinsky sprang round the desk and snatched the phone from Matt's grasp. Anticipating a blow, Matt flinched, but Buzinsky stepped back, shaking with anger, and pressed a button on his desk. Two bodyguards burst into the room. He spoke to them in Russian and they jumped forward. One held Matt in a vice-like grip while the other patted him down, took off his jacket and searched his pockets, removing his phone and wallet and handing them to Buzinsky.

The tall bodyguard with the shaved head made Matt take off his shoes and examined them. Finally he stepped forward and ripped the belt from Matt's trousers. He turned it over and examined the buckle, permitting himself a smug smile of satisfaction as he pointed out the antenna to Buzinsky.

'You should have stuck to being a newspaper hack,' Buzinsky taunted as he passed the belt back to the bodyguard, who crushed the device under his boot. He took Matt's and Anna's phones and put them in small safe by his desk. The door clicked closed. Matt wondered if his phone was still transmitting and if it could still pick up their voices. The bodyguard pulled two pairs of handcuffs from his pocket, pushed Matt's hands behind him and locked him to the chair.

Buzinsky shook his head. 'You journalists are scum. You think you can do anything you want, don't you? Surveillance devices, sting operations, phone hacking...'

'Like you,' said Matt,

Buzinsky sprang forward and hit him in the face. A warm, sweet taste filled Matt's mouth as he licked the blood from his lips.

'And you nearly got away with it,' said Matt.

'Yes. It would have been perfect except for that fucking Russian whore.'

'No. I had already worked out that you killed Tony. I knew what you and Sahin were up to.'

Emma jumped from the sofa, sprang across the room and slapped him hard across the cheek. 'You liar!' she said.

'You didn't know everything. There is a lot you don't know,' said Matt.

'Don't kid yourself,' said Emma. 'You told me everything you were doing. I knew every move you were making. I couldn't believe how easily you fell for it. You think you're smart but you fell for the honey trap, didn't you?'

Buzinsky interjected. 'What does he mean, there is a lot you don't know?'

'You'll find out,' said Matt.

'What don't we know?' snarled the oligarch, staring at Emma.

'Ignore him,' she said, 'he's bluffing.'

'Who else knows about the phone?'

'Nobody. He was never going to let anyone near that until he broke the story. When I found out he was going to see Barker's solicitor I thought he might be taking him some evidence, but he wasn't. Your boys grabbed his backpack but there was no phone in it. He never even met the lawyer. He was taken straight to hospital.'

Buzinsky's cold eyes locked onto Emma in a piercing laser stare. When he spoke he spat the words out. 'He was seeing the Russian whore. She gave it to him. You didn't know a thing about it!'

Emma's cheeks flushed. 'It was you that was careless with your bedroom talk.'

'What the fuck do you think I pay you for, bitch!'

He walked across the room to the sofa, pulled a gun out of his pocket, put it up against her head, and fired. The only sound was a slight plop and Emma slid onto the floor, blood streaming from her head.

'Jesus Christ!' Matt screamed. He tried to jump up, but the chair tipped over and he fell to the floor, staring at Emma's crumpled body. He became aware of his heartbeat thrashing in his ears as he watched the blood and tissue oozing from her head to form a dark red pool on the pale cream carpet. The shock had slammed though his body like a massive electric charge, the shooting still a freeze frame in his mind. Every pore in his body tingled. He couldn't take his eyes off her slim, lifeless body. She had betrayed him, but she had been his lover. 'Oh no,' he groaned.

The tall bodyguard walked over and pulled Matt into an upright position. He was shaking uncontrollably. He looked round the room, desperately hoping that at any moment the door would burst open and armed police clad in black would come charging in. Where were they? Had they heard the shot? Was the police app on his phone working? Had the police placed a bug in the office? But no-one came. Buzinsky's security people had probably swept his office clean. The stark reality hit him and he slumped in the chair. The police hadn't heard anything. It had all gone wrong. He was on his own.

Buzinsky walked towards him, pointing the gun at his head. 'Where is the whore?'

Matt tried to pull himself together, to keep his wits about him. He breathed deeply and tried to clear his head. 'I have no idea. I'm the last person she would want to tell.'

'Who else knows about the phone?'

'Emma was right. Nobody.'

Buzinsky whipped him round the head with the pistol. Matt felt the crack ricochet in his head and blood dripped down his cheek.

'You're not that stupid. You must have made a copy. Where is it?'

Matt lifted his chin defiantly. Buzinsky pressed the barrel of the gun hard into the centre of his forehead. 'Where is it?' he snarled.

Matt's tongue felt like coarse grade sandpaper. He turned to see Emma's inert body and swallowed hard. 'Locked in my hotel room safe,' he croaked. 'Fuschia Hotel, Bloomsbury, room 304, safe number 3821.'

The oligarch strolled back to his desk, picked up the phone and barked orders for the copy to be collected. His two henchmen stood motionless by the door, waiting for their next order.

Matt reckoned that it would take at least thirty minutes for someone to get to the hotel and find nothing in the safe. Then his time would be up. His chin sunk onto his chest and blood streamed down his face and onto his shirt. He looked up at Buzinsky and shrugged. 'So, you win.'

The Russian's face showed only the slightest hint of gloating. The only sound in the room was Matt's groan as he crumpled like a punctured balloon. He looked up at last. 'But just tell me this. Why did you have to do it? You had the best manager in England. You were winning. Why?' he said in a thick husky voice. Buzinsky raised his hands in an arrogant and condescending gesture. 'You don't know me, do you? I get what I want. Sahin knew that. He said, "I know you want to win the Champions League. You probably can, but I could make sure you do." He told me how he could fix games. I believed him, so I paid and he delivered.'

'But it all went wrong when Tony found out?'

'Yes.' Buzinsky shook his head as if it really was a matter of regret. 'Emma told me he had worked out what Sahin was doing, but she wasn't sure if Barker was going to expose it. It would have ruined the club of course, and Barker didn't want that. But I couldn't take the risk. So I had him killed.'

'Suicide,' said Matt. 'It was clever. I give you that. And it fooled everyone, the pathologist, the coroner – everyone except me. But I never found out how you got the police to cover it up.'

Buzinsky smiled. 'That was easy. My head of security is ex-Met. He has contacts. He is looking for a new number two and a man like Maclean can find early retirement and a new career with us very attractive.'

Matt answered with an understanding nod.

'But was Sahin in on it? I was so sure for a long time that he had done it.'

Buzinsky was like a cat playing with a mouse now. He sat back in his chair, legs stretched out, black boots on the antique desk, the gun cradled in his arm, still pointing at Matt. 'Sahin? You think I'm stupid? How do you think I survived in Russia? The fewer that know the fewer to dispose of. Only three men knew anything, and they are all in this room. Sahin had one use for me: to fix the matches we had to win. At that he was very good.'

'Aren't you worried that his connection to you will come out? He's singing like a canary.'

Buzinsky threw back his head and laughed. 'You don't know anything about Russia, my friend. Do you think he prefers to be dead or serve two years in a comfortable French jail? There is nothing to prove that it was me who paid him to fix City games. It can never be traced.'

'Did you know that Sahin was also paid by his Singapore gambling syndicate to fix your semi-final in Greece?'

'Did he? So what? What else he did, I don't care.'

'And Varta? Did you kill him?'

'Varta? He was an eighty-million euro asset. I didn't want him wiped out. Sahin panicked when you told Emma you were going to frighten him. He thought Varta would tell you everything. He knew that Sahin was fixing referees and that Zhang Wei was fixing players for him. I didn't think Varta was a risk. I could have dealt with him, had him transferred to China, but then you poked your nose in.'

'And Zhang Wei? Did you kill him?'

Buzinsky threw back his head and laughed. 'I'm sorry to disappoint you. No, not that one. Not Zhang Wei. For once the police were right. He was taken out by a Triad drugs gang he had double crossed. But none of this is ever going to be any use to you, is it? You are just a journalist who is out of his league, and now you are out of time.'

Buzinsky rose from his chair, walked over and stood behind Matt. He felt hard steel rammed against the back of his head. A bead of cold sweat slid slowly down his forehead and dripped into his eye.

The distant thwacking of rotor blades caught the Russian's attention. He stopped and listened, then walked over to the plate glass window. Matt wondered if it was the police helicopter or just a private chopper heading up river to the Battersea heliport. They had the place surrounded, didn't they? What were they waiting for?

The chopper had clearly spooked Buzinsky. He scanned the sky, saw nothing, then jerked back from the window. On the roof opposite, a ray of bright sun glinted on a telescopic lens as a sniper in a flak jacket broke cover for an instant to take a better position. Buzinsky saw him immediately and grabbed his phone, speaking rapidly in Russian. Slipping the phone into his pocket he barked orders to the two bodyguards. They rushed forward, unlocked Matt from the chair, roughly twisted his arms up behind his back and cuffed his hands together. He screamed in agony at the pain in his side.

Buzinsky strode to the bookshelves lining the wall, touched a button and a panel slipped back to reveal his private express lift. Matt was bundled in by one of the bodyguards and the four men made a rapid descent.

CHAPTER SIXTY ONE

The lift opened into a private garage that housed the Russian's personal fleet of luxury cars. Matt was pushed roughly past Ferraris and Porches but, to his surprise, instead of being bundled into a car, he was thrust through another door into the fading daylight. In front of him he saw a small private dock where a fast red motor launch lay waiting. With his arms tied behind his back, Matt stumbled and fell as he was shoved into the boat. The tall bodyguard took the controls and the engines roared into life. The other man cast off the ropes.

Before Matt could get to his feet, the launch had turned east onto the open river. The driver opened up the throbbing engines and within seconds the boat came up onto a plane, flying over the water at forty knots, a spume of white water spraying out behind them. Buzinsky was screaming at him to go faster. Static crackled from the Motorola MTH 800 Tetra handset as the bodyguard searched the airwaves using the digital tracking scanner. Fifteen seconds later he found the police frequency. The static cleared and the calm voice of the Metropolitan Police Commander came over the airwaves.

'Go ahead Central One. MP over.'

'We've entered the building. The subject has flown. We must have missed him by a minute. He has taken the informer. Likely hostage situation. We have one dead female. The building is surrounded. He must have had a hidden exit to the river. Central Two and Three have gone around to the waterside.'

'Understood. India 99 is airborne and we'll alert the Marine Police Unit at Wapping.'

'MP over.'

'MP. India 99. Permission?'

'Go ahead India 99. MP over.'

'We are heading for Canary Wharf. Over.'

The tall bodyguard with the shaved head shouted something to Buzinsky, who nodded, looked at his watch, and spoke into his mobile phone. No one was taking much notice of Matt as he struggled up off the floor and fell into a seat. The boat had taken him by surprise, but it was a smart move by Buzinsky. He felt helpless but he was confident that the police would have a backup plan. Buzinsky could be heading for a ship downstream. Or perhaps he was planning a rendezvous with a fast car positioned somewhere along the river which would then disappear into the labyrinth of London, taking him with them. But for how long? He would be held hostage only as long as he was negotiating currency. He shivered as he imagined the worst scenario, then pulled himself together. The police had massive resources. Their helicopter would be able to track Buzinsky's every move, but where was it? He looked up and saw only an airliner overhead. What about City Airport? That could only be ten or fifteen minutes away. Perhaps Buzinsky kept his private jet there. Would the police know that? He breathed in deeply. He hoped so. Russia had no extradition treaty with the UK, and if Buzinsky could escape to Mother Russia he would be free and clear. There was no reason why he would take him to Russia. They would probably shoot him as they boarded the aircraft.

Matt stared up at the shapes in the dark clouds and saw images of boys from the playground taunting him. *"Your dad's a fucking loser. You're a fucking Nodad. Your dad topped himself cos he was no good. You're a loser. Loser!"* This was not the way it was going to end. He had to find a way to escape. Above the high whine of the boat's engines the radio crackled into life again.

'MP, India 99.'

'Go ahead, India 99.'

'We have sight of a motor launch heading east at 40 knots: red hull, white half-cabin, twelve metres long. Four males on board.'

The EC-145 police helicopter, fitted with an on-board video camera, zoomed in on the getaway boat and beamed its signal back to the Metropolitan Police Commander at the control centre. He stared at the screen. 'OK, India 99. I see it now. Close in. MP over.'

The launch had rounded the Isle of Dogs and was just passing the O2 arena when the harsh throbbing noise shattered the air. The chopper swung in and hovered over them. Buzinsky kicked his bodyguard, screaming at him. The man opened a locker, took out an AK 47, put it to his shoulder and fired, forcing the chopper to sheer away violently.

Matt guessed they had been on the river for over five minutes already. Time was running out.

They sped downriver towards Greenwich. Matt could see a cloud of spray in the distance. Two boats were coming towards them at high speed. As they got closer he could make out two RIBs – large, black, rigid inflatables packed with men in black. He tried to slip his hands out of the cuffs but all he did was take the skin off his wrists. Buzinsky's driver shouted and pointed at the RIBs.

In the failing light, a searing searchlight from the chopper picked out Buzinsky and, even over the noise of the rotors, a voice boomed out over the water. 'This is the police. Cut your engines immediately. We are going to board your vessel.'

In response, the guard with the AK47 fired at the helicopter again, but it was out of range. Buzinsky barked orders to his driver to hold his course and speed as the boats hurtled towards each other at a combined speed approaching 100 knots. A collision seemed inevitable. At the last minute the RIBs, which had been almost alongside each other, swung out to opposite banks of the river and pulled round in a tight circle to try to come up along each side of the Russian boat. The man with the AK47 opened fire. As the police closed in, the Russian driver pulled his boat into a 360 degree turn, engines screaming, and the boat heeled hard over. Matt was thrown from his seat into the side of the boat. He hit the gunwales with such momentum that he was able to heave himself over the side and roll into the water. The bodyguard with the AK47, also caught unawares, was flung across the boat, his gun clattering into the scuppers. The police boats were outmanoeuvred. One lay low in the water, badly damaged, and there were casualties. Buzinsky's launch raced away.

Matt sank under the water, his hands cuffed behind his back. The sounds of screaming engines, the throb of helicopter rotors and crackling rifle fire vanished. There was only silence and darkness. At first he struggled to reach the surface, but with his hands tied behind his back it was useless. The exertion was a serious waste of breath. But the urge to breathe soon became irresistible and he began to swallow foul water. The pain growing in his chest felt like a vice which was gradually being screwed tight. The gulps became more frequent and the pain became unbearable. His will to live seemed to be extinguished. But then the pain gradually eased and the gulps came at longer intervals. It seemed to Matt that he was slipping into a dream in which he had a vivid recollection of the boys in the playground. Tomkins staring into his face. *"Your Dad's a loser."* No! No! From deep inside he summoned up the will to fight back. Somewhere up there would be hands waiting to pluck him from the water. He kicked his legs, driven by some unseen force, until his head broke the surface. As he gulped for breath he swallowed more water and he was sucked under again.

One of the tactical support team positioned in the bow spotted Matt as his head bobbed up for a second time. He jumped in and held him up. Someone threw a looped line and he slipped it under Matt's body and pulled it tight. Helping hands reached out to hoist him aboard. One of them began pumping his chest to expel the water he had swallowed. Somehow the pain in his ribs didn't matter anymore. He vomited, coughed, spluttered, and began to breathe. He looked into the face of the figure dressed in a black wet suit and smiled. 'You saved my life,' he choked, then collapsed again.

The police helicopter pilot continued to track the launch from a safe height, the observer following every move and the radio officer feeding information back to control.

'MP, India 99.'

'Go ahead, India 99.'

'Exchange of fire! We have men down on Marine One. One male in the water. Marine Two is providing rescue and assistance. City Airport could be the destination. TOA would be in five.'

'India 99. Understood. We've already put them on alert. All flights in and out are on hold for the next two hours. They will give you clearance to approach. Emergency vehicles will be standing by.'

The SCO19 commander at the MP control centre had indeed covered every option, using all the assets at his disposal. In addition to the EC-145 helicopter and Delta TX RIBs, he had also marshalled armed response vehicles on both sides of the river. To cover the now likely, and highly dangerous, scenario of an attempted escape from City Airport, he had called up the CTSFO. The Counter Terrorist Specialist Firearms Officers were the Metropolitan Police's crack unit, used to storm buildings, planes, buses and trains and handle hostage situations. Each BMW X5 ARV was equipped with specialist GPS and communications equipment, and the team of five highly trained officers were armed with Heckler & Koch carbines and Glock 17 pistols. Their call sign is Trojan. The commander updated the leader.

'MP, Trojan One.'

'Trojan One receiving.'

'Subject almost certainly heading for City Airport. What is your best TOA?'

'First ARVs should arrive in seven minutes.'

'Trojan received. MP over.'

The SCO19 controller glanced at his watch and winced. He looked back at his monitor and watched the armed response vehicles scything through the city traffic, homing in on City Airport. 'Come on. Come on! Faster, damn it!'

At City Airport all incoming flights had been diverted and flights due for takeoff postponed until further notice. The runway was clear. A white Gulfstream private jet began to taxi from the parking apron, rapidly picking up speed as it headed for the runway take-off area. Radio calls to the Gulfstream from an iridescent air traffic controller were met with total silence. Alarm sirens shattered the air and red lights winked in the gathering darkness. Uniformed officers rushed out and jumped into police vehicles, emergency lights flashing and tyres screeching as they raced off to intercept the Gulfstream.

With all eyes focused on the private jet it was only an alert air traffic controller that noticed the powerful four-cylinder BMW S100RR motorbike racing towards the other end of the airport. He alerted the SCO19 commander who instructed one of the airport police cars to give chase.

Buzinsky's launch screamed into the marina at the end of the runway just as the leather-clad driver of the BMW motorbike skidded to a halt by the dock. The oligarch jumped on the back of the bike and they roared off, the police car trailing two hundred metres behind.

The EC-145 helicopter was now overhead and flying low over the bike, sending its pictures to SCO19, its powerful rotors chopping up the stretch of water on each side of the runway and drowning out all the other sounds. The police commander gritted his teeth as he watched his BMW X5 ARVs closing in. Just two minutes to arrival they estimated.

The Gulfstream was on the runway, engines screaming, ready for take-off. The passenger door was open. Strong beckoning hands were waiting to pull the two Russians onboard as the BMW S100RR hurtled up the runway. At the other end of the airport the two leading ARVs raced onto the tarmac, sirens blaring, the officers cradling their Heckler & Koch carbines in their arms. They were only five hundred yards from the Gulfstream when a refueling tanker going quietly about its business pulled out from behind a hanger. There was nowhere for the motorbike to go. It smashed into the tanker at a hundred miles an hour. The explosion rocked the airport buildings and a ball of fire lit the sky. The pillar of black smoke could be seen as far away as Canvey Island. The tanker driver was flung clear by the explosion. He was recovered, badly injured, from the runway. The charred remains of Buzinsky and his driver were unidentifiable.

EPILOGUE

Matt rushed down the platform at Manchester Piccadilly station just in time to catch the 12.34 p.m. train to London. He had been at a celebrity charity fundraising dinner, run by a former Manchester United star. Despite the glamour and glitterati, and the undeniable size of the funds raised for children's hospitals in Africa, Matt discovered that only a small percentage of the money raised was finding its way to sick children. A new story was unfolding.

He looked over his notes, then sank back in his seat, watching the Cheshire countryside fly by, pondering the extraordinary events of the last year. Since that terrible day that had ended with Buzinsky's death, he had been caught up in a whirlwind of events. Anna had disappeared into the witness protection program and he would never see her again. He was sure that somewhere she would be beginning a new life with her own fashion company. Perhaps one day she would be married and have children. He often thought about her and wondered where she was – Rio de Janeiro? New York?

Sahin had been sentenced to two years in a French jail but, following an agreement between France and England, he had been extradited to the UK to stand trial for Varta's murder. D.S. Maclean, along with several high-ranking Scotland Yard officers, had been suspended while a top level police investigation took place.

Matt's information had already led to the ongoing exposure of Tan's European match fixing network. It had ensnared dozens of players, coaches and officials throughout Europe. No country had emerged unscathed. A surge of interest in the murky world of agents filled the back pages.

Henry Tan, wanted by the police in most major European countries, had remained in Singapore. The European crime agencies had been unable to bring him back to face charges as they had no extradition treaties with Singapore. The Singaporean authorities had initially been uncooperative claiming that, until they had evidence that a crime had been committed on Singaporean soil, they were powerless to act. Some critics suggested that this was because there was a high-level conspiracy to protect the master fixer living in their midst. A breakthrough had come when two members of Tan's syndicate turned on their boss. Their written testimony, along with evidence of phone records, money transfers and bank accounts from Judge Quentel's investigation, had finally led to the Singaporean police moving in. Twelve men were arrested. Five were released on bail, while Tan and seven others were kept in custody. But the defecting members of the syndicate were too scared to testify in person, so the police had used draconian security laws from the 1950s to keep the men in custody.

Evidence against the syndicate had been gathered and presented behind closed doors to the Ministry of Home Affairs and an advisory council before a decision was finally made by the president. It was agreed that the gang should remain under preventive detention. Henry Tan and his associates would be held for years without ever having the evidence tested in a court of law.

Under huge pressure to act, the Singapore government had responded, but in its own way. Matt's in-depth story for the *Telegraph* was headlined SINGAPORE CUTS THE HEAD OFF THE SNAKE. It was being hailed by the media as the clean-up that had purged football of its greatest challenge. Matt remained in constant demand for media interviews as the full scale of his involvement in Buzinsky's downfall became known.

Then, in December, almost one year after Tony's death, Matt was presented with the prestigious Press Gazette British Journalism Award for Sports Journalism. In the words of its chairman, the awards "recognised journalists who hold those in power to account, and give a voice to those who don't have one." Of the seventeen award categories it was the only one given to sport. Matt was humbled as he stepped onto the stage to accept his award "for brave and must-read journalism."

In his short acceptance speech he had said, 'I was rather stunned. I didn't expect it when the standard of entries was so very high.'

By way of celebration Matt had taken Tania, James and Julia for a long overdue dinner at the Wolseley in Piccadilly. He had ordered Dom Perignon and raised his glass. 'I want to thank you all for the help you gave me to uncover the truth and get justice for Tony.' They had leaned across the table and clinked glasses. 'And let's drink a toast to absent friends. To Anna,' he had said. 'Without her bravery, it would never have happened.' They echoed his toast. 'And finally,' he said, 'I want to thank you all for putting up with an impossible man who always thinks he's right, and never takes no for an answer.' They had laughed and clinked glasses again.

The Manchester train pulled into Euston exactly on time at 2.44 p.m. It left Matt plenty of time to get the tube to Fulham, collect Callum, and catch the 6.00 p.m. Eurostar to Paris. For the first time in many months he was relaxed and looking forward to the pre-Christmas Disneyland treat he had promised Callum.

THE END

Enjoyed reading *Fatal Fix*? Then please do leave a review on Amazon or Goodreads to help others find it and enjoy it too.

ABOUT THE AUTHOR

Graham Morse had a career in advertising and marketing before retiring to become a blue water sailor with his wife Janet. After crossing the Pacific and visiting small islands, mostly still untouched by civilization, he wrote his first book, *The Islands Time Forgot*. His next book was a biography of his father-in-law, the first manager of the English national football team.

Sir Walter Winterbottom, The Father of Modern English Football was shortlisted for the British Sports Book Awards in 2014.

A lifelong love of football and concerns over the huge influence of money in football, prompted him to write his first crime thriller, FATAL FIX, set in the world of modern football.

Much-travelled, Wiltshire-born Graham is married to Janet. They have four children and nine grandchildren. Graham and Janet now live in the Caribbean.

Printed in Great Britain
by Amazon

46512784R00210